THE FERAL CHILDREN

ANIMALS

DAVID A. SIMPSON

WESLEY R. NORRIS

Wise Pug Publishing

ALSO BY DAVID A. SIMPSON

Novels

Zombie Road: Convoy of Carnage

Zombie Road II: Bloodbath on the Blacktop

Zombie Road III: Rage on the Rails

Zombie Road IV: Road to Redemption

Zombie Road V: Terror on the Two-Lane

Zombie Road VI: Highway to Heartache

Anthologies

Tales from the Zombie Road: The Long Haul Anthology

Undead Worlds: A Reanimated Writers Anthology

Treasured Chests: A Zombie Anthology

Trick or Treat Thrillers: Best Paranormal 2018

Trick or Treat Thrillers: Best Horror 2018

Coloring Book

Zombie Road: The Road Kill Coloring Book

The Feral Children
Animals
A Zombie Road Tale
Book 1 in the Feral Children series

This is a work of fiction by
David A. Simpson
and
Wesley R. Norris

ISBN: 9781099338960

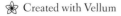 Created with Vellum

The Feral Children

Animals

A Zombie Road tale

Dedicated to my dearest partner in life:
The nitpicky, OCD, grammar-Nazi, Robin.

PROLOGUE

WINTER

K odiak wrapped the buffalo skin robe tighter as the wind swirled gusts of snow around his feet. The stone walls of the burnt-out church provided little shelter from the snow storm that raged and wailed and dumped its fury on this forgotten corner of the world. Snow clung to his eyelashes, eyebrows and his hair, which was getting too long, as he watched and waited.

He knew the storm gave them perfect cover if the other tribe chose tonight to attack. If they came, it would be from this direction. Right into his trap. The cables strung across the road were concealed beneath the fresh snow that blanketed the asphalt, ready to be pulled tight at a moment's notice. They were invisible in the dark, benign and harmless on the off chance someone else was traveling the road, but deadly when pulled into place.

His ears strained over the howling wind to hear the whining of the snowmobiles the others rode. If they came, it wouldn't be to talk. If they came, they would be counting on the storm to mask their approach. He leaned against Otis, soaking in his warmth. The big bear would smell and hear them long before him. The wind died down a little and its shrieking through the collapsed roof eased. The pair waited with a patience learned from hard lessons and shared an easy companionship. They looked like snow-covered mounds of fur.

Kodiak had tried to avert trouble, had went out of his way to avoid a fight but his efforts were perceived as weakness. Things escalated as things do and a life had been taken. The others had thought they were weak, thought they'd be an easy target but they had been wrong. Now they were coming for payback. It might be tonight, it might not be, but he knew they were coming. They wouldn't forget the insult and they wouldn't forget about the girl.

The boy defied them. He stood against them. The child warrior and the colossal bear that towered by his side would defend his people. His tribe. The innocent boy once called Cody Wilkes was long gone. There was no one left alive to remember who he had been. The ugly, new world started in September when the old world died and the warrior king known only as Kodiak arose from the ashes.

He pressed closer to Otis, the 1200-pound bear, seeking the additional warmth he offered. He was scarred and fearsome and had a roar that made his living enemies quake in terror. His massive claws could decapitate a zombie with a single blow. His jaws had immense power to crush bone and rend flesh.

Maybe that was the difference, he thought as the big bear chuffed softly at him, ruffling the feathers and beads in his hair. *We have the animals to give us purpose. Keep us sane. Love us as we love them. Protect us as we protect them.*

There was enough of everything for everyone left alive for

a long time, there was no reason to fight. No reason to go to war. They had warehouses full of food. Water was abundant. The war should be with the undead and the Savage Ones. The animals who'd always avoided man before the zombie virus swept the world but now attacked in droves, all fear of man lost. The coyotes and the vultures, the hyenas and the crows and all the other carrion animals. The ones that lived on the dead. The ones that were driven to madness from unrestrained gorging, eating the easy pickings from the stumbling buffet.

The other tribe wanted control, they couldn't live and let live. They wanted the girls and they wanted servants to do the work that was beneath them to do. Like any war, it started out small. Small disagreements, small arguments, small trespasses. Then came the escalations, the yelling and the fights. Pushing and shoving turned into killing and dying. It was always the same whether it was two kids on the playground or global nuclear powers playing brinksmanship. Somebody always blinked. If they came tonight, Kodiak would end it.

He'd shown mercy and kindness in the beginning. He'd tried to keep the old ways where children didn't bludgeon each other to death with homemade battle axes or spears. The old ways were gone, though. It had taken him a little longer than the others to realize it but now that he did, he would be as ruthless and unforgiving as they were. The next time they met, blood would spill.

He hoped they would come, that it would end here tonight. The boy and his beast would fall into them with claws, jaws and steel.

No more mercy.

No more wasted words.

Let them come.

Kodiak ran his hands over the cool iron of his Warhammer.

He watched.

He waited.

He remembered....

1

SEPTEMBER

MR. BAYNARD

R obert Baynard slipped out from under the covers as his alarm clock buzzed its good morning serenade, enjoying the feel of the cool air on his skin. After silencing the ride of the Valkyries, he slid from the bed, wasting no time as he smoothed the sheets and made it with military precision. He transitioned into his morning stretching routine. His years as a United States Navy sailor may have been long over, but he still carried the habits ingrained in him from twenty years of service to his country.

Robert was not a large man at only five feet seven inches and one hundred thirty-three pounds, his ideal perfect weight for his height. He prided himself on his physical conditioning and strict regimen. Not much he could do about his thinning hairline, but his waistline was easily kept in check.

Adequately stretched he dropped to the floor and pressed out his morning routine of pushups and sit-ups, noting with some satisfaction that he finished a full seven seconds ahead of his usual time. Stepping into the bathroom he turned on the hot water then headed for the kitchen. It would be heated to precisely his preferred showering temperature by the time he started the coffeemaker, grabbed the morning paper from the front porch and returned.

Exactly seven minutes and forty-five seconds later, Robert exited the shower as the last drops of coffee made it from the machine into the pot. He didn't have to check; he knew it with certainty.

Even though it was a Saturday, he dressed in his usual work attire of starched khakis, sensible brown shoes, button down Oxford and one of his many animal themed ties. Today's was a bit more festive than usual; it featured a collage of Macaw parrots. Returning to the kitchen he poured his first cup of coffee: black, no sugar. He set the skillet on the stove top and turned it to the medium heat setting and headed for the fridge. Robert knew that by the time he had all his normal breakfast items laid out in neat rows, his cup of coffee would be just the right temperature to drink and the skillet would be just the right temperature for cooking. Robert loved consistent, methodical orderliness in his life and had his morning routine mapped out to the second.

Today's breakfast, like every other morning, consisted of four strips of crispy bacon, two lightly buttered pieces of wheat toast and two eggs over easy, fuel for his day of molding young minds.

He broke from his routine and read the labeling on the package as he opened it. It was a different brand than he usually bought. There had been a meat shortage for weeks and the cause had never been made clear. Something about a labor dispute and company mergers but the new bacon looked the same as the old bacon. No extra fat or unevenly sliced pieces. He laid the strips of thick cut in the skillet and took his first sip of coffee. Perfect, he thought as he loaded the toaster with two slices of whole wheat bread. As soon as he lifted the bacon from the skillet to cool and drain away the excess grease after exactly six minutes, flipped only once, he would depress the plunger on the toaster and crack two eggs into the bacon grease. The toast would pop out as he scooped up his over easy eggs and breakfast would be exactly on schedule.

Minutes later, Robert sat down to eat and mentally went over his day as he browsed the headlines in the morning paper. A few riots in the big cities, he noted. Flu-like virus was sweeping the country causing psychotic behavior in people. He would be sure to discuss this with his students. Viruses were always making interspecies jumps, and this could be another example.

He was a high school biology teacher in addition to leading an extracurricular zoology program. The program was designed for students who were interested in careers in veterinary medicine, game and fish law enforcement, or animal biology. The group discussed topics such as how loss of habitat and the encroachment of man were forcing both man and beast to adapt to a rapidly changing world.

One of his students, Harper, had nicknamed him Mr. Barnyard, playing on his last name. At first it had annoyed him but he had grown to secretly like it, even though he'd never admit it to the kids. Today he was taking her and an assortment of the best and brightest of these students on a field trip to the Piedmont Animal Sanctuary to study some of the many animals housed there. Each student would be free to spend the day observing the animal species of their choosing and submit their findings to the group for discussion at their next meeting for an extra credit grade.

He remote started his car with the key fob and cleaned

up his breakfast dishes, satisfied in the knowledge that his car's engine would be at its optimum operating temperature when he slid behind the wheel.

As he left his house precisely on schedule, he marveled at his own efficiency. Robert was as predictable as the sunrise and a creature of habit that very rarely made changes to his routine.

"Although," he thought as he drove toward the school to meet his favorite students, *"That new bacon was delicious."*

2

___

CODY

The sun peeked over the tops of the tall maple trees rapidly bringing warmth to the early fall Saturday morning. Cody Wilkes was already working up a sweat despite the cooler temperatures as he finished scooping up the last shovel full of dung left behind by Millie, the black rhinoceros. She was a huge beast who generated equally huge piles of waste. Weighing in at nearly 1100 pounds but as gentle as a lamb, she was an old girl at thirty-five and blind in one eye. The part time job had its drawbacks, that was for sure, but he didn't complain. It sure beat cutting grass or, God forbid, babysitting. His mom wasn't a pushover like some other parents. If he asked her for fifty bucks to buy a new game, she'd make him do so much work around the house that it came out to about ten cents an hour. Nope. He'd rather hang out with the animals. Pay was way better, too. Cody was careful to keep her in his peripheral vision when he worked on her blind side. She wouldn't intentionally hurt him but her limited vision made her hazardous to work around in the confines of the pen and having his foot stepped on would not be his preferred way to start the day. Her short tail swished back and forth to chase away the pesky flies constantly buzzing around her.

Millie was a popular attraction at the Park. Her gentle nature and willingness to tolerate the masses of children that visited every year made her a crowd favorite among the flocks of kids lining up to feed her carrot after carrot, her favorite treat. As soon as she heard the first car approaching, she would leave her pen and spend the rest of the day grazing the fence line along the walking path and waiting for a tasty handout from the tourists.

At almost 400 acres the Piedmont Animal Sanctuary sat up against the mighty Mississippi River on one side and the Minnesota border on another. It was located just a few miles outside of New Albin, Iowa, a small town with two claims to fame. It was the hometown of Milt Gantenbein of the Green Bay Packers and also the farthest northeastern town in Iowa.

Many of the residents in the park were retired circus animals needing a safe place to live out their golden years. A few, like the black panther, were animals that had been owned by people who didn't realize the commitment it took to keep large exotic pets and found themselves unable to deal with them once they passed the cute and cuddly stage.

Despite its middle-of-nowhere location, it was considered one of the premiere care facilities for aging animals or ones that no other zoo would take. The gentler creatures like Millie, Bert the giraffe and Ziggy the ostrich had large areas to roam in the daytime and returned to their enclosures at dark. Others like the wolves, bears and the panther had handlers during visiting hours, so the guests could get up close and personal with the animals. Even though almost every animal in the park had been born in captivity and were used to being around humans, it never hurt to be cautious with the toothier species.

"Catch!" Kelly yelled as Cody looked up in time to snag the bottle of water out of the air. She smiled at the sight of her fourteen-year-old son leaning on his shovel. Tall and handsome like his father, he was the center of her world. She missed Todd and wished he could see the man his son was becoming. Cody was still a small boy when his father died along with three other firemen when the roof collapsed in a warehouse blaze.

"Thanks Mom." Cody said as he twisted off the bottle cap and took a deep swallow.

"Hon, when you're done here, will you feed the hyenas? They are kenneled on the other side of Bert's enclosure, the old cages where the lions used to be. Derek will be down shortly to sedate them and inject their microchips. Keys are in the golf cart." Kelly said as her radio chirped to life.

"Sure Mom," Cody sighed. He missed the old lion and didn't care at all for the two newest additions to the park.

Kelly keyed the mike on her radio. "Go for Kelly."

As the primary veterinarian at Piedmont she was constantly on the run. Today was shaping up to be even tougher because of the staff that had called in complaining of flu like symptoms. The capuchin monkeys were always getting loose and stuffing themselves on junk food or Bert was dealing with an upset stomach. The big giraffe loved to eat maple leaves but the heavy tannic acid in them played havoc with his digestive system. Bert was famous for his noxious gas. It always drew giggles from the children when he ripped a big loud stinky one while mom and dad were trying to get a picture of their kids with the long-legged critter.

"Kelly, this is Will, we've got a visitor complaining of

fever and a headache up here by the snack bar." the radio squawked.

"Copy, have Anna come, she's with us all day today." Kelly responded.

Anna Rimes was a part time volunteer at the park who worked as a paramedic with the fire department.

"Roger that," Will answered back. "She's in route, I called you because he appears to have a bite mark on his forearm, and I thought you'd want to take a look at it, see which of our residents decided to snack on the paying customers."

"On my way," said Kelly. "Cody don't forget the hyenas; I'll be back in a bit."

She took off at a run, worried about the bite and wondering if it was going to be one of those days. None of the petting animals had ever bitten anyone before, she hoped it was just an overly friendly slobber from one of the goats. Life at Piedmont was never boring.

Tossing the shovel in the back with the rest of the buckets and tools, Cody chugged down the last of the water, gave Millie a pat on her enormous head and hopped on the golf cart. He drove over to the feed barn to grab some cuts of meat for the hyenas from the walk in cooler and some extra grub for his pal Otis. When it was loaded in buckets and stowed in the cart, he headed down to the enclosure near the river to find the bear.

Otis lay in the shade of a giant maple tree but lifted his head and chuffed as he watched Cody approach. The boy always meant a scratch in those itchy places and something tasty to eat was heading his way, so he pushed himself to his feet in anticipation.

Otis was a 1200-pound bear of questionable lineage that had performed in Las Vegas in his younger years to sellout crowds. Cody's mom thought he was a Kodiak and Grizzly mix but whoever his parents had been, he'd taken after the bigger one. Otis was an attention lover of the highest order; he still did a few tricks for the crowds of kids to hear the applause. He was gentle enough for them to ride him around but it wasn't allowed, of course. He'd never intentionally hurt anyone, but you couldn't convince the insurance companies of that.

Cody grabbed one of the buckets of beef and stood looking eye to eye with the big bear. He reached up and rubbed Otis between the ears and got a satisfied groan of pleasure for his efforts. He pulled a large roast from the bucket and held it out for inspection. Otis gave it a big sniff and gently took it from the boy in his cavernous jaws. He turned and ambled back to his spot in the shade to enjoy his breakfast as Cody tidied up the enclosure. He shoveled what needed to be shoveled, cleaned out his drinking pool then reclined against the bear's ribs as Otis lay sprawled out, gnawing happily on the bone. He scratched him idly behind the ears and smiled at the contented sounds he made. He was like a giant pussy cat.

"Enjoy buddy. I'll see you later." Cody said after a few minutes and stood, gave Otis a good back scratching and left the enclosure. He'd rather spend the day lying in the shade with Otis, but he didn't want to keep Derek waiting. Cody plopped in the golf carts seat, pressed the pedal and headed towards the hyena kennel.

The two hyenas came to their feet and stared at him as he approached with the bucket of meat, mouths drooling and pacing back and forth in the pen. They were huge, hunchbacked and a mottled, tawny color. Their mouths were oversized, they seemed too big for their heads and it looked like they were smiling a devil smile when they barked their creepy laugh. Cody was wary of them. They looked mean and cunning and even had evil sounding names: Diablo and Demonio, Spanish for Devil and Demon. They'd only been on site for a couple of days and were nasty beasts. The pair had been seized by the DEA when they busted a gang affiliated with one of the Mexican drug cartels. With no other facility willing to take them, they had been transported to Piedmont. Rumor had it the gang's leader had fed the two beasts a steady diet of people who crossed him. Kelly dismissed it with a laugh when Cody asked her about it. She said hyenas had gotten a bad rap ever since Disney vilified them.

Cody wasn't so sure. He was uncomfortable with the way they stalked the bars and eyed him. Like he might be what's for dinner. He didn't bother trying to hand feed them, their meat got tossed in the dirt.

As he chunked the slabs through the bars of the pen, Derek rolled up on his cart and began unloading his gear. He started prepping his tranquilizer stick that would sedate the animals so he could check them over and insert the GPS locator microchips that all zoo animals were required to have.

"Cody my man," Derek said with a smile. "Come to hold these bad boys still while I chip 'em?"

"No way." Cody said. "I'm not getting anywhere near those things. Who names their pets Devil and Demon anyway?"

Derek laughed, "Yeah, they aren't exactly kid friendly names. We'd have to do something about that if we were going to integrate them into the park, but honestly, I think we'll end up putting them down. We've been trying to place them in a facility that's designed for truly wild animals, but no one wants them. Everyone has heard the stories and most of them are probably true. These two are just too vicious for a place like this. It's a shame the way some people raise their animals, they really are magnificent creatures."

Cody was usually troubled over talk of an animal being put to sleep, but in this case, he felt a sense of relief. They were battle scarred from where they'd been beaten and tossed into cages with fighting dogs. Animals born and bred into killing had a taste for blood and it couldn't be tamed, no matter how nice you treated them. They would always be dangerous.

Derek jabbed each of the hyenas in turn with the tranquilizer stick and a minute later both were snoozing, heads on their paws.

"That will keep them out for about ten minutes or so," Derek said as he prepared the smaller syringes that contained the GPS chips.

"So, buddy," Derek said, "Since you're the man of the Wilkes house I have a question for you. You know me and your Mom have been seeing each other for a while now. I was thinking about something a little more public and permanent if you catch my drift."

Cody knew where this was headed. He'd caught the glimpses between Mom and Derek when they thought no one was looking and he was cool with it. He knew about their spot down by the river and their late nights at work. So, did everyone else, it was the worst kept secret in Piedmont.

Derek was a great guy, always quick with a joke or a laugh and he always treated Cody like a man and not a boy. He and Derek had shared a couple of beers a week ago down by the Mississippi as they waited for a catfish to take the bait drifting at the end of their fishing lines. Mom would have flipped out if she knew, but Derek said it was a rite of passage and what Mom didn't know wouldn't get them hurt. He'd given Cody his old Zippo with the Coast Guard emblem engraved on it. A memento from his days of service when he was fresh out of high school. Cody carried it with him everywhere now.

"Go for it man. I know about you two, everyone does." Cody said with a grin.

"Cool," Derek said and put out his fist. "Just wanted to make sure you were okay with us going out to dinner and movies and stuff."

Cody bumped it and a smiling Derek stepped toward the sleeping hyenas.

He unlatched the kennel door and slipped inside, knelt beside Diablo. Cody stayed outside with a hand on the gate, ready to close it the second the job was finished. He didn't want to be anywhere near them. Derek used the battery powered clippers to shave the fur at the injection site and swabbed the skin with an alcohol pad. As he prepared to jab the sleeping hyena his radio squawked to life.

"Derek!" Kelly's voice came over the radio. "We need you up here NOW at the gates! People are attacking each other, HURRY!" She yelled desperately.

She sounded like she was on the verge of hysteria. She sounded scared.

Derek keyed his mike. "I'm on the way!"

Cody jumped out of the way as he flew out of the kennel and slammed the self-latching door.

"Gotta go. We'll finish this later. Can you gather my gear?" he said, as he jumped on his cart and hurried for the front gate.

Cody watched as Derek rode off then picked up the tranq sticks. He reached through the cage to get the clippers and the GPS syringes. No way was he going inside. He loaded them in his cart then hurried to see what was going on and if there was anything he could do to help. He'd never heard his mom sound like that, she was usually cool headed. Trouble in the park wasn't unheard of, usually the result of some impatient tourist agitated with waiting in line or the constant flux of children flitting about like bees. *It couldn't be too bad,* he thought. *Probably a couple of overly excited guests in a shoving match over a snow cone or something. Maybe the radio just made her sound panicky.*

Neither one of them noticed the barred door had bounced back open an inch. The old safety latch on the seldom used cage hadn't caught.

3

HARPER

T he shuttle bus pulled to a stop in the parking lot of the Piedmont Animal Sanctuary and as soon as the driver opened the door Harper Alexander sprang for the exit and was the first one out. The rest of the kids were right behind her, rushing for the gates to be the first in line. Mr. Baynard just shook his head at their exuberance to get inside the park the second it opened. It reminded him of his military days: Hurry up and wait. He waved the driver away and operated the wheelchair lift himself, a fine line of perspiration on his upper lip despite the cool morning. Murray Sanders took off as soon as his wheels hit the ground with a *Thanks Mr. Baynard* thrown over his shoulder. He was hurrying to grab his place in line the other were saving for him.

"Care to join us?" Baynard asked the driver. "I have enough passes to get you in too."

The bus driver just grunted and waved him off.

"Nah, I've got stuff I need to do." he said and pulled out his phone.

He was feeling lucky today. He had two hundred bucks

left in his checking account and he was going to double it. Maybe triple it if Lady Luck held and the online poker game didn't cheat him again.

"Suit yourself," said Baynard, wincing at the sudden pressure behind his eyes as he joined his eager students near the head of the line.

"Ok, guys and girls. Everyone have their phones? Snack money?"

There was a chorus of excited acknowledgements as the gates swung open and the parks ticket taker slid open the window to his booth.

"Good, stay in touch."

He had to raise his voice to be heard over their excited chatter. "Remember, study your animals. How they move, interact with their environment. That's important. Many of them are not native to this country, so how they've adapted to their surroundings is part of your research. Sketches, photos, videos and any data you can collect will factor into your grade. Be thorough and have fun!"

"I'll be around to observe each of you in a while. Now get out of here." he yelled at the retreating kids and watched them scatter.

He could feel a killer migraine coming on, his head was throbbing and the light was hurting his eyes. He made his way towards the gift shop where he was sure he could find some cheap sunglasses, a bottle of water and surely, they carried aspirin.

Harper made a beeline for the giraffe enclosure. She had seen Bert once before with her parents on the guided tour. He was magnificent. Easily sixteen feet tall and in his prime at 15 years old. She stared up in awe at the kind but funny face of Bert while he surveyed the park. A staff member had answered all her questions and her parents nearly had to drag her away to keep up with the group.

He had come to Piedmont via Venezuela eleven years ago. A zoo outside of Caracas fell on hard times and began selling animals for big game hunts. The resulting uproar and outcry of animal activists around the world saw the facility shut down and all the surviving animals relocated to other zoos. Bert was lucky enough to find a home at Piedmont.

Harper had no problem with hunting, she understood how the money from sportsmen funded conservation and protected habitats. Careful management of wild game kept the population healthy. She came from a long line of outdoorsman but slaughtering tame zoo animals was just wrong.

Finding Bert this morning wasn't hard. All she had to do was look up. She spotted him with his head up in a tree, pulling leaves into his mouth with his eighteen-inch purple tongue. Picking up her pace, she was soon standing a few feet away from the bull giraffe.

"Hi Bert, I'm Harper. I doubt you remember me, but I think you are amazing. If you don't mind, I'm just gonna watch you awhile and take some notes and a few pictures." she said.

The girls at school would snicker and make jokes if they were to see her now but Harper didn't care. She didn't care about most things teenaged girls obsessed over. Boys, clothes, music and social media didn't dominate her life. Thirteen years old and easily the prettiest girl in school, she preferred comfort over fashion and usually had her nose in a book instead of someone else's business.

She studied the fence that separated the walking path from the animals. It was eight-foot-tall and no one was watching and this might be her only chance before too many people arrived. She stuck her foot in one of the four-inch squares that made up the wire and started climbing. The ever-alert Bert abandoned his quest for the perfect leaf and stepped her way. Another foot higher, then another, she found herself at the top staring at his long neck. Bert lowered his head towards the girl, sensing no ill intent from the small creature with the tasty looking straw-colored hair. She felt the warm air expelled from his nostrils as he stared into her eyes mere inches away. Letting go of the fence with one hand, she raised her phone and snapped a selfie of her and the friendly giraffe. She giggled as he extended his long tongue and touched her hair with it. Deciding he didn't care for the taste he pulled it back in. Girl and giant stared unblinkingly at each other for a few seconds. The magic of the moment was broken by the putt putting of a golf cart.

"Miss, I'm going to have to ask you to get down from there, please."

Harper climbed down as Bert returned to his foraging. She faced the man on the golf cart. His shirt said Derek on it and she knew there was a friendly smile just below the surface of the stern look he was giving her.

"I'm sorry. I'm his biggest fan. He gave me his auto-graph," she said as she wiped giraffe drool off her cheek.

Derek tried to hold the frown but couldn't. "It's ok," he relented. "I was more concerned about you falling than Bert eating you. Enjoy your day and try to stay on the ground. I've got a date with two hyenas, so I'm gonna trust you won't try to steal my giraffe while I'm working."

Harper laughed and gave him a wave as he motored away. Looking at Bert she smiled. "Now, where were we?"

Harper followed him as he ambled along, sampling various trees at random. She made rough sketches of him foraging and tried to capture the way his tongue curled out to snag the leaves. He always picked the ones farthest away, the highest he could reach and she wondered if there was reason for that. She made a note to research it further and laughed as his behind erupted in one of his famous thundering farts. She took more photos, added detail to her sketches and carried on a one-way conversation with him.

She looked up when she saw Derek motoring as fast as the golf cart would go; he passed her with a quick wave and left her in a cloud of dust. She shrugged and went back to writing observations in her notepad.

A few minutes later, Bert whipped his head toward the front entrance as the sound of screams and honking horns shattered the stillness of the morning. His mane bristled, and he snorted at the disturbance. Harper gathered up her things, told Bert she'd be back and headed to see what all the fuss was about.

4

VANESSA

Vanessa Talley made her way through the sanctuary chewing her ever present bubble gum. She blew a bubble as big as her face and inhaled it quickly when it popped, avoiding having to peel it off her cheeks. At ten years old, she was the youngest of Mr. Baynard's zoology group, but she held her own with the older kids. She had already been advanced a year ahead in school once and was smart enough to skip another. She could graduate at 16 and be in college shortly thereafter. Her dad, however, didn't want her to grow up too fast and always be the youngest of her class. She breezed her way through school, turned assignments in ahead of time and finished whole textbooks while her classmates were in the early chapters.

She thought she looked older than her ten years, she certainly felt it. Her high cheekbones and confident poise garnered no doubt that she was a descendent of African royalty somewhere in her lineage. She was proud of her ancestry and her one goal in life was to help end hunger in poverty-stricken nations through smart resource management. Poaching animals provided one meal one time.

Proper management meant many meals many times. Her father called her idealistic but she felt that part of the answer lay in the ostrich. Ugly to most, but beautiful in her eyes, she adored the species and its potential to improve lives. She had argued her point with her father and Mr. Baynard more than once. It was a bird that could adapt to practically any environment found on the African continent. They were low maintenance with a highly adaptive digestive system. A female ostrich could lay up to sixty eggs a year and it was an egg that could weigh five pounds! The meat was protein rich, the skin yielded high quality leather, and the feathers were a market in themselves. There was also its significance in African folklore; the ostrich was considered the King of the Birds. They also possessed a set of four-inch claws at the end of their feet that could gut a lion so the highly social flocks of the giant birds were fully capable of defending themselves. She would sum up her argument by saying it was like having a velociraptor that gave you the world's biggest omelet for breakfast. Her passion made it hard to argue with her.

Her goal today was to spend some quality time with Ziggy, a female ostrich. Ziggy toured for a while with one of the last traveling circuses in the country. When her owner retired to Florida, she spent a couple of years entertaining children on the boardwalks at the beach.

Her trainer used a laser pointer to paint a target and using her massive beak and long neck she busted piñatas full of candy for the enthralled children, popped balloons floating in the air and occasionally took an adventurous child for a ride on her back as she ran down the beach, clucking and chirping.

When her trainer passed away, Ziggy was willed to Piedmont with a large endowment to make sure she was always cared for and could spent the rest of her days entertaining children and adults alike.

Vanessa watched her walk along the fence hunting for snacks. She darted her head quickly and gulped down the unwary cricket. She was an efficient hunter and her eyes, the largest of any land mammal, easily picked out the small prey that she loved to munch on. Vanessa shot some video of her hunting and narrated along remarking on the powerful legs and graceful motion. No effort was wasted as the large bird sniped cricket after juicy cricket.

The sound of crinkling cellophane brought Ziggy to full focus on the girl. She knew that sound. Ziggy loved popcorn. She anxiously awaited the toss and when it came, she snatched the fluffy treat out of the air, ready for more. Vanessa tossed her two at once and Ziggy snagged them both. She shared the bag with the ostrich, glad for the time she had with the magnificent strider all to herself before the park became crowded. She tossed Ziggy the last piece but as she darted for it, her head swiveled toward the front gate when the screaming started. The popcorn fell forgotten to the ground.

Vanessa grabbed her stuff and headed for the gate as Ziggy kept pace on the opposite side of the fence. Her daddy taught her to always be aware and ready for danger. She had no idea what could be going on, but she was going to find out.

5

SWAN

S wan Michaels skipped along the tour route, stopping to pull a pretty yellow flower from the wild patch growing beside the road. She tucked it over her ear and gave a quick apology to Mother Earth. She recited aloud the poem she was working on about all the people and all the animals living in harmony with each other. *It wasn't very good*, she thought, but whatever, it was a work in progress.

Swan was the child of globally aware nature lovers who were quick to sign a petition or attend a protest for causes they believed in. Her mother was a spokeswoman for the Meskwaki Indian tribe and her father was an environmental management tech who had been smitten with her from the first time he'd met her on the reservation. They both encouraged her activism. Her long raven colored hair hung straight and glossy. She had a carefree, thrift shop chic look that she managed to pull off with her Ugg boots, Save the Whales t-shirt and knee ripped jeans. A strict vegetarian, except for the occasional chicken nugget, she sometimes felt guilty about all the lettuce that gave its life for her salads.

She'd begged her parents for a trip to observe pandas in the wild for her upcoming thirteenth birthday. Her passion was conservation and she had inherited some her parent's radicalism. When she got older, she wanted to take on Japanese whalers, big game hunters, loggers, real estate developers, oil company pipelines and anyone else who might harm an animal.

In her young mind, it was perfectly natural for animals to prey on one another, just not man. Man had no business interfering with the natural order of things. She had been proud to carry a homemade sign outside of a meat packing plant, protesting the wholesale slaughter of animals and the deplorable conditions in which those animals lived out their short lives. Sure, people had to eat too, but she believed there had to be a better way. More harmonious and in tune with nature. She believed strongly in spaying and neutering to prevent unwanted litters. She loved baby animals and hated to see them discarded by careless owners and she cried every time a commercial came on TV about animal cruelty.

The walls of her room were covered in posters of cute animals and she sent ten percent of her allowance to PETA without fail every week. Most weekends she volunteered at the animal shelter and would have adopted all of them if she could. In an ironic twist of fate, her mother was allergic to dogs and her father, cats. She was relegated to caring for a solitary goldfish named Terry, but Terry lived as well as any goldfish ever had, so there was that.

Her biggest passion though was wolves. She loved them! The pack mentality and the mating for life: It was so romantic. All those dumb ranchers out west raising a stink about a few missing sheep drove her nuts. They were wolves! What else were they supposed to eat? Personally, she couldn't imagine eating a fluffy little lamb, but wolves needed meat and more importantly, wolf cubs needed meat. They were so cute! It was the circle of life and that was cool with her. Mother Earth knew what she was doing.

Swan reached her destination and stared through the enclosure at the magnificent male Timber Wolf laying in the shade. His eyes were alert and darting as he surveyed his surroundings and kept an eye on his mate as she fed on a chunk of raw meat. She admired their thick silvery gray coats and the large canine teeth. Sinewy limbs built for speed and endurance. Graceful and effortless in their motions, they were truly apex predators and she loved everything about them. It saddened her to see them in their enclosure, even though it was very nice by any zoo standards. They should be free to run wild and hunt. Zero was definitely an Alpha and with his mate, Lucy, by his side, he would easily rule over any pack.

Zero and Lucy had been born in different petting zoos thousands of miles apart but were together now, mates for life. She snapped a few photos with her phone and posted it to her Instagram account. Later in the day, a handler would appear and lead them out to greet visitors. Despite their size and the sharpness of their teeth, the two were as gentle as puppies. They had been born in captivity as had their parents and their parents before them. They'd never known the wild and were as friendly as any family dog. Later the crowds would come but for right now she had them all to herself.

Inspired she pulled out her notebook and started writing bad poetry about the majestic hunters. *"Now, what rhymes with wolf?"* She asked herself.

After several minutes of deliberation and eraser chewing, she decided to file the poem away for later. Great poetry couldn't be rushed.

Honking horns and what sounded like a scream broke the silence and Zero stood quickly and looked toward the front of the zoo. Hackles raised and lip curled, he let out a low growl. Lucy moved in beside him, guarding his flank and protecting her mate and there was a low rumble in her throat too. They didn't seem so cute and cuddly anymore as Swan snapped another photo of the two regal animals ready for battle. She was surprised but pleased to see the wild in them come out. She had kind of hated that they seemed so docile and gentle, they were wolves after all.

She gathered up her bag and gear. She had all day to visit with them and whatever the disturbance was, it sounded serious. People were so stupid sometimes, she thought. Animals didn't engage in petty behavior; if there was a problem, they solved it right then and there. They ate when they were hungry, they drank when they were thirsty and they mated when they wanted to mate. They didn't fight for petty reasons but if they did, they fought to kill. Only people got angry over little things that didn't matter.

6

ANNALISE AND TOBIAS

The twin brother and sister duo of Tobias and Annalise Richter made their way through the sanctuary eating the snow cones they had purchased at the snack bar. Pale blue eyes, hair so blonde it appeared almost white and alabaster skinned, they were an eye-catching pair. They evoked thoughts of elven children from some frozen fairy realm. Tall and slender, elegant in their movements, they had an air of aloofness as if they were visitors to this world and not just a couple of twelve-year olds from Iowa. They were an odd pair, preferring each other's company to that of others, quick to finish the other's sentences and communicating at times with just their facial expressions. They had the same uncanny bond that most twins shared and their ability to sense each other's thoughts seemed like telepathy at times.

According to their online genealogy research, they were descendants of the Nordic peoples. Their Scandinavian forefathers were Vikings and explorers. Mighty warriors and fearless women. They were proud that their ancient ancestors were the first people to set foot on the continent of

North America, not Christopher Columbus as so many people erroneously believed. They preferred to think of themselves as children of the Norse God of Thunder, Thor instead of Dennis and Tina Richter. Not to be confused with Thor from the comics and movies, although Annalise thought he was hot.

As similar as they appeared, they were very different. Annalise was filled with humor and compassion, whereas Tobias tended to be snarky and serious. She took things lightly, not letting much bother her while he tended to be hot headed. He suffered no affronts to his sister and fists would fly when someone dared to make a rude comment about her unusual appearance.

They arrived at the polar bear enclosure where Popsicle and Daisy were tussling over an old tractor tire. The cooler fall temperatures made the bears more active. They were rescue animals who'd been at Piedmont many years. As orphaned cubs in Greenland with a knack for raiding garbage cans and showing no fear of man, authorities were concerned that as they grew they could become dangerous. Not wanting to put them down, inquiries were made to different animal sanctuaries and Piedmont was quick to take them.

Popsicle was an impressive 1200 pounds and ten feet long from nose to tail, although during the cold Iowa winters he and Daisy both would gain another fifty or sixty pounds as the frigid weather was more suited to their natural habitats.

Daisy, at 750 pounds and seven and half feet long, was no slouch in the size department either. She slid effortlessly into the pool and swam to the other end, climbed out chewing on a fish and gave a huge shake, spraying the delighted twins with water.

Their enclosure featured a swimming pool that the staff kept stocked with live fish and an icemaker purchased from a defunct commercial fishing operation. It dumped a steady stream of ice directly into the pool during the warmer months.

Annalise and Tobias chose to do their study on the polar bears because sometime in the past they thought their ancestors had probably fought with and against, or maybe even worshipped the mighty giants.

Tobias's youthful mind conjured images of their ancestors charging into battle astride the magnificent beasts, swords and battle axes clenched in the fists of the Northmen, the riders and their mounts one in mind and purpose as they raided the frozen country in search of honor, riches and glory. He wasn't sure if people actually rode polar bears, but he liked the thought of it.

The twins dreamed of working side by side studying the effects of global warming. Maybe winning the Nobel Prize for their work. After high school they would attend college together, move right into research and when each found their respective mates, they would all live under one roof. They had it all planned out.

The twins watched as Popsicle rose to his hind legs, ears perked and fur rising along his back. Daisy lowered herself and rumbled a deep growl as the light breeze brought a smell to their sensitive nostrils that signaled danger.

Screams of agony drifted on the breeze, snapping each of the twins from their daydreaming. Tobias raised an eyebrow and Annalise responded with an almost imperceptible nod. The pair took off at a dead run, their long legs eating up the distance as they headed for the sanctuary entrance.

7

MURRAY

Murray Sanders stopped his wheelchair in front of the haunted mansion. Halloween was still a month away but the staff were already decorating the visitors' center in preparation. It was an old rambling house, its Victorian architecture giving it an appropriately spooky vibe as the starting point for the haunted hayride. He approved of the grinning pumpkins and ghosts in the upstairs windows. Vampires, werewolves, zombies and chainsaw wielding maniacs thrilled him to no end. Even before his accident, he spent a lot of time staying up late watching every scary movie he could find and slaying monsters by the thousands with his Xbox controller. He was a huge fan of movies and spouted pop culture references whenever he was excited or nervous, though most of his quips went over people's heads.

Most of his old friends didn't come around anymore to see him; it was just too awkward for everyone. When he took the dare on his bicycle to jump the homemade ramp at the bottom of the hill, they all cheered him on. None of them saw the van that took away all of the feeling in his lower body until it was too late. The driver sped away in a panic instead of stopping and calling an ambulance. He was never caught, never had to stand trial, never apologized to the boy he had crippled. Murray knew it was his own fault as much as the drivers', he shouldn't have been in the street, but he couldn't help but feel bitter that no one ran to help him. That he had been alone and afraid for what seemed like a long time.

When the van hit him all of his friends ran away. They were all young and scared and pedaled home to tell parents as fast as they could. He didn't blame them; they didn't know any better. They didn't think to run up to the nearest house and pound on the door. What did kids know about spinal injuries? They didn't know you were supposed to lay still and not move. They thought they were doing the right thing, riding away to get help as fast as they could. He was worried about a car coming and running over him and his instincts told him to get off the road. He had been able to crawl to the sidewalk before the first grownup noticed him but by then the damage had been done. He hadn't felt the bones grating against his spinal cord and finally severing it as he struggled up the curb.

After the accident, he simply gave up. He lost all interest in gaming and the movies that he loved. He refused to see anyone and barely ate. He sat in his room and listened to the other kids running and playing. The sound of skateboard wheels on asphalt or the hum of bicycle tires drove him further into himself.

He was smart, almost gifted, and had an aptitude for all things mechanical. The bicycle ramp at the bottom of Cedar Hill road, the one that was supposed to send you flying through the air but land softly on an incline, had been his design. He could do three-digit multiplication in his head, he understood Algebra and he'd dreamed of becoming an engineer before his life changed. His parents tried to treat him just like before the accident, to pretend it was just an inconvenience to be overcome and not the end of the world. What did they know? They weren't the ones trapped in a chair. He heard his mother cry when she thought he was asleep and he saw the crumpled-up wads of paper in the trash where his father had been trying to find ways to pay the high costs of his medical bills. He knew he was useless and a drain on everyone around him.

Bitter and angry with the world, he watched in disgust as the volunteers installed a wheel chair ramp on the front of his house. They might as well hang a glowing neon sign in the yard: HELPLESS CRIPPLE LIVES HERE.

He resented them for their pity. He wanted to run them off, curse them and show them he didn't need their help but running was no longer an option.

No one was able to break through the wall he'd built around himself. He refused to do therapy. What was the point? He fell behind in his classes, even the ones he used to ace without a problem. He used any excuse he could to get out of going to school where he heard the whispers and people made way for his wheelchair like it was contagious. Nobody knew what to say to him and he didn't make it easy for them. Finally, everyone stopped trying and he was fine with that. He hated the world, the world hated him back and that was just the way it was.

He continued his mental and physical descent until the day his dad wheeled him into the van modified for his wheelchair. His father ignored Murray's grumbling and questions about being dragged from his self-imposed prison. Murray's sour attitude was answered with silence as the van carried him somewhere he'd never been.

When they arrived at the YMCA Murray complained and tried to argue that he didn't want to go. He didn't need to attend yet another program for cripples. His dad ignored his protests and wheeled him inside.

Rows of folding chairs had been set up in the gymnasium facing a man in a wheelchair wearing an Army t-shirt. His arms were corded in heavy muscle as he rolled his chair back and forth across the hardwood floors of the basketball court and he had a little brown monkey sitting on one shoulder.

He saw other people in wheelchairs like his own and a lot of them were military veterans. They had stumps of legs sticking out where IED's had brutally amputated them. Others, like him, whole, but broken.

The man introduced himself as Sergeant Walker, grinned at the irony, and began speaking. Murray went from morose to riveted. The Sergeant told the crowd about putting a gun his own mouth, ready to end his life after the incident that paralyzed him. He told them how he'd given up hope for a productive life. Murray hung on every word and knew exactly what he was talking about. He felt the same way. But this guy had gotten past it, he was a real beast. He wasn't letting the chair own him. He owned the chair. It was a tool to keep him in life, not out of it. He'd lost the use of his legs, but his mind was as powerful as the massive arms he flexed at the crowd. He told them how he competed in wheelchair races, climbed mountains and entered body building contests. The whole time his little monkey capered and fetched him different things he wanted to show them. The little fellow dragged over a white board for him to draw on. Fetched a golden trophy his basketball team had won in the State championship. He picked up a marker he'd dropped and even put money in a soda machine and brought back a diet coke.

"I haven't been able to teach him to read," the soldier lamented. "He still can't bring me an Orange soda when I want one."

He was pursuing his PhD. He'd even been in an Ironman competition, completing the swimming portion with just his arms to move him through the water. He'd come in last place but that didn't matter he said. He had been on the field and he had given it his all. He finished his presentation with the little monkey putting on a Teddy Roosevelt hat and smiling his toothy smile as Sergeant Walker quoted the twenty sixth president.

"It is not the critic who counts; not the man who points out how the strong man stumbles, or where the doer of deeds could have done them better. The credit belongs to the man who is actually in the arena, whose face is marred by dust and sweat and blood; who strives valiantly; who errs, who comes short again and again, because there is no effort without error and shortcoming; but who does actually strive to do the deeds; who knows great enthusiasms, the great devotions; who spends himself in a worthy cause; who at the best knows in the end the triumph of high achievement, and who at the worst, if he fails, at least fails while daring greatly, so that his place shall never be with those cold and timid souls who neither know victory nor defeat."

Everyone was inspired by his story and Murray fell in love with the monkey.

As his testimony wrapped up Murray impatiently waited his turn to speak with the man. A renewed Murray refused to let his father push his chair when they left, he would propel himself. No more feeling sorry for himself, he vowed. His father whispered a silent prayer of gratitude for the wounded vet who finally got through to his son when everyone else had failed. He didn't mind a bit when he handed over his Visa card to pay for the workout gear Murray picked out at the fitness store.

Murray had asked his parents about getting a capuchin monkey as a service animal to help him and he'd been working towards it for nearly a year. They had agreed if he got his grades up, if he learned everything there was to know about them and he raised the money himself to buy one. They weren't cheap.

He'd buckled down and brought his grades up, that was the easy part. He'd joined Mr. Baynard's animal studies group to learn about them and had started crafting clever articulated wooden monkeys to sell on Etsy. He had nearly five thousand dollars saved up and soon they could start seriously shopping for one. Murray pumped iron. When the new school year started, he added biology classes to his workload. He held his head up when he rolled down the hallways in his school. He made amends with old friends and added new ones. He owned this chair; it would never own him again. His body ached and his muscles strained from the intensity of his workouts. His skinny arms doubled in size and his belief in himself grew with his muscles.

His father changed the smooth street tires out for some with off road treads and the dirt paths and gravel trails around the town park became his training course.

His dream was to take his interest in mechanical engineering and infuse it with the study of starfish and lizards that regenerated their lost or damaged limbs. He would figure out how to apply that to his damaged spine either through biological or mechanical means and get out of this chair. He'd give his advancements to the world, make sure that people like the soldier who'd changed his life would get the chance to be whole again. He'd be like Wolverine, regenerating from traumatic injuries and righting wrongs wherever he found them.

Moving past the haunted house, he rolled onward to the monkey cages. Piedmont had four of them in residence. They were wonderful animals that never ceased to cheer him up. He envied the way they moved, their speed and agility he could never come close to even if he wasn't sentenced to life in this wheelchair. Soon he would have one for himself. There were programs that lent the little creatures to incapacitated people but he wanted one of his own, not one he would have to give back whenever they wanted. It was worth the wait, maybe by spring he would have enough money if his sales were good. Who knows, maybe he could get it a little outfit and be an organ grinder, maybe go to children's hospitals or something. Maybe get a YouTube channel and raise money for charities. The future wasn't what he'd planned but it didn't look half bad from where he was sitting.

He watched them scamper back and forth across the bamboo monkey bars, chittering at each other as they played a game of tag. China, Sage, Elmo and Ernie were nearly everyone's favorite animals and he knew he wouldn't have much time to study them before the crowds of little kids showed up.

He watched them play, long limbs and tails swinging them across the pen and sketched their faces, noting how each was different. They never missed a hand or foothold. Never faltered, the enclosure mapped so thoroughly in their brains they could do it blind. He laughed at their high-speed pursuit and tried to capture some of it with his phone.

The small simians scampered for the safety of their nest as a scream pierced the air, followed by more screams. Their chatter stopped as they pushed each other in an attempt to get deeper inside to hide in the shadows.

Murray spun his chair in the direction the gate. *Special effects for the haunted house,* he wondered? It made sense, but they were too real, too desperate and pain filled for that he quickly decided.

Praying it wasn't one of his friends in danger or hurt, he put his dirt track practice to use and propelled toward the yells and shouts, now joined by the sound of squealing tires and honking horns.

8

DONNY

Donny Lin skirted the edges of the park, sticking to the shadows and the less traveled places, avoiding any staff that might have questions for him. He knew he'd been seen a few times, no more than a fleeting glance, but if he wasn't careful, eventually someone would figure out that he was not paying the gate admission every day. Once the crowds arrived, it was easy to blend in and become invisible. He made his way towards the modern 'outhouses' at the back of the park to take care of his morning business. He kept away from the main bathrooms near the gates, too many staff were there and there weren't enough people yet where he could hide in plain sight. He couldn't let anyone find out that he was living there because then the authorities would be called. He had a secret spot in the hayloft of the barn in the petting zoo where he could sleep. He had a little niche carved out in the very back and it wouldn't be discovered until hundreds of bales were used first. He figured he had until early spring before they got to the back of the loft. He wasn't proud of it but there were storerooms of supplies and no one would miss cans of food or a little fresh meat intended for the animals. There were always plenty of leftover people food too. At the end of the day, the concession stands and little restaurant tossed their unsold food in the dumpster and garbage truck only came twice a week.

If he had choices, this wasn't where he would have chosen to be but it was better than being in the foster care system. He was too young to get a job and start living a sort of normal life so he was in a holding pattern for a few more years. He'd been bounced around through the system since he was an infant with no idea where he came from or who he really was. Nobody wanted to adopt the half Asian boy who couldn't speak. Most people treated him as if he were mentally disabled instead of mute. Nothing could be further from the truth; he'd just never had a chance at being a normal kid. He didn't know who his father was and all he knew about his mother was that she'd been Chinese.

There was no way was he ever going back, he'd sleep in a dumpster with the rats before he let another adult sneak in his room late at night like his last foster dad. Being mute and unwanted, he'd always been a target of bullies and perverts looking for an easy victim. The night his foster dad came for him, he had busted his nose with a solid kick, grabbed his few belongings and ran. He drifted through different towns, ate from dumpsters behind restaurants, shop lifted when he had no choice and kept on the move. He was invisible to grownups as long as he didn't look dirty and they didn't see him during school hours. He avoided the big cities and the predators that lurked there. He took clothes from Goodwill bins, walked into birthday parties at Chuck e Cheeses and ate his fill, paid attention to church billboards and their advertisements of potluck dinners.

Winter was coming and he really should be heading south but he liked this place. He'd found it by accident but it had everything he needed. The barn was warm, the food was plentiful and he had the run of the place at night. There were no cameras and the one old man who was the security guard never left the house once he closed the gates.

He stared at his big toe poking through the worn-out thrift store tennis shoes. He was going to have to 'borrow' a bicycle and ride up to the nearest little city to get himself supplied for winter. La Crosse was about thirty miles north and it was big enough to have a few donation boxes around town. He'd never had name brand anything, just cast offs, hand me downs or stuff he took from thrift shop donation boxes. His clothes were worn but clean. He alternated between the two sets he had and washed them in the bathroom sink with hand soap after the park was closed.

The barn was an ideal spot to hide out during the day where the chances of being caught were almost zero. Once there were a crowd of kids in the petting zoo, he could walk over, make sure no one was looking and disappear into the empty goat stall. From there he could scurry up the ladder and be out of sight in the loft. While he waited, he lay beneath an old elm in the wooded area behind the panther enclosure where he'd spend the morning lounging and reading one of the books he borrowed from the visitor center library. The risk of daytime discovery scared him, but the night was his. He could roam freely, finding leftover food, dropped sunglasses and change in the coin slots of the vending machines. He'd even found an iPod once, but his conscience prevailed and he put it in the lost and found box.

He'd begun sharing his spoils with the panther who he discovered loved corndogs and hamburgers. He didn't know what the zoo called the big black cat, but to Donny, he was Yewan, one of the few Chinese words he'd learned. Night in the language of his mothers' people. The panther, like him, was most active after dark. He'd listened to one of the staff answer questions about him and learned he'd been bred in captivity and had been a family pet until he got too big. One night, with a pounding heart and more than a little fear in him, he'd climbed over the fence with his offering of corndogs. The panther may have looked fierce and vicious but it was just a big kitten. It longed for human touch, it had grown up being cuddled and loved and missed playing and roughhousing. Donny spent most of his nights in the enclosure after that first timid meeting and had taken to bringing his blanket and curling up with him near dawn to sleep together.

He daydreamed of setting him free and the two of them racing through the night on the hunt, their prey never knowing what hit them until powerful jaws closed around their throat or his spear pierced their heart. Like the panther he was fast and strong. Lean and wiry like a distance runner, he knew together they could rule the forest. Man and beast, tooth, claw and spear, striking fear into the hearts of the lesser animals.

His fantasy of roaming the jungle with the big cat was interrupted by the screaming from the front gate area. Donny felt panic surge through him. Screaming meant something bad happened, someone could call the police. If they started poking around they might discover him, start asking questions he couldn't answer even if he wanted to. He considered abandoning his new home, but he finally felt like he had a place to call his. He couldn't leave, Yewan was the only friend he'd ever had, but he needed to know what was happening. Horns began to honk as people screamed and a strange keening sound filled the air.

Donny raced along the edge of the wood line to a better vantage point. His eyes widened in disbelief when he saw what was happening at the front gates.

9

MAIN ENTRANCE

R obert Baynard white knuckled the edges of the sink. The water and aspirin weren't helping, if anything he felt worse. His head was killing him. He was drenched in sweat and his insides felt twisted up. Uncontrollable rage coursed through him in waves. The bathroom door swung open as a man entered and the sunlight hit the mirror Robert stood facing. He grimaced as the light reflected into his eyes, the pain like white hot daggers and he felt a growl in his throat begging for release. He forced it down and splashed more water on his face.

"Hey buddy, you don't look so good," the man said.

Robert ignored him.

"You need some help or something?" the man asked.

Robert tried to tamp down the rage building inside of him and remained speechless, teeth gritted, once again gripping the edges of the sink as hard as he could.

A hand touched his shoulder and a concerned voice asked, "You want me to get you some help?"

Pain flared through his body at the contact and before either man realized what was happening, Robert whipped his head around and bit down savagely on the man's fore-arm. He yelled in surprise and pain, shoved Robert away and fled the bathroom. Robert was flung backward, stumbled over his own feet and fell, striking his head on the edge of a urinal. He lost consciousness as the zombie virus continued to course through his veins. Robert Baynard, proud veteran and school teacher, died on a bathroom floor as something new and hungry took control of his body. His eyes shot open, black and lifeless as an uncontrollable need filled him. A need for blood, a need to bite and rend. A need to replicate, duplicate and populate. An insatiable craving for human flesh. He smelled them and heard them only a few feet away and sprang to his feet.

Kelly stepped into the nurses' station, concerned over the prospect of a guest being bitten by an animal. It was shaping up to be one hell of a day. They were short staffed, most of the crew had called in sick. There were already lines forming at the gates as families and tour groups took advantage of the nice weather before the days grew cold. And now this. It wasn't unheard of for some of the animals to get a little rowdy, but nothing had ever warranted the panic she'd heard on the radio.

The nurse's station was near the main entrance near the visitors' center. This area consisted mostly of park benches, the snack bar, gift shop and a playground for the kids. The closest creatures were the barnyard animals in the farm display that doubled as a petting zoo. There were a few goats, the chickens, a pair of cows, some free roaming peacocks and an old alpaca. They'd never had any trouble from any of them.

Although, it could be one of the capuchins, she thought. The little monkeys occasionally darted out of their enclosure if a handler was careless and would start begging or stealing junk food from the guests. Along with their wallets, watches, earrings or any other thing they could get their paws on.

A burly man sat on the edge of the examination table. Blood dotted his t-shirt and jeans. Anna held a compression bandage to the wound on his arm, a tube of antibiotic cream in her free hand.

Kelly bustled in, washed her hands and approached the man who was trying to be cavalier about the whole thing and maybe do a little flirting with the pretty aide.

"Sir, may I see?" asked Kelly.

He nodded and massaged his forehead with his free hand. Sweat ran freely from under the bill of his John Deere cap. He was in a lot of pain, much more than a simple bite would cause, and was starting to have trouble maintaining his air of nonchalance.

Anna pulled the bandage away and he drew his breath in sharply at the pain. Black streaks were spreading outwards from the bite mark. A huge chunk of flesh was missing, the human teeth impressions plainly evident.

"How did this happen?" Kelly asked as she studied the wound. "Was there an altercation?"

"I guess," the man said. "I was just trying to help. Some guy in the bathroom looked sick, he was sweating and looked like he was about to throw up. I was just trying to see if he was okay and the jerk bit me."

"We'll dress this for now but you need to get to the emergency room and have a doctor look at it." Kelly said. "We'll call you an ambulance, this really needs to be examined."

Anna shook her head and tried to convey something without the man seeing as he agreed, his good humor fading fast as the waves of pain became worse.

She had the man lie down on the examination table as she dressed the wound then pulled Anna aside so they wouldn't be overheard.

"What is it?" she asked.

"I've tried contacting EMS, the Sheriff and the fire department." Anna said barely above a whisper. "No one is answering. I think this might be serious. I think the biter might be carrying the virus that's been all over the news."

"I thought that was only in the big cities." Kelly said. "And they're not sure what it is, Anna. Some are saying it's just opportunists taking advantage of the situation and starting riots so they can loot."

"Well, that's no ordinary bite. It's moving too fast, Kelly. It only happened a few minutes ago and he's already feverish. You saw those black strands of infection spreading away from the wound. I've never seen anything like it."

"Me neither." Kelly said worriedly. "Where is the man who attacked him?"

"Still in the bathroom, yelling and beating on the door. He's gone completely insane. Derek and Will are over there now to make sure he doesn't get out."

"If you have this under control, I'm going out there to see what's going on." Kelly said.

"Go, I'll try to get his fever down and keep calling EMS," replied Anna.

Kelly arrived at the bathrooms and heard for herself the guttural growls and pounding coming from inside. Derek stood by the door but there wasn't much he could do to secure it. There wasn't a handle on the outside, it was a push door. She pulled out her phone and dialed 9-1-1. The man sounded completely deranged and they needed professional help.

"I sent Will to try to find the keys so we can lock it."

Derek said "If there are any. I don't remember seeing them hanging on the board."

She quickly filled him in on the situation as the phone rang and rang. If the virus was that contagious and took hold as quickly as it had with the man at the Nurses station, they should consider shutting the park down.

"I think you're right." Derek agreed. "Something is wrong. Big time wrong and this guy trying to tear the door down kind of scares me."

The phone continued to ring then abruptly disconnected, leaving her with a dial tone. She tried again but instantly got an *all circuits are busy* message. She bit her lip and her eyes held worry, edging on fear.

A few people had gathered around the bathrooms, curiosity piqued by the banging and growling coming from inside.

Derek tried to defuse the situation. "Apparently, he ate some bad Mexican food folks, go enjoy yourselves, we'll have this sorted in a minute. There's another set of restrooms by the haunted house right over there," he pointed at the visitors center a couple of hundred yards away.

He got a few laughs as the people drifted away, most of them dismissing the incident without a second thought.

Will came hurrying up to them and shook his head.

"No keys," he said. "These doors never get locked; they've probably been lost for years."

"Maybe it's just the cell phones." Anna said, hitting the redial button for 9-1-1. "I need to get back to the infirmary to see how our patient is doing and I'll try the land line. Maybe I'll have better luck."

"I'm going to let the boss know we need to shut this place down." Derek said, wincing as the man inside the bathroom screamed and slammed against the door again. "Will, make sure no one tries to go in there."

"Okay." Will said and eyed the steel door dubiously. "As long as he doesn't figure out how to open it."

He pulled out his own phone and tried to call his wife.

Kelly was reaching for the door of the first aid station when the bitten man slammed it open and barreled out. She was knocked off the porch into the hedges as he howled and flew down the steps, blood staining the front of his shirt. He sprang off the porch and launched himself at a young couple staring open mouthed and dumbfounded. With snapping teeth and keens of hunger, he tore into them rending flesh and spraying hot blood across startled faces. It took a moment for anyone to react but when they did, panic ensued and screams echoed through the park. Terrified parents grabbed their kids and ran for the entrance. The fear in the air was tangible and catching. There was something terrible and final about the gurgling screams from the couple and people ran away from the sounds of death and whatever was causing them. Those who hadn't seen the carnage didn't have to. They knew a lion or tiger or something equally vicious had escaped and was killing people. They heard it. Heard the horror, the shrieks of sheer terror and ran for their cars.

The man slashed and bit then leaped away from the dying couple in a frenzy. His infected brain drove him to seek new victims and he took down an elderly man who stood there paralyzed, mouth agape at the brutality and speed of the blood covered man.

Kelly scrambled from the hedges and dashed into the first aid station. All hell was breaking loose and panic was threatening to overwhelm her. Anna was sprawled on the floor, her throat torn out, her blouse torn open and a huge pool of red soaked into her hair. Anna fumbled for her radio, she had to warn Cody, had to tell him to hide. To get inside a cage and lock the door behind him. Anna twitched and sat up, her eyes were black, her lips were curled and a hissing sound was coming from her shredded throat.

"Go ahead, mom," came a voice over the radio and Anna launched herself towards the noise. She flew across the room, easily jumping the fifteen feet, fingers clawing for the fresh blood.

Kelly screamed and threw up her hands to shield her face as she backpedaled through the door. One of the Anna's legs tangled in the IV stand and she smashed to the floor, breaking the fall with her face. Teeth skittered across the tiles and she lunged for Kelly again as she tried to slam the door. Hands clawed for her and broken teeth gnashed for tender flesh. Kelly screamed at the monster and with adrenaline charged strength, shoved her weight against the door, finally latching it when Anna's feet slipped on the blood slicked tiles. The rampaging monster hurtled herself against it, into the safety glass, and it spider webbed into hundreds of tiny cracks. She banged her head repeatedly against it, her skin shredding and black blood splashing across the window. The reinforced door held and Kelly watched in horror at the thing that had been her friend only moments before destroyed her face against the unyielding glass.

Across the park, Demonio and Diablo shook off the effects of the tranquilizers. They woke up slowly, their noses filled with the scent of the man who hurt them with his pointed stick. They licked at the stinging needle marks and sniffed the ground, followed the footsteps to the gate. Diablo shoved his toothy snout against the bars and it inched open. They slunk out and smelled the wind. The scent of the man and was strong, his aftershave astringent and unique to them. Lips curled in a low growl and they padded towards the smell. Towards the revenge. It was all they knew. They had been trained to fight, trained to kill anyone or anything that tried to hurt them and the man with the strong smell had hurt them both. The shaggy hair on their hunched backs stood on end as they slipped down the trails towards the front of the park.

Will was really, really starting to get a feeling that things were spiraling out of control when the inhuman shrieks and the banging on the door finally stopped. Thank God for small favors. He could hear screams from other parts of the park now, though. He stared at the useless phone in his hands. Things were going nuts, he couldn't get ahold of his wife, nobody answered his 9-1-1 calls and the sounds of terror made his blood run cold. He needed to go, to get home. He needed this job too and his sense of duty wouldn't let him just abandon his post. He needed to check on the guy in the bathroom, maybe he had died. Maybe he had finally knocked himself out or something.

He pushed the door gently inward and dared a peek. The thing that once was Robert Baynard lunged, sunk his fingers into Wills eyes and bit into his face. Will added his own scream to those all around him as he felt the flesh pulling free. The zombie savaged him viciously then left him dying on the floor as he sprang out of the door in search of fresh prey.

Moments later, Will's body lurched upright. An unnatural hunger consumed him and drove him to his feet. He barely noticed his dangling eyeball and a face that was raw, oozing meat as he joined the hunt.

Derek saw Kelly fly off the porch into the bushes as he was hurrying towards the Visitor center and the offices there. He ran for her, ignoring the man screaming and tearing into an old man when he saw a young couple that had to be dead leap up from the ground. They were covered in bites and slashes and blood and there was no way they could be alive. There was no way they could be running and screaming after a woman struggling to run with her toddler out the front gate. There was no way they were leaping on all fours like animals. There was no way they ran her down and tore into her, sending gouts of blood spraying across the asphalt.

But they did.

The parking lot was utter chaos as the zombies fell on the fleeing guests. The blind fury of the freshly turned undead was relentless and brutal. Windows were smashed. People were torn from cars. The fastest runners were easily brought down with inhuman speed and strength. One became five. Five became ten. Engines fired up and revved to the limit joined the sounds of killing and dying. Screams of terror and screams of rage were drowned out by screeching tires and crunching metal as dozens of cars all tried to squeeze through the same exit. Keening, clawing, biting monsters were there ripping into the broken cars and tearing bodies apart in their insatiable hunger.

Kelly turned away from the bloody glass and the undead thing that kept trying to bite through it as Derek ran up the steps.

Her eyes were wide, on the verge of panic, but seeing him brought her back from the edge a little. He was something sane in an insane world. Something solid she could cling to. Something that kick started her brain to get it working again and get out of the continual loop of *this can't be happening. This can't be happening.* The last of the bloody, ravaged things had chased the terrified people out into the parking lot and wholesale slaughter was happening out there. But not inside the park.

"The gate! We've got to close the gate!" she screamed and sprinted for the big wrought iron fences before any of the gibbering things in the parking lot came back.

"Get the left one!" he yelled and ran past her to the farther of the two, his eyes on the parking lot, the smashed, smoking cars and the screaming monsters attacking them like savage animals. They had to hurry, had to get the gates closed, had to keep those things out. Derek grabbed it and started pulling but was slammed from the back. Jaws closed around his knee and he felt it snap, heard the bones break before he realized what hit him. His arms flailed and another toothy maw clamped down hard on one and pulled in the opposite direction. His arm snapped like a dry twig and his shoulder popped from its socket. Useless random facts flitted through his brain as he watched in disbelief, the pain and shock so extreme he didn't even feel it yet. A hyena's bite was three times as powerful as pit bulls. With eleven hundred pounds of pressure per square inch, nothing could withstand them. They could snap wildebeest femurs as easily as a human biting into a cracker. His head slammed against the ground and the pain hit him, forcing all thought except desperate survival out of his mind. They ragged him back and forth, pulling on him like a play toy and he saw his arm tear free from the elbow.

Derek screamed, a raw, throat shredding scream as the pain kicked in and Demonio dropped the arm. His maw spread wide as he clamped his teeth around Derek' dislocated shoulder. His canines sank deep and more bones snapped and popped as Diablo finally tore his lower leg loose and blood pumped freely from the slashed arteries.

The hyena let go of the leg, barked his laughing bark

then yelped as he was suddenly flying through the air. The impact broke the fiberglass nose of the golf cart and nearly sent Cody tumbling over the steering wheel. Demonio released his hold on Derek's shoulder and crouched low at the new threat, his gurgling, phlegmy sounding growl drowned out by the keens of the undead in the parking lot, many of them turning towards the movement and noises. Kelly slammed her side of the gate closed and stood paralyzed as she watched Derek's life pump out of him and the Hyenas crouched to spring at her son. The clanging of iron on iron pulled their attention away from the human on the silent machine. It was a sound they knew. It meant they would be trapped again.

Caged.

Beaten.

Starved.

They saw the freedom of the trees across the parking lot and as one, turned and ran for them as the undead started running for the humans gathered at the gates.

Cody wanted to run to his mother, run to Derek and run away all at the same time. Everything was happening too fast; it was too much. He needed a moment to think, to scream, to cry, and to hide but there wasn't time for any of that. There were only seconds left in his life if those things rushed back inside. He jumped from the cart, grabbed the tall steel gate and pulled. Another boy, a dark-haired Asian kid, joined him and together they got the thousand-pound gate swinging closed on its well-oiled hinges. It slammed into place and Kelly locked the catch as the first of the torn and bloody people from the parking lot smashed into it. They backed away as the gate shuddered when the undead ran into it at full speed, hungry arms reaching through the bars.

It would hold. It was old and heavy and solid, almost like a prison cell door with the name of the park across the top of the two halves. Kelly only watched for a second before she tore herself away from the screaming mass and ran to Derek. He was a barely recognizable mess, the hyenas had savaged him, literally torn him limb from limb in seconds.

He was fading fast, his world growing cold and dark as the last of his lifeblood pumped out in a weak trickle. He smiled as Kelly knelt over him, tears streaming from her eyes and tried to tell her not to worry, he was okay. It didn't hurt. His mind was muddled and he couldn't remember what happened exactly. Had he fallen off a ladder? She brushed the hair away from his forehead and stroked his face. That was okay, her hands felt warm and he was so cold. He'd just close his eyes for a moment and wait for an ambulance. He was so tired. He should ask for a blanket, he was starting to shiver.

10

KELLY

Kelly had to pull herself together. Derek was gone and the whole world had taken a hard turn into mayhem and insanity. If she didn't do something, if she didn't start acting instead of reacting to everything, everyone else was going to die. She felt as if she were in a B horror movie. *This is impossible*, kept running through her head, *this is all impossible.* Yet it was happening and she was thrust in the center of it. The blood on her clothes and dripping from her hands, the screaming things reaching for her through the gate and the fire and smoke billowing up from the parking lot told her it was all real. It was all happening and happening fast.

She forced herself to stop staring into the madness on the other side of the gate and let her training take over. She'd seen ugly before. She'd seen torn up animals, she'd been covered in blood, and she'd been calm under pressure. *Nothing like this* her mind shrieked. *You've never seen nothing like this!* She told it to shut up. Her eyes darted past the undead gate crashers and found Cody. He was what was important now. He was the only thing that mattered.

He stood with a handful of other kids, all of them wide eyed, tear streaked and staring at the remains of Derek or the ripped and ravaged people trying to squeeze through the bars.

They were shocked and confused, not sure what to do next. They had run towards the noises out of curiosity or maybe to try to help but now what? They couldn't get out and didn't know which way to flee. She ran her fingers through her hair, trying to clear her head, trying to think. Grasping hands reached for her, only yards away. Biting, snapping faces tried to force their way between the bars to the kids standing there in unmoving fear. There were a few girls, and boys, a kid in a wheelchair, an odd-looking pair of twins and others. Where were their parents? Were they banging on the gate to be let in so they could finish off their own offspring? She shuddered at the thought. *Not my child,* she decided. *He gets out alive.*

There were others huddled near the snack shack staring at the only way out, the only exit to their cars, blocked by snarling, bloody people. Fear was written plainly on their faces. A couple with a pair of teenage boys and a young family with a little girl and a baby in a papoose slung across his father's chest kept looking at each other, then at the parking lot. None of them knew what to do, they stood transfixed, unable to decide where to flee.

She had to step up. Take charge. Fix what she could and give these people a chance. The undead slammed and keened at the gate, fresh meat so close, just a couple inches of iron bars separating them from the blood that they craved.

"Cody, take everyone to the visitors center," she barked. "We've got to get away from them."

She looked at the families and kids as they all turned to

stare at her, hope in their near panicked eyes. She had on a uniform. She knew what to do. She was an official.

"This is my son, he'll get you somewhere safe. Lock all the doors behind you."

No one moved.

"*Cody!*" she yelled and he started, his eyes seemed to come into focus. "Get going, take them to the center. Hurry!"

"But Mom..." Cody started and pointed towards Derek.

"*No buts, just do it!* She shouted, her 'I'm-not-in-the-mood-to-take-any-crap' voice cutting through their indecision. "*Do it now.*"

"I'll be right behind you," she added, as they started moving.

"Come on." Cody said and took off in a jog. "They won't be able to get in, the doors are solid."

The kids stuck together she noticed. The pale white twins grabbed a handle on either side of the boy in the wheelchair and sped him along as the others circled around him forming a fragile wall of protection. It wasn't much, it was a little thing but it spoke volumes about them.

As they disappeared around the snack shack, Kelly moved to Derek's corpse. She checked the time on her watch. Sixteen minutes since Anna had been dead and then came back and lunged for her. Her entire world had been ripped apart in only a quarter of an hour. The man she loved was gone. The country she lived in was being destroyed. Everything she knew about science and medicine had been rendered null and void in a matter of moments. The rules didn't apply when blatantly dead people were trying to eat living people. It wasn't just here in this isolated part of Iowa. The virus that cropped up out of nowhere a few days ago had spread at an insanely rapid pace. She couldn't imagine being in a big city, there was no chance, no escape and no hope. Here... maybe. Just maybe. Her mind raced and she knew she didn't have much time. This safari could work, could keep them alive. It was fenced and secure, there were plenty of animals for a food supply and there was water. She had to move fast, though. Time was ticking away and things had to be done.

Derek was a large man, but she managed to drag him into the golf cart. She nearly vomited when she picked up his dismembered limbs and put them in the back but she forced it down. She'd seen worse she kept telling herself. She ignored the twisted faces and hungry cries at the gates, they weren't an immediate problem. Tick tock. She didn't have time for niceties or to be dainty. She had a mission that *had* to be finished. It just had to. She hopped in and pressed the pedal to the floor, racing against the clock. Four minutes later she stood on the bank of the Mississippi in their favorite getaway spot. She had a lot of memories here lying on a blanket, talking about nothing and everything. No time for them now, though. She wrestled his body to the muddy water, waded out to her waist. She leaned over and pressed her forehead against his for a few seconds, allowing herself a moment to say goodbye before she pushed him out as far into the current as she could. The slow waters carried him away as she tossed the other parts of him as far out as she could. She did throw up then, heaving bile into the muddy water. She splashed her face, washed her hands and waded ashore. She felt like he would approve. As a younger man, he'd done a stint in the Coast Guard. She looked at her watch again. Twenty-eight minutes.

She took the long way back, racing along the trails looking for any more of the zombies but there were none to be seen. If they were here, she was sure they would come after her, killing people seemed to be their only motivation. She bailed out of the cart and approached the door to the first aid station where Anna stood swaying. She paid no attention to the woman staring in at her and Kelly nearly wailed. She'd been hoping she was wrong. Hoping the sunlight being blindingly bright and the throbbing in her head was just stress. Just a migraine coming on. She'd hoped the black streaks running up her arm from the tiny little nip Anna had given her when they fought at the door was just dirt. Or scratches. Or anything other than the virus racing through her system but it wasn't. She'd supposed she'd known all along; it was what gave her the strength to do what she'd done. Anna ignoring her was the last confirmation she needed. She was already infected. Already one of them.

From the few minutes she'd had dealing with the undead, she'd learned a few things fast. *If* they killed you, you came back instantly. If they bit you, it took a little more time. The first man they'd been treating in the station had lasted for ten or fifteen minutes and his bite was large and terrible. Anna had turned almost instantly when her throat was ripped out. She only had a nick, it barely broke the skin, but she'd been feeling the cold spread of the disease almost since it happened. She could feel it in her head now, icy fingers curling around her brain. Derek hadn't been killed by the undead and none of them had bitten him so she was pretty sure it wasn't in the air; it was through direct contact. Bites or maybe even scratches. The newly turned were vicious and fast and inhumanly strong. A hundred people had fallen to it in a matter of minutes. She knew why the phones hadn't been answered. She knew no one would be coming to rescue them. She knew they were on their own.

She couldn't leave Cody to deal with Derek's remains

so she had to get rid of them. Her boy was close to breaking already. She couldn't leave Anna locked up for him to deal with, she had to get rid of her. She couldn't turn into one of them on this side of the gate, she had to get rid of herself.

Kelly opened the door and pushed Anna aside, latched it securely behind her and grabbed a pen and paper from the desk. Her arm spasmed with a shooting pain and she knew she had to hurry.

Cody,

I'm so sorry I can't be here for you. I got bit when things went crazy. I'll be one of them soon, I feel myself getting sicker by the minute. Don't let them bite you no matter what. I love you son. You have been my whole world since the day you entered kicking and screaming. Never stop. Never stop kicking and screaming no matter what. Your father was a brave man. You have his strength. He would be so proud of you. I don't know what's coming. I think you are on your own. I don't think help will ever arrive but I want you to promise me you'll kick and scream the whole way. You can do this. Don't leave the park, it's fenced and safe. Try to protect the people and the animals for as long as you can. Do what you must. Do what's right and what's necessary, even if it's hard.

I'm leaving now and I'll try to lead the rest of them away but I'll always be with you.

Love,

Mom.

She had so many more things to tell him, so much more advice to give, but there wasn't time. She looked at her watch but couldn't read the hands, she wasn't sure what they meant anymore. Her writing had gone from neat and curly to barely legible, her mind was getting foggy. She left it on the counter where he would find it and stumbled to her feet, tears nearly blinding. She grabbed Anna by the hand and led her outside.

She tried to hurry as she led Anna towards the entrance gates. With nothing to hold their attention, some of the undead were still at the bars but most milled aimlessly around the parking lot. She pushed a few out of the way, stepped through then double checked that the door was secure behind her. She swayed for a moment, lost in darkness, her mind completely blank. Kelly felt the dryness of her throat and mouth and had difficulty swallowing, sweat poured in rivers down her body as the fever raged, the virus attacking her at the cellular level. It wouldn't be long now. She winced through the pain in her skull as the sun stabbed into her eyes, the pupils nearly fully dilated. A small part of her came back, the dying bit of human that still remained and she shook the gate one last time. It held and she grabbed Anna by the hand and pulled her away from the zoo. She began singing the lullaby she sang when Cody was a restless infant, the notes raw in her throat. The undead lurched towards her, the ones at the fence running toward the sound. Their dead minds were confused, they heard a human but smelled one of their own kind. They sensed the infection coursing through her veins but they followed her singing and shambled along behind her. She wanted to get as far away as she could before it was too late. She led them away, past the burning wrecks at the entrance and turned south where the road meandered for miles before it came to the next town. She cried and sang as she led them away from her baby and after she died, when the virus completely took her, she climbed back to her feet and followed the shambling crowd.

11

THE CHILDREN

"I can't get a call out," the father with the papoose said in exasperation.

His wife was frantically dialing her own cell and ignoring her traumatized daughter crying and clinging to her leg.

"How can all the circuits still be busy?" she asked, the panic making her voice shriller and shriller. "How come nobody is answering?"

Her husband ignored her and tried redialing his own phone. 9-1-1. All circuits busy. Hang up and try again as fast as he could. He needed someone to answer. Someone to reassure him help was on the way.

"We can't stay here," the other man said.

He was older, graying around the temples, had a deep tan and the build of a man who worked with his hands for a living. A plumber or carpenter. Maybe a heavy equipment operator.

They were in the visitor's center, the original house that had been built near the turn of the century, with the doors locked and the curtains drawn.

Cody paced and tried to shut them all out. He wanted to run to his mom, help her deal with Derek and Anna, get some kind of answers to what was going on. What were those things? What made people go crazy like that?

Everyone was in the spacious lobby and on their cells, either trying to call emergency services or family

"Snap chat is working," said one of the kids.

"Twitter, too." Another answered and everyone gave up trying to dial phone numbers.

They went to the internet, it was still up and working. Chaos was everywhere as they heard panic and screams coming out of the tinny sounding speakers from a dozen different news feeds. People were attacking other people. There was murder, riots, looting and anarchy all across the nation, especially in the east coast towns. The big cities were tearing themselves apart from the inside out and it had been going on for hours. No one had heard from the president. The military were supposed to be on red alert but the reporters hadn't heard anything from them, either.

"Someone should declare martial law," one morning show host declared.

"Someone should declare a mandatory curfew," opined another.

Anyone that started their mornings with television or listening to the radio hadn't ventured out of their houses to enjoy a day at the zoo, they were riveted to the TV until the stations started going off the air. Some did the worst thing possible, they ran to the stores to stock up on supplies. Most never made it back. No one in the park had turned on the news until now, they had all been blissfully ignorant as the world fell apart until it happened to them. If they listened to anything at all that morning, it had been streaming music, cd's or mp3 players filled with their favorite songs.

Cody peeked through the curtains trying to see his mom or any movement outside. He'd heard the golf cart come flying by a few minutes ago but couldn't see it or her. He knew she was counting on him to keep these people safe but he wanted to go to her. There were adults here, they could take over now. It was too much. Too much to ask of him.

"It's everywhere," Murray said holding up his phone. "Des Moines is burning, people are looting and rioting, and the zombies are attacking anything that moves!"

"Zombies?" the younger father said. "Zombies aren't real; those people are high on something, or sick. That virus has been on the news for a couple of days now."

Murray looked at him, "Don't you know what's happening? This is it, the end of the world as we know it. One of them bites somebody, who bites somebody else and pretty soon we're all living in sewers and scavenging for cat food! Don't you watch movies?"

The older man scoffed, "Look, I don't know what's going on, and I don't care. We're leaving. I'll run down any of those crazies that get in my way, that's what a brush guard is for. I've got a safe full of guns at the house. Druggies, sick people, the walking dead, I don't care what you want to call them, if they come around my place, me and my boys are gonna light 'em up."

The two boys nodded in agreement, excitement tamping down their fear. Their dad was always talking about being prepared, you never knew when everything could go to hell in a handbasket. He'd mostly meant the government getting out of control, about the Tree of Liberty being watered with the blood of tyrants, but a zombie uprising was just as bad. Maybe worse.

The older man looked at the couple with the two children. "If you want to get out of here, you're welcome to come with us. Same for all you kids, there's no room for everyone in my truck but I can come back and get you. We'll get you back to your parents and in a few days the cops or National Guard will have this under control and it will all blow over."

The younger couple whispered to each other and both nodded at the older man. "We're with you."

Murray wheeled his chair in circles anxiously. "You leave, you die, and if you let those zombies in the gate they'll kill us. C'mon, look at the news, this is everywhere. The world is dying."

"Kid, you should lay off the video games. This ain't nothing but some bad drugs getting passed around and some crazies using the chaos to get a new flat screen and some Air Jordans."

"Those people aren't looking for a flat screen." Murray said and pointed towards the front gate. "I think they're looking for brains."

"Come on, let's go," the man said and headed for the door, ignoring the kid who obviously watched too many horror movies. Zombies weren't real.

The other family and their small children fell in line behind him.

Cody stopped pacing and stepped between him and the door. "Please, my mom said..."

"Kid, no offense, but your mom ain't in charge of us. We're leaving, we've got family to check on so decide right now whether you want me to come back or not but get out of my way."

"My family is already here." Cody said lamely and stepped aside. "I have to stay."

The man looked at the other kids who looked at each other.

"I guess we will, too." Murray said. "Our parents know where we are. They'll come get us, right guys?"

There were nods from the others, slow and unsure at first but once they thought about it, it made sense.

"We'll stay, Mister but thanks for the offer." Harper said "My dad would be mad if he came for me and I wasn't here."

"Makes sense," the man said. "Lock up behind us."

They checked to be sure none of the crazies were anywhere around and the families left the house, hurrying to the parking lot while it was still empty. The kids made their way to the living room with the overstuffed furniture and went back to their phones, trying to get in touch with their own families. All but the lean Asian boy, he clung to the shadows. He had nowhere to go and there was no one who cared if he was safe or not.

Cody watched the small group leave, heard their cars start up a few minutes later then slipped out of the door. He scanned the area, listened intently for the keens or screams of the crazy people and looked for any sign of his mom. She was nowhere to be seen. He left the porch and edged towards the snack shack and the front gate. He wanted to make sure they had closed it behind them. Derek's body was gone and the golf cart was parked haphazardly in front of the nurse's station. There was a lot of blood staining the cargo hold so it was easy to figure out what she'd done but that didn't explain why she hadn't come to the house.

The area around the front entrance and parking lot was empty. The gift shop door stood ajar, a tipped over postcard rack blocking it open. The park was unusually quiet, the only sound was the breeze rustling the leaves and the crackling of flames barely heard from the car fire near the road entrance. No chittering from the monkeys. No cries of the peacocks or bleating of the goats. Even the chickens were quiet. Everything was hiding, being still and silent.

He heard them as they joined him to stare out at the parking lot. An hour ago, there had been a line of happy people waiting to get in, their biggest concern was sunblock and hoping the animals were active so they could get some good pictures. Now there were a half dozen smashed cars and a school bus burning brightly, the parking lot had pools of blood and shredded clothes littering it. Discarded shoes and purses were everywhere. Flies were gathering at the puddles and drinking their fill. They watched in silence for a few moments before the oldest looking girl finally said something.

"I think that's Mr. Baynard," she pointed to a form crawling towards them, its lower body broken and burnt but the remnants of a flashy necktie could be still be seen. His head was still smoldering, wisps of smoke curling up from the burnt hair. They watched as he scratched his way toward them, pulling himself slowly along. Something had torn him open. A car bumper or maybe another crazy and his entrails were spilling out, sliding across the asphalt behind him.

"I don't think its drugs making them crazy. No kind of drug can make you act like that," a young black girl said and moved in a little closer into the group.

"It's zombies." Murray said. "There is no other explanation. Prove me wrong."

No one tried because no one could. He was right. They watched the slow progress in horrified fascination, saw it tried to scream at them but no sound came from the burnt things mouth.

Cody was the first to tear his eyes away from the slow-moving horror.

"I've got to find my mom. She will know what to do."

"We can help," an Indian girl said. "Do you think we're safe in here?"

"Should be." Cody said, "We're surrounded by fence. Good fences that keep the antelope in so it ought to keep those things out. They don't seem to be very smart. I don't think they can climb."

"Where should we start searching?" the pale boy said and his sister nodded at his words.

Cody bit his lip and looked to the nurse's station with its gore stained, spider webbed window. At the bloody cart parked in front of it. She should have come to the house unless something was wrong. Unless something had happened to her. Suddenly he felt really glad the kids were with him, he didn't want to be alone. He was afraid of what he'd find when he looked inside. He pointed, his throat too tight to speak and they understood.

"Um, dude." Murray said. "We need weapons. I know she's your mom and all but, you know, maybe she's not anymore."

Harper gasped and swatted him for being so insensitive but he didn't back down.

"Just saying, that's all," he defended himself.

"He's right." Cody said. "She might not be..."

He swallowed the giant lump in his throat and finished "herself."

He pulled the door open to the snack shack and handed everyone a long knife or barbeque fork before they made their way over. The office was trashed. Blood, broken bottles, smashed cabinets and spilled desk drawers cluttered the place but no one was inside either living or dead. The quiet Asian boy handed him a note as they turned to leave.

It had been laying on the counter and everyone else had overlooked it.

12

CODY

Piedmont House was commissioned by Theopolis James Piedmont in 1897. Construction began that spring and the last nail was driven flush in the winter of the same year. Three stories tall with a large open floorplan for entertaining the elite members of society, it featured indoor plumbing and was one of the first houses in the region to have electric power. In addition to having its own telegraph lines, it was also the first to utilize Alexander Graham Bell's new-fangled device called the telephone. With its lavish design, modern conveniences and the Piedmont flair for aristocracy, it was the envy of north eastern Iowa.

Now, over a century later, it was the visitor center and staff offices of the Piedmont Animal Sanctuary. Each year for Halloween, the park staff decorated the first floor with a macabre collection of ghosts, ghouls and scary music. Vampires and werewolves ushered people out of the creepy waiting area and onto the haunted hayride that included thrills and chills of all kinds. Monsters waited to leap from the shadows to scare small children, give teenage boys a reason to put their arms around their dates and cause the occasional adult heart to skip a beat or two. Giant, hairy spiders sprang from trees and animatronic zombies clawed the earth with their skeletal hands as they tried to rise from the grave in search of brains. Running from the first of October through Halloween, it was a huge tourist draw and every year the park added a few more scares to the delight of visitors.

The second floor was utilized as office space for the park personnel and the third floor had eight spacious rooms that were used mostly for storage. Utilizing much of the original furnishings, it was a step back to a simpler time when gossiping on the telephone party line was the height of societal scandal.

Inside the old house, Cody sat with the stained note in his hands and ignored the other kids. He read it over and over, looking for something he missed. The sentence that said *I'll be right back, everything is fine.*

It wasn't there. The cold, hard, ugly, black truth was all the note held. No happy ending. Just death and sacrifice. A last goodbye that told him to buckle up and take care of things. She'd said it nicely, she'd said it in a mom way, but that's what she meant. It's up to you, buddy. It's your burden now to carry on by yourself. He heard the others talking, heard their voices and the tinny voices coming from six different phones and it registered with him even if he didn't want to acknowledge it. The zombie outbreak was happening all over. No city, no state, no country was spared from the horror of raging infected sweeping through them. *Stay inside, help is on the way*, they repeated over and over but they never said who was coming to help. Or when. The weather radio in the kitchen played the same Emergency Broadcast message over and over, the recorded message growing monotonous in its urgency. The world really was falling apart out there. Still fighting back his emotions, he wondered how to deal with what was happening outside the fences and more importantly, how to keep it from getting in. Was he sure it wasn't airborne? Was it really only spread by a bite? Were some of them already carrying it? There were too many questions, and no answers for any of them.

He looked around at the other kids. Most of them were alternating between phone calls and texts to relatives or redialing 9-1-1. Occasionally someone would get up and wander around the house, peeking through curtains. About an hour ago Swan, the dark haired Indian girl, had gotten through to her mother who was stuck in traffic on the interstate. She frantically tried to fill her in on what happened, tell her she was fine but they all heard her mom start screaming and then there was nothing. She sat on a couch in a daze next to Cody. She had her knees hugged to her chest and rocked slowly back and forth. Dried tear streaks were on her cheeks and everyone talked in whispers. She and Cody knew their parents were gone. The others could hope their families were fine but none of them really believed. They'd seen how fast it happened. How brutal and vicious. The virus had started and spread and killed a hundred people in a matter of minutes. A half hour from start to finish. They hoped but they didn't believe. She sat beside him staring off into nothing. It was going on early afternoon and the animals had forgotten their fear, come out of hiding and could be heard chittering and cawing or bleating their animal sounds. No else had been able to get a call through, not to 9-1-1, not to family, not to anyone. All circuits were busy the automated voice told them or they just rang until voicemail kicked in. The internet had been slow and sluggish all morning, pages taking forever to load or refresh but now it was quick again. There wasn't any new content, though. Their Facebook posts reaching out to friends went unanswered. Their Instagram pictures went unnoticed. No one replied to their tweets. Texts messages sent were never seen.

Donny Lin didn't have a phone and grew restless watching the others. He paced around the house, peeked through every curtain and didn't see anything unusual aside from the park being completely empty. None of the undead things were inside the fences and he slipped outside to look around. To make sure. As he hurried down the paths, he began to notice a pattern. All of the animals ran towards him and paced along until they were stopped by their barriers. They were nervous, too. They took comfort at the sight of a human, something that had been a constant their whole lives. He realized something else, too. They were probably hungry. He'd noticed that the caretakers usually fed most of them after the park was open so the guests could watch them eat.

When he slipped back into the house an hour later, they jumped from their seats and asked him where he'd been. He should have told them if he was going outside. He wasn't used to the attention or anyone missing him when he wasn't around and was a little taken aback. They peppered him with questions and admonishments until Cody finally said, *"Well? Aren't you going to say anything?"*

He pointed to his mouth and shook his head and they realized they'd never heard him utter a word.

"You can't speak?" Harper asked "What happened?"

"You didn't see any zombies out there?" Murray asked.

Donny shrugged, ignored her question, shook his head emphatically at Murray and mimed an animal, pretended like he was eating and pointed outside.

Cody exclaimed and slapped his forehead. "I forgot all

about the animals. They haven't been fed yet. Can you guys help me?"

A chorus of yes's and okay's and anything is better than sitting around here answered him as Swan dug an ink pen and a small notebook out of her bag and handed it to the Asian kid.

"Okay, thanks. I'll show you the storeroom. There are charts on the wall telling who gets what and how much. Who are you guys anyway?" Cody asked. "You all know each other?"

Introductions were made and when Donny wrote his name on the pad, Swan announced it to everyone.

It didn't take long to get organized and soon they were loading up the golf carts with buckets and bags. The way the feeders were designed, they didn't have to enter any of the enclosures or cages to add the food or refill the water troughs. Many of the animals were fairly self-sufficient and didn't need daily care. The antelopes grazed and drank from the ponds. The chickens and peacocks could fend for themselves and as Cody fed the Jersey cow, he worked on auto pilot, his mind racing and still trying to come to terms with the new world he was living in. It was hard, nearly impossible to imagine, but it was over. The world he knew that morning was gone. They'd heard the news reports, they'd seen the videos. It was all gone. His mom was gone. His friends were gone. There would never be any new episodes of his favorite shows. There wouldn't be any new video games or superhero movies. There weren't any more cops or army or president. There weren't any more people except for maybe small groups like theirs that had been lucky or smart. He pushed the big thoughts out of his head and concentrated on the small thoughts. What were they going to do? Should they try to leave or stay in the park?

What were the other kids going to do? How was he going to take care of the animals all by himself if they left? Should he set them all free? He thought about the rest of the animals and which ones would be fine in the hundreds of acres of fenced land. Most of them, he concluded. They only had a few hunters in the park, he would have to keep them penned up, but most of the animals were herbivores or ate insects. They'd be fine turned out to take care of themselves. They'd be easy to hunt, too, if things started getting really bad. He pushed the idea out of his head, he didn't want to eat animals that were nearly as tame as pets but once he thought it, he couldn't unthink it. Last resort option he told himself. Things would have to get really, really bad.

They trickled back to the main house as it was getting dark and when Cody walked in, Donny was adding wood to the oversized fireplace in the parlor. Temperatures were falling as the sun started its descent into the western sky and the old house was cooling rapidly. The flames felt good and they seated themselves on the floor to absorb its warmth. The talk was quiet but animated as they shared stories of how they fed "their" animals. Swan said the wolves let her touch them and loved being scratched behind the ears. Murray said he'd gone inside the cage of the monkeys and they had climbed all over him and searched in his pockets looking for treats. The others had similar tales, they all had smiles and Donny was practically beaming. He had pointed to Charon, the black panther on the chart, and made it clear he wanted to feed it. The big predator was gentle as a kitten and Cody figured he'd probably figured that out, had discovered the oversized cat like to have his belly rubbed. It didn't even occur to him to be alarmed or worried about them getting injured. Otis would never hurt anyone and despite what the grownups were always saying, he didn't think any of the others would either. Caring for the animals had let them forget their own worries and lives and losses for a while and they were still basking in the simple beauty of it.

Murray finally broke away from the animal talk and declared himself starving to death.

"Got any people food in here?" he asked Cody.

"Let's finish off whatever is in the fridge before it goes bad." he said, and they all headed for the kitchen, pushing away any thoughts that they were eating other people's lunches. People that were dead and running around killing other people.

They ate sitting around the fire and traded for the best sandwiches or bowls of microwaved soup, candy bars and fresh fruits. They talked quietly about the day and what had happened, how the world they knew no longer existed. They were kids, the oldest of them only fourteen. They'd grown up on dystopian video games and apocalyptic TV shows and end of the world movies. They'd seen hundreds of hours of zombie shows. They'd witnessed the screaming undead with their own eyes and they didn't pretend they hadn't. In case they forgot, in case they thought they were having a waking dream, all they had to do was walk out to the front entrance. Mr. Baynard was there clawing at the bars, his burnt and melted face not much more than a blackened skull. Others had wandered in during the day and there were probably ten or fifteen of those things pressed against the gate. They knew they were the lucky ones and they didn't think the families that left was still alive. They knew they were safe where they were at and they knew no one was coming to save them. Cody took a poll just to make it official and no one wanted to leave, even if they could.

Their families knew where they were. They would come if they were still alive. The safari was their new home.

"Okay." he said, "I can show you everything I know about the park tomorrow. We'll have to figure out what to do with all the animals but I've got a few ideas. I think we'll be okay here, it's pretty secure and it's off any main roads. You have to be looking for this place to find it."

As the fire died down, phone batteries went dead, bellies were full and eyes got heavy, Cody told them there were rooms upstairs they could claim if they wanted. No one did. They pulled cushions off of couches and chairs in the offices and used them for makeshift mattresses as he and Donny went to the gift shop to grab armfuls of Mexican blankets and souvenir cushions they could use as pillows.

Murray claimed the couch and rested the weather radio he'd grabbed from the kitchen on his chest. The parks crew had never changed the frequency but it had a couple of different settings. There were a lot of weather stations from different parts of the country and the emergency channel but it didn't have regular radio. Vanessa turned off the lights and they listened in the dancing firelight as he scanned through the stations looking for any kind of news. Any voices in the night. He caught the same broadcast warning occasionally distant, echoed and automated. He'd listen for a while before turning the dial but no one ever said anything new. It was all the same warning, nothing was updated. By the time he gave up and turned it off, most of them were fast asleep.

13

DAY ONE

Ever since the accident that left him in the wheelchair, Murray had been an early riser. He was embarrassed by the shriveled twigs that were now his legs and being walked in on in the bathroom caused him a great deal of embarrassment. He'd developed the habit of being the first up to tend to his needs in the mornings. He was fully capable of taking care of himself and found it demeaning when someone offered to help him with his toilet duties, even his parents.

He wheeled himself in circles around the lobby, a habit he had when he was anxious or excited. His mind raced, one idea jumbling over another as he intermittently paused to check his phone or scribble in his notebook. This is it. The big one, TEOTWAWKI as the doomsday preppers on TV called it. The End of the World As We Know It. Unable to contain himself any longer, he rolled over and shook Cody.

"Get up man." he said in a loud whisper, "We got stuff to do. We are running out of time."

He watched as Cody shook off the fog of sleep.

Confused at his surroundings, the boy looked around and his face fell when he saw that nothing had changed from the previous night. So much for it all just being a bad dream. Donny was coming in from outside with an armful of wood and started stoking the fire to burn off the early morning chill.

Cody padded back into the room, having ignored whatever it was that was so important until he could go to the bathroom. Everyone else was stretching and yawning, wrapped in colorful blankets and looking sleepy-eyed. Murray was scribbling furiously in his notebook but when he looked up and saw everyone was mostly awake, he announced loud enough so they all could hear.

"We don't have long. The power grid is gonna fail, internet and cell phones will probably go first. Are there generators here? How many? How much fuel? What about guns and survival gear?"

Cody shook his head in confusion and some of the others frowned at him, not understanding or maybe not really wanting to understand.

"Listen to me man, I've been gaming the apocalypse for years now. These may not be crawling out of the graveyard trying eat your brains type of zombies, but they are zombies. We know this. We gotta get a plan. No one's coming to save us. They're either all dead or like those things outside. Which, technically, they're dead, too, I guess."

His animated voice snapped them out of their sleep stupor and they listened as he ranted.

"Slow down," Vanessa said, "and tell us what you are talking about."

Murray rattled off one thing after another like it was inevitable. Like it was a fact. Like their whole terrible situation wasn't temporary and things would soon be fixed. It's not like after a hurricane or earthquake or flood or forest fire. Things were bad then but things got better. Somebody always came to help.

"Nobody is coming!" he exclaimed. "There's nobody left. That wasn't fake news last night. You guys gotta see the big picture, man. We don't have much time before everything shuts down. If we don't download all the knowledge we're ever going to need right now, it'll be lost forever."

He had their attention then went on to explain, drawing his knowledge from books, movies, video games and the hundreds of internet searches he'd been doing for the last few hours.

"Electricity runs everything." he said. "Without it, we're back in the dark ages. We only have a few days at the most before the power grid crashes and the world goes dark."

"I think you're getting carried away." Harper said. "C'mon, Murray. Everybody's not dead. We can't be the only survivors. There're probably whole cities that are safe. This can't be everywhere."

"We don't have time to pretend!" Murray exclaimed. "If I'm wrong, then it's no big deal, we spent a few hours downloading stuff. We can delete it later. But we need to get everything we can about survival. What kind of plants are edible or medicinal, how to grow crops, smoke and cure meat, first aid, how to build snares and fish traps. The list is endless. We have to save it offline because in a day or two, everything online, the complete knowledge of everything in the world is going to be lost."

They were generation Z, they'd never known a world without high speed internet, facetime or instantaneous answers to any question they might have. Most of their skills and talents were rooted in technology and as they listened to Murray talk about planting seeds and learning how to spin cotton into cloth, they hugeness of yesterday settled down on them.

They looked at him like he'd grown an extra head. No one was in a rush to do anything, they still looked shell shocked and unsure.

"I'll make you a deal." Murray said. "If you can find one other live person out there, anybody we can talk to on Twitter, Facebook, Snapchat...whatever, find one other person and I'll admit I'm wrong, maybe I'm jumping to conclusions."

"My battery is almost dead." Swan said. "I can't waste it on nonsense."

"They sell chargers in the gift shop." Cody said. "I'll get some."

"I don't think we have to worry about spinning wool to make clothes." Harper said. "If everybody is dead, there will be plenty at the mall."

"Yeah, okay, point taken." Murray said "But regardless, we're going to lose the internet soon. Maybe even today and when it goes, so does all of the information. We need to save as much survival stuff as we can."

Cody returned a few minutes later with a handful of charging cables and one by one they finally had to admit what they already knew in their hearts. They scoured every far corner of the internet they could find, they watched live traffic feeds from a hundred different cities and everywhere it was the same. The undead wandered about unchecked and unchallenged. Donny watched for a while, knew by the looks on their faces what Murray said was true, then went outside to check the fence line. He wanted to double check the spot where he'd slipped under was secure.

It didn't take long for the rest of them to set down their phones and stare listlessly into the dying fire.

"What are we supposed to do?" Vanessa asked. "Why bother doing anything, we're all dead, it's just a matter of time."

This was one bet Murray would have gladly lost but he'd had hours to wrap is head around their situation. He had sincerely wished he were dead more times than he could count so he knew how some of them were feeling. They had a chance, though. They were lucky to be where they were, isolated from big population centers and surrounded by a strong fence. Now they had to get over their grieving for friends and family. They didn't have time to be despondent over the death of the world. He had to get them talking, get them to join him in saving knowledge before it was gone and fortifying the park if it needed it. He spoke quickly, told them they didn't have time to be sad, they could do that next week. He laid out his argument, expounded on their need to be fast and urged them to help him gather everything they would need to start rebuilding.

"Does anybody have a credit card?" he finally asked. "We can buy a bunch of prepper eBooks."

No one did.

"Aren't there websites about that?" Harper asked. "Just get it for free."

"Loads of them." Murray said. "I've been scouring them for the last couple of hours, my phone is almost full, but it's only bits and pieces here and there and it takes time to find good articles. Time we don't have. We need to buy every book on Amazon about gardening and making tools and fixing machines and first aid. We need to download them and make copies and save them, it'll be the only thing that prevents us from reverting back to cavemen."

They were all wide awake now and realized what he was saying was probably true. Most of it, anyway. They wouldn't be swinging clubs, grunting at each other and wearing rough furs if they didn't get all the information he was ranting about but while it was available, they should try.

"Okay." Cody said. "In the office is the main computer, I don't know how big the hard drive is but it's got to be bigger than all of our phones combined. You want to take charge of that, Murray?"

"Find me a credit card. It might be the only thing that can save our lives." he said dramatically and wheeled off.

"There's probably a purse or wallet laying around outside." Swan said. "I'll go look."

"I'll help." Vanessa said and followed her out. "We'll find one, don't worry Murray."

"I've got to milk the cow." Cody said. "She'll start bawling if it's late, I guess it hurts her or something."

"We'll figure out something for breakfast." Tobias said and his twin sister nodded.

"Oh yeah, if one of you want to come with me, we can get the eggs from the chickens." Cody said and Harper volunteered.

As Cody worked methodically filling the pail with warm milk, he considered what else they had inside the walls of the sanctuary. There was a generator and the fifty-gallon fuel tank for it they used for the meat lockers in case of a power outage. The electric golf carts had solar panels on their roofs as trickle chargers for the batteries but he knew from experience if you forgot to plug one in at night, the little solar charger didn't really do much. One of the carts had a cigarette lighter on it that could charge their phones, the panels could probably keep those in power.

There was a hand pump in the kitchen that pulled water from the old well. It still functioned as it was a part of the historical tours to let people see how water was drawn from the ground when Piedmont house was first built. He didn't know how good the water was but it had to be better than drinking from the Mississippi.

Donny met up with the girls and searched everywhere, even in the bathrooms, but the only purses or wallets they saw were laying out in the parking lot. The undead milling around the front of the park went crazy when they saw them and slammed into the bars, hands reaching, faces pressed hard and tried to squeeze through. They slipped back behind the snack shack so they were out of sight and the keening died down a little.

"Did you see the lady in the hiking outfit?" Swan asked with a little shake in her voice. "The one near the ticket booth?"

Donny and Vanessa peeked back around the edge and saw the one she was talking about. A woman with filthy cargo shorts, a shredded plaid shirt and a rugged leather satchel slung over one shoulder.

"You think that's her purse?" Vanessa asked already figuring out what the other girl had in mind.

Swan nodded

"We have to get it." she said. "We have to. They're depending on us."

The other two agreed and they started trying to come up with a plan, taking occasional peeks around the corner to make sure she was still there and trying to force her way through the steel. Donny pointed at one of the golf carts and mimed his idea. The girls made horrified faces but it would probably work. And it was a lot less dangerous than anything else they'd thought of.

They picked out a four-seater and Swan took the wheel since she'd done a little kart racing and then Donny climbed in the back, ready to snatch it when they got close. Swan circled behind the row of buildings that housed the nurse's station and gift shop then lined herself up beside the fence. The cart, like the rest of those is the park, was electric and silent. She gave the horn a short toot when they were in place and Vanessa stepped out from behind the snack shack and waved her arms. The undead surged harder against the bars as she came closer. They snarled and snapped their teeth, stretched out hungry arms and reached for her with blood crusted hands. Swan floored it and steered close to the gate, scraping the fiberglass body and steel framed windshield support along it. She gritted her teeth as pieces of the cart broke and flew off. She nearly screamed when she hit the first outstretched arms, breaking them with a horrible chicken bone snapping sound. They twisted in a way no arm was supposed to bend and she slammed the brakes right in front of the hiker woman. Donny reached through the bars and grabbed the satchel and tugged but the strap didn't break. Twitching, broken hands tried to grasp at him. Fingers pawed but were unable to grip. They clasped weakly on his arms and he opened his mouth to scream a silent scream. The cold flesh grabbing him was revolting, it was clammy and disgusting and he was going to throw up. The girls were yelling at him to hurry and he was trying but every time he jerked on it, the woman just slammed harder into the bars. An arm snaked up from the ground, one of the crawlers being trampled by the others, and grabbed at Swans ankle. Another misshapen hand tangled itself in her hair, reached for her eyes. She screamed her own scream then and mashed the go pedal. The hand on her ankle was strong and would have pulled her out of the cart if she hadn't had a death grip on the steering wheel. Donny managed to get a double grip on the satchel as they lurched away from the bloody, mangled horde and watched with horror as the strap finally slid up over her head. It caught her neck, snapped it and nearly jerked him out of his seat.

Swan didn't stop until she was back at the main house and then just sat there shaking, her fingers white in a death grip on the wheel. The others came running, they'd heard the commotion and her screams. Donny threw the satchel on the seat and sprang out, running for the bushes to throw up. The feel of those clammy dead fingers scrabbling against his skin was the most vile and disgusting thing he'd ever felt in his life. It was like cold spiders creeping over him and trying to burrow their way in. When he rejoined the group, Vanessa was triumphantly holding up the wallet and a half dozen credit cards.

14

CODY

They helped Cody with the rest of the animals and when they gathered for the late breakfast the twins had whipped up, they were feeling a little better. Even though Donny and Swan thought they'd never be hungry again, it smelled too good and they dove in like the rest.

"Any updates on the computer?" Annalise asked as Murray rolled in and took his place. "Any new news?"

They all turned to him and knew the answer before he shook his head then spoke softly so they had to strain to hear him.

"Nothing. I mean nothing official. Not overseas, not here in America, not any news channel, not any blog. There were some new twitter posts but it was from people like us. I answered all of them and a few answered back but there isn't anything from anybody that's in charge. Just people spread out all over, all alone and with zombies surrounding them. Nobody knows anything, really."

Nobody had anything to add to that dour news and they ate in silence for a few minutes. It wasn't like it was a big surprise but they had almost managed to forget when they were taking care of the animals.

Cody broke the quiet and started talking about his ideas to free most of the animals, to let them run wild in the open areas. They could pretty much take care of themselves. Some they would need to keep penned in, the farm animals from the petting zoo and the predators like the panther, the bears and the wolves. They would need daily care, they would have to be fed and watered. The meat lockers would last a little while after the power failed but after the generators exhausted their fuel supply what was left would spoil quickly.

"That will be a problem." he told them. "None of the hunters know how to be wild. They were all raised in captivity and we can't just set them free. That would be cruel. They might do okay here inside the fences, all the antelope and gazelles are trapped, but outside they'd starve to death. The panther would lick a rabbit to death before he tried to eat one. The polar bears probably couldn't catch a fish out of a kiddie pool."

"Can we do that?" Tobias asked? "Teach them how to be wild again?"

"Can we adapt them?" Harper cut in "I mean, can we claim one as a pet? I love Bert, I'd take care of him."

Cody hadn't thought about any of them wanting to take any of the animals under their wing and be their protectors like he was going to do with Otis. He'd thought he might have an argument on his hands trying to get them to help with their care and feeding. He should have known better, they had all been on a field trip to the park on a Saturday instead of playing video games or watching movies. It was because they all loved the animals.

"Um, okay." he said. "Me and the bear are old pals but you guys can take any of the others, make them your pets."

"I prefer to call them my spirit guides." Swan said and everyone else chimed in with terms like *partner, companion, helper* and a few others.

Cody held up his hands. "Okay, okay. No offense intended. You're the caregiver though. They're your responsibility but we'll have to share the workload for the rest. Some of them are too old to be turned out and probably wouldn't want to leave their pens anyway. Teddy the buffalo is almost twenty and mom has him on supplements to keep him healthy and Mille is blind in one eye and can't hardly see out of the other. There are some others that need special care but I think most of them will be okay running wild."

The talk of the animals took their minds off what was just outside their gates, the fact that none of their families had come to try to rescue them and the realization that they were alone.

The panther and the wolves needed meat as their primary diet but there was plenty in the cooler for now. Otis and the polar bears were a little more flexible since they would eat virtually anything. There was plenty of pellet food for most of the park animals as well as a loft full of hay for the winter months. The grass hadn't started to die off yet so grazing was still good and if they turned them out now, the bagged food should last them through the winter. They'd worry about getting more when the time came, they had themselves to think about too.

The mood in the house lightened. The highly adaptive nature of kids had pushed aside last night's fears. They weren't going to get torn apart, they had a safe place to stay and they had a basic plan to stay alive. While they'd been busy with their tasks all morning, Murray had been on the computer downloading all the free books he could find and deleting files that were useless to them now. Forty gigabytes of accounting information, tax records and old invoices were no longer deemed important. The credit cards had bought all the important information that could be downloaded and he wanted to get more. He wanted the classics and histories. He wanted every book ever written that would tell them how to do something, solve a problem or fix a machine. He wanted knowledge and he knew anything he didn't save could very well be lost forever.

Resolve settled in that they were on their own and a sense of excitement seemed to spread through them. Each still harbored sadness for their families but there wasn't time to sit around and mourn. They had things to do if they didn't want to join them. Murray gave them a sense of urgency about the preparations they needed to make and Cody gave them the excitement of having something wild and exotic as their very own, an unthinkable thought yesterday.

Cody talked as they ate, filling them in everything he could remember about the Park. There was wild game inside the fences: a lot of rabbits, squirrels and raccoons. They flourished without any natural predators. The river had fish and as gross as it sounded, they'd grow fat and plentiful with all the dead bodies that were probably floating in it. Unfortunately, the carnivorous animals had never needed to stalk their prey, it was always scooped into a dish for them. Cody was certain that they still possessed the predatory instincts of their ancestors. They just needed to be awakened. They could teach them. As they talked of the animals and gave Murray lists of books they needed, Cody leaned back and took it all in. He tried to see the big picture, not just the day to day things they were talking about. He tried to see where they'd be and what they'd need by Christmas when the snows could be a foot deep and their only heat was the fireplace.

He looked at their clothes and mentally inventoried the human food stores. Mostly junk food in the gift shop and souvenir store. He'd helped unload the delivery truck for the snack bar and knew there would be cans of chili and nacho cheese, frozen cases of hamburgers, french fries and hot dogs but all of that would spoil if Murray was right and they only had a few days of power left. They'd have to cart it all over to the meat storehouse but even then, they'd only have another week before the diesel ran out. They needed canned goods. Soups and veggies and things like that. They'd have to go into town sooner or later. They'd have to make a supply run for food and clothing but he didn't even want to think about that.

Water was abundant thanks to the hand operated pump in the old house, unless the pipes froze. *Too much, there's just too much that can go wrong and leave us helpless*, he thought.

Winter was coming. Everyone was dressed for early fall. Shorts and hoodies, tennis shoes or high tops. They needed thick clothes, heavy jackets, good boots, gloves and hats. There were a few items in the gift shop, like sweat shirts and animal themed blankets, but nothing that would sustain them through a long Iowa winter.

Cody needed some fresh air and a reprieve from the excited chatter. He pushed his chair back and stepped outside. The morning was still cool and brisk but the sun was up and the day would be pleasant.

He stared at the gate in the distance, nearly hidden from view by the snack shack. They were still there and still wanted in. He would have to come up with some way to deal with them. The things knew they were inside, he supposed they could smell them or something but they just kind of swayed back and forth. They didn't go into a rage unless people were visible and then they went nuts.

Cody wasn't from Putnam, they had lived a few miles out, but he was certain that he recognized some of the shambling monsters from his trips into town. One looked like the girl from the pizza place and he was pretty sure the old man in the mechanics clothes was the guy that changed the oil in his mom's car. It was hard to tell, most of his face was gone but the gray hair looked familiar. They liked to bunch together, he noticed. Every time one came shuffling down the road, it would hear the crowd and come join them. They would have to figure out an easy way to kill them off. He didn't want the horde to keep getting bigger and bigger. If it got to be in the thousands, they might spread out to the weaker chain link parts of the fence and be able to tear it down.

15
―――

CODY

The days passed. They fell into a routine. No one came to rescue them and they knew no one would. They stopped sneaking glances to the parking lot every chance they had. They stopped straining their ears listening for a convoy of soldiers come to help. They were on their own. Their parents were gone. Their friends and family had all fallen before the unrelenting tide of undead. Some adjusted quicker than others. They all shed their tears in private or with faces buried in animal fur, breaking down while stoking their chosen companions. Cody, too, while he spent an afternoon with Otis, trying to teach the bear to grab fish out of the water. He let it all out and the big Kodiak took it all in then licked his salty tears with a rough tongue. He tried to be strong, not show any weakness around the others. He was the oldest and they were counting on him. Looking at him as a leader and not a boy in the shadow of manhood, just as lost and confused as they were. He finally stopped his sniffing and feeling sorry for himself, sighed and leaned back into Otis's massive frame as they reclined near his pool. The afternoon sun felt good on his face, but the brisk fall wind prickled at his skin. It was already October, getting colder day by day and the only jackets they had were blankets from the gift shop with holes cut in them to make ponchos. He readjusted his so it covered his arms and whiled away the rest of the afternoon enjoying Otis' warmth and musky bear smell.

True to Murray's prediction, they had lost power on the third day. That was okay. It was enough time to get everything any one could think of downloaded. The lights had flickered once and darkness enveloped them. The twins were ready with the candles and dinner continued but there was a hush to the conversation. They knew the power would never be coming back on.

Now, almost two weeks in, they were still eating like kings with hamburgers and hotdogs for every meal. Today was the last meat meal, though. The genny was out of fuel and the stuff in cold storage was gone. They gave smaller portions to the animals and tried to teach them to hunt but they had used the last of the meat this morning. They were saving the canned chili, usually used for the Coney's, because it wouldn't go bad. Tobias and Annalise had gathered all the junk food in the shops, smashed out the glass in the vending machines and had boxes of chips and candy bars but they couldn't live on that. They needed nourishment. Real food. The chickens in the petting zoo gave eggs every day but it wasn't enough to feed eight rapidly growing children. The cow gave them plenty of milk and Murray said you could make butter out of it by skimming the cream. The twins were eager to try it and had started a list of things they needed when the group went into town. A butter churn from an antiques store was added to it. The pair knew their way around a kitchen and had taken over the cooking duties. For a brief couple of months, they had decided they were going to be world famous celebrity chefs and had wreaked havoc in their parent's kitchen. Between the cooking shows and the recipe books, they had learned a lot and gotten pretty good before they lost interest.

Cody had been formulating a supply run plan. There was a seldom used access gate on the back of the property that would put them a couple of miles outside Putnam. Otis and he had checked it out and found no undead hanging around. The crowd at the front gate had swelled to nearly a hundred. They just milled about in the parking lot until one of the kids captured their attention then they renewed their assault on the gates. He wondered how many it would take to overcome their defenses. That was something he didn't want to find out. They would have to deal with them sooner or later, but they were weaponless. Murray assured them that a bullet through the brain would shut them down permanently, but there were no bullets. There were no guns to fire them. All they had were pitchforks and shovels. Cattle prods and tranquilizer guns. There were a few kitchen knives but nothing that would slow down the screaming undead if they shoved a section of fence over. They had tried a few different things against them but so far, they had avoided the whole problem. They couldn't keep doing that, though. They needed to come up with a solution. Harper had jabbed one of them with a tranq stick but it had no effect other than increasing the attack on the wrought iron bars. The cattle prod made them dance but that was about it and it only worked on one at a time.

Each of them had been spending their days tending and befriending the animals, teaching their companions to hunt or at least eat fresh killed meat with the fur still on it. They had learned how to rig snares from one of the books and were introducing the animals to freshly killed rabbits with the blood still hot. They had let most of them out to roam free but many of them came back to their pens every night and Millie never wandered far.

The golf carts were dying. The short days and the weak sun would barely charge them enough for ten or fifteen minutes of power before they came to a stop. Murray extended the solar panel cables and spliced them all together so they directed their energy into one battery. It was enough to keep a cart and their phones fully charged. They pulled the invertor from the generator, hooked it to the oversized battery for 110 power. It gave him juice to run the computer but laptops and external hard drives were on his list of things to get from town. He wanted backups of backups.

There were plenty of downed trees, branches and brush inside the fences and Donny designed a crude harness to hook up to Teddy. With only a little coaxing, he was dragging whole logs out of the woods and up close to the work areas. The old buffalo seemed to enjoy the work and certainly the attention he got. The apples Vanessa found on one of her trips to the edges of the park helped with his motivation, too. With each of them taking an hour long turn each day with the axe, they had quickly amassed a couple of cords of firewood to keep them warm all winter. They scraped out a big firepit a good distance from the main house and got in the habit of having a campfire every night with the brush they trimmed off the logs.

Swan and the wolves had become inseparable. They shadowed her and were never far away. She would hurry through her chores of cleaning the barn stalls or spending an hour chopping wood but when they were finished, she'd run with her wolves. Her second family. They would play and hunt and chase the antelope but they never caught anything. Even the rabbits eluded them as they darted this way and that then finally disappeared down a hole. Sometimes they curled up together in the tall grass and slept, her between them, warm and protected. She was filled with delight when Cody told her that the swell in Lucy's belly was babies. There would be wolf cubs soon.

Vanessa and Ziggy prowled the vast acreage of the park searching for edible berries and nuts, using some of the books Murray had put on her phone. The Ostrich towered over the ten-year-old, nearly double her height at a little over eight feet. Vanessa led the giant bird with a leash for the first week or so but the more time they spent together, the less time Ziggy wanted to spend apart from her. Cody thought the old mother bird had come to consider Vanessa as the child she never had. As the only one of her species in the park. She may have been lonely and not even realized it. The two became inseparable and Murray helped her rig up a saddle. Ziggy hardly felt the girls sixty pounds on her back and with her able to run thirty miles an hour, they could reach the far corners of the park faster than anyone else. She was protective, too. Her sharp eyes were constantly on the lookout for anything that would harm her or her chick. One evening, eating their last burgers around the campfire, Vanessa told them how Ziggy had defended her from a strange attack. They had been at the blackberry patch along the fence near the road. An opossum had come at her through a hole burrowed under it.

"I was gathering berries and Ziggy was hunting for lizards or something." Vanessa said. "and that creepy little thing tried to bite me. Not just once, it acted like it was hungry and I was the main course. It was savage! I screamed and started to run but she was there almost instantly."

She stroked the bird's neck as it was nestled beside her.

"Didn't you girl? You slashed that thing but good."

The four-inch claws on Ziggy's feet had eviscerated it, nearly cut it in half.

"But why would it attack you?" Murray asked. "They don't eat people, they eat road kill and rummage through trash. They were bad at our house. My dad had to make a cage to keep them out of our garbage cans."

"Not much road kill any more. Or trash." Swan said. "You think it had rabies?"

"I don't know, I hadn't thought about it. It was just weird, that's all. I was proud of Ziggy for killing it."

"Were there any zombies by the fence?" Tobias asked.

Vanessa shook her head. "Not really. There was one in the ditch but it was all busted up and most of it was gone. It could barely move."

The twins exchanged a look and nodded to each other.

"What?" Cody asked. "What are you two not telling us?"

"We noticed it a couple of days ago." Annalise said. "The coyotes and possums and vultures are eating the undead. We were on the roof of the aid station, watching the ones at the front gate and trying to figure out a way to kill them. If you're quiet, they don't notice you. They never look up."

"That's gross." Harper said. "But maybe that will solve the problem. Maybe that's nature's way of getting rid of them."

"Maybe." Cody said. "But what if it's contagious? What if the animals are turning into them? What if that possum was the first and the rest of them come after us?"

Nobody had any answers for that and all they could do was hope it was an anomaly, just a crazy possum.

"Maybe you got too close to its nest and it was trying to

protect its babies." Murray said. "Has anyone else seen any of the others acting aggressively?"

No one had, the only weird thing was the animals that usually ate road kill were now eating the zombies.

"Same thing only different." Cody finally said. "Dead and rotting is dead and rotting, right?"

"We'll just have to keep a close eye on them." Swan said, an arm around each of the wolves. "Maybe the Savage Ones will be content to eat the undead. Stinky meat is what their used to, right?" They shouldn't bother us, we're not dead."

Most of the scavenger animals were normally nocturnal and avoided humans, but they'd taken to feeding at all times of the day. They paid no mind to the living, gorging themselves on the abundance of zombies. They ignored each other, too. Some were natural enemies but with more food than they could ever eat that stood still and let them feed, they left each other alone. The coyote didn't need to try to kill a raccoon for dinner. Dinner was standing at the front gate. After a few bites, dinner would fall to the ground and they could tear into the soft and squishy parts.

No one had seen the hyenas since they fled the zoo and they had mostly forgotten about them. Out of sight, out of mind.

Donny and the Yewan were at the fire every night, listening and watching, but he wasn't sleeping in the house anymore. He preferred to bed down in the hayloft with blankets and the panther for company and warmth.

It hadn't taken long for the animals to start reverting back to their true natures. Swan was teaching the wolves to chase rabbits, the panther was stalking birds and going up trees after raccoons. They made sure to keep the gates closed to keep them out of the petting zoo as the instincts to hunt continued to evolve. Their daily supply of eggs and milk wasn't much, but it helped, and they didn't want to lose them.

The two polar bears were content to eat fish. The twins had built fish traps and the Mississippi was generous. Their coats had taken on a glossy appearance from all of the oils in the fish and they were something to behold. Like Vanessa, the twins had used leashes at first to lead them to the river and back but the bears had always known humans. They learned quickly and soon the two nearly albino children were frolicking with them in the cold water and riding them around the park. They had to teach them to fish by wading out into the shallows and standing still. The fish that darted off came back after a few minutes and the bears learned quickly how to spot them and paw them out to the bank.

Otis on the other hand, showed no interest in hunting or stalking prey. He was happy eating human food. Especially Spam. He'd chuffed and bobbed up and down like an overexcited puppy after his first taste. He'd devoured the two cans they'd found stuffed in Derek's desk and begged for more. While he didn't care for the hunt, he was quick to show the other animals who was the dominant creature in the park. After a dustup with Popsicle, he'd walked away with one chewed up ear, and a new scar on his snout, but Popsicle didn't challenge him again and the other animals in the strange family recognized him as the alpha. It had been frightening for them to watch, the giant bears battling for supremacy. They couldn't stop them, they couldn't inter-fere, and a single swipe of a paw would have killed them. When it was all said and done, it had mostly been growls and roars. Mostly posturing and neither animal came away from the fight with much damage.

Cody had watched the strange twins and the polar

bears diving into their pool chasing the fish they'd pulled from the traps in the river. They seemed almost oblivious to the cold water as they splashed and played with the two big bears, eating and sharing the raw fish with their ursine friends. He was the oldest and part of him wanted to tell them it probably wasn't a good idea to eat uncooked meat but what was sushi? What was steak tartare? And who was he to tell anyone what to do? If grownups were here, they'd be yelling at him for letting Otis inside the house and if the truth be told, when he actually thought about it, he really didn't think they would survive for long. Winter was coming, they were surrounded by zombies and all the grownups were dead. They were all being a little crazy, a little irresponsible, but it was okay. They were living in a crazy world and he tried not to think about it.

The twins were an odd pair to begin with, but the absence of any adults had exacerbated their behavior, maybe more than everyone else's. They'd taken to drawing Nordic runes on their bodies with permanent marker, touching them up often as the sun and dirt worked to fade and erode them.

Murray zipped around in his chair, always in motion and the little capuchin monkeys became attached to him like he was their second mamma. At first, they hid under his coat when the panther or one of the bears would pad alongside his chair but they grew comfortable around the predators when they realized they had no interest in eating them. He taught them to fetch things for him and they were eager to please, chittering merrily and jumping around swinging on things. He didn't even try to keep them on a leash when he first freed them. They could smell the undead, as did all the animals. They sensed everything was different somehow and clung to the humans that still were human.

Their entire lives, it was all any of them knew. The humans had always been their caregivers, had always given them food and water. They would be lost without them.

Murray dug through the tool sheds, opened closets, rifled through desk drawers. He was always in search of anything that would give them an edge, always scrolling through his tablet looking at one of the thousands of books he had on it. He inventoried everything, jotted down notes and considered possible alternative uses for each item. The park had a fairly well-equipped maintenance garage where the caretakers had kept the various mowers and carts in good running order. There was just about any tool they would need but without any machinery to fix, there wasn't much use for most of them. He was organized and methodical and Cody was thankful. Murray would have a list of all the things they needed when he finally swallowed his fear and they ventured out for a supply run. He'd been putting it off for as long as possible because some of them, maybe all of them, might not make it back. When he first started thinking about going to town, he hadn't even considered taking the animals, they might wander off and they'd never see them again. He'd changed his mind, though. They had all been working with their companions for hours and hours every day and the bonds were strong. He wasn't worried about any of them running away anymore. He didn't think they could drive them off if they tried.

Harper was the next oldest to Cody, she was thirteen and sometimes he couldn't help but notice how long and tan her legs were. He caught himself staring more than once after she took a quick, cold shower with the pull bucket they had rigged up. Her scream from the icy water and giggles afterward made him smile as she rushed to the fireplace to warm up beside it, her t-shirt sticking to the pointy places on her chest. She was really pretty and he'd get a little tongue-tied if he thought about her as a girl and not as one of the crew. If he thought about what it would be like to kiss her and not shovel cow manure beside her.

He'd always been awkward around girls at school, they were a mystery with their own ways and the ones he liked probably wouldn't want to talk to him anyway. Besides, what were you supposed to say to them? Did you see the new Star Wars movie? They'd probably laugh at him. With her it wasn't a big deal. He had to talk to her and everybody else, she was just one of the crew. It wasn't official or anything but everyone sort of looked to him for guidance or to settle an argument. He depended on Murray to keep things organized and everyone did the jobs they were supposed to do without him having to remind them. It wasn't like before. If you didn't do the dishes or mow the yard when you were supposed to, the worse that would happen is you would get yelled at. Now, if you didn't do your job, something bad could and probably would happen. Didn't milk the cow? She might die. Didn't water the chickens? They might die. Didn't walk the perimeter looking for breaches in the fence? You might die. Everything was a lot more serious now.

Harper made him laugh when she told him she had every intention of riding Bert right through a horde of zombies, high on his back, out of reach of their grasping hands.

"Bert will knock them all over like bowling pins and I'll have a morning star to make sure they stay down."

"A what?" Cody asked.

"Morning star. You know one of those ball and chain spikey things. Just swing it and kaboosh. Bye-bye Mr. Zombie head."

"Brutal." he said with approval.

Cody and Murray had inventoried the animals in the park and considered which ones were edible and how much meat they would provide. No matter what kind of math they did, the answer was not enough. There were a few gazelles and antelope no one would mind losing if they got desperate, they were truly wild and kept their distance but if they started eating them, all of them would be gone in a matter of weeks. There were the goats and sheep from the barnyard that would keep them from starving a while longer, but they wanted to breed them and create large herds, enough to be sustainable. The twins said they could even make cheese from the milk. The rest of the animals weren't really edible and he'd go hungry before he tried to eat Millie or Teddy. They didn't have a way to preserve the meat anyway, not that there would be much left if they could catch one of the antelopes. The bears and wolves ate a lot.

The fish traps were bringing in a basket of fish everyday but the panther and the bears were devouring them as quickly as they were caught and were still hungry now that the storehouse meats were gone. There just wasn't enough.

Murray wanted a smokehouse but they didn't have everything they needed to build it. All their plans and ideas were kind of moot anyway until they left the park for supplies. The town might be crawling with the undead with no way to get near any of the shops.

None of them had lived in Putnam, only knew it from passing through on the main road. They knew there was a grocery store, all their parents shopped there but they didn't know much else about the town. There were mostly boring antique or record stores and candle shops. Things they saw when they passed through but never paid any attention to.

The kind of places where they'd rather sit in the car and play on their phone while their moms went inside.

As they sat on the banks of the river, Cody leaning into the warm fur of Otis, he decided the time had come. That night he would tell the others they were going on a raid. Putnam was close enough that a fully charged cart would make the trip. If they were careful, if they were quiet, maybe they could find enough stuff to get them through. They needed food for them and the animals, warm clothes and some weapons to protect themselves. Going into town to see what was available would give them an idea of how hard the coming winter was going to be.

Maybe they'd find a town barricaded by military personnel, thriving and safe but deep down he doubted it. Most likely, the town would be crawling with undead and before the day was out, he and his crew would join them. There was no other choice though. They had to go now while they were strong and had options. If it was really bad, they could quietly retreat and figure out something else. They couldn't wait until they were weak with hunger and desperate.

They were on their own and he'd made his mom a promise to look after the park and its survivors. He wouldn't let her down. Wouldn't break the promise. He didn't know what he'd do if he walked out one day to see her at the fence, clawing and growling as she tried to get in.

He ruffled his hands through Otis's fur then climbed to his feet. Committed to his plan, they started back towards the house where he began gathering brush for the fire. It would feel good, burn hot and bright and chase the chill of the night away while he explained to the other kids his plan to either save them or get them all killed.

16

KERRY

K erry Lovell peeked through the blinds, looking for any sign of her husband. She was drinking the last of the coffee scavenged from their neighbor, the caffeine taking the edge off of her hunger. Chris had been gone too long. Worry set in. What would she do if he didn't come back? There wasn't anything left to eat, they'd even finished off the canned cat food from Mrs. Lowell. They'd been holed up and hiding since everyone went crazy. They had been one of the lucky ones, Chris had late classes that day at the University and was planning on grading papers all morning. They'd decided to keep Caleb home from school because there was a bug going around and he'd just gotten over a bad cold. She volunteered to watch her sister's kids if she wanted to keep them out of classes and Sharon had agreed. She had enough stress in her life, she didn't want her children coming down with whatever was going around.

They thought the madness would pass quickly. The Army or the police or somebody, anybody, would restore order. The sick would be taken somewhere to get well and life would go on. They were wrong. It got worse. They lived fifteen miles south of LaCrosse where her husband worked.

Had worked.

They had moved away from the city and into the same subdivision as her sister a few years ago. It was far enough away from town to be called country and the Rolling Hills Estates were considered gentleman's or hobby farms. The houses sat on five to ten acre lots and many of the families had a horse or other 4H animals.

Things had gone from normal to insane in a matter of minutes. Her sisters' kids had spent the night, had stayed up half of it giggling, and were still sleeping when everything went wrong. She and Chris were sitting on the front porch enjoying coffee and some quiet time before the children woke up when their neighbor across the street came tearing down the road in his car. He was driving like a maniac and screeched to a halt in front of his house. He ran inside, yelling for his wife to get his gun. He was bleeding from his shoulder and a screaming mob came running down the road after him.

They sat and watched, too shocked to move as he came back out a moment later blasting away at the people. He shot them dozens of times but none of them fell to the ground. They only screamed louder. They smashed through the windows and they heard his wife's shrieks become gurgling and liquid filled. They attacked in a frenzy, ignored the bullets ripping through them and started biting and tearing at him. Their fury died down as quickly as it started and they watched with wide staring eyes as their neighbor stood up and began shuffling around. Instinct told them to stay still, don't get noticed. They barely breathed as they watched the bloody, ragged crowd walk aimlessly around the house and yard until they heard another scream. This one came from four or five houses down, a good quarter mile away. The mob turned towards it instantly and started running, keening and screeching until they disappeared over the rise.

They went inside, locked the doors, shuttered the windows and tried to make phone calls. They kept quiet and watched the world burn on the television and computer until they lost power. After that, more of the same. Stay quiet, ration food, filter the pond water the best they could and steal eggs from the Walters two houses down. Their doors were swaying in the wind, bloody footprints covered the sidewalk. They wouldn't be needing them.

They were out of everything though. It had been weeks and Chris had raided all of the neighbor's houses. He'd brought back a wheel barrow of food but it hadn't lasted long with five mouths to feed. You'd think the so-called farmers would have pantries full of canned goods fresh from the garden but nobody did. Thousands of dollars' worth of food went bad in their deep freeze, nobody did their own canning anymore. By the time the undead had cleared out of the neighborhood and it was safe to venture out, all of the penned-up animals that had been trapped in their stalls were dead and bloated.

On one of his raids he had found a battery powered radio with shortwave and weather bands. He spent hours with it, rotating the dial slowly through each setting and never getting anything but static until he tried the AM band. Low on the dial and late at night he found a message being broadcast on a loop. It repeated the same few sentences over and over but it gave him hope. A group of truckers were headed to Lakota, Oklahoma and they were going to set up a safe area. All were welcome.

They needed supplies if they were going to make the

trip. He had cleaned out every house for miles and they hadn't provided much anyway. Usually just a handful of canned goods the wildlife couldn't get into. Mice and squirrels and insects were taking over and tearing into the boxes of cereal or bags of rice or cartons of noodles. The children were thin as rails and had been sleeping a lot, they were all slowly starving to death. They needed sustenance. They needed food. They needed to be strong. Anything could happen along the way and they needed to be able to run if they had to. The trip might take days, maybe even weeks. They had no idea what the roads would be like or how many of the undead they would encounter. They might have to backtrack a lot to avoid the hordes.

Chris was going farther this time, they needed real food. He was going to take their truck and go into town to the store, make a big haul, get everything they needed. He wasn't a mechanic and didn't know much about cars. He took it to the dealer to get serviced and called triple A if he had a flat. He could figure things out, though. He knew he needed more between him and the undead than a thin pane of glass. He covered the windows with strips of metal and added a big push bar to the bumper to protect the radiator. The truck didn't crank when he was ready to test it, the battery had drained. He had to take one out of a neighbors' old Ford tractor.

"All of the batteries will be dead." he'd said. "I should have thought about it and disconnected them. The cars clocks and computers and who knows what else is a constant drain on them. I'll stop at a parts store and get us a new one."

He should have been back an hour ago.

She checked on the children. Caleb, Landon and Clara were playing with Legos in the basement. Caleb was her only child and the other two were her niece and nephew but they were hers now and had started calling her mommy. At the tender ages of six and seven, they were inseparable, Caleb and Landon born only days apart and Clara, less than a year younger.

They'd been locked inside, mostly staying downstairs and being quiet for what seemed like months. The kids learned quickly that it wasn't a game. They saw for themselves a few days after it all began and Landon and Clara were still crying for their mother. A horde came screeching down the road chasing somebody in a car. A neighbor down the way making his escape. They saw the bloody crowd with ripped open bellies, torn off faces and missing arms. They heard the keens and cries of hunger and watched in revulsion as the broken things too damaged to walk dragged their way down the road leaving smears of gore behind them.

They stopped asking about their mother and they became very, very good at keeping quiet.

Chris been gone too long, she thought again for the thousandth time. It had been hours since he'd left that morning with his homemade armor. She had sewn pieces of carpet to the sleeves of his work jacket to stop those things from biting him. It was already after lunchtime and Putnam was only a half hour away. He should have been back, been with her and the children by now. She gripped the key fob to the BMW parked across the street. If he came running with the crazies on his tail, she'd hit the alarm, hopefully distracting them enough for Chris to make it to safety. If there was any juice left its battery.

Where is he? She repeated to herself over and over, glancing at the clock on the mantle every few minutes.

17

PUTNAM

Putnam, Iowa was a typical small midwestern town. The old courthouse with its weathered clock tower dominated the skyline while elms and maples lined the sidewalks. Their leaves exploded in the brilliant colors of fall and the hues of gold, orange and red invoked images of a Norman Rockwell painting. Now, the trees stood in silent witness to the devastation that the virus had wrought on the small slice of heaven. Trash and debris nestled against their trunks and white plastic shopping bags were tangled in the lower branches. Fallen leaves covered the streets. Store front benches, already starting to rust, sat empty and forlorn. The old men who whiled away the mornings with hot black coffee were long gone. The stores and businesses sat deserted and dark, a few had shattered windows with glass shards on the sidewalk. Smashed cars with open doors sat at intersections, traffic lights swayed on the wires above them.

Flies still buzzed around the delis and ice cream shop, their perishable items long spoiled and reeking. Birds flew in and out of the open windows while mice skittered back and forth, chewing into the boxes and bags of food. Ants marched in single file lines carrying their spoils like a conquering army. A few stray cats and half-starved dogs wandered the alleys, their owners either part of the undead hordes or long gone and never coming back.

Putnam was laid out in a square design like many other turn of the century towns across the country. Its buildings were brick and mortar, no fancy glass and steel, just classic architecture in the old square. Easy access to the Mississippi, with its barges moving products on the river, and the fertile soil made for an ideal agricultural site. Bypassed by the interstate in the early 1970's, it sat off the beaten path and died a slow death as lifestyles changed. They youngsters went away for school and never came back and the downtown became boarded up storefronts and second-hand junk shops. For a generation it was forgotten, a relic of a bygone era withering away. The digital age changed all that, the antiques store no longer needed local customers to stay afloat, he could sell his wares globally on eBay. The inexpensive houses near the riverfront found a resurgence in popularity when people worked from home and gentrification brought in new businesses.

Like so many other small towns the square offered an eclectic mix of the old and new. Situated beside the feed store was the Verizon hub. Across the square, Mixon's barbershop sat next to Bowman's software engineering office. The owner of Maroni's Italian Restaurant had worried about the new Subway shop when it opened but by setting out a sign advertising his lunch specials, he more than made up for lost business. Not that it mattered anymore, Sal Maroni shuffled along the road a hundred miles away in an unending quest to find fresh blood. He didn't know where he was going or where he'd been. He didn't feel the rain or the cold or the bones of his feet as they scraped along the asphalt, his shoes and skin long worn away. He wandered with dozens of others, mindless and adrift, always hungry and always searching.

Donny jogged ahead of the rest of them, scouting for danger. Harper drove the cart with Murray seated beside her, his wheelchair folded in the back. The others walked silently down the road, ready to turn and run for the safety of the park at the first sign of trouble. They had drawn straws to see who would stay. Somebody had to if the trip were a disaster and none of them came back. Somebody had to free the animals if that happened. Vanessa had walked with the strange parade to the rear gate and made sure it was latched then watched as they disappeared. If none of them came back, she knew what to do.

Murray brought China, one of the capuchins. He insisted that her knack for getting in and out of places might come in handy. She perched on his shoulder, looking through his hair for anything that might provide a snack, grooming him affectionately as if he was one of her own pack. He swatted at her as she stuck her finger in his nose. Undeterred, she kept probing.

Zero and Lucy padded softly beside Swan, ears up and alert, while Cody and the twins brought up the rear.

Welcome to Putnam the sign read *Iowa's friendliest town*. There was a compact car crumpled against the base of the brick structure, the doors still open where the driver had either fled or died. There were dark stains on the seats that looked a lot like dried blood and they looked away as they passed.

By group consensus they had decided to skip looking in any houses unless they didn't find any big supplies of food at the stores. They might get a few bags from homes but they were much more likely to find the dead inside. It would be better to try to score big, maybe find whole storerooms of canned goods, more than they could carry. Walking beneath the trees that lined the streets the stench of decay was heavy in the air. Occasionally they saw a curtain flutter in a house as a shambling shape brushed against it. They didn't talk, not even to whisper. They used military hand signals learned from a book. Swan had to shush her wolves more than once when their deep rumbling growls started to get loud. Putrid bodies lay decomposing in the streets, empty eye sockets filled with mucky water. A lot of them had holes in their heads, dried brains and blood crusted around the wounds. There were empty bullet casings littering the ground, a lot of them, but they didn't see any guns. Whoever had been doing all the shooting had won the fight. At least, this one. All the bodies showed signs of having been fed on, bones exposed and weathering as they returned to dust. They didn't know if it was from the zombie attack or animals scavenging their remains but none of them cared to look closer to try to find out.

Donny fell back to join them as they continued their slow walk into the downtown area, the cart crunching over leaves and broken glass, all of them gripping their makeshift weapons and staring in all directions. The desire to turn and run back to the safety of the Park was strong. Inside the fences, they weren't afraid. Inside the fences, they were safe. But inside the fences, there wasn't any food. They heard thrashing up ahead and Swan urged Zero and Lucy forward as she slunk along in a crouch beside them. Unconsciously baring her teeth and growling deep in her throat with them. Cautiously, the group followed the growling trio. Tobias and Annalise readied their pitchforks and advanced slowly, eyes wide, breathing fast and ready to lunge. A zombie in a deputy sheriff uniform lay pinned underneath an overturned patrol car, his clawing fingers ground down to splintered stumps. It snapped at them, biting the air with his yellowed teeth and struggled harder to free himself.

"Kill it before others hear him and come running." Murray whispered. "Hurry."

China hid herself under his shirt and shivered.

"We are warriors." Tobias told his sister.

Mouth grim, she nodded and they both thrust their pitchforks into the biting things face.

It fell still instantly and the wolves stopped their quiet growls, sniffed at it and snorted. Tobias's eyes were huge in his rune painted face and Annalise seemed even paler as they pulled the tines out and looked at the black blood dripping from them. It was their first kill. She waited for a moment to see if she would feel guilt or shame. She had just taken a man's life. But she hadn't, really. The man was already dead and they had done him a mercy. She gripped her pitchfork with greater resolve and a small, tight smile spread across her lips. It matched the one Tobias wore.

The closer they got to the square, the more evidence there was of a battle. The zombies had won, that was obvious, but a lot of them lay dead with blown open heads. Windows were shattered at the municipal building and the doors were broken down. Someone had tried to make a last stand but it hadn't worked. There must have been thousands fighting to get in, the entire town. Cody wondered what happened to them because so far, they hadn't seen any wandering around. The place was long abandoned.

The nose of a pickup was wrapped around a utility pole and a lone black crow was focusing on the driver as it cawed and shifted anxiously from side to side on crumpled hood. The woman inside was pinned: trapped by the steering wheel and the crushed roof from the broken off pole. She was half way through the windshield, her body bent in an unnatural manner. Her face was a ruined mess, eyes and lips gone, cheeks shredded from the crow that dipped down and tore at the easy meal, feasting on the rotting flesh. She still struggled and chomped but her movements were feeble and the black-eyed crow easily avoided her broken teeth as he ate. Vultures circled overhead in slow lazy circles, awaiting their chance to feast undisturbed on the dead.

Putnam had everything they needed if they could get to it without getting shredded by the zombies. They weren't equipped to fight the undead, not yet anyway. The first thing on Murray's list was Armor and Weapons.

"We have to find a sporting goods store or thrift shop first." he told them. "We need to find protection. We need leather gloves and football pads or soccer guards. Anything that will prevent us from getting bit. That comes first before we look for food."

A block from the center of town, Replay Consignments had mannequins in the windows bedecked with football equipment. It was a second-hand sports shop and Swan took the lead, her two protectors staying close. The bell over the door tinkled and everyone froze but nothing came lunging out. The wolves entered warily, sniffing around in curiosity but not alerting to danger. The rest of them slipped in quickly and as soon as he found a display with baseball equipment, Cody grabbed some catchers gear and hurried back out to Murray. The leg guards were perfect, nothing was going to bite through them. It didn't take them long before they were decked out with a combination of hockey, soccer, lacrosse and baseball guards and they all felt a little safer. They had a fighting chance now; a zombie would have a lot tougher time finding flesh on them. The modern armor was nothing like the steel and chainmail of old. It was lightweight, easy to move in and quiet.

"Weapons next on the list, right?" Annalise whispered as they eased out of the store, still trying to move silently. For all they knew, a huge horde could be a few blocks away.

Cody nodded and pointed to a hardware store half a block up. The first thing they thought of when brainstorming their raid was guns of course. They argued pros and cons for a long time and in the end, they decided against them. Nobody had ever shot a real one and what if it drew in zombies? The world was so quiet now with no cars or airplanes or even the hum of electrical wires, a gunshot could probably be heard for miles and miles in any direction. And worse, what if it frightened their companions? Animals had to be trained to guns and they couldn't risk panicking them, scaring them so bad they ran too far away and got lost.

In the survival books, they had found plans on how to build war hammers and sawblade battle axes from threaded pipes and other common materials. Weapons they could tailor to kids. They knew from chopping wood they would never be able to swing an axe fast enough to protect themselves from attack. Baseball bats were too blunt.

"You've got to pierce the skull!" Murray kept telling them. "We have to have long sharp instruments. Spears when we can, spiked hammers for when it gets close. Knives aren't heavy enough to pierce the skull and the weapons have to be our size, not our parents' size. We have to be able to swing them hard and fast."

Swan swept the store with the wolves and when she gave them the all clear signal, Cody and Donny slung Murray over their shoulders and hustled him inside. The twins stood guard with the pitchforks as Harper grabbed his chair and followed, the little monkey scampering beside her. There were bloody hand prints on the swinging doors. Something dead had been inside but it was long gone now.

They found flashlights and packs of batteries then made their way to the plumbing section. Everything they needed was there and with a sigh of relief, they got started assembling the various pieces of threaded pipe, T-fittings and caps into deadly child sized war hammers. They capped off one end of four-foot sections of black pipe and duct taped steel marker stakes into the other end, their pointy tips made deadly thrusting spears.

"Make sure you grab some flat files." Murray said, checking his list. "And paracord to wrap the handles."

Fine tuning and improving their weapons could be done back at the Park but it felt good to have something besides a pitchfork to fight with.

China found the bags of peanuts near the register and was chattering excitedly as she tore them open. The wolves and the panther paced the store, vigilant and sniffing the air. It only took them a few minutes to assemble the weapons and Cody motioned for Donny to help him in the farm supply department. It wasn't well stocked but there a lot of things a hobby farmer might need. Food for chickens and goats, various feeders and incubators and light farm equipment. Mostly implements that could be attached to a riding lawn mower. They needed to get the biggest two wheeled garden cart they could find to hook to the back of the golf cart. It would double their carrying capacity. They added a few sacks of grain for their cow and goats and Murray made note of how much was left on the shelves. They knew where to come when they needed more.

Armed, armored and with the few tools they needed, they made their way back outside and were ready to hit the grocery store. The town was eerily quiet with only the tweeting of birds and their footsteps crunching on leaves breaking the silence. They could hear the flap of vultures' wings overhead.

"Where did everyone go?" Annalise whispered as they passed another empty shop, its door broken and hanging askew. "Something must have made them run off."

"Maybe some survivors were in a house and when they ran out of food, they drove off." Harper said. "Maybe all the dead people chased after them."

It was as good a theory as any and the longer they were there, the more confident they became. The town wasn't that big, only a few dozen streets long with the same number of cross streets. It only had two traffic lights and a roundabout at the town center. Near the river was a small industrial area with a few warehouses and shops but they didn't bother going down there, a grocery store was next on their list. They had a few choices, there were a couple of health food shops, a good-sized chain store and a little mom and pop that reeked when they approached it. It had been the best butcher shop for miles around but all that meat was spoiled, rotten and still stinking. Clouds of flies swarmed around it.

They crossed the road to avoid the smell and spotted the other grocery store halfway down the block of a side street. Cody signaled and they made their way towards it, the cart humming along quietly as they swung their new weapons, trying to get used to the heft and feel of them.

It was a pretty big store, the largest one for ten or twenty miles in any direction and supplied the rural families in three counties.

There were dead inside.

They spotted a few zombies wandering aimlessly up

and down the aisles, trapped when the electricity went off and the automatic doors stayed closed.

They huddled around the cart to decide what to do but they already knew. They couldn't go back empty handed. They needed the food and what good was having weapons if they were too afraid to use them?

"Okay." Cody said. "Donny and I with the spears, Harper and Swan pry the door open and you two make sure it doesn't open too wide. Just enough to stab them when they try to get us. Ready?"

Wide eyes and nervous head nods. They were as ready as they'd ever be.

The woman near the magazine rack heard them as soon as Swan shoved a tomahawk blade between the doors to pry them apart. Harper got her spear in the slot and the door slid open a few inches. She turned her black eyes to the sounds and smelled the untainted blood flowing through their veins. She screamed and launched herself at the two boys standing on the other side of the glass, her greasy, dank hair flying behind her. Other keens and screams took up the call and pounding feet came up the aisles sensing fresh meat. Her vein mottled face hit the frame and a reaching arm shot through, clawing the air and grabbing for flesh. Tobias had his shoulder against the door and Annalise had her Warhammer wedged in place but it still shuddered and slid open another inch. Cody thrust his spear, aimed for her eye and grunted with the effort as it broke through the thin wall of bone and pinned her in place. Her flailing stopped almost immediately, her legs crumpled and he had to jerk back hard to free his spear.

Before she hit the floor, two more were fighting to be the first at the children. Old brown blood stains covered a man's jacket, his yellowish shoulder bone poking through the shredded skin. Donny jabbed at him and the point tore into his cheek, slid off bone and flayed open a deep gash along his head. The man snapped at the steel, tried to bite through it and only broke his teeth. Pieces of them flew as the boy pulled back and stabbed again, this time aiming for the wide-open mouth. Filthy, clutching hands in a homemade carpet covered jacket reached for him, tried to dig dirty fingernails into flesh. The end of the spear burst out of the back of his head in a spray of black and yellow goo and before Donny could pull out, the man was shoved aside by a woman scrabbling over the fallen bodies. The door gap was wider now and the twins tried to force it back but the wild haired woman already had her head and shoulders through. She thrashed and screamed a dry scratchy scream then shoved it open, knocking both of them aside. Her frenzied flailing knocked Cody's spear away and she launched herself at Donny. Harper screamed. Her bloody mouth was stretched wide as her hands grabbed his shoulders and she fell on him, snapping at his face. A black blur hit her, sharp claws slicing through skin like paper, snarling fangs closing around her neck and snapped it like a twig. Yewan's mighty leap knocked her ten feet away from them and she savaged her mercilessly, ripping and shredding until the lifeless corpse lay still.

"Watch out!" Murray yelled and they all turned away from the panther, back to the door. A toddler was climbing over the bodies, his hungry black eyes fixed on them as he snapped his milk teeth, the hunger driving him forward. Tobias tried to shut the door but the bodies blocked it. The baby keens were getting shriller the closer he got and Cody picked up his dropped spear. Donny scooted away on all fours as the thing came at him.

"Stab it! Stab it!" Swan yelled but Cody hesitated. It

was just a baby. It was inhumanly fast and was grabbing at Donny's foot as he tried to get away, tried to kick at it with his falling apart tennis shoe. There was a guttural growl from behind him then the wolves shot past and tore into the scuttling little monster. Lucy and Zero sank fangs and clamped down, both of them ragging and pulling on the thing like it was a toy. A leg and an arm tore off and they dropped them and went after it again. It was still keening and trying to crawl towards Donny, its little mouth still working in hunger. Black blood oozed from the wounds but didn't spurt out like they expected. The heart wasn't pumping and very little was spilled. The wolves grabbed the baby again and when they were finished, it was finally still.

Swan knelt between them, draped her arms over their shoulders and rubbed her face in their fur. Zero licked at the tears she didn't even know she'd been shedding. No more of the undead came screaming out of the darkness of the store and they all heaped praise on the animals. They had hoped they would protect them, they had hoped they would fight for them but until it happened, they weren't sure. Now they were. The animals had the same instincts as a family dog would in protecting his master.

They drug the bodies out to the parking lot, left them by a truck then pulled out their flashlights and started loading up the garden cart. They piled the back of the golf cart high with boxes and boxes of canned goods and bags of dog and cat food.

The wolves and panther wouldn't like it much but it would keep them from starving until they learned how to hunt. They avoided the meat and deli section; the reek was almost unbearable. Worse than the smell of the zombies. Murray rolled his chair up and down the aisles making inventory notes as the rest of them hurried back and forth to the cart with the pilfered supplies.

It didn't take long until they were loaded almost to the point of being overloaded and the group started their trip home. They moved quietly but with more confidence. They had met the enemy head on and destroyed it. They had fought and killed and their animals had too. They were a team. They were bad asses.

Eyes and ears were alert. Even though the place seemed abandoned a wandering dead thing could be hidden anywhere. Aside from their quiet passage down the streets and the crunching of leaves, the scurrying of small rodents and the calls of the crows were the only signs of life.

There was one more stop on their list, they had to get clothes and good shoes. The Outdoor Store should have everything they need. It carried everything from high end camping, hiking and fishing equipment for the well-heeled in town along with military surplus and old war paraphernalia for the collectors. It was already fall season and they hoped winter jackets were in stock.

They gathered around the single glass door and tried to peer inside but the store was dark and cluttered with too much stuff. Tobias rapped on the glass pane with his pipe hammer and the response was instantaneous. They heard a snarl and low scream from the back of the store then the clatter of things being knocked over as something surged to the front. It was a fat man with a gray hair and beard. At one time he was probably jolly and loved children. He was probably the guy who played Santa at the VFW Christmas party or threw candy to the kids during the Parade. He slammed into the door and despite themselves, they jumped back a little. He still loved kids, which was apparent, just not in the same way he used to. He pressed his face against the glass and tried to chew through it. The three predators crouched low, ready to spring, and there was a low rumble of warning coming from them. Donny and Tobias had to struggle to get the door open enough, he kept slamming into it trying to force his way through. Once they shoved it open a few inches, a hand came out and a spear went in. Cody pulled back quickly before the thing fell and took the spear with him. He was learning. They drug the Santa Clause looking man out onto the sidewalk and left him. This would be a place they would be coming back to from time to time and there was no use letting the body stink the place up.

Once Murray was inside, they spread out to go shopping. The Outdoor Store was big. It was overstuffed with auction lots of military gear haphazardly stacked beside displays of expensive hiking boots from Timberland, Keen and Columbia. Arc'teryx and North Face jackets hung next to military issue ACU's. Mannequins wearing World War Two uniforms were standing on boxes of Mountain Home long term storage food. China found a bag of beef jerky and Murray had a captive audience once the wolves and the panther smelled it.

"Great." he grumbled. "I'll just wait here, feeding your animals. You guys have fun!"

"Thanks Murray." Swan said as she disappeared into the gloom, completely missing, or maybe ignoring, his sarcasm.

"Don't forget Vanessa!" he yelled after her. "Size six!"

China grabbed the bag out of his hand and darted to the top of a pile of old BDU uniforms tossed in a bin, chittering happily as the wolves watched their food disappear. They tried to go after her and things started falling over, clattering to the floor and starting a small chain reaction.

Cody chuckled and headed to the rear of the store as

Murray cursed, the monkey chittered and the wolves whined. Yewan ignored them all with a flick of his tail and padded after Donny.

The animals hadn't alerted to any more undead but he wanted to be sure, wanted to check the bathrooms and managers office before he completely relaxed and started hunting for a pair of hiking boots. He shone his light around the door leading to the storeroom and saw the dirty handprints, blood smears and scratch marks on it. The jolly zombie had been trying to get in. Cody turned the knob and pulled opened the door, his hammer ready to bash something in the head if he needed to. The smell nearly made him gag. It wasn't a dead smell; it was a bathroom smell. A raw sewage, unflushed toilet and unwashed body smell that may have been worse than the rotting meat of the zombies. There was a stack of boxes blocking the pathway but he easily shoved them aside. The room was crammed with more military stuff and a set of small, dirty windows set up high in the block wall let light filter in.

"I've got a gun. Move one more muscle and I'll blow your stinking head clean off." A trembling voice came from deep in the shadows.

"Whoa." Cody said. "I didn't come to steal your stuff. We didn't know anybody was here."

"What happened to that thing outside the door?" the voice said and Cody zeroed in on it.

"We killed it."

"Bullshit. Those things are invincible. It's been out there for months. It doesn't eat, it doesn't sleep, and it scratches on the door day and night, week after week. You can't kill them."

"We've killed a bunch of them."

"Liar." the voice spat.

Cody kept the flashlight trained on the wall of junk in front of him but his eyes were adjusting to the gloom. He spotted a kid no older than himself huddled in the corner with a machete in his hand.

"Don't look at me." he barked "I'll shoot you! I'll blow your friggin' brains out!"

Yewan walked up, curious about the new voice and Cody spun the light full the kid. He was blinded but not before he saw the giant, black cat. He squealed and dropped the blade. Yewan stood beside him, as tall as his waist, his baleful yellow eyes pinned the kid to the spot. A wet spot spread across the front of the boy's camouflage pants as he covered his face and whimpered.

"Don't let him eat me." he begged. "Please don't let him eat me."

"Dude, chill out. He's harmless." Cody scratched the cats' neck then pushed him towards the door. Yewan left with a flick of his ears and small snort. He didn't like the smell either.

"Geez, you've been trapped in here since the beginning?" Cody asked, trying to put the boy at ease. "That had to suck."

He was repulsed by what he saw. The kid had made a toilet out of a wooden ammo crate and liquids were oozing out of it, staining the floor in one corner. His makeshift bed was only a few feet away, a bunch of clothes thrown on the ground. There were old girlie magazines laying on it, open to his favorite pictures. There were empty MRE packets and other garbage strewn around but not a trash can in sight. Stacked against one wall were cases and cases of the standard military field food. Probably recently expired and bought cheap at a surplus auction.

"You really got rid of the zombie?" the kid finally asked when he realized he wasn't in any immediate danger.

"Yeah, easy as pie once you know how." Cody couldn't help but brag a little.

"Who are you talking too?" Swan's voice drifted back to them from the shoe section.

The boy's eyes got big when he realized there were more of them and at least one was a girl. He looked quickly around the room, at the open toilet, the squalor and his filthy clothes. He'd even pissed his pants. He looked like a cornered animal, not grateful somebody had freed him but mortally embarrassed that they were going to see how he'd been living.

Cody hesitated before he answered. Would he want to be found like this? No, he guessed not. Who knew what the kid had been through? He wouldn't humiliate him any further.

"Myself!" he yelled back. "Did you find a jacket for Vanessa?"

"Working on it." Came the reply, far away and echoed.

"Look, we have a pretty good place if you want to join us." Cody told the boy.

"You guys have food? Is it safe?" he asked

"Yeah, completely fenced in and we have food now, we just raided the store. Besides, we could always use more help."

"I'm not going to be your slave." the boy said, getting some of his bravado back.

"I didn't mean it like that." Cody replied, a little exasperated. "I mean, it's a big place, we all have work to do and somebody else helping out would make things easier for everyone. You don't have to, you can stay here. I don't care."

"No, it sounds good. I'll come." he said, afraid the boy with the panther would change his mind.

"Okay. Cool." Cody said. "Um, if you want, go ahead and get cleaned up. I'll wait for you outside."

The boy eyed him coldly as he backed out of the room, shut the door and took a deep breath of the fresh air. How could anybody live like that? Why hadn't he just killed the zombie and been done with it, there was only one. Why hadn't he at least used a plastic bag for a toilet and tossed it out the window? Cody went over to the military boots section and started prowling around, looking for his size.

The kid took his time getting cleaned up. Cody had given up waiting around the back of the store for him, had loaded his boots and coats into the cart and was helping Murray back to it. He told them about the boy he'd found, glossing over the grossness of it, and finally finished by saying he wasn't sure if he would be coming with them or not.

"If he doesn't show up in the next few minutes, let's go." Cody said as he laced up his new boots.

"I want to get back before dark and he may have changed his mind. I think the animals scare him."

Swan snorted. "He won't be much good at the Park then. Let's go."

"Give him a chance." Harper said. "He's been trapped for weeks. Poor guy."

Donny signaled *you want me to start?* Indicating him and Yewan would lead the way.

Cody shook his head. "Let's all stick together. Those things could be anywhere, more may have wandered in while we were here and be on the road."

Donny nodded and waited, one hand gripping his spear,

the other scratching the panther behind an ear. The twins spotted a tattoo parlor and slipped over to peek inside.

"We'll be back in a sec." Tobias said and they were gone before Cody could say anything.

The door finally opened and the kid stepped outside on the sidewalk. He stared at them, at their animals, at the cart and trailer loaded up with supplies and announced "I'm ready."

He was wearing all new military gear that didn't quite fit. The pants legs and sleeves were too long. He had on brand new shiny black boots, not the dull brown ones or hiking boots everyone else had chosen. He had a machete on both hips tucked into a belt and a big oversized pack stuffed full of things on his back. Even though the uniform was too big, his belly still hung over the belt. The baby fat, as his mother called it, on his cheeks reddened as they stared at him and didn't say anything.

"This will need to go in the cart somewhere." he said as he came over to them. "I guess we have to walk? How far is it?"

Cody hid his annoyance and signaled Donny to get him started on a slow jog back, running point and looking for danger. The big cat loped along beside him.

The twins came back out of the tattoo shop and sprang to their mounts. They had grins on their faces and a bulging satchel.

Harper introduced herself and stuck out her hand from the driver's seat.

"Gordon Lowery." he said and handed his pack to Cody to put on top of the stuff in the already overloaded cargo area.

"Gordon Lowery, the guy that owns half of the county?" Murray asked

"That would technically be my father but since he hasn't been heard from in a few months, yes, I suppose it would be mine now." Gordon replied.

Cody caught his time reference again. It had only been a few weeks, not months, since the outbreak. Maybe being trapped in the store room messed with his head.

Swan rolled her eyes and led her wolves to the rear. She didn't bother to introduce herself and was already wishing Cody hadn't invited him to join them.

18

TRIBE

The flames licked at the night sky as the bonfire burned brightly. Smoke drifted lazily on the breeze. Everyone was boisterous and cheerful, happy they had something new and different to eat. They sat around the fire roasting Vienna sausages or marshmallows on sticks celebrating the success of their first raid and their new member. Otis smacked his lips in anticipation of the tasty treats Cody shared with him.

Gordon tried to be pleasant with the group but was in a foul mood. He looked on in disgust as Cody and Otis shared the tiny sausages. The bear was obviously a danger to everyone, it was running around without a chain or muzzle or anything. His feet hurt, he had blisters. Nobody told him he'd have to walk miles and miles. They should have let him ride, he could have drove or the cripple in the wheelchair could have rolled along, he didn't have to worry about getting blisters. Nobody had really spoken with him, they stayed separate on the endless trudge back to the Park. The animals didn't like him much, either. That was okay. He didn't like them. Cody had promised him food and warmth.

This wasn't food, not like he was accustomed to before the world collapsed. Junk food and canned meats. Potato chips, snack cakes, and stale crackers. Cody had made it sound like they had a good setup, that it was nice and almost normal like it was before. It wasn't much better than where he had been staying. The only good thing he'd seen so far was there wasn't an undead thing constantly scratching at the door. He was already thinking he should have stayed in town. If he'd have known all the zombies were gone, he probably would have. There had to be better places than this crappy zoo left in the world. There wasn't any electricity or hot water. There weren't any steaks or ice cream and that creepy quiet kid actually ate cat food. He wrinkled his nose as he watched the mute boy spooning some out of a can and smearing it on crackers, eating one and giving the other to the huge black panther that never left his side.

The house was old and drafty. The rooms dusty and the floors creaked with every step. They seemed content, but the whole situation felt beneath him. They all slept in the same room, too. There was no privacy. You had to carry a bucket to the bathroom to flush the toilet or walk to one of the fancy outhouses along the trails. Cody told him there were rooms on the top floor if he wanted and that was probably just a ploy to get rid of him so they could talk about him behind his back. He told them he had blisters but nobody seemed to care. One of those weirdo albinos told him there was an aide station if he wanted to get some Band-Aids but nobody went to get him any. They all acted like they were too busy unpacking the cart and feeding the animals. Nobody had cooked, either. They were eating junk. He hoped it wasn't like this every night. What was the use of all that food he'd had to help lug into the house if nobody was going to whip up something good? He sat by himself and listened to the talk as they worked on improving their weapons. Most of them had dangerous animals right beside them. He'd tried to join in to different conversations but they were talking about stuff he didn't care about. Easier ways to file spear points. Fish traps and logs they'd spotted for firewood. Proper ways to wrap a handle so the paracord wouldn't come loose. All they cared about was work and the stupid animals. What was with all the mediaeval weapons? Why didn't they all have machine guns? And didn't anyone play video games anymore? His iPad was full of them and when he found out they had a way to charge it, he wanted to plug in. They said he had to wait, Murray needed the charger for his book reader.

The twins made him uncomfortable. They were strange. The kid in the wheelchair was always amped up, fueled by energy drinks and junk food, the monkeys always climbing on him and making noise. It was disgusting to watch him take a bite out of a candy bar and then share it with one of them before taking another bite himself. Savage Ones, he'd heard the term used about the scavenger animals, but to him it seemed like these kids were pretty savage in their own right. He eyed Harper, now that was a good-looking girl. He liked blondes. All of his favorite girls in the magazines he'd brought were blonde. The other girls were pretty too, but other than Vanessa, she was the only one who didn't weird him out. Swan and her wolves were creepy. Annalise, her polar bear and the tribal tattoos she drew on her arms was a little disturbing. He moved closer to the fire and a little closer to Harper. At least she didn't have some animal sitting beside her. She'd said she had a giraffe and he'd almost laughed at her. Out of all the animals here at the Safari Park, she couldn't pick out one more practical? A dog maybe?

Cody was talking about food and his ears perked up.

"If we ration carefully, we picked up enough food to last us at least a month on this trip. One or two more raids and that should be enough to carry us through the winter." Cody said.

"Now that we know what kind of stores are in town, I have some ideas for some projects we can build," interjected Murray. He was wrapping paracord around the handle of a homemade war hammer. "We can even build a windmill to pump water."

Cody nodded. "Food first, then we'll worry about that. We also need to do something to insulate the chicken coop and goat pens before it gets too cold. Hopefully in the spring, we'll have some new chicks and it won't be long after before we have plenty of eggs to go around."

Swan lay on a blanket and stared up at the clear night sky. There were no artificial lights to interfere with the view anymore. The stars looked close enough to touch. She stretched a finger towards one.

"You know," she started. "We are all connected. The stars lined up perfectly to bring each of us here so that we could survive. Some of us were strangers, but now we are a tribe. We are a part of everything; everything is a part of us. Mother Earth provides everything we need if you will look and listen for it." She traced designs in the air with her fingers. The wolves lay on either side of her, lazing in the warmth of the fire. The others paused in their work or idle chatter and listened.

"Squirrels gather nuts, store them for the winter. They lose a few along the way and a new tree grows. The tree provides shelter for more squirrels. More squirrels means more for my wolves to eat. They make sure the squirrels don't overpopulate. It's a perfect design when people don't mess it all up." she said with a sigh.

Donny lowered the file he was using to sharpen his spear point, Yewan curled protectively around his feet. It was an odd speech but she was a strange girl at times. Her mother had been active in the tribal council and she'd been attending gatherings and pow wows her whole life. She was proud of her heritage and its closeness to nature. She saw mankind as a negative influence on the natural world. Her wolves could shred some small animal they'd managed to catch and she didn't bat an eye but if talk turned to taking down one of the gazelles for meat, she became agitated and would often storm off to be alone. The subject of hunting had been broached a few times during Mr. Baynard's discussions before the fall and she visibly bristled. They had no right to hunt the creatures of the forest, we should become vegetarians she'd insisted. She wasn't so vocal about it anymore. She knew the store shelves would be empty sooner or later and her wolves didn't eat vegetables. They were lousy hunters, it was only luck if they ever caught anything by themselves and she didn't know how to teach them.

She talked on about harmony and balance, about the trees and the bees in her melodic voice and how maybe this was all a big reset from Mother Earth. Man had grown too greedy, took too much and the world had had enough of it. They'd forgotten how to live in unity with nature. Nature always provided if you knew how to see it. Some of it made sense to them. Cody thought a lot of it was wistfulness and hopefulness. No one had any idea what had happened to cause all of this. All they really knew for sure was that they were alone and outside their protective fence was a world full of death.

19

DONNY

Every night after he got the spear Donny and Yewan would slip out of the back gate and attempt to bring in some fresh game. He'd spent hours throwing it at haybales and finally had it perfectly balanced. It flew straight and true and most of time he could get pretty close to the bullseye. He'd filed the blade to a fine point and it could cut cleanly, penetrate deeply and take down an animal before they knew what hit them. He couldn't call to his cat so he'd taught him to obey different sounds he made by tapping his ring against the steel of the spear. They were simple commands they could both remember. A double tap meant come. A scraping of steel on steel meant stay. They were basic but it was all they needed to understand each other.

They'd spent night after night stalking prey or waiting to ambush an unwary deer. On this, the ninth night of luck-less hunting, the rising full moon cast the forest in a dim glow as they sat unmoving on the limb above the game trail. It was just past twilight, full dark barely settled in and he was feeling good about their chances. He'd spotted fresh tracks on the trial so he knew it was frequently used.

Donny shifted slightly, careful not to let his improvised armor creak. His mind was still and clear as he tried to channel his ancient ancestors, tried to have patience and peace. Dressed all in black with pads and guards of various sports gear, he was protected from bites but could move easily. He had modified it to look a little more like Samurai armor. Like the rest of the crew, he was exploring the freedom from society's constraints. A few months ago, none of them would have even considered painting their faces or tattooing their skin. It simply wasn't acceptable. The old rules didn't apply now. There were no grownups telling them what to do or protecting them from being frightened, hungry and cold. They had killed the undead who were trying to kill them. They had stolen from stores and ran with wild animals. Everything was different now and the ways of the past were gone. It didn't matter if you knew how to do algebra, it mattered if you knew how to milk a cow. Actions they took now had real consequences. Life and death hung in the balance and there was no fallback plan. If any of them made a mistake, it could kill them all.

If they were to be magically transported back to September as they were now, back before the outbreak, their family and friends wouldn't know them. They moved differently. They looked at things differently. They listened differently. They could be violent and even the smallest among them would never be bullied again. The other children would shy away, they would sense the savage and the wild just below the surface. They looked untamed with the best movie quality Halloween costumes any kid ever had but they weren't costumes. They were functional tools and the weapons they carried weren't plastic. The blood stains on them weren't fake.

The twins had embraced their Nordic heritage and looked more like Vikings every day. Swan looked every bit like an Indian warrior and Donny was trying to emulate his brave and fierce ancient ancestors. His hair was getting long again. He'd kept it short during the summer but now it was already over his ears. By the time the winter snows came, it would help keep him warm. He had taken to wearing his armor all the time and if felt as natural as a shirt or pair of blue jeans. So far, the park had been secure but anything could happen at any time. The speed and fury of the outbreak had shown them that. Beside him, Yewan sensed something coming and twitched his tail in anticipation, his golden eyes focused and unblinking. They were both learning patience, the panther learning his commands by sound and touch.

A pair of whitetail deer walked along the game trail towards the tree that concealed the hunters. They moved cautiously in the low light, stopping often and sucking up the acorns that littered the forest floor. With their sensitive noses analyzing every scent and their keen eyes alert, they searched the night for predators. They sensed something was amiss but their noses and sharp eyes weren't registering anything. They didn't look up. Lowering their heads, they continued their walking graze inhaling the fallen acorns by the mouthful.

Donny laid a hand on Yewans neck, trying to transmit his thoughts to the black panther. *Not yet*, he thought. *Not yet.* Impatience had cost them a chance at a kill more than once over the last few nights. They couldn't rush in and chase them down. Donny wasn't very good throwing at a dead run and the deer were wily and quick. Yewans speed would have helped him in an open field but the brambles and underbrush slowed him while the deer bounced right through it with graceful leaps. As the pair moved beneath them, Donny removed his hand from Yewans neck and stepped from the limb.

Before the startled deer could react, Donny dropped the ten feet and drove the spear through the ribs of the one right below him. Yewan landed on the back of the other, sank his claws into its sides, his fangs into its neck and rolled it to the ground. Sharp teeth sheared through the spine, instantly paralyzing the deer as the taste of warm blood filled his mouth.

Ancient instincts flared to life as the flow of fresh blood reawakened them. He hunched low and let out a growl, guarding his kill. His first but now that he knew how, it wouldn't be his last. Donny's heart hammered as he looked at the results of their ambush. Not one, but two fine animals that would help sustain the carnivores and feed his tribe. After weeks of trial and error, of chasing and waiting, of fruitless nights that ended with disappointing results, they had finally figured it out.

Donny gave him time for the blood lust to calm, then dropped to a knee, rubbing Yewan behind the ears. The big cat leaned into him and boy and beast reveled in the glory of their first kills. He bled and gutted them so they'd be easier to carry then shouldered the first one to haul it to the back gate and the golf cart waiting for him there.

He pulled up near the campfire where the other kids sat assembled with some of the animals and felt himself swelling with pride as they gathered around the back of the cart, congratulating him and Yewan on their hunt. Otis shuffled up cautiously, giant nostrils overwhelmed by the smell of fresh meat. Donny stroked Yewan who was growling a warning to the big bear. Otis ignored him as he continued his inspection, his mouth watering at the delicious smell of something other than dog food or a tiny rabbit.

They decided it would probably be best to get the fresh meat away from the animals before they started fighting over it and hurried it over to the storehouse. They strung them from the ceiling and chose the one Yewan had chewed up for the animals. With saws and hatchets, they carved it up and carried chunks of the still warm meat to their companions. The wolves and the bears tore into it hungrily as Cody carved off slices for the foxes they kept penned up at night to keep them from being too tempted by the chickens.

Swan watched, battling her feelings about hunting innocent animals and couldn't help but feel slightly repulsed by what Donny had done. She had felt the anticipation and trembling of Lucy and Zero when he'd first pulled up though and realized how much they needed the meat, especially Lucy to feed the cubs growing inside of her. They couldn't keep eating dog food. The world had changed and if she wanted to live, she had to change with it. She had to put aside yesterday's thinking that killing any animal for any reason was wrong. Those were childish thoughts; she was part of a pack now and it would be getting bigger soon. Her wolves still couldn't hunt, still couldn't take care of themselves and it was her fault. They needed her to teach them like Donny had taught Yewan.

Donny sensed her watching him and turned to meet her stare.

"Teach me to hunt," she said, "so I can feed my pack."

He nodded once. She turned away and went back to her wolves.

It was cool enough so the meat wouldn't spoil, it was already dropping down below freezing some nights. Tomorrow they could break out the books, follow the directions and carve the other deer properly so they didn't waste any of it.

After the others left the storehouse Donny cut the heart loose and carried it out to the campfire. The deer kills meant something big and they knew it. They had entered a new phase in their lives. They wouldn't be reliant on fish and the occasional rabbit. They wouldn't have to butcher their goats to survive the winter if a horde moved in and they couldn't get to town. He held it up for all of them to see then sank his teeth into it and tore off a small piece. He swallowed it down before he lost his nerve and gave the rest to the big panther standing at his side.

They wanted to cheer and clap to honor their hunter and the first kill but that wasn't appropriate, they'd learned to stay quiet and not make unnecessary noise. Cody pulled his Warhammer from its sheath and held it high in the air. The others followed suit with their spears and tomahawks, Gordon holding his machete aloft along with the rest. Donny smiled and bowed slightly to them. He wiped the blood from his chin, picked up his own spear and left the warm glow of the fire. Yewan followed him silently on padded feet and the pair disappeared into the night.

Gordon watched the others and sat back down when they did. He'd learned to try to blend in, to pretend he didn't hate it here, that they were all crazy to spend so much time with wild animals. These kids weren't right in the head, he'd decided. After a few weeks, Cody had said he'd throw him out of the park if he didn't stop complaining and start doing his share of the work. They'd do it to. He believed him. He wasn't afraid of them, not really, he had his machetes. He didn't trust them not to sic one of their bears on him though. Or those wolves of Swans. He hated them and they never missed a chance to growl at him if he came too close. They'd be happy to tear into him.

20

SWAN

Like Donny, Swan had also abandoned the house for the comfort of the pack on the warmer nights. Nestled beneath her blankets, cuddled with the wolves, she would stare at the sky, wandering if her Mom and Dad were still out there. Maybe they had found sanctuary.

As the days passed and the chill November winds blew in, she moved back into the house. This time the wolves came with her. Lucy was preparing for the birth of her cubs; her natural instincts had her hunting for a protected spot and Swan built her a den in the corner of the unused office.

Swan sat with Lucy's head in her lap, the first-time mother panting with the exertion of giving birth. Zero approached, submissive in his posture and lowered his head to lick her muzzle. Lucy growled at her mate to keep his distance. Cowed, Zero backed away but kept watch over her and the soon to be born cubs.

The first pup came minutes later, followed by two more. Swan cried at the sight of their tiny, mewling bodies. They were so helpless with their eyes still closed and their legs moving in uncoordinated ways. Her pack was growing. She swelled with pride and stroked Lucy's head.

Lucy pulled away and began licking her cubs. Cleaning them and forming the emotional and physical bond that let them know she was their mother. The puppies whimpered, blind and helpless as she guided each of them to her nipples so that they could take their first meal. Swan was in love with them already and began thinking of names. *River, Valley, and Meadow*, she decided for the two males and the female greedily suckling their mother.

The other children gathered at the door, anxious to meet the new arrivals. All but Gordon, he knew better. He took advantage of a rare opportunity when everyone was preoccupied gushing over the babies and hurried into the kitchen. The creepy twins were in charge of the cooking and they were stingy with the food, especially the good stuff. He opened the pantry and pulled out a handful of Twinkies, making sure he closed everything back up before sneaking them up to his room. He had the only one that locked and that's why he'd chosen it. He found the key hanging on a rack in the kitchen but now he wore it around his neck.

Swan finally shooed them out of the room to give the new parents some time to themselves and joined the rest as they gathered around the fireplace in the living room. The babble was excited and Murray was skimming through his eBooks, trying to find out about polar bears and if they would be having any babies soon. Swan ran her fingers through her black hair. It was wild and growing longer than she'd ever worn it. She'd never been fashion conscious, preferring loose baggy clothing that hid her developing body and maintenance free hairstyles, usually opting for a braid or a ponytail. She had an idea for it but would need Annalise help her pull it off.

Swan had been hunting with Donny twice so far but had been unsuccessful in her efforts taking anything larger than rabbits or squirrels. The wolves hunted differently than the panther, preferring speed over stealth to take prey. She found lying-in ambush to be boring, the wolves hunted by sight and smell, preferring to run their game down. She couldn't sit still and quiet for hours barely moving a muscle. That was Donny's way of hunting but it didn't work for her.

She needed to learn the bow and arrow but she still struggled with the one Tobias had taken from the sports store. He had given up on it when he found it too hard to pull. It was all he could do to cock it and lock an arrow, his skinny arms trembled with the effort. He abandoned it and once she decided she was going to learn to hunt, she'd been working with it. With Murrays help, they changed the settings so the compound bow was easier for her to pull. She did pushups to build her strength and practically ran everywhere she went, also wearing her armored pads, developing muscles that would help her in pursuit of the fleet footed game they pursued. She couldn't let her wolves run down game like they would in the wild, though. She couldn't keep up; they might travel thirty miles without tiring and they could run twenty miles an hour. She didn't feel safe that far from the Park, there were hordes of undead roaming around. She needed to get better with the bow, it would let her bring down bigger game like the deer that were in abundance. Gordon had said they were stupid for not using guns. He said it would make life so much easier. She agreed with Cody, though. There were a hundred undead at the front gate trying to get in. It was solid steel and the fences at the front of the park were the best and strongest, a reassuring sight for the tourists. In the back of the park, where they would be shooting, the fences were old and rusty. They were only there to keep the gazelle inside and if they attracted a huge horde of the undead with gunfire, they could probably tear right through it.

Swan had a pair of tomahawks she'd taken from the sporting goods store. A sharp blade on the front edge and a spike on the back gave her a double opportunity at landing a fatal blow. She'd picked them up because she thought they looked cool and it was a weapon her ancestors had carried. She'd learned how to be deadly with them though. At first, she hurled them at the barn door, her aim wild and all over the place. Once she learned how to make them stick every time, she moved to smaller targets. There was a science behind the skill, the hatchet rotated as it was thrown. You just had to be the right distance so it had time to spin and hit the target with the head and not the handle. Once she figured that out, it was no harder to learn to hit the bullseye than it was throwing a basketball through a hoop. Now, after a month of practicing hours every day, she could hit a fence post from thirty feet in a full sprint. She got better every day and could kill a scampering squirrel with the lethal steel most of the time. Her wolves were eating better and on a good day, there were a few extra for the twins' stewpot.

21

KERRY

Time had passed slowly for the first few days when he hadn't come back, each minute dragged on for hours. He'd given her very specific instructions and she promised she would do them. If he didn't return, she had to run. She had to take the kids and go. They'd die here if she didn't.

Don't come looking for me because we both know what it means if I'm not back in a few hours. But don't worry he'd added. *I'll be careful. I'll be back. Really, it's no big deal, I know how to deal with those things.*

They were down to the last bag of dog food. Chris had skipped over the Alpo and Old Yeller when he was looking in the neighbors houses for food but she didn't. It wasn't so bad when softened with water and cooked with eggs. The children had long since stopped complaining about the food, they would happily eat a can of spinach if it would take away the empty ache in their stomachs. They asked about Chris for a day or two but finally stopped. She had forced a smile and told them a lie none of them believed.

"Daddy will be home soon. He's fine."

She dozed fitfully in the chair, keeping a vigil every

night, feeling the ache of loss deep inside her. Her tears were quiet and when the sun rose, she knew her wait was over. There was frost on the ground. It had been weeks; he was gone and they were dying. There was nothing left to eat and winter was coming. If they didn't go now, they never would. Chris had put a fresh battery in her minivan, stolen from Mr. Hardy's big Kubota tractor, and had filled it with siphoned gas

"Just in case." he'd said when he kissed her goodbye. "But don't worry. I'll be back before you know it and we'll be having spam steaks for dinner."

There was nothing for breakfast but the kids wouldn't complain. They had aged a hundred years in the past few months.

"Hey guys, I need you to gather up your backpacks." She said as she woke them. "We've got to leave. We're going to Lakota."

They didn't ask about Chris and she didn't say anything about her plan. She knew it was a long shot, knew she wouldn't find him, but she had to try. She had to at least look. Just a quick drive by of the grocery store, it wasn't really out of the way.

She led them into the garage. She'd packed the van with the few supplies she had which was only their clothes, some blankets and a gun. She was stoic and kept her eyes dry. She couldn't show them fear and she couldn't succumb to it herself. If she started crying, she might never stop. They had seven hundred miles to cover in a minivan long overdue to be traded in for something newer. She would have to find gas but she knew how to siphon, Chris had shown her. They'd be okay. They had to be. There was no other choice. They loaded quickly and strapped in. She had known this day would come and had been preparing. She'd blacked out the back windows to protect the kids from seeing any of the horrors they might encounter on the road. She made sure they had their ear buds in and switched on the DVD player in the headrest. Something to occupy their minds, distract them and keep them from looking around and asking questions. She had no allusions of battling a horde of zombies, fighting valiantly and overcoming overwhelming odds. She would try, she would do everything she could to make it to Lakota but if she couldn't, if they got surrounded, she had an option. She double checked the load in the gun Chris had brought home from one of their neighbors. Six bullets rested in the chamber, enough to do the job. Enough so they wouldn't have to become one of those screaming undead things.

She sat facing the garage door and thought about Chris one last time. This trip was supposed to happen in the truck, the one he'd armored up and had extra gas cans in the bed. The one he'd taken into town for a quick supply run. *I just need to test it out before we hit the road, you know, run down some zombies so I know it works. If the town's empty, I'll grab some food from the supermarket. If not, I'll come right back. No worries.*

They should have stayed together, tested out the truck along the way and made the trip on an empty stomach.

Steeling herself, she hit the key, not a hundred percent sure it would fire up until it did. *Please*, she prayed. *Don't let me down this time.* It had given her problems; it had been in the shop twice this year but there never seemed to be enough money to fix it right. They could only afford one car payment at a time and there had been two more years on the truck before it was her turn for something new.

She hopped out, double checked through the little

windows to ensure nothing was around and slid the door open.

She dropped the van in gear and didn't bother to close the garage door. She'd never be returning. To come back was slow death by starvation.

The van protested and shuddered for a few minutes before it smoothed out and started running right. It was the first time it had been started in months. As she eased out of the subdivision, she passed wrecked cars and open doors in the houses. Curtains flapped in broken windows and long dead bodies were on overgrown lawns and driveways. The GPS was already programmed for Lakota, she followed the mechanical voices instructions, driving around abandoned cars and checked the gauges. Three hundred sixty-four miles until empty. That would put her past Des Moines and out in the middle of nowhere. It would be an easy place to find food and siphon gas.

She turned south as she exited the Rolling Hills estates and gripped the wheel tightly. There was no traffic at all. No kids playing on swing sets. Nobody mowing their lawn. No one working in their garden. She hadn't expected to see people but the stillness of everything was disturbing. Leaves covered the road and one set of tire marks was still barely visible in places.

She was following Chris' path.

Occasionally she saw a car in the ditch or just pulled to the side with the door standing open. In one of them someone was still moving, struggling to get out. It was half eaten by something and the seatbelt held it in place. Its empty eye holes tracked her as it reached out in desperate hunger, its jaws snapping open and closed. She shuddered and sped up. She would be in Putnam in a few more miles and at least she would know what happened to him. The truck would be easy to spot.

What if she saw him all ripped up and gnashing his teeth at her like that thing back there? Her mind was awash in uncertainty. No, she told herself. He had the carpet coat. He'd killed those things before, he'd had to put a few down when he was raiding the nearby houses. He could be safe. He could be trapped on a roof or something. He could be waiting on her to come rescue him. She blinked the tears out of her eyes and ground her teeth. She could see his tracks cutting through the downed branches, leaves and pine needles. He might be there she told herself. There was a chance, stranger things have happened. She smiled a little, almost convincing herself it might be true. The van thumped and the wheel jerked hard towards the ditch.

Everyone screamed as she twisted it back on the road, barely avoiding an abandoned car. The van careened wildly for a moment as she sawed the wheel back and forth, over correcting and sliding on the damp leaves every time. Steam was hissing from the radiator and she almost started screaming in frustration as she brought it to a halt. She sat there for a moment frozen with indecision, not knowing what to do. Putnam was only few miles away, they were close. The van would make it to the grocery store and the truck. She had the spare key on her ring, the battery had to still be good and it was fueled up and ready to go. Maybe Chris was still there and he'd be waving from the rooftop. She could save him and they'd be on their way.

It could happen.

It could be like that.

She calmed herself, hushed the kid and opened the door. She had a plan. She must have hit one of those branches in the road. She'd make sure it was clear then they'd be on their way. She stepped out then screamed as cold hands snaked out from under the van and rancid teeth sank into her calf. She jerked away and the upper half of a rotten zombie came with her, fingers sunk deep into skin and its jaws open wide for another bite. Kerry danced and jumped but the thing kept biting, kept climbing up her leg with inhuman fingers as liquefying intestines were pulled out and stretched along the road, it's bottom half still jammed under the van.

She grabbed the thing by its greasy hair and tried to pull it off as it took another bite. She didn't even feel her ripping skin being torn loose; her mind was a red cloud of mind-numbing terror. She tried to run but it tangled in her legs and she fell. It lost its grip and she crabbed away kicking at its face when it clawed after her. The kids were all screaming louder than her and the thing turned its gaze towards them then reversed direction, dragging itself back to the van.

"NO" Kerry yelled when she saw what it was after and jumped to her feet. She ran faster than it and threw herself in the drivers seat, slamming the door on the reaching hands. Bones crunched and she hit the gas, dragging the thing and leaving a long, bloody trail on the road. She had a death grip on the wheel and tried to shush the kids, maneuver around the fallen branches, control the pain starting to throb in her leg and calm her racing heart. Steam still poured out of the broken radiator. She was dead and she knew it.

Oh my God. The kids. She was at the verge of panic. Of completely freaking out. She was gonna turn, she'd seen her neighbors do it. She wouldn't eat her own flesh and blood. She had to keep moving. Get them to some kind of safe place, some empty house where they might be okay. The kids were crying, ignoring the Disney movie and her leg was trembling, making it hard to keep steady pressure on the gas pedal. She had three chunks of it missing and in that things belly. It was bloody but not spurting. At least she wouldn't die of blood loss. She could feel her leg growing colder, an iciness spreading through it. The virus. She wondered how much time she had. Probably not much. She had to protect the children, make sure she didn't kill them. She was a little amazed at how clear her mind was working. She would have guessed she'd be a jabbering, incoherent wreck unable to think from fear but she was calm now. She knew she only had a few minutes to act and her babies would live or die based on what she did in those minutes.

She slowed the van and spoke calmly to the kids.

"Caleb, honey. Go in the back of the van and get mommy that rope. There's a big coil of it in Daddy's pack."

When he brought it up to her, he started crying again when he saw her shredded pants and bloody leg but the coldness was moving faster, she didn't have time to coddle him. She lashed her right hand to the steering wheel with the stout cord as she talked, telling them they all had to be brave. She pushed the old van and the temperature gauge continued its slow creep towards the red line.

She wasn't sure if she could last until they made it to the supermarket and if she did, they wouldn't be going anywhere else. Chris was dead. She knew it with certainty now. Those things moved so fast, one had killed her in just a split second. She had to find a house the kids could hide in, hopefully one with enough food to last them a while. She felt feverish, nauseous and the skull pounding throb of the worst headache she'd ever experienced. She kept talking to them while choking back the urge to vomit. Kept telling them they were going to have to take care of themselves now. In the few minutes they had she tried to tell them everything she could, any little thing that could help them live.

"Listen to me. Mommy is sick. I may act crazy soon. I can't hurt you though. See I have my hand tied up. When that happens, I want you to run. There are scary people out there. Stay away from them. Do you hear me? Stay away from them. Look for nice people. Tell them you need help. Tell them I got sick and you need a place to stay. Do you understand?"

"I want my Mommy," Clara cried.

"I know sweetie. I know, but Mommy's not here and I need you to listen to me. Can you do that for Aunt Kerry?"

"Yes," she sobbed.

She battled another wave of nausea, pressed the accelerator harder as the steam from the cracked radiator billowed from underneath the hood and tried to find a promising house. Something off the road and sturdy. She told herself it would be okay. Kids were tough. If she found them shelter and food, they'd be all right. They'd figure it out.

She didn't believe it. They were seven years old. They would be dead in a week if not sooner and the tears rolling down her face wasn't from the pain of the bites or knowing she was dying. It was for them.

She saw it then. Her children's salvation. Faint smoke off in the distance. Someone was still alive; someone had a fire burning.

22

NEW ARRIVALS

I t was a lazy Sunday and everyone was loosely gathered around the campfire. Chores were done and the twins were working with their polar bears using fish as treats for well performed maneuvers. The pair had quickly adapted to the saddles they had rigged up.

Vanessa and Ziggy were playing a game. She'd blown up some balloons and would hit them with her laser pointer. Ziggy waited to see which one was next and would attack, either popping them with her beak or gouging them with her sharp claws. Every balloon destroyed earned her more of the popcorn she was so fond of.

The boys were practicing spear or long hammer spinning, twirling them around their arms and necks and doing karate poses. Maybe showing off a little. Otis and Yewan dozed, completely uninterested in watching them dance around. Donny had gotten really good, even mastering some of the outlandish moves he's seen in old Kung Fu movies. His spear never left his side, even when he slept, and its point had tasted deer blood often.

Swan was working a piece of deer leather, softening it

up so she could make herself a buckskin shirt as her wolves and cubs enjoyed the warm sunlight.

Murray was playing toss with his monkeys but more often than not they wouldn't bring the tennis ball back and he had to coax them in with snacks. They seemed to like the game of keep-away with the foxes better than fetch.

Harper was filing down the end of a bolt to make it pointy. She was making herself a morning star and was bound and determined to teach the giraffe how to follow simple saddle commands.

Gordon sat near the fire toasting a marshmallow just to show them he wouldn't be shut out and that he didn't care what they thought but he was fuming inside. He'd been working for hours chopping wood, doing his share of work, but Swan had sneered at the pile he had when he was finished.

"Vanessa can cut twice as much in half the time." she'd said. "And she's only ten. We need to change the rule from how long you cut to how much you cut."

Cody had stepped in before they wound up in another shouting match.

"Gordon is still getting used to the work, he had blisters for weeks, remember? It takes a while to toughen up."

Gordon hated him for butting in and pointing out that he was soft. He flipped them both off when they turned to leave. He hated this place. It was too much work, the animals needed constant care and he couldn't understand why they didn't put them outside the gate and forget about them. Every time he tried to tell them a better way of doing things, Mr. High and Mighty Cody would act like he was considering it and then tell him no. Sometimes he wouldn't even think about it, like when he kept telling him they should move to someplace easier to maintain. Someplace that wasn't so much work. *You can leave if you want but we're staying* was the only answer he got to that suggestion.

The squeal of tires and the tortured sound of an engine on its last legs brought everyone to their feet and the monkeys scurrying for safety under Murrays' jacket.

A minivan swerved into the lot and there was a roar from the undead milling around the front gate. It bounced off the wrecked school bus, slid sideways into the parking lot and rolled to a stop. It lurched forward again and jerked left and right; the driver seemed to have no particular destination in mind. It hit a few of the fast zombies then sped away, smoke billowing out from under the crumpled hood. The kids sprinted to the front gate and saw the van circle the expansive parking lot with the undead chasing behind. It looked like it was going to lead them away, get back on the road and go, but it swerved at the last second and took off down the long straight stretch leading to the oversized parking area at the far end of the lot. It was empty now but, in the summer it was a place for campers and trucks and RV's to easily maneuver and sometimes spend the night. The van swerved sharply again, tilted precariously to one side, then raced right back towards them. Its motor was clattering and they could smell the burning rubber of overheated hoses. Halfway across the lot, there was a clang of metal breaking, something deep and fatal in the engine and a different kind of smoke started pouring out but the driver didn't let up.

It was all or nothing. Kerry could see them, the people at the gate. She was right, it had been a campfire. Part of her was steering the car and keeping the gas mashed, getting her babies to safety. The other part was roaring and jerking towards the fresh flesh only a few feet away behind her. The screaming and crying little chunks of meat that would be filled with warm, red blood. Kerry fought it harder than she'd ever fought anything in her life. She sank her teeth into her bottom lip, completely tore through it hoping the pain and the blood would satisfy the craving for just a few more seconds. She was close. So close. She kept the wheel straight, her foot to the floor and saw them with clarity for a second.

It was kids staring at her through the iron gate. Wild looking children with warpaint and spears and there were animals standing with them. Bears and panthers and wolves. She saw foxes and monkeys. Her eyes dimmed to black and she smiled a bloody smile. Her babies would be safe, she had found a warrior tribe of feral children who would teach them to be fierce.

They watched as the woman behind the wheel slumped over and the van slowed to a crawl. The undead were halfway across the parking lot, screaming and keening in a hungry frenzy. The engine made a final wheeze and seized up, bringing the smashed-up minivan to a halt near the sidewalk. Without the grinding, gasping sounds of the motor, they heard crying and then the driver sat bolt upright. She snarled and launched herself towards the rear and whoever was in it started screaming in terror. They watched wide eyes and speechless as the thing was jerked back into its seat, held in place by rope around the steering wheel.

"GO!" Cody yelled before he could think of any of the ten thousand reasons they shouldn't.

"Wait!" Gordon yelled but the others were already sprinting through the gate, racing the undead for the prize in the van.

"Get the kids!" Cody yelled at Harper and Vanessa. He was running straight for the fastest of the runners, Otis overtaking him in a few quick bounds. The giant bear knew who the enemy was. He could sense the unnaturalness of the screaming things, the same as the rest of them. If his master was running to kill them, then he would kill them too. Donny and Yewan passed them, the pairs speed unmatched by any one else and they met the first sprinter head on. Yewan sprang and claws like butcher knives sank fast and slashed deep. Donny's aim was true and the next one flew off its feet when sharpened steel drove through its head. The twins thundered by riding high on Popsicle and Daisy, a battle cry on their lips and saw bladed axes in their hands. They swung them with wild abandon, their tattooed bodies as pale as their mounts, their fearlessness unmatched. The bears roared their challenge and slammed into the horde, bowling the undead aside with their huge shoulders. Cody and Otis fought side by side, claws and hammers finding faces and heads. Their mottled gray bodies broke and bled, were torn apart and crushed, destroyed with fury and rage.

The thing in the driver's seat was thrashing wildly when the girls ran up.

"I'll cover you, get them out!" Swan yelled and put herself between the two girls and the first of the undead running at them. She gripped her tomahawks, one in each hand and crouched, adrenaline and fear making her heart pump fast. Zero and Lucy stayed by her side, growling and snarling their warning. Their lips peeled away from long, sharp teeth as they tensed to spring. Swan had the same snarl, same wrinkled nose and same low growl in her throat. When the first one was twenty feet away, she loosed her tomahawk. It spun once and buried itself with a dull thunk into the thing's forehead. It dropped and the second screeching woman stumbled over him. She almost got her balance again but Zero sprang at her, driving her to the ground. She snapped yellow teeth at him and he tore most of her head off when he popped her skull in his powerful jaws.

Ziggy hovered protectively around Vanessa, her throat swelling as she cried out her warnings and she danced and flapped her wings.

Harper ignored the torn lipped thing lunging at her from the driver's seat and grabbed the sliding door handle. She could hear at least two kids, maybe three, shrieking in terror at the frothing monster only a few feet away from them. She saw the ropes digging into the flesh, peeling the skin away as the black-eyed thing jerked and raged. The blood-soaked jeans and the bite marks on her leg told the story. Harper yanked with all of her adrenaline-charged strength and the plastic handle snapped in her hand. The door was locked from inside and she almost fell over backward when it gave way. Neither girl was armed, they had both run out with nothing, hadn't thought to grab a weapon. Harpers half-finished morning star was where she'd left it and Vanessa only had the laser pointer still gripped in her fist.

"Ziggy" she said to catch the big bird's attention and pointed the red dot at the glass window in the sliding van door.

. Ziggy reared her head back on instinct and her long neck propelled her beak against the glass. It disintegrated into a million shards, revealing three very scared children. Tear streaked faces yelled even louder when they saw the giant eyed bird staring at them.

"Hurry." Harper said and held her arms through the opening. "If you want to live, we have to hurry."

She pulled each of them through the broken window as fast as she could as Vanessa pointed them towards the gate and told them to run. It was closed but Gordon was there, he'd open it. The second the last little boys' feet touched the ground she yelled for the others to come back. It was hard to be heard over the sounds of battle but they'd been listening for the retreat order. They had killed their way through the first of the runners but the main horde was bearing down on them and was only seconds away. They couldn't fight those kinds of numbers, they'd be overwhelmed. Cody shouted ahead to the crazy twins and Annalise acknowledged with a wave of her axe. They had aimed their bears into the heart of the horde and a thousand pounds of pissed off Polar's were plowing them down, running full speed through the midst of them with the wild-eyed kids whooping, swinging their battle axes, screaming in defiance and sending blood sprays in high arcs.

Donny rang his spear twice with his ring, the metal on metal a signal to his panther to come. Yewan heard and obeyed. He crushed a head in his jaws then heeded the call. He ran for his pack brother. The man cub who taught him to hunt and kill. The boy who showed him his true nature.

Cody yelled for Otis and ran, he didn't wait around to see if he followed. The horde was almost on top of them and the bear could take care of himself.

Donny caught him easily and they saw the others stacked up at the gate as soon as they rounded the van.

"Get inside!" he yelled, breathing hard. "What's wrong?"

Are we locked out? Was the first thing that crossed his mind. *How did that happen?*

He felt Otis bound up beside him as they left the parking lot and ran along the walkways to the ticket takers booths. The gate opened suddenly and everyone poured through it, humans and animals alike sensing relief at being behind the fences. Away from the unnatural things. The twins came in last, only yards ahead of the horde and dismounted with a flourish as Cody and Donny rammed the gates shut and turned the lock. Mottled, weathered faces slammed against it, arms shot though, hands reached for the warm meat that was so close. The children hurried away from the mob as they stacked up, away from their cries of hunger and away from the stench of rotting bodies. Across the parking lot, dozens of broken undead crawled forwards on shattered bodies. Dozens more lay unmoving with splashed open or missing heads, snapped spines and crushed backs.

As they neared the fire pit, Cody rubbed his bears' ears, put his forehead against Otis's and held it there for a moment, thanking him for his help.

"We couldn't have done it without you, buddy." he said and tried to convey his feelings, to let his friend know how he felt. The feelings of love and relief and gratitude were almost too much. The bear sent a big wet tongue up his cheek and Cody laughed.

"Gross." he said and wiped the slobber off.

He swung a leg over his back and gigged him closer to the others. Otis obliged for a few paces then twisted, sending him rolling towards the ground. He wasn't like the Polar's, he didn't like anyone riding him.

Swan stood over Gordon with a Tomahawk in each hand, ready to sink one into his face. Zero was by her side snarling a warning and ready to rip into the boy if his mistress willed it.

"You son of a bitch, you nearly got us killed." she shouted.

Cody grabbed her arm before she could swing

"Whoa, whoa, whoa!" he said and pulled her away from

the boy whose lip was bleeding and already starting to swell. "What's going on?"

"That bastard locked us out!" she yelled, pointing a tomahawk still dripping with black blood at Gordon who was struggling to his feet.

"I had to check for bites!" he shouted right back. "One bite is all it takes to kill us all!"

"You could have checked after we were inside!"

Swan was livid and had a right to be but Gordon had a point.

"Stop it, both of you." Cody said. "He's right. Everybody check each other out. Swan, take Zero and go for a walk before he kills Gordon."

"I wouldn't shed a tear." she said but stalked off with the wolf trailing her.

When everyone calmed down and started examining each other, Cody eyed the boy coldly.

"Never put the lives of the tribe in danger." he said quietly.

"But..." Gordon started to protest

"Never put the lives of the tribe in danger." Cody repeated then turned away.

Harper and Vanessa were fussing over the newcomers who were trying their best to stop sniffling and crying. They weren't babies anymore, they'd seen things over the past few months. They'd grown up hard and fast since September. You had to or you died.

The three children stood in awe of the older kids and the magnificent animals. It was like something out of one of those movies they weren't supposed to watch but did anyway after their parents were asleep. The chittering of monkeys caused them to turn their attention to a boy in a wheelchair. Four cute little brown furballs were hanging off of him, peeking at them with open curiosity.

"Welcome to Piedmont Animal Sanctuary." he said, in his best impression of John Hammond, welcoming his guests to Jurassic Park. He laughed as the monkeys swarmed over them, checking their pockets and hair for something to eat or steal. Clara shrieked but it turned to a giggle and the capuchins chattering and playfulness made them forget, for just a moment, the horror they'd just survived. The foxes were curious too and came close, their inquisitive noses sniffing out the new smells, their long, bushy tails wagging happily when they started being petted. They were used to attention from hundreds of kids a day in the petting zoo but hadn't been getting much lately. They relished the human touch and curled themselves around the trio, whining happily and licking away the salty tears.

23

GORDON AND HARPER

"Hi, Harper."

She turned to find Gordon staring at her and wondered how long he'd been there. She set the pitchfork aside, brushed her long blonde hair back out of her eyes. She'd been working with Bert, mucking out stalls and lugging water buckets for the petting zoo all morning. Her back ached and her hands were calloused from the daily routine. Her clothes were dirty and in need of a good wash. She loved it. She loved the zoo and the animals, especially Bert.

Teddy, the buffalo lowered his huge head to grab a mouthful of feed pellets from his freshly filled trough. Cody had been working him all morning dragging downed trees out of the woods. The shaggy beast was old and tired and deserved his rest but not until he devoured his lunch.

"Hi, Gordon." she forced a smile at the boy, although her patience was running thin. Most of the others didn't even try to be nice to him anymore and the room temperature seemed to drop about twenty degrees whenever he and Swan were in it together.

He'd either skipped out on his chores or half assed them again. No way was he done this early in the day. He leaned casually against the gate post of the buffalo enclosure, hands in the pocket of his khakis. He wore a multi pocketed vest and a button-down shirt, his hair carefully combed. He looked like he was posing for an LL Bean catalog. He never wore his armor, she wasn't even sure he had any, and all the clothes he'd taken from the surplus store were overpriced brands that didn't hold up very well to everyday work. They were for city people who wanted to look like they were outdoorsmen. Too many pockets and zippers and buttons. He was supposed to be cleaning out Millie's pen. Cody had taken him off of the wood chopping detail and had him working with the animals. They'd hoped he would settle in and bond with one of them. So far, that hadn't happened.

She sighed. They'd get nothing out of him again today. Until it was time to eat anyway. Then he'd load his plate with food and return for seconds. When he was done, he would go to his room to do whatever it was he did up there.

"Aren't you tired of this place? The flies and the crap and the creaky old house?"

"I like it here." she said, running her hand over Teddy's head. "It's safe. We have everything we need, and I get to spend all the time I want with Bert."

"Bert," Gordon snorted. "He's gross. Always farting and drawing flies to him."

Harper cut her eyes at him disapprovingly.

Sensing he was losing ground, Gordon changed his tact. Even with her messy hair and dirty clothes, she was still the prettiest girl left alive. The only one who had a little something in the chest department pressing against her armor.

"Yeah, he is pretty cool to watch, maybe if you changed his diet, he wouldn't be so gassy."

"Maybe," she answered.

"But, you know, there's a whole town right down the road. There are some pretty nice houses just sitting empty. A couple of generators from the hardware store and we'd be set." he said slyly.

"I don't think Bert would like living in town, hitting his head on stoplights and all that. This is the best place for him and all of the other animals too."

"It's not too far to visit." Gordon pressed. "They could stay here, we could live in town. Have you seen the stuff just sitting in the jewelry store? There's gold necklaces and diamond earrings and platinum watches just waiting to be plundered."

"I don't care about that kind of stuff." she shrugged, wiped her hands on her dirty tactical pants and armor pads. "It's kind of useless, really."

"Yeah, but surely you'd rather wear something besides those clothes and hockey pads."

"They're comfortable, and once you get used to the pads, they aren't so bad. You should get you some, just in case the zombies ever get inside the gates." she told him.

He scoffed. "I wouldn't be caught dead in those rags."

He tugged at the hem of his vest, trying to draw her eyes towards him. She obviously had the hots for him. She never looked him in the eyes. She was hiding her feelings. *Probably didn't want to break Cody's heart*, he thought smugly. He knew they all but worshipped Mr. High and Mighty.

"I guess what I'm trying to say is, we should leave, just you and me. You can come back anytime you want and visit Bert. We'll live it up, eat good food, have hot water and surround ourselves with all the finest things. Sooner or later someone is going to come through and rescue us. We can move into one of those fortified towns and live like civilized people. If we stay out here, we'll miss them."

His tone was sharp, almost condescending. He'd watched his Dad reduce people who owed him money to tears and begging with the same tone and he copied it the best he could. Maybe she just needed a firm hand to get her priorities straight. Maybe she needed to be told what to do.

"You think we aren't civilized?" she smiled, but there was no warmth in it.

"No, not you," he said, backtracking a little. "These other kids. Sleeping and eating with the animals. It's just nasty. You deserve better than that. You deserve better than that creepy house. It makes so much noise I can barely sleep for all the creaking. It's going to fall or burn down someday; I don't want you to be in it when it happens. That's all. We should think about going someplace better."

"I'll be just fine, Gordon. We'll be just fine. I don't need to be rescued and I don't want to live in town, there's no protection from the zombies if they wander through. We have a good life here, and you could too if you tried just a little."

Harper wanted him to join them, not be an outsider. She wanted for everyone to get along and be happy. For everyone to do their fair share, it wasn't that hard if everybody pitched in and helped.

"It doesn't matter who you were before this happened." she continued. "All that matters is who you are going to be. I don't want to go to a fortified town and have people trying to tell me what to do. I'm not going to give up Bert or go back to being a cheerleader. My parents are dead. All of my family are dead. If we did find a town, they would put me in foster care or something and split everyone up. This is my family now, Gordon. It can be yours too, if you would try. We don't ask for much, just do your part."

Gordon shook his head and she could see he would never understand the gift they'd been given. He would never be happy *living like animals* as he thought of it. He wanted the old world back but it was gone. She almost felt sorry for him.

"Look, I've got a lot of work to do and you probably do too."

Bert strolled lazily towards them. The giraffe angled slightly in his direction, in an attempt to mash him between his body and the gate. Gordon stepped swiftly aside. He wasn't finished talking to her but the stupid giraffe filled the space between them and put his back towards Gordon. He lifted his short tail and dropped a load of manure in the boy's direction. Gordon jumped out of the way but didn't avoid getting dung splattered on his pants. He hated the giraffe.

Harper stepped around him and headed for the barn with Bert following close behind. Her bodyguard. He gritted his teeth in frustration but grabbed the pitchfork and headed over to knock out the jobs Mr. High and Mighty had assigned him for the day. Putting on his best clothes had been wasted on her, she hadn't even noticed. He'd play along, though. He'd bide his time and wait for his chance. He'd prove to her once and for all that he was the man for her. Once he got her away from all this drudgery and back to civilization, she'd change her mind. She'd never want to come back and he certainly never would. Not unless he had a gun to put a bullet in Bert's head.

24

GORDON

Gordon was miserable and smelled like animal dung. He'd been trying for a week or so but his plan of going along to get along was just too much work. He hated it here. It was cold, his room was drafty and he never seemed to be able to get Harper alone. If he didn't know any better, he would think she was avoiding him. Sure, this place was maybe a little better than the room where he'd been trapped for months but not by much. Or weeks, as they kept correcting him. Whatever. It felt like months. He had nothing in common with the others. After his little talk with Harper he'd tried to fit in but he was simply too civilized to be with these people. They all thought they were Tarzan or something the way they ate, slept and bathed with the filthy animals. Hell, they were becoming animals. Even the new kids were running around with the foxes and wolf cubs like they were harmless puppies, not dangerous animals that could turn on you. It only took them a week and they were nearly as savage as the rest of the idiots.

He was tired of hauling feed and cleaning up after them. He ought to just refuse. He'd chop wood, he could see the sense in that, but there was no reason to keep these stupid animals. They should drive them all out of the gate and be done with them. What would they do if he just stopped working, let Swan beat him up? She'd just got lucky last time. He hadn't been ready. If she tried it again, he'd knock her teeth out.

The only job he didn't really mind was stabbing zombies at the front gate. Whenever they started piling up, wandering in off the road for some unknown reason, they would have to go to the entrance and spear them in the head. The coyotes and buzzards and whatever else ate dead things would drag them off and have a feast. Gordon liked that job and would even volunteer for it. The others would get it over quickly, it stank pretty badly up there, but he liked to make it last. He'd jab them in the eyes, watch the gooey orbs run down their cheeks and was fascinated as they ignored their blindness and still tried to snap at him. Sometimes there was a woman zombie that wasn't too messed up. He didn't care if she was missing an arm or something, he'd learned to ignore bones sticking out and things like that. If they weren't all rotten and gross, he'd hook the spear and rip their clothes off. He'd stab them in their hairy parts between the legs or poke their saggy boobs to see if they would deflate any more. Once he'd tried to count how many times he could stab one but got tired after fifty. It had holes everywhere but still tried to bite him. He wondered if he could tie one up, one that wasn't too gross, and have a little grown up fun. The few magazines he'd brought with him were getting pretty worn out. He was fifteen, almost sixteen, the oldest of them all, and he had needs. But still, he didn't think he could. He'd need help tying her down and besides, what if he caught something? What if the zombie virus was like an STD and his dong started rotting off? What he needed was for Harper to come to her senses and run off with him.

The rhino had nearly stepped on him twice while he daydreamed and cleaned out her enclosure. Stupid blind creature, and the flies! Buzzing around her ass then landing on his face. It was disgusting and demeaning. Then to top it off she had sideswiped him and knocked him down right into a pile of dung. Sure, he'd given her a little jab with the pitchfork to make her give him some working room, but it didn't hurt her with that thick hide. *Ungrateful half blind bitch*, he thought.

They should be back in Putnam living it up. He'd been embarrassed when he saw the empty streets and the stores standing deserted after his rescue. All that food for the taking and he'd been surviving on army rations that were barely fit to eat. If he'd known there was only one of those zombies or how easy it was to kill, he could have gotten out. He would have, too. He would have figured it out sooner or later. He hated that Mr. High and Mighty had seen him living like he'd been. He'd seen all the girly magazines with the sticky pages. It was worse that he hadn't told the others, like he had some big secret and was lording it over him. Like he was blackmailing him and would tell everyone if Gordon didn't do everything he said. If he didn't cut wood or clean the stalls.

Yeah, Gordy was so chicken he pooped in a box, slept right next to it and looked at dirty magazines all day. Speaking of chicken, did you choke yours very much, Gordy?

They'd all laugh at him and snicker behind his back. He hated them all.

The town had been deserted; he could have been a king when they came instead of a prisoner. All the zombies had chased the survivors down the road and had never come back. The few that were there were locked in the deserted buildings.

He cursed his father who'd run out and abandoned him and he cursed himself for not staying home that day. He'd gone along with him because the old man was going to kick the store owner out. He was going to shut him down for breach of contract and Gordon wanted to watch it happen. He wanted to see Gordon Lowery Senior, known as the Bulldog in certain circles, lower the hammer and watch the old shop keeper beg for another chance.

"He was late with the lease payment for the second time and that is grounds for termination." His dad explained on the drive down to Putnam in his new Mercedes. "When I had the contract drawn up, I made sure our lawyers put that in the fine print. I've been waiting for over a year for him to be late again. That old junk shop he's been running for the last decade has become prime real estate. I can double the rent with a health food store. We're going to demand for him to immediately vacate the premises. I'll show you how it's done, son."

The old shopkeeper had been wearing his stupid *Proud Veteran* hat and eating a greasy takeout breakfast at his desk when they confronted him. He'd done everything his dad had predicted and Gordon had a hard time keeping the grin off his face. He'd blustered, he'd gotten mad and finally he'd begged. His father had come down on him so hard the old man had gotten sick and had run to the bathroom. They had done a little fist bump when they heard him retching and his dad had mouthed *pathetic* then went out into the store to determine how he wanted to remodel it. Gordon had stayed in the office and was peeking in the drawers when he heard the snarl of something inhuman and his dad scream. There was a scuffle and when he looked out, his father was running out of the front door. Gordon yelled something, he couldn't remember exactly what, and the bloody old store keeper turned towards him. He slammed the door and had been trapped for months. Or weeks as they claimed. Whatever. It felt like months.

Jokes on you Dad, he thought as he tossed another scoop of rhino dung into the wheelbarrow. He was probably out there wandering around with the rest of the undead in his expensive suit, shuffling around in his overpriced shoes, self-winding Rolex still keeping time on his wrist.

He leaned on the shovel and thought about last night. He finally got her by herself but that hadn't worked out so well. He knew it wasn't visible, but he still felt the imprint of Harper's hand when she'd slapped him. He just wanted a kiss. She was the only one old enough for him to be interested in, the only girl that had boobs, and she should be grateful for his attention. She didn't have to be such a tease. She was always teasing Cody too, laughing at his jokes or agreeing with whatever he said. The infallible Cody. Mr. High and Mighty. What a prick.

Cody said we need more firewood.

Cody said we should each pick a skill and learn it from the books.

Cody said clean out the stall.

Cody said you have to cut hay.

Cody said it's your turn to walk the fence.

Cody said you have to kill zombies at the front gate.

Cody said this.

Cody said that.

Cody, Cody, Cody.

Who put him in charge anyway? So what if he'd been a Boy Scout and had a few skills? So what if he knew the zoo better than anyone else? It was the end of the world and rules didn't apply anymore. *I'm almost a year older than him, it should go by seniority.* Gordon thought. *And we should be in town or back home. There were probably survivors there, it was a gated community.*

But, no.

Cody says we're gonna keep a low profile.

Cody says it's safe here in the freaking sticks out in the middle of nowhere.

Cody says the animals need us, and we are gonna need them if those zombies ever get in.

Last night, he'd listened to everyone drone on and on around the fireplace as they discussed the weather, Christmas coming up, supplies on hand, training they were doing and things they'd learned. If they lived in town, they wouldn't have worry about all this survivalist crap. There was plenty of food and they wouldn't have to take care of all these stupid animals. When Harper had made another trip to the kitchen to pull the brownies out of the oven, he volunteered to help. She was the only one who was nice to him and he knew why. She had probably been thinking about getting away, thinking about him and how easy life would be in town. After all, she had baked them because he said chocolate was his favorite. If that wasn't a blatant come on, he didn't know what was. He was the oldest, the richest and had a plan to get them out of this zoo. Of course, she had the hots for him.

She'd acted surprised when he'd slipped up behind her and wrapped his hands around her waist then went to kiss her neck. She acted like she didn't like it, that she was offended. She'd spun and slapped him.

He'd ran off to his room when what he should have done is slapped her right back and told her things were going to change. He should have taken charge, told them all that he was the oldest and he would be calling the shots from now on. Angry at the memory, Gordon threw his pitchfork on the ground. He didn't care if Millie hurt her hooves on it or not. He hoped she did, dumb animal. He still seethed at the little tease, one of the others had probably put her up to it. Swan, most likely. She hated him for no reason. That was okay. He hated her back. One way or another there was going to be a change of leadership around here. Lowery's gave orders, they didn't take them.

Gordon lashed out at Millie, kicked her hard and she ambled off. He was incensed, working himself into a full-blown rage. He was through cleaning out stalls and doing everything Cody said. He was a survivor, he had lived through the outbreak and he'd done it on his own. He hadn't had any help. He had as much right as any of them to make decisions. More actually. He was the oldest and he had been born and groomed to be a leader in the community, not a go-fer or shit shoveler. He came from money, prestigious parents and expensive schools. He was their better and deserved to be treated as such. He paced back and forth, getting angrier by the moment. He'd tried to do it their way but that was over. They were going to do things his way from now on. He was the biggest and if he had to, he'd beat the crap out of all of them. He touched the machete handles tucked in his belt, nodded to himself, then set out in search of Cody.

25

CODY & GORDON

Cody and Harper stood in the kitchen of the old house giving Otis a promised treat. He opened the last can of Spam and tossed the jelly coated hunk of compressed meat to his pal. Otis caught it out of the air and gulped it down, waiting expectantly for more, it was his favorite snack.

"That's the last of it," Cody said and wiped his hands. "I'll look for more when we go back into town."

He poured Otis a bowl of dog food. The Kodiak chuffed, but ate it anyway. It would hold him over until someone brought in some fresh meat. Swan and Donny were getting good at hunting and it was rare when one of them didn't have something hanging in the storehouse.

Great, Cody thought as he watched Gordon storming towards him. He reeked like dung. How could he get covered in it? All he had to do was scoop it out and dump it in the fertilizer pile. Murray had plans for a big garden in the spring so they were keeping all the droppings together instead of spreading them anywhere out of the way. Cody's wrinkled nose at the smell pissed Gordon off even more.

"I'm not feeding them or cleaning up after them anymore. We should either move into the town and get some real weapons and a real place to live or send a scout up to my old neighborhood. I told you it was gated and private. Most of houses have solar panels and generators. I have family there, you could probably have your own house. A mansion with a hot tub, not a dump like this! This place is just a flop house, my God, you all sleep in the same room. I can hardly even go in the den anymore because it stinks like animal," fumed Gordon.

"The town isn't safe, Gordon." Cody explained again. "We've been over this. It's empty now but those hordes are on the move. What if a huge one wanders in out of LaCrosse or Cedar Rapids? What would we do then?"

"At least we would be on a main road!" Gordon exclaimed. "At least we'd be somewhere we could get rescued if help comes. They'll never find us out here."

"Nobody is coming to save us." Harper said flatly. "You're living in a fantasy world. There is nobody else out there with a city like it used to be. Nobody is scouring the countryside looking for survivors. If there *are* other people, they're doing the same thing we are, just trying to make it through the winter."

"But we hear them on the radio!" Gordon practically screamed. "We know there are others."

"We hear bits and pieces of people talking on CB's or something." Cody said. "Murray told us they're using super powerful radios, probably stuff that was illegal before, and it's bleeding over onto the emergency channels. We don't know where they're at or what they have. It might be only two or three people and they could be anywhere in the world."

"Fine." Gordon said. "But we can't stay here. We need

to send somebody up to scout out my old house. I'm telling you, we had security guards and high fences, better than these, and everyone had generators and lots of food. They still have electricity. We could live normal again!"

The twins came in to start dinner and made a face at Gordon when they saw he had tracked dung all over their floor. He ignored the two weirdos.

"Who's going to go check it out?" Cody asked, trying to get Gordon to see reason. Trying to let him realize he was grasping at straws. "You?"

"Donny is the fastest." he replied. "He could get up there in a week. Heck, once he finds people somebody there can come get us. They'll have cars."

"What makes you so sure they would want you back, Gordy?" Swan asked as she came out of the den holding one of the cubs. "If I were them, I sure as hell wouldn't."

"Nobody asked you, dog girl." Gordon said and glared at her.

Swans lips curled away from her bared teeth and a slow, guttural snarl came from her throat.

Gordon stepped behind the island, putting a little distance between them but he wasn't finished. He needed to make them see reason.

"Look at her." he said and pointed. "This place is going to your heads. She thinks she's a wolf."

"And look at them." his angry finger went towards the twins. "Is that normal? They've got tattoos all over their bodies and they're only twelve years old. They look like circus freaks and I've seen them eating raw fish with those bears. You've got those little kids we rescued starting to act like animals, too. Normal people don't act like this. Normal people would have you all locked up for child endangerment!"

Gordon had to get it off his chest, had to make them see they were all going crazy, they had to get out of here and back to civilization.

"You're all turning feral and acting like cavemen. Have you looked in a mirror lately, Cody? You look like an extra on some survivor show. What's with the beads in your hair and that stupid necklace? This place sucks. The animals suck. My family would be appalled to see me living like this, eating this garbage you call food." he finished angrily.

"Then don't eat our cooking." Annalise said, "make your own."

Tobias nodded his head and set his jaw. He would get not one bite of their meals anymore. He'd toss it to the zombies first.

Cody was running out of patience, but tried one last time to reason with Gordon, "We aren't going anywhere. We have a great setup here. Besides, the animals..."

"The animals!" Gordon screamed cutting him off, spittle flying from his lips.

Everyone was against him. Everyone hated him. This argument wasn't going as planned and he was getting so mad he was out of control, just lashing out.

"Always the damned animals! It's a goldmine out there and you want to stay here and play with your teddy bear. People are gonna hit the towns to take the food and all the good stuff. Nobody is coming here. We'll never be found or rescued if we stay here. These stupid animals don't matter. The zombies don't eat them, and they can fend for themselves."

"Then go," Cody said coldly. "Get your gear and go. You'll be home in a week."

He'd had enough. "I won't stop you, but I won't be there to save you next time either."

"Save me? Save me?" Gordon nearly shrieked.

He was livid, more afraid that Cody would tell them how he found him cowering in his own filth than he was of being thrown out. He was ashamed of the others finding out and couldn't let him say anymore.

"You didn't save me, I was doing just fine by myself. I don't need you. I don't need any of you!"

Harper placed a hand on Cody's shoulder. "He's upset, just let him cool off. He'll come around."

"You always take his side! He's hiding from the world instead of trying to find other survivors. All for some stupid promise he made to his dead mama." Gordon screamed and mimed a shuffling zombie.

Before he'd realized it, Cody shoved Harper aside and swung on Gordon. His fist slammed the other boy hard, Gordon's lips split open and he fell to the floor. Blood poured freely down his chin and onto his chest. Otis reared up on his hind legs, banged his head against the ceiling and roared, shaking dust down from the rafters. Cody was livid, was tempted to let Otis rip the bastard apart but saw the wide, fearful eyes of Clara staring at him from the den. He put up a calming hand on Otis' chest and stopped the bear from attacking.

Gordon pushed himself to his feet and stood, fists clenching and unclenching, murderous rage in his eyes. He dropped his hands to his machetes but before he could pull them Swan had a tomahawk in each hand, her fists choked up near the head, ready to slash into him. Annalise and Tobias both had instantly gripped big carving knives and were ready to spring. He stared at Cody with tears of impotent rage in his eyes and blood streaming down his chin. He raised his hand and mimed a pistol. "POW," he said softly, turned and ran up the stairs to his room.

Cody fought the urge to chase him down and finish kicking his ass. Grab him by the hair and drag him out the gate. Gordon had brought nothing but trouble to the group. He complained about everything, what chores he would do were half assed and he ate twice as much as anyone else. He was careless around the animals, he left tools laying around that could cause injury and they all shied away from him. That spoke volumes to the rest of them.

For some reason, he resented Cody. He'd only tried to help the boy, but he had a chip on his shoulder the size of Kansas. He was always angry and upset whenever he didn't get his way. They heard him slam the door to his room and tensions eased. Weapons slid back into holsters or knife racks. Otis dropped down to all fours and went back to his favorite spot in front of the fireplace.

"It's okay, Clara. The boys were just arguing. It's over now." Harper kneeled in front of the little girl and pushed hair out of her eyes. "Boys just being boys. You want to help with dinner?"

Donny caught Cody's eye and turned his body away from everyone else so they couldn't see what he said. He pointed to himself, made a slicing motion across his neck, pointed upstairs then raised his eyebrows in a question. Cody shook his head and Donny nodded. It was over, it was just a fight. They weren't savages. They didn't kill people just because they were mad at them. Cody grabbed a potato and started peeling, a mindless job because his mind was on something else. What Donny had asked scared him a little. If he would have said yes, he had no doubt the silent boy would have walked calmly up the stairs and killed him. If Gordon had pulled his machetes, Swan would have sunk her steel into his head. It was a sobering thought because nothing would have happened to them. No repercussions for murder. No police. No courts. No jail. No nothing except someone would have to drag the body out and bury it or toss it to the coyotes.

His hands shook a little and he had to concentrate to control them. He had the power over life and death. That was a scary thought. Maybe Gordon saw that tonight. Maybe he finally understood the old ways were gone. The problem with Gordon was that he thought he was better than everyone else and had shown disdain for them once he was safe behind the gates. Harper was the only one he wasn't constantly arguing with and something had changed with that. Even she didn't stick up for him this time and she had always been the peacemaker. Maybe she'd finally had enough of him too. He wasn't even mad at him anymore; he was afraid for him. Afraid of what would happen to him if he didn't change his ways.

26

MURRAY

Murray sat alone in the lab section of the zoo's animal care center. He watched the virus cells on the slide under the microscope. He knew what normal cells looked like, according to the pictures in the books. He had some of his own blood on a different slide. This looked nothing like his. There was no healthy cell activity in this sample, just a strange looking glob moving lazily about. He was worried about the animals in the zoo becoming infected if the virus jumped across the species. There was no way they could handle one of the bears or the other carnivores if they became infected and there was a really good chance of exposure since the animals had engaged with the zombies.

He ignored the chomping of the decapitated head in the basket on the counter. He had asked Donny to bring it to him and to keep it to himself. He didn't want to cause any more stress on the others. They were busy stocking the zoo for winter and gathering wood. Things he wasn't able to help with, but he felt he had to do something to pull his weight, and this was too important to ignore.

He referenced one of the books from the shelf on

animal medicine. He compared the picture of healthy cells to the sample he had taken from a sleeping Otis the night before. Otis appeared healthy with no sign of the foreign invaders in his system. He breathed a sigh of relief.

He had a test in mind, though no way would it be totally conclusive, but with his limited knowledge of viruses and the equipment at his disposal, it was the best he could come up with.

He lifted one of the brown mice from the aquarium. Another gift from Donny, the six mice scurried about seeking cover while he captured one of them. The small furry creature looked at him with its beady eyes and let out a small squeak.

Donny lifted the syringe filled with the zombie blood and injected it into the mouse.

"Sorry, little guy." he said.

He put a small white band around the rodent's leg and returned him to the aquarium. He scooped up another mouse and this one was injected with saliva from the undead head still gnashing its teeth in the basket. That wasn't something he was interested in doing again anytime soon. Even in its decapitated state, the head still wanted to bite, and he'd come close to losing a finger when he drew the sample. Completely disconnected from its circulatory, respiratory, and central nervous system, it was still animated, something still drove it to attack

The second mouse got a blue band and Murray put him back with the others. Now to wait and watch. If they attacked the others and the virus spread to them, the tribe was in a world of trouble.

Murray made sure the lid was secure to the aquarium, popped the top on a warm Dr. Pepper and flipped through the pages of a book he'd found in the house. A novel about repo men in California, something to take his mind off of heavier things. He turned to the dog-eared page he had marked and continued reading.

Murray watched them on and off for hours while he finished his book. He wondered if the author was out there amongst the undead or holed up somewhere safe, either way, he didn't see a sequel coming anytime soon. The mice showed no signs of aggression, no change in their movements or behavior. Just mice being mice. They were huddled together in one corner of the tank, sleeping. He breathed a sigh of relief. It was rudimentary by any means, but he was pretty sure the virus wouldn't jump to the zoo animals from battle wounds. He made a mental note to try and get hold of one of the Savage Ones. It would be interesting to see what their blood looked like under the microscope.

27

GORDON

There was an uneasy truce and most of them tried to forget about the fight. The twins would glare at him when he took food from the community dishes they cooked but Cody must have told them not to say anything. Swan pretended he didn't exist and wouldn't even look at him. He was fine with that, too. He hated her and the stupid wolves more than all the rest of them combined. All Cody had said the next morning was *the new chore list is up*. They watched him, waiting to see if he would refuse to do anything, probably hoping he would so they would have some lame excuse to throw him out. He was smarter than that, though. His dad had taught him a thing or two. Sometimes you had to do things to lull the competition into thinking you were defeated, that they had won. Sometimes you had to swallow your pride, smile in their face and plot your revenge. When they weren't paying attention is when you would swoop in with a lower bid or bribe the right official to hassle them with zoning codes or maybe leak those pictures your private investigator took of that mistress in a hotel room. Gordon could play the game. After all, he was a

Lowery and the Lowery's owned this county. He had to bide his time and make his plans. He pretended he'd been taught a lesson but under the cool exterior he was filled with icy anger. Everyday his rage toward Cody grew as he watched him act like the big high and mighty leader. He had dared hit him! He had dared to lay hands on a Lowery. In a normal situation, he'd be in a jail cell and his father would make sure the judge threw the book at him. They were golfing buddies and Judge Brady knew where his bread was buttered. He knew where his campaign contributions came from. Mr. High and Mighty would be facing twenty years of hard labor.

Every day he watched *her* but always at a distance. She was the one he thought about when he stared at his magazines with a flashlight when everyone else was sleeping. He wondered what she looked like under her clothes. He could never get her alone to talk, to explain that he hadn't meant anything by grabbing her. He knew she was purposely avoiding him but she couldn't keep it up forever. She was the oldest girl here and since he was the oldest boy, they should be together. It was only right. Older people had needs, adult needs, and they should be taking care of each other. Surely he could make her understand and see the sense of it.

He would take her with him when he went back to his home to live. They could make the journey together. Maybe they could ride that stupid giraffe, it was high enough so any undead they ran into couldn't get them. The only problem with that was Bert hated him for no reason. When she wasn't hanging out with Cody or any of the rest of them, she was with the giraffe. He would aim his noxious ass in his direction, or swipe at him with his big head if he got anywhere near Harper. She would tell him to go, he was upsetting the stupid thing. She refused to leave it and come talk to him alone. *We're training* was always her excuse.

He needed to make her understand that Cody was wrong, being slaves to the animals was wrong and acting more like them every day was wrong. If she left with him, they could go back to where people were civilized. He was sure his old community was safe behind their walls. They had to be. The more he thought about it, the more convinced he became. This group was acting like savages in a jungle. They called themselves a tribe, they hunted animals with spears, they swam in the frigid water with the polar bears, they cavorted with those ridiculous monkeys and they slept with the furry creatures like pack animals. They'd turned the living room into a barn stall.

If she left with him, he would bring her the finest clothes and drape expensive jewelry, just sitting there for the taking, around her neck, wrists and on her fingers. They'd leave this place with the animal noises that kept him awake at night and the never-ending lists of chores. There were other survivors back home; he knew it in his bones. His community wouldn't have been overrun so easily. He had family there and it was gated and fenced. Million-dollar homes with separate servants' quarters. You can bet they weren't living in a barn with wild animals stinking up the place. It was a virtual paradise and all they had to do was get there.

Sooner or later, someone would come to Putnam and find a ghost town. They'd load up the stores of food and valuables and be gone, leaving him behind in this hellhole with no way to replenish supplies. Putnam was the only place close enough for a cart to go before the battery died and if it got cleaned out, they'd starve to death. If they wouldn't risk traveling north to his home, they should at least be there. If they weren't going to bring all the food to the park, they should at least be in town to defend it against bandits. No one was coming to the safari on purpose, it was too far off the main road. Nothing else was out here. Nothing worth taking anyway.

Gordon daydreamed as he filled the wheelbarrow with buffalo dung. He plotted and planned, thought of ways to get even and ways to escape. He knew he couldn't take Cody in a fair fight, even though he was bigger and stronger. If he had a gun he could, but there was still the bear to contend with. He didn't think a few bullets would stop the thing if it was mad and if he shot Cody in the back, it would probably be mad. If he was honest with himself, he knew he'd never convince Harper to run away with him by herself. He'd have to convince the whole group to leave. Going by himself was out of the question, there was no telling what kind of trouble he might run into on the road. If he brought a whole group, he'd arrive home like a returning hero and his dad had hunting rifles. They couldn't use their animals to bully him anymore and he'd make rugs out of most of them. They'd do what he said or he'd kick them all out.

It all came back to the Cody problem. He knew he couldn't do anything to him, hell if Mr. High and Mighty stubbed his toe halfway across the Park, they would find a way to blame it on him. Cody wouldn't leave as long as it was safe and without him, none of the others would either. He would have to force their hand somehow, take away their reasons for staying. Make it so they had to find some-place new and he would be just the guy to take them there. If he could engineer some bad luck, maybe a few accidents here and there, he could kill two birds with one stone. If they didn't have all the stupid animals to take care of, they wouldn't be trapped here. If he could blame it on bad decisions made by Mr. High and Mighty, they wouldn't think he was so great and do everything he said. All he had to do was start taking out the animals and he was fine with that. Nothing would make him happier than to see Swan blubbering over her dead wolves.

Gordon grunted with the weight of the wheelbarrow as he made his way over to the compost pile. There would be no more hauling crap around, either. They'd leave this dump and these stinking animals and in time everyone would realize he had been right all along. All the girls would be his and the boys would do whatever it took to stay in his good graces. He smiled at the thought of Harper sitting beside him, Vanessa and Annalise bringing his meals and seeking his attention. Swan would be on permanent cleaning duty and he'd have those wolves of hers turned into rugs. He'd make her do all the worst jobs like cleaning the bathrooms. He'd make sure he missed every time he used the toilet, too. If she didn't do a good job, he'd make her clean it with her tongue. His smile was huge at such pleasant thoughts.

He'd banish Donny the freak. He couldn't be trusted; you never knew what he was thinking. Tobias would be kept in check by the hold he kept on the boy's sister. The young kids would fall in line if they knew what was good for them. Murray, that pathetic cripple, had his uses so he'd keep him around. He grinned through split lips at the thought and actually started humming as he plotted his revenge on all of them. Yes, life would be good.

He'd be patient. He'd wait, and when the time was right, he'd strike. The book hidden under his mattress held the key to changing everything.

28

VANESSA

Vanessa wiped the dust from the mirror on the vanity before her and stared at her reflection. Pride swelled her bosom as she reflected on her actions of the past months. She wasn't the studious little girl she had been. She had killed monsters. She had saved lives. She'd dashed fearlessly towards those stranded children with no thought of her own safety. Ziggy had performed flawlessly, shattering the glass so they could drag those three kids to the security behind the iron fences. Her daddy would have been so proud of her. He was selfless like that. She remembered him buying food for homeless people when they were out in the old neighborhood where he had grown up. He paid no mind to their dirty clothes and unwashed smell as he chatted with them, learning about their lives. She'd watched quietly, sitting on tree shaded benches as they ate and he talked to them, listened to them and shared a little gospel. Most people walked by society's forgotten cast offs, ignoring their requests for change or offers to work for food. Not her dad though, he had a big heart and always told her it was her responsibility to look out for the less fortunate. To be a bright light in a world of darkness. She missed him so much sometimes. She prayed often that he had survived somehow and was safe with a group of good people.

She'd done all she could to be that light. She'd sat up late the first night as the three small kids cried for their mama. She answered the best she could when they asked her why their mother and aunt had tried to get eat them. She sugar coated it a little but not much. The kids had seen things, they weren't dumb and they were old enough to know the truth. Telling them lies could get them killed. She'd held them until sleep took them and the skulk of foxes helped. They sensed the unhappiness, chose the child and comforted them with their presence. She had colored page after page with them in books taken from the gift shop, read them stories and made sure they did their chores. *Always give more than you take*, she'd encouraged them. *We all have to do our part to survive. Never go outside the fences, never open the gates. It's safe in here. The tribe and the animals will protect you.*

It had been her idea to put them in charge of the petting zoo. The helpless animals were invaluable to their long-term survival. The chickens supplied them with fresh eggs, the goats would be a steady source of meat and cow gave them milk.

She'd laughed along with them when Bessie had knocked Cody from his stool into a pile of manure as he instructed them on how to milk her. He'd dusted himself off, and continued as though nothing had happened, his face red with embarrassment. *Squirt, squirt, squirt and the bucket gets full* he sang a little song to get the rhythm as he worked their teats back in forth to fill the plastic pail.

They'd taken to the foxes or in actuality, the foxes had

adopted them. They were the smallest of the omnivorous creatures in the zoo and it was a good fit. They were playful creatures and weren't big enough to hurt them accidentally. The spent hours together, their worries shoved aside as they chased and wrestled with the little red balls of fur.

They'd done well at their tasks. As time marched on, they cried less frequently at night about their parents and instead asked questions about fighting the zombies and going on scavenging runs. They did their chores and tagged along with the older kids as they tended to the other animals. They moaned and groaned about the lessons that she, Harper and Murray gave them. They didn't care about reading or learning math. It didn't matter they argued. She'd chastised them. Of course, it did she'd reassured them. Without reading, how do you know what you are eating is safe? Without basic math, how did you know you were giving the animals the right amount of food? They'd given in and were decent students. She'd never thought much about teaching before the world ended, but found she enjoyed it. She'd also discovered parts of her heritage she'd never read about as she devoured the books on African history gathering dusts on the shelves of the vast library in Piedmont House.

She was fascinated by the changes of her group over the past few months. They'd gone from typical kids who usually couldn't be trusted to set the garbage out without being reminded a few times to cunning and savvy survivors. They knew what had to be done and knew the consequences of not doing it. They had all gone a little wild but their situation warranted it. They weren't living in ordinary times anymore. There weren't any adults to tell them what they could and couldn't do and there never would be again. There were things at the gate that were trying to kill them. They had figured out how to manage on their own and they had learned to fight back. They learned from their companions, their animal friends who showed no fear, knew no restraints and didn't have remorse. They matched violence with violence. Death with death. Savagery with savagery. Their weapons, their animals and their wits were all that kept them from becoming one of the shuffling undead and they never forgot it.

Tobias and Annalise had always been a little different with their pale skin and nearly white hair but now they didn't try to suppress their unusualness. They embraced it and like the Viking ancestors they claimed, they started covering themselves with strange tattoos. Intricate knot work and rune patterns gleaned from downloaded books covered their arms and legs, drawn on with permanent marker. She'd watch them painstakingly recreate them by the glow of the fireplace every evening, experimenting with different patterns before they made them permanent with the tattoo gun. They looked like relics of the Viking age with their braided hair and battle axes.

She thought about Swan and her face paint. The buckskin clothes and the decorations she wove into her hair. The girl never spoke of it or bragged of her heritage; she didn't have to. Her native American blood was evident in her straight raven black hair and the dark complexion that was bronzed by the days spent in the sun. Even her choice of weapons, the tomahawks and the bow, were a nod to the Indians of the plains.

Donny had a lot of Chinese in him but he'd developed a range of skills that borrowed from many of the Asian countries. His armor looked vaguely like a Samurai's. He fought with the spear and could spin it like the fighting staff of a

Shaolin monk and he'd taught himself to move as stealthy as his panther.

Cody and Harper were as American as apple pie and neither knew much about their ancestors. *I think we came from Germany,* Cody had answered when asked about his forefathers. Harper had just shrugged and said *Iowa.*

Vanessa picked up the battery powered clippers that once belonged to Derek. She'd found them in the back of one of the golf carts amidst empty Dr. Pepper bottles, empty feed sacks and foul-smelling buckets that had been used to lug raw meat around. She stared into the mirror at her dark, nearly ebony skin. Her full lips and high cheekbones. Her father had called her his Nubian Princess. She didn't know much about her history beyond her grandparents. They were simply Americans. She didn't know where her ancient fathers had called home but she knew it was somewhere in Africa. They may have been slaves or they may have been free men but she knew they had once been warriors. They had once lived or died by their skills, their cunning and their wit, and now she did too. Like Donny, the twins and Swan, she embraced her people's history and drew from it to give her courage and strength.

She touched her hair, ran her fingers through it one last time. It was long and unruly, the tight, kinky curls refused to be tamed without creams and conditioners. Her kind of hair couldn't be put in a ponytail and forgot about. She had to be careful not to get it soaking wet or it could start to mold. When she tried to wear a hat, she had to have it so tight it hurt her head or it would fall off. Braiding it was too much trouble. Dreadlocks could easily be snagged by reaching, undead hands and besides they stank. *No wonder the African women kept it short*, she thought, *they didn't have time to mess with it every day.*

She turned on the clippers and pressed them to the skin above her ears, shearing backwards carefully. Within minutes she was running her hand over the smooth sides of her head and staring at her new mohawk in the mirror. She smiled. She liked what she saw.

She unscrewed the cap on the white makeup and dipped three of her fingers into it, dragging horizontal lines down each side of her newly exposed scalp. It made her look fierce, she thought.

That was the easy part, she said to herself then picked up the razor blade sitting next to the small can of ashes taken from the bonfire. She'd read everything she could find about ritual scarification, a practice by warrior tribes to attest to their prowess in battle. The scars of the warrior reflected at a glance their skills in battle.

She had saved three, had risked her life for theirs and it was fitting that the first marks on her flawless skin would be for them. A reminder to her and the world that even if she never did anything else worthy of honor, this she would have forever.

She made an incision beneath each eye, wincing at the pain and the reflected image of blood pouring down her cheeks. She cut slow and deep, felt the sharp burn and ignored it. This was nothing, this was but a scratch and she would not flinch. She dabbed her fingers in the ash then worked it into the cuts to promote swelling. When it healed, it would leave a prominent scar. She wondered how many more self-inflicted cuts she would bear before the world resumed some form of normalcy.

She sat and watched until the blood finally stopped running and the ash sealed the wound. She wiped the remnants of blood from her face and stood. She looked different and she felt different. She was leaving her life before the fall behind. Her clothes were different, her attitude was different and now her face was different. She let her machetes find their place on her hips, grabbed her spear, slipped the laser pointer into her pocket and went to find her ostrich.

29

SWAN

The children all giggled incessantly at Murray as he sucked in another mouthful of helium from the tank and his high-pitched voice rang out. The animal sanctuary had always been a popular place for kids' birthday and other events so rounding up some party items had been an easy task. Balloons floated against the high ceilings while others were tied off to chair backs. The youngest children chased each other in a high-speed game of tag through the hallways. Otis lay in front of the fireplace, soaking up its heat and snoring heavily. Yewan was curled in a window sill absorbing the last rays of warmth as the sun made its slow descent into the western sky.

The monkeys chattered excitedly, bouncing from cabinet to chair to shoulders and swinging from the light fixture above the massive oak table in the formal dining room. They leaped for the balloons floating lazily against the high vaulted ceiling. Sage, one of the feistier capuchins, tried to mimic Murray and breathe in the helium. Her own voice scared her and the rest of monkeys and they all darted for the safety of Murrays' jacket. An assortment of gifts lay sloppily wrapped on the table. This was supposed to be Swans surprise birthday party, she was a teenager now, but she was late. Harper had been secretly planning it for weeks and made sure Cody's job roster had her on fence detail. It only took a few hours to make the rounds, she should have been back before dark. Maybe she was getting a few more rabbits for Lucy who was still nursing the cubs.

Donny kept watch at the window, looking for any sign of her and the wolves. He caught a glimpse of her in the lengthening shadows and motioned for everyone to take their places and get ready. The house fell as silent as a tomb as children tried to stop giggling and ducked behind doors or into empty cabinets ready to leap out and yell surprise.

Swan entered the front door, followed by Zero padding softly behind her. Candlelight lit the big house, casting long shadows. She saw no sign of her friends, just the snoring bear in front of the fireplace and the black panther dozing in the window.

She sighed and hung her jacket on the coat rack, surprised no one was hogging the fire. Well, if you didn't count Otis but he was always hogging it. Hunting for survival was hard. She was a little miffed at herself for missing a sprinting rabbit not once but twice. Both toma-hawks had fell short and stuck harmlessly in the ground. The experience was real, it was tough, nothing like she'd imagined. Trying to outsmart one of Mother Earth's creations wasn't as easy as she thought it would be. Every creature had a will to live and even the most adorable animals had the instincts to fight back when cornered. The concept seemed ok to her, a small mistake and they didn't have fresh meat that day, success and her pack feasted. It was fair, she didn't have guns and an unfair advantage. She didn't shoot an animal from a half mile away where it had no chance. She hunted with her pack and they killed for need, not sport.

She thought back to her first success with the compound bow and still felt the adrenaline rush of their first kill. A small buck had finally fallen under one of her arrows and she'd watched as the wolves ran down and finished off the wounded animal. She'd thanked the deer for its sacrifice and fell in beside the wolves as they feasted. The meat was hot and bloody. She'd only tried a taste before the wave of revulsion hit her but it was an important ritual with her pack. They hadn't warned her off. Zero had moved aside to give her room, acknowledging her as alpha. She let them eat as much as they wanted from that hunt before she gutted it and carried the remains back on her shoulders. She much preferred her venison cooked.

Her mouth watered at the memory of the tender venison they'd roasted in aluminum foil buried in the camp-fire coals. She wondered what the twins were cooking for dinner and headed for the kitchen. When she passed through the dining room, a crowd of children exploded from cover screaming surprise. Zero and Lucy went into a defensive stance, teeth bared and hackles raised, startled by the sudden noise. Swan crouched, had both tomahawks in her hands and a snarl on her lips when she saw the shocked looks on everyone's faces.

Embarrassed, she lowered her weapons, spoke softly to calm the wolves and smiled as her eyes drank in the presents, balloons and the cake with the thirteen candles. She didn't think anyone remembered. Didn't think it even mattered with the world dead. Most days she didn't know or care what the date was anymore. Murray kept up with that kind of stuff, not her. She was focused on caring for her pack and honing her skills.

"Thanks guys," she said with genuine gratitude.

Hugs and happy birthday wishes were given as each of her tribe made their way forward. She stood there, armed and armored and smiled happily at the outpouring of love. She smelled of wood smoke and sweat and her face was darkened with soot. A black triangle shape extended across her forehead and blended with her hair. It covered her eyes and tapered down to her chin, giving her a wolf like profile in the dim light of the candles. Her hair was twisted into a long braid with acorn beads and a raven feather woven into it.

She wiped at her eyes, overwhelmed by the love and support of these other orphans. Thrown together by chance they were strangers who became a family. A family who became a tribe. They were all so different, yet here they stood as one, laughing and eating cupcakes the twins had whipped up.

She stood at the head of the table and took them all in. The cogs in a wheel, the members of her tribe, each with an ability and skill that helped them survive.

Tobias and Annalise, with their ethereal appearance of almost white hair braided and beaded with the intricate tattoos covering their alabaster skin, were the fishermen and the cooks. They were berserkers on polar bears.

Vanessa, with hand-crafted ostrich plume earrings dangling from her ear lobes, her mohawk and ritual scars was their quickest when she rode Ziggy. She could dart into town and back for a bag of supplies in less than an hour and she had learned to lead the dead away from the front gate. They'd give chase and she would get them started on the road north then cut back through the woods. They kept going once they started running and were never seen again. New ones stumbled in, usually one or two a day, but she kept their numbers manageable and covered a lot of territory around the Park.

Cody, tall and handsome with the hair he was constantly brushing from his face had shown them how to live with their companion animals. He had held them together and kept them alive during those first chaotic and frightening days and continued to lead them and make wise choices.

Harper was the sister she'd never had, the peacemaker and smile bringer who could see farther than anyone when she rode high atop Bert.

Donny, strong and silent was her hunting partner who didn't fear the woods and kept them in fresh meat.

Murray, the boy with the books who always had an answer for everything and could figure out how to fix anything.

There was Caleb, Landon and Clara, the triplets they had started calling them, who had completely taken over the duties of the petting zoo, freeing up the older kids to do other work.

Then there was Gordon who was finally trying to fit in and be friendly. He would smile and laugh with them but it sounded forced. He was trying too hard. His lips were scabbed over and still healing from where Cody had hit him. *Should have hit him harder* she thought. *Or hit him more.* No matter how nice he was trying to be, she didn't trust him and didn't like him. It had started on the first day they met and he'd made them wait forever while he packed his stuff. She didn't like the way he looked at her either. It felt like he was always trying to imagine what she looked like under her clothes.

She reached for one of the cubs who were playing at her feet, held the small creature to her lips and kissed it softly.

She returned the wolf to his littermates when Cody hollered over the din that it was time to open presents. She took her place of honor at the head of the table as Landon and Caleb struggled to slide her heavy chair forward. Clara placed a homemade cardboard crown on her head, complete with glued on macaroni designs and crude wolfs head drawings.

She squealed with delight as Murray handed her his gift, a pair of fine sharpening stones and oil for her toma-hawks. Harper gave her a heavy winter cloak with Mother of Wolves embroidered over the breast. She hugged her tight and swung it around her shoulders. It would be warm and quiet and wouldn't restrict her movements.

Custom tooled knee-high leather moccasins from the twins came next followed by a fine bladed field dressing knife from Cody. She unwrapped the gift from Vanessa, a pair of high-end sunglasses that would certainly come in handy when the snows fell.

Caleb, Landon and Clara gifted her with pictures of Lucy and Zero taken from coloring books in the gift shop. The wolves were rendered in greens, reds, blues and pink and were scribbled outside of the lines. She loved them.

Gordon gave her a handful of arrows for her bow and told her happy birthday, although a little stiffly. She thanked him. He was trying at least. Maybe that punch to the face had knocked some sense into him.

Donny came last. She tore open the wrapping and pulled out the present. Pieces of antlers from the first small buck she'd taken were drilled out and threaded on a leather cord. He'd polished each piece until it shined. Over-whelmed, she threw her arms around him and hugged him tightly.

They sang happy birthday to her at the tops of their

lungs and Cody lit the thirteen candles one by one with the old Zippo lighter. She closed her eyes, took a deep breath and blew them out, whispering her wish as the last flame was extinguished.

None noticed when Gordon slipped away from the party for a few minutes.

She fell asleep that night so thankful for her tribe. She'd been on every trip to Putnam and they didn't stop at any of the stores where her gifts came from. They went in and out fast, loading up the golf card as quick as they could hurrying back to the safety of the Park. She had tickled Clara until she was breathless with laughter and threated to tickle her until she peed her pants if she didn't tell how they did it. She finally got the answer after tickle torturing Caleb and Landon. Vanessa had ridden in on Ziggy. She could be there and back in no time and could outrun any zombie no matter how fast it was.

As she drifted off with her wolves bedded down to either side of her and the cubs snuggled up for warmth, she hoped her parents were thinking of her, wherever they were.

30

TEDDY

They stood around the buffalo, huddled in their winter coats, as it wheezed and tried to push itself to its feet. Teddy, named in honor of President Theodore Roosevelt, was lying near Bert's feed trough. The great shaggy beast's chest heaved with the exertion of trying to draw in breath. He usually stayed in his enclosure at night, it was the only home he knew. He'd been living in it for almost twenty years and rarely wandered very far on his own. For some reason, he had traveled halfway across the park. No one had an explanation or knew what to do for him.

There was worried, quiet talk about the virus jumping species to infect the animals despite assurances from Murray that it wasn't possible. Donny and Vanessa stood ready with their spears in case it turned into a 1000-pound version of the monsters outside the gates.

Murray insisted it wasn't the virus, Teddy didn't show any signs of zombie infection. He flipped frantically through the veterinary manuals on his tablet but there just wasn't enough information to go on. He hated the feeling of helplessness as he watched the majestic animal suffering.

The buffalo drooled heavily, thick mucus streamed from his nostrils and his eyes rolled back in his head. His body fought against whatever was destroying him from the inside but he was losing.

"I don't know, I just don't know." Murray muttered as he searched one book after another. "This doesn't make any sense; he has the symptoms of food poisoning."

Teddy took a deep, wheezing gasp and let it out with a shudder. One last plume of breath fog came from him, dissipated in the cold air and his chest didn't rise again.

Confusion ran through the children and Swan knocked an arrow as Harper ushered the triplets away. They had to be ready if Murray was wrong, if it was the infection. They would have to put him down quick. They waited, weapons at the ready and fear in their hearts but after several tense minutes, Teddy remained where he lay. It wasn't the virus and they all felt relief. They couldn't imagine having their companions turn on them.

Gordon tried to look as shocked and upset as the other children. It wasn't hard, he was good at pretending and he actually was surprised. The giraffe was supposed to be the one lying dead on the ground. It was a useless animal and she spent entirely too much time with it. Besides, if Harper had a broken heart then he would have been there to offer comfort. His plan hadn't worked as expected but that was okay, maybe it was better this way. Without their beast of burden to drag logs for them, they would have to work that much harder and longer to get wood. Something they wouldn't have to do if they left this place and went somewhere civilized.

The Dangerous Plants of the Midwest book hidden in his room had given him the idea. It had been one of the thousands in the Piedmont House library and he'd secreted it away when he'd been thinking about poisoning Cody. There was nothing deadly enough that he could find to get rid of Mr. High and Mighty but there were other ways to get rid of someone. Better ways. Make everyone think he was incompetent and then take his kingdom away.

He'd mixed a double handful of chokecherry leaves with the fresh alfalfa he left in Bert's feed trough. Highly toxic to animals and growing wild in the woods of the park it was easy enough to make it look like an accident. The stupid buffalo must have followed him and the smell of alfalfa last night when he went by his pen. They didn't bother locking the grazing animals in anymore, they let them wander freely although most of them went back to their homes every night.

When Harper called for him, they saw Bert peek his head up down by the river. He ignored her and went back to foraging, looking for anything still green or tender that grew along the shore. At least he was okay and they were starting to think Murray was right. Teddy must have eaten or drank something. Maybe he got into some rat poison or antifreeze somehow.

Cody stood there, saddened and shocked by the unexplainable death. He felt guilt over the fact that he'd once considered eating Teddy before they discovered that Putnam was deserted. Otis sniffed at the buffalo's snout and chuffed, backing away. He wondered what disturbed his big friend. Teddy was an old animal, but this didn't seem like death from old age. This was something different.

"We need to double check all the sheds and the garage." Cody said. "Make sure they're still locked up. Maybe he got poisoned from one of them. Do you think he would eat weed killer? Is it sweet to the taste maybe?"

"Never tried it." Murray said "but I wouldn't think so."

They all stood and stared, wondering what to do next. They couldn't just leave him lay there. Swan squatted by the deceased animal, the wolves taking position on either side of her as she caressed the shaggy head and hummed a melody that only she knew the words to. She asked for the Earth to reclaim him and for his spirit to move on, unburdened and at peace. Cody pondered the situation. Teddy was gone, there was no bringing him back. The meat would go a long way to feeding the carnivores, but Otis had already sensed something wrong, something tainted so they had to get rid of the carcass. They had no way to move him, he was simply too big and heavy. He groaned inwardly at the thought of digging a hole big and deep enough for him.

When she finished her ceremony, she stood with the rest of them for a few moments in silent farewell. He had been a gentle giant who had been an immense help and had worked tirelessly for hours on end dragging logs for them.

Harper wiped tears from her eyes and led the triplets away.

"Come on, guys." she said. "Let's check the outbuildings then we'll gather eggs for breakfast."

Swan leaned over, spoke softly to Donny and he nodded his agreement.

"We'll take care of Teddy." she said. "I've already committed him back to Mother Earth. He may be contaminated, we can't risk our animals catching whatever it is."

Cody turned to the others. "Let's check everything, make sure the sheds are secure and make sure none of the others are sick."

Thankful for the opportunity to be anywhere else as Swan and Donny began their grisly task, the children hustled off. They'd seen enough death already in their short time on Earth and hoped they wouldn't find more.

31

TRIAL AND ERROR

"Cody is going to be so mad." Clara whispered and tears sprung up in in her eyes.

The chicken coop resembled a slaughterhouse. At least half of the hens were dead. Butchered and mostly eaten, reduced to a few piles of feathers. Harper had sent them ahead to gather the eggs while she checked the garage and storage sheds. The gate had been standing wide open to the petting zoo area and the foxes were doing what foxes do. They chased them out but the damage was done. They surveyed the carnage and didn't have any idea what to do.

"I'm scared." Landon said, on the verge of breaking down. "Cody told us we had the most important job in the zoo, and everyone was counting on us. I know we latched the gate last night. I know we did. I gave it a shake like he showed us to make sure."

"He did, I saw him." Caleb said nodding in agreement with his cousin. It didn't matter if he did or not, he was gonna back up Landon regardless.

"We should hide, Cody might kill us like he did those

monsters. Or let Otis eat us." Landon said wide eyed, his youthful imagination getting the best of him.

Terrified at the prospect of being eaten by the bear, they were making plans to run away when Harper came up behind them and gasped.

"What happened guys? How did the foxes get in to the hens?" Cody asked.

The tribe was seated at the big table and there was a definite shortage of eggs when the twins brought the breakfast platter out.

"You won't hurt them will you Cody?" Clara asked, her hands twisting and turning her napkin. "You won't kill our foxes?"

She couldn't meet his eyes or anyone else's. All three hung their heads in shame and fear, not sure what the punishment would be. She stared at her nervous hands and sniffled.

"That's your biggest concern, your pets?" Cody asked sternly and looked around at the others. Some had small smiles of pride and nodded their approval.

"Yessir." she whispered. "Please don't hurt them."

Cody let them shift around uncomfortably for moment and kept a frown on his face as they snuck peeks up at him. The chickens were a loss but he didn't blame the foxes, they were doing what foxes do. They could probably get more chickens, there had to be some still alive at the nearby farms. Like the others, he was touched about their concern for them. They didn't care if they got punished, they cared about their animals.

Gordon stood off to the side waiting for Cody to scream at the kids. To explode and really tear them a new one. He'd left the gate open last night when he snagged the armload of Alfalfa. He hadn't planned on the foxes doing the damage they did but that was just an added bonus. More dead animals. Another failing of Mr. High and Mighty.

"Nobody is going to hurt your pets." Cody finally said. "We would never do that. But who left the gate open? Did you forget with all the excitement of the birthday party?"

Relieved, all three children tried to speak at once. They swore it wasn't their fault. They'd been careful. Followed the rules. Locked the gate. Double checked it and gave it a shake. It wasn't their fault.

Cody listened to their voices running together making excuses and tried to think of a suitable punishment. He believed them, that they thought the gate was closed, but he also believed they must have been in a hurry to get ready for the party and had made a simple mistake. He decided the loss of the chickens would be enough of a reprimand. Every time they ate breakfast, they would see the results of their carelessness. They would see there weren't enough eggs for everyone, let alone any for the wolf cubs. He let them make their excuses and shed their tears for a few moments and was getting ready to tell them it was over, just don't let it happen again when they caught him by surprise.

"Please don't let Otis eat us!" blurted out Caleb, real fear in his voice.

Cody looked confused for an instant, then laughed. He crouched down and pulled them all into a hug.

"Don't be silly." he said. "Otis won't eat you. He loves children. But from now on, I want all three of you to check the gate when you leave. I want a triple check, you understand?"

They nodded, assured him they'd really, really, really make sure it never happened again.

"Good. You need to clean up the mess, though. I know it's gross, but it's your mess. Dig a hole and bury them."

They hung their little heads, relieved at not being eaten by a bear, but still pretty sure they'd latched the gate. Grownups never believed anything a little kid said but it wasn't so bad. Nobody seemed to be mad at them.

Gordon silently cursed a blue streak as he waited to load up his plate. He'd expected Cody to lose it with the kids. At least scream at them some. Cause some friction, maybe some lingering hard feelings but it had turned into a hug fest. Hell, the kids were starting to believe that they'd been in a hurry and hadn't closed it properly. Everybody took tiny little portions of the scrambled eggs but screw that. He was hungry. He took what he normally would and if they didn't like it, they could kiss his ass.

He thought about the chokecherry leaves as everyone wolfed down the meal. The ruckus with the buffalo and then the chickens had everyone running behind with their duties. He still had some hidden in a sack under his mattress. Nobody got mad about the dead buffalo. Nobody got mad about the dead chickens. Nobody was fighting and thinking they needed to leave or maybe get a new leader. If anything, the killings had brought them closer together. He needed a new plan and he thought he knew just the thing.

If he couldn't turn the others against Cody, he'd turn him against himself. Otis was the key. Cody would tear himself apart if something happened to the bear. In the aftermath, he could get rid of the other animals one at a time. There would be a new death every week until they finally gave up and abandoned this place. They'd never figure it out and after a few of the animals had passed on to the great hunting ground in the sky, they would be glad to leave. They'd be too afraid to stay. He smiled at the thought. Otis loved that nasty canned meat. He'd put the poisonous leaves inside of it, toss it to him then wait. Wait for the bear to die and Cody to fall to pieces. He felt confident, this was the answer that had eluded him and he wondered why he hadn't thought of it sooner. He ate slowly, ignored the conversation around him and let the others finish and leave to go do their chores for the day. Mr. High and Mighty had him on perimeter duty and that suited him just fine. The bear would be in front of the fireplace hogging all the heat. All it did was sleep, sometimes for days at a time. Hibernation light is what the cripple called it. Whatever. He'd wake up if he smelled the Spam then he could spend the rest of the day checking the fences. No one could blame him for what was about to happen. By the time he'd finished eating he had the house to himself. He hid his grin as he swiped off his plate with his sleeve, set it in the clean pile and practiced his sad face.

32

HARPER & CODY

The November wind blowing out of the north ruffled Cody's hair and tossed it around his face. It was getting long and hung down to his collar. Longer than he'd ever worn it. Like the others, he was starting to look a little wild. Not as much as the twins or Swan or even Vanessa but he was embracing the animal's nature, becoming more like them. Harper had twisted a few small braids into his hair and adorned them with beads. A small ostrich plume was woven into one of them. It had been a gift from Vanessa. She'd told him it was what a chief should wear.

Cody and Harper were checking the fish traps in the Mississippi since the twins were making a run outside the fences to look for more chickens. Their polar bears were as tame as horses, almost as fast and about a hundred times deadlier.

They sat together on the bench overlooking the muddy water and Harper slid in close. She shivered a little from the northern winds and he slipped an arm around her for warmth. They wore their armor whenever they left the house and it made bundling up cumbersome. Winter coats didn't fit over it very well and it was too restrictive if they strapped the pieces on over heavy jackets. Soon they would all be wearing capes like Swans, she had shown them how practical they were.

"You didn't seem too keen on the buffalo robe they said they were going to make." she said.

"I dunno, just seems weird, I guess." Cody shrugged. "I grew up here, saw Teddy every day. Brushed him, fed him, and cleaned up behind him. It just seems wrong somehow."

"I think it would be ok. I think he'd be glad you had it."

"I know, I heard Swan. *We are a part of everything, everything is a part of us"*

"Don't forget *Mother Earth provides*." Harper added, imitating Swans voice. "But seriously, it's ok Cody. Teddy doesn't need it anymore. I'm sure he'd be proud to know that after all the years you've taken care of him, he could return the favor. It will keep you warm and those monsters can't bite through it. Besides that, it sets you apart as our leader."

Cody balked at the words. He didn't consider himself a leader, not really. He didn't want a throne to sit on or for anyone to call him your majesty or anything. He knew what needed to get done and let everybody know. They all had to work together to survive. He thought of himself as part of a team where everyone had input. Murray was much smarter than him and Donny had become a master hunter, providing fresh meat for everyone. Swan was always so confident, even if she was a little weird. Vanessa, the youngest of their core group, had a natural way with the small children. Any of them were just as suited, if not more than him, to lead.

He snapped back to the moment, missing what Harper had just said. "Huh."

"I said, what do you think really happened to everyone? What made them turn into monsters?"

"I don't have a clue. Maybe it's like Swan said and the earth just had enough of our pollution and destruction. Maybe it's something that a scientist created in a lab and it got loose. Doesn't really matter at this point. We're safe in here. It's secure and off the beaten path so we don't get too many zombies wandering in. We have each other. Food is easy to come by. I do miss my PlayStation though." he grinned.

"Do you think there are more people out there some-where?" she asked.

"There has to be. We found Gordon and the little kids came from somewhere, so there's gotta be pockets of people still alive."

"I miss the old world too," she said "but if it had to end. I'm glad I'm here."

"With you." she added, barely above a whisper.

He looked at her. They'd just been talking, friend to friend and she was easy to talk to but the way her voice became soft caused something to click and shut his brain down. He was suddenly aware that his arm was around the most incredible girl he'd ever met. She stared into his eyes and all he could think about were her lips, so red and soft and slightly parted. He wondered how they would taste, how they would feel. His heart started slamming into his ribs and he couldn't think of anything to say. She leaned a little closer and he could feel her warmth, saw the flush in her cheeks and moved a little closer himself. Her eyes were only inches away, their noses almost touching and he breathed in her scent. They stayed that way for a long time, too unsure to move any closer but knowing they didn't want to move any farther apart.

"Cody." she breathed and, on her lips, it was an adoration.

A confession.

A declaration.

He closed the short distance before he lost his nerve and his lips found hers. Soft and gentle, unsure and hesitant. She rose to meet him, pushed against him brought a hand up to twine in his hair.

Gentleness became more insistent. Uncertainty fell away and he pulled her close, armor against armor, and his tongue found hers. It was so easy, so natural. All the questions he had about kissing girls, what you did with your nose or did your teeth bash together and did it hurt if you pressed too hard were answered in an instant. None of those things mattered and it was the most wondrous feeling he'd ever had. He could kiss her for hours.

For days.

Forever.

"Get a room, you two." Gordon said and glared as he stomped by on his long journey around the fence line. "And put a condom on it, last thing we need is another mouth to feed."

They pulled apart quickly, plastic armor got entangled and they fumbled to loosen it. Both of their cheeks burned in embarrassment and they looked anywhere but at each other.

Cody stood quickly, muttered something about checking the traps and practically ran for the river.

Harper was mortified. It was the first time she'd kissed a boy, a real kiss not a birthday peck on the cheek and Gordon had to ruin it. She kind of understood why Swan didn't like him now. He didn't have to be so hateful. She resettled her armor and smoothed her hair. Well, at least she wasn't cold

221

anymore and a smile crept back across her lips. It had been nice. So nice. She would get him alone again and pick up right where they had left off. Maybe after the Thanksgiving meal, wasn't there a tradition of kissing under mistletoe? Who said it had to be only at Christmas? She set off to find Murray, he would have a book with pictures of it and he'd know how to find some.

33

BUSTED

Swan needed her sharpening stones, the grizzly job her and Donny were doing was a lot more work than they had anticipated. The buffalo was huge, a thousand pounds at least, probably closer to two thousand. They had only dressed deer before and they weighed maybe a hundred and fifty pounds for a big one. Moving quietly had become second nature to her, something she did without thinking and her choice of armor and clothes helped her move silently when hunting. It was something she'd learned from Donny and her wolves. She stepped over the creaking second step on the porch out of habit. She avoided the warped board by the planter because it squeaked and before she opened the door, she stopped when she heard Gordons voice.

"Wake up lazy ass." he said and she heard a thwacking sound. She stepped to the side, peeked through the living room window and saw him hit Otis again with a poker from the fireplace.

The bear grunted but didn't open his eyes. He slept a

lot, it was his hibernation season, but it wasn't true hibernation. He'd wake up and mosey around every few days.

"C'mon you big stupid idiot." Gordon said. "Got something tasty for you. Yum yum yummy, it's your favorite food."

He tossed a chunk of meat right in front of his nose and Otis grunted again then opened a bleary eye. Swan moved fast, ran back to the door and shoved it open. She heard the back-door slam and hurried over to see what Gordon had been trying to feed the bear. She snatched it up as his big tongue was reaching out for it and he snuffled a surprise when it wasn't there. There were a handful of leaves stuffed into the greasy lump of Spam and her eyes narrowed. She double checked, made sure there were no more then carried the whole mess into the kitchen. She put it in a Tupperware container and snapped on the lid before she headed upstairs to the third floor. His door was locked but she kicked until it broke open. She wrinkled her nose and went immediately to the window to open it. The room reeked of unwashed body and something else. Something she couldn't identify but it smelled dirty. The bed was unmade and the sheets were filthy and stained. There were nasty books on the floor and some of them were open to pictures of blonde girls spreading their legs wide. Some of them looked like he'd been spitting on them or something. She was thirteen, she wasn't stupid but it took her a minute to realize what she was looking at. Her girlfriends had giggled over video clips on the internet of men and women doing the things men and women did but this was gross. This was disgusting. She looked around the room, averting her eyes from the disturbing images her mind was conjuring up of Gordon hunched over the pictures that looked like an older version of Harper and... and...

She couldn't even think it, shuddered and started opening drawers using her cloak so she wouldn't have to touch the handles. If he had any more of the leaves, she wanted to find them. She didn't know what they were but if he was trying to feed them to Otis, they had to be something bad.

Swan wasn't subtle. She dumped out the contents of the desk, the old chest of drawers and pulled everything off the hangers in the closet, everything off the shelves. She didn't particularly try to smash his iPad but didn't bother to step over it either. The screen shattered under her foot. When she was finished, she had a small collection of trinkets gathered on the desktop. One of her feathers she used to braid in her hair. It was jet black, a ravens, and she thought it must have come loose and she lost it in the woods. Vanessa's bracelet she'd made from pieces of hand sanded oak beads. Harpers locket on a gold chain that went missing and they had blamed on one of the monkeys.

She hadn't found any more of the leaves but there was one more place to check. She went all the way back downstairs to get a fireplace poker to pull the blankets off and toss them aside. When she tipped the mattress over her eyes widened.

"Bingo, you bastard." she said.

She ignored the other magazines and pulled out a Ziploc bag of leaves that had the same coloring as the ones in the Spam. She was surprised when she looked up to see Donny standing in the doorway. He was wondering what was taking her so long and now he knew. He had a question on his face and she held the bag up.

"Know what these are?" she asked

He shrugged and mimed smoking a cigarette.

"No, I don't think so. It's not dope. Gordon was trying to feed some to Otis."

He raised an eyebrow and mimed the wheelchair sign and she nodded.

"Yeah. Let's ask Murray."

He pointed to a book she had tossed on the floor along with the sticky magazines and she picked it up. It was from the library downstairs and was about dangerous plants.

By the time he got back, the bear should be dying or dead. Gordon practiced his surprised look, his concerned look and finally his commiserating sad look. Should he put an arm around Cody and say something like *I'm so sorry, buddy*? Would that be pushing it a little too far? He'd play it by ear. Meanwhile, he had enough leaves left to get rid of two or three more animals. The wolves for sure. They'd definitely be next. After that, if he had any left, he could get rid of the panther.

He walked slowly along the trail worn along the fence line, taking his time and stopping to relax often. He was supposed to do some other stuff when he finished his rounds, he couldn't remember exactly what, but whatever it was would be forgotten by everyone else when the bear got sick. Probably mucking out more stalls. It was cold when he was in the shadows but not too bad if he stayed in the sunlight. He moved away from the fence line, away from the overhanging branches and didn't bother checking for holes from something burrowing under it. Zombies didn't dig and he had always thought it was a waste of time to do the checks every day. A few times a month would be more than enough. His mind drifted back to how it would be in another few weeks. How he'd lead them all back to civilization inside the gated community. He walked right past a fallen branch bending the chain link fence nearly double.

He had forgotten to bring the saw and ax in his hurry to get away from whoever had been coming in the house. Whatever. Whoever made the rounds tomorrow could cut it up and fix the fence if they wanted. He ambled along, lost in his delicious thoughts of Harper and the fun they would have once he got her away from the Park.

It was nearing dinnertime when he got back, he had stretched the walk out as long as he could. He'd even gotten a little nap on one of the benches that was in a patch of sunshine. There wasn't any commotion happening as he neared the house and he wondered if anyone had even discovered the bear was dead. All it did was sleep so maybe they hadn't. He'd have to play it cool, maybe he could notice the bloody foam coming from his mouth when he went to the fire to warm up. He had the perfect alibi so why not? He could be the hero who tries to save the beast.

When he stepped inside, they were gathered around the table and it wasn't for dinner. They turned to stare at him and he saw the bag of leaves sitting on the polished wood. He froze and his mind raced. He should run. Right now.

Donny ghosted in behind him with Yewan silent by his side.

Running was out of the question.

"What's up?" he asked and started taking off his heavy winter jacket.

"I ran into some trouble at the back of the Park," he said. "There were some branches over the fence and it took me a while to fix everything."

No one answered, they just stared and they had hard looks on their painted faces. He had to think fast but he had to know what they knew so the lie would work. He adjusted his armor, settling it in to more comfortable positons.

"We having salad for dinner?" he asked, buying time.

"Come in and sit down." Cody said.

"Uh... sure, bud. We having a meeting?"

As he approached the table, he saw a handful of the chewed up leaves they had cut out of Teddy's stomach and the glob of Spam with the leaves still stuffed into it. The book he'd hidden under his mattress, Dangerous Plants of the Midwest was opened to the page he'd earmarked about chokecherries. The little pile of stolen treasures was there, too. He froze and a spear point prodded him forward. Not gently, either.

"Have a seat." Cody said coolly and Swan pulled the one at the end of the table out for him.

She smiled a wicked smile and her teeth nearly glowed under her soot blackened face. Cody's face was striped in war paint too. All of them were, even the little kids had their faces shaded so they looked like their fox companions.

Gordon sat and swallowed hard. This had the feeling of a tribunal; some primitive court room and he was the one on trial. Whoever he'd heard on the porch had found the poisoned meat meant for Otis. They'd searched his room and found the rest of the leaves and then cut open the buffalo to see what killed him. There was no way he could lie his way out and that was why Swan was all smiley.

Gordon feared the wild girl but tried not to let it show. Out of all of them, she had to be the craziest. The twins were tattooed up like circus freaks but they didn't ooze crazy like she did. She had gone feral and like her wolves, he didn't think she knew how to feel remorse or guilt. She would happily sink one of her tomahawks into his head if she had a good reason. He had only poisoned a stupid animal, though. They might be mad but you didn't kill people for that. Normal people didn't, anyway. You could never tell what this group would do.

"Chokecherry." Murray said reading from the book. "Highly toxic and will kill animals who ingest it. Herbivores will eat it by mistake while grazing."

They all looked at him, waiting for a denial or an excuse or an apology. Something. Anything.

"Yeah, it's mine." he finally said, grasping at an idea that might work. "I was doing some research on how to kill the Savage Ones. You know, we have to thin them out, more and more come every week and they're getting aggressive. I was doing my part, trying to help out."

The more he spoke, the more plausible his story sounded. He slapped his hands on the table like he'd seen his father do and stood, raising his voice.

"I don't appreciate what you're trying to do here." he said indignantly. "It looks to me like you're trying to blame me for Teddy's death. I found those chokecherries and he could have too. If anything, blame Mother Nature."

Swan sat back in her chair and slow clapped a few times.

"That's admirable." she said. "Except you left out the part where I saw you trying to feed them to Otis. You left out the part where you mixed the chokecherry leaves with the alfalfa during my birthday party and snuck out to feed it to Bert. You left out the part where Teddy followed you and ate it instead. And finally, you left out the part where you didn't shut the gate behind you and the foxes killed half the chickens."

"And let us take the blame for it." Landon added.

Gordon stammered but couldn't find words. His story had unraveled and there was nothing left to say. There was no lie he could come up with they would believe. Realizing the ruse was up, he went for the one thing he could always fall back on. Righteous anger.

"Yes, I did it!" he exploded, yelling at them, trying to make them back down. "Ok, is that what you want to hear? Because I did and I'd do it again. I had to!"

"You aren't fit to lead!" he pointed at Cody and jabbed his finger at him. "You're letting these people, YOUR so-called people turn into a bunch of cavemen! Look at them! You're failing them in every way. We could be in nice houses with solar power and generators instead of this septic tank you call home!"

He opened his arms to all of them, imploring them to understand.

"I'm trying to save you from yourselves don't you see? I did it to open your eyes. We have to get out of here! All I asked for was a scouting team to be sent to my old home. It's safe, I know it is, but he won't even allow it. He wants to keep you here and you are all gonna die if you stay! Follow me! Let him stay if he wants, I'll show you a better life!" Spittle flew from his mouth as he ranted.

He pointed to the youngest, the triplets, then at Swan.

"Do you want them to grow up to be like her? Thinking they're an animal? She thinks she's part wolf now!"

No one came to Gordon's defense. No one nodded their heads in agreement. They sat there and stared, unmoved by his speech. He waited for someone to say or do something.

Cody looked at the tribe. Gordon had made his case; it was up to them to decide.

"Does anyone want Gordon to lead us?" Silence.

"Does anyone want to leave and go with him?" More silence.

"What do we do with him?" Cody asked.

Swan spoke first. "Kill him."

Donny slammed the shaft of his spear on the floor in agreement.

Gordon's eyes got big and he looked around fearfully. They were crazy. They would do it and he couldn't get away. He didn't even have his machetes with him, they had been forgotten in his room.

"Banishment." Murray said

There was a murmur of voices and a few heads nodded. No matter what Gordon had done or tried to do, they weren't murderers. They wouldn't hang him or cut his throat. Most of them, anyway.

Cody gave them a moment then said "Show of hands. Who wants death?"

Swan and Donny were the only two to raise them.

"Banishment?" he asked

Everyone else held their hands high.

"It is agreed, then. Effective immediately."

"But you can't." Gordon blurted. "It's getting dark. You have to wait until tomorrow at least. What am I going to eat?"

Cody turned to the pale faced boy who had tried to ruin everything. Had tried to kill Otis.

"Get out, Gordon." he said. "You have five minutes. If you're inside the fences after that, I'll let Swan and Donny have you."

They both smiled at him, toothy grins in blackened faces, and Swan drew her tomahawks slowly out of their holsters.

"What time is it, Murray?" she asked.

He was the only one that still wore a watch.

"It's five fifty-seven." he said.

"Tick tock, Gordy." Swan said and her smile grew more animalistic.

34

GORDON

Gordon ran from the painted faces. The grim ones and the smiling ones. He didn't even think to grab his jacket as he bolted for the front gate. When he rounded the corner of the snack shack, he skidded to a halt. There were dozens of the undead pawing at him through the bars and he suddenly remembered what his other job had been today. Spearing the zombies. It was starting to get dark and the savage ones were coming out for their evening meal. A coyote ragged viciously on a keening woman's leg and tore a chunk out, peeling skin away all the way up to her knee. It slunk off to feed in peace but he would be back for another bite. The red eyed possums were wallowing in from their hidey holes for the walking buffet. Their mouthful of sharp little teeth slashed and tore at the foul-smelling meal as they grew fat and lazy with such a plentiful supply.

Donny and Swan moved quiet as shadows but he saw them and their horrible companions move into position and watch him. Swan had Murrays watch in her hand and she tapped a finger on it, reminding him time was ticking away fast. The back gate was the only way out, there weren't any of the undead around it. Was there? He couldn't remember. He hadn't been paying any attention when he walked past it this afternoon. It was too far away, though. He'd never make it before they caught and killed him, he couldn't outrun them and he knew it. They knew it too by the looks of satisfaction on their faces. The others were coming out on the porch to watch. He wanted to pull his hair in frustration but there was no time.

"It's not fair!" he screamed. "It's not fair!"

"Should have done your job today." Swan said.

"Shouldn't have tried to kill Otis." Cody said, raising his voice to be heard over the screeching of the undead.

Gordon turned in circles, feeling trapped. Caged and about to be executed. He saw the golf carts by the nurse's station and ran for them. He could make it to the back gate with one of them, he could get away. Murray yelled a warning but it was too late, he was in the first one and had his foot to the floor. There was a crashing sound as he sped off and when he glanced over his shoulder, he saw dangling cords and solar panels smashing along the trail behind him. Murray had wired all the panels together to charge one battery at a time otherwise it took days of good sun just to get a few hours drive time. Gordon didn't slow, he only had minutes to cover miles. Wolf girl and Panther boy wouldn't be able to keep up with the cart but if they turned their animals loose, they probably could.

The clattering and banging of the panels finally stopped when the last cord broke and the cart seemed to pick up speed. He kept it floored and stayed on the trail that was the most direct route to the back gate. It was a service entrance that had long been out of use. The gravel driveway that led up to it off the main road was over grown and filled with potholes. It took him long minutes driving full out to make it through the winding paths and across the open field. The gazelle and antelope ran from the bouncing cart and he knew his five minutes were up. He knew the two biggest psychos of the tribe were hot on his trail, running like the wind with wolves and an inky black panther tracking his scent. The sun had dipped behind the spidery branches of the winter trees and it was getting dark fast. Cold, too. He topped a gentle rise and spotted the gate a quarter mile off and turned towards it. In the distance he thought he heard the howl of a wolf and he urged the cart to go faster.

He slid to a stop next to the gate and jumped out. It was locked. The fragging gate was locked! He'd never noticed the chain and padlock before but it must have always been there, it was old and well worn. He looked up and knew he'd never be able to climb over. He'd never make it through the barbed wire at the top.

Maybe the river. He could make it down to the river and swim around the end of the fence.

Right. And die of hypothermia. It was already down in the forties and would probably drop below freezing again tonight. He grabbed the gate and shook it, noticed the bottom was loose. The wires holding the chain link to the metal frame were rusted and some of them broken. He looked back over his shoulder and saw two dark figures top the rise. The animals could be anywhere in the tall grass, they might only be yards away. He ran for the cart and backed it up about thirty feet then slammed it into the forward gear. It picked up speed slowly but it hit the gate in the weak spot and punched its way through. The metal fencing dragged along the roof, ripping the last solar panel off and gouging holes in the plastic but he was on the driveway and picking up speed. He turned around and flipped them off, nearly plowed into a tree when he hit a big pothole and cursed as he swerved back on the road.

He kept the pedal mashed for nearly a half hour before it finally died. It had been getting slower and slower as the battery ran down and he kept it pointed north. He wasn't far enough away if they chased after him but he didn't think they would. Mr. High and Mighty had said he was banished. He was allowed to leave. He didn't say the psycho's would be allowed to hunt him down. They might do it on their own, though. He knew they hunted in the north woods but they'd be more concerned about fixing the fence than chasing him. It was full dark and freezing cold before he came across a house. He approached carefully, trying to stay quiet and hidden but his teeth kept wanting to chatter. The front door stood wide open and one of the windows was broken. That was a good sign, it meant nobody was home. Living or dead.

Gordon slipped inside and jammed a chair against the door to keep it closed. The house had been empty for months, and from the moonlight he saw evidence of breakfast remains on the counter. The empty packaging had never made it to the trash can. The owner had been eating a greasy breakfast, he guessed, from the moldy cast iron skillet left sitting on the stovetop. He wondered if there was something in the food, if that's what had started the outbreak. He was too exhausted to think about it and too afraid to stand there in front of the window where he might be seen. He found the bedroom and burrowed under the covers, shivering for a long time before he fell into fitful sleep. A deep, thundering boom that was miles off woke him in the middle of the night and he only wondered about it for a moment before dozing off again.

When he awoke, he was afraid. Afraid of being alone.

Afraid of those things that came out of nowhere, snarling and hungry. They were untiring and relentless with no capacity for mercy, no understanding of how important he was and his potential in this new world. He was afraid of being wrong. What if there weren't any survivors back home? What if it really was something in the food? No place would have been safe. He couldn't go back to Putnam; they would find him there and one of them would kill him. Or worse, let their animals tear him apart. He had to go north. Maybe he could find another golf cart, a gas powered one, or maybe a quad. He could ride one of those. His older cousin had one and let him drive it on occasion.

He was angry with all of them, all of the savage little kids who thought they were *one with their spirit animals* or whatever that loon Swan was always going on about. They had run him out and he'd only been trying to lead them to a better place. They'd get what was coming to them one of these days.

He crept around the house quietly once the sun was up and prowled through all the drawers. There were jackets in the closet and winter clothes in boxes on the shelves. He found a nickel-plated revolver in the nightstand. It took a minute to figure out how to open it but when he did, he found six bullets in the cambers. A full load. He practiced pulling it out of his belt in front of the full-length mirror and it didn't take long before he learned the trick of pulling it out quickly without snagging it on his clothes.

"What was that?" he asked the image facing him. "You think I should leave?"

He whipped out the pistol and shoved it into the face staring back at him.

"I don't think so Mr. High and Mighty. I think I'm taking over."

He whipped the gun to the left and said *pow, pow* then shoved it back towards the face. In his mind, the two wolves' heads exploded and Swan fell to her knees screaming in pain and sorrow.

"Shut up, bitch." he said coldly "or I'll blow the cubs away too."

"No!" she cried. "Please don't Gordon. I'm sorry. I'm so sorry. I'll do anything you ask, please don't hurt them."

Donny came from the shadows at him, his spear cocked and ready to throw and the panther leaped for him, a snarl on its lips. Gordon whipped the gun around and fanned the hammer faster than an eye blink. He sent a dozen rounds into the panther and Donny and everyone shrieked as they were sent flying across the room and crumpled to the floor. Buckets of blood poured out of them, painted the walls red and saturated the carpet. The rest of the animals fled away or cowered in the corners.

"Anybody else want to try me?" he asked as the smoke curled up from the barrel of his gun and framed his face.

Cody fell to his knees and the rest followed his lead. They bowed to him. He snapped his fingers at Harper and she came. Hesitant at first but she melted when he wrapped his arm around her and pulled her close.

"Things are going to be different around here." he said, "I'm running the show and if anybody gives me any trouble..."

Gordon aimed the gun right between the eyes of the image in the mirror then screamed and dropped it when it went off, shattering the glass and creating a deafening roar in the room. He snatched it off the carpet and ran. Gunshots attracted the undead, that's what Cody always said. Who knows, it might be true. He wasn't going to hang around and find out.

It was true.

Gordon heard them coming, heard their keening cries of hunger and got off the road. He went down the embankment and slipped behind a root bundle of a fallen tree near the icy waters of the Mississippi. Sound carried for a long way in the stillness of the new world and he heard them run by, flapping shoes slapping the pavement or bare feet worn down to bones making their own haunting sound. He waited for a long time after he heard something dragging itself along the asphalt but no more came. Just that half dozen or so. They had been close, maybe at the next farmhouse up the road so it was probably a good thing he'd fired off that shot. If he hadn't, they might have caught him by surprise. Gordon smiled despite the cold because the fates were taking care of him. They always smiled on a Lowery. He dragged himself out of the mud and cut through the woods until he found the road again and started the long trek north. A half mile later, he saw where the runners had come from. There was an old-fashioned country church and from the tattered clothes and shoes around the front door, it looked like they had been hanging around it for a while. He wondered if there were survivors inside and crept closer to listen. He heard them milling around and chanced a peep through a stained-glass window set high in the stone wall. It was full of the undead, scores of them, just bumping around the pews and stumbling over each other. There would be no shelter there. He snuck away and kept moving north.

Before the world went to hell Gordon and his friends would have ruined a punk like Cody. They would have ridiculed and scorned him for his Walmart clothes and his job shoveling dung. They would have made his life in high school miserable. What kind of people even thought about work until after at least four years of college? *Trash, that's what kind,* he thought with disdain. The platinum Visa still in his wallet had ensured Gordon never wanted for anything. That was the difference between him and them. They didn't know any better. They were content to wallow in the muck and eat garbage food and live like animals. He wasn't. He was a Lowery. He knew better. He knew living like a medieval peasant in some drafty old hovel wasn't his lot in life. He deserved better and he would have better.

He walked all day, eyes constantly searching for danger. He'd seen the pack of coyotes following him, always at a distance. He had been tempted to take a shot or yell at them but he didn't. He was afraid of what the noise might attract. The houses were few and far between on this desolate stretch of road and some of them had people inside. Dead people. He could see them wandering around, wearing a path in the rug. At one of the farms he found a small utility vehicle, some kind of John Deere ATV but it wouldn't start. The key was in it but nothing happened when he turned it. He couldn't tell if there were zombies in the house and he didn't want to chance it. He slept in the barn that night wrapped in a smelly horse blanket. The owner was in his stall but he didn't stink much, he'd probably been dead since right after the outbreak. Starvation most likely.

He found a house the next morning he knew was empty. The door was hanging on one hinge, a rotted body was on the porch and he could see brown stains of old blood on the walls. There was canned food in the cupboard and he ate cold creamed corn while staring at the mummified corpse with half its head blown off. He didn't find any more guns and there wasn't a car in the driveway. Whoever had lived here was long gone and from the looks of the place, they had left in a hurry. He found an oversized ski jacket that fit over his armor and slipped it on. It had a furry hood and would be warm if he had to spend a night outside.

He wasn't moving very fast, it seemed like he had to run off the road and hide all the time. Sometimes he'd heard a zombie or two shuffling along with no destination in mind. Sometimes it was the wind playing tricks on him. A few times it was the coyotes and he'd watched them tear into a crawling woman as she ignored them and kept moving south. They followed her, taking bite sized snacks. They weren't skinny coyotes, either. Not at all like those he'd seen in movies or in pictures. They were fat and waddling, stuffing themselves on the easy meals.

He found a bicycle with air in the tires and thought long and hard before throwing a leg over it. It would be faster but he might ride up on a horde of them. When he was walking, he could stop and listen often. On the bike, it might be too late and he knew once they got the scent, once they started chasing something, they never stopped. He would have to ride until he got there. No breaks, no stops. Just keep pedaling unless they would catch him. Not worth the risk, he decided. It might take him another day or two at the rate he was going but at least he would make it there alive. He would be welcomed home, back to his people. His tribe.

The closer he got, the more devastation he saw, the less confident he became that he would find the welcoming gates of Smiths Landing standing firm against the outside world. If the infection had been in the food like he was beginning to suspect then no one would have been safe. When the long stretches of farmland and woods became more populated with houses his pace slowed to a crawl. He darted from corner to corner, watched and waited and listened before running to the next. He would never admit it but he had learned a lot from the little kids at the Park.

His months of forced labor had hardened him. His chubby cheeks and belly fat were gone. He'd learned how the undead moved and "thought". He knew they were stupid, felt no pain and would never, ever, ever give up if they caught your scent. As much as he hated them, he was afraid to be without the snotty little brats. He was afraid to be alone. They were good fighters, they could have protected him and if he had convinced them to come, even if the Landing was over run, they could have cleaned it out.

The sky was overcast and snow flurries danced in the wind. He was cold, hungry, afraid and full of self-pity. He hadn't had a decent meal in days and eating stale crackers and cans of nearly frozen vegetables had his stomach cramping. He'd seen nothing but empty houses and wandering dead since he left. No smoke from fires, no human noises, no people or cars. This had been a mistake. He should have believed Cody when he said the rest of the world was dead. Maybe he shouldn't have tried to kill off the animals, at least the twins whipped up some pretty good meals. His fingers and toes were numb. He'd been standing as still as a shadow for over an hour while a group of twenty or thirty dead things shambled aimlessly down the street. They were moving a lot slower now that the cold weather had set in but when they wanted to, he knew they could still run. Easily outrun him and drag him down. He had to wait until the last dragging crawler was long gone before he dared move. His guts roiled and he was afraid he was going to mess himself before it was safe to drop his pants. He snuck into an empty house and barely made it to the bathroom in time. He sat there shivering for a long time and when he was finally finished, there was no toilet paper.

He wanted to cry. He was going to die out here all because of those damn kids who wouldn't see reason. Days of walking and nights of no sleep had left him too exhausted to be mad. Too fatigued to care about anything anymore. Constantly on alert, always listening and looking had left his nerves frayed. He didn't know what he would do if Smiths Landing was crawling with the undead and the closer he got, the more sure he became that it would be. Everything was dead. Only he and the kids had survived. Even if he could make it back to the Safari Park without getting killed or dying of hunger, they would never take him in. Maybe he could beg. Maybe he could promise he'd never doubt Cody again. Maybe he could be their slave and do whatever they said. Anything was better than this. Tears and snot started streaming down his face and he was ready to give up. Ready to curl up and die. He sat down on a musty couch in the living room, pulled a comforter over him and sobbed himself to sleep. Cody had won. Cody had broken him.

35

SMITH'S LANDING

Gordon woke up with a scream as something bit into him. It was full dark and a thousand needle sharp teeth ripped at his hand. He sprang up and flung the thing off, heard it slam against the wall and felt his flesh rip away. He stumbled over another furry body that had latched on to his leg and ran for the door. In the moonlight he saw them; a grin of opossums with their beady red eyes and rat like tails chased him out of the house. They were attacking him like he was one of the undead, looking for an easy meal. He stomped at the one on his leg, heard it squeal and felt the bones crush under his boot. Gordon ran. He ran blindly and they gave chase. They smelled his blood and they were as frenzied as the zombies. He didn't have time to think, he could hear their skittering claws on the pavement coming for him. He sprinted for blocks, unsure of where he was going, he only knew he had to get away. They were worse than the undead, they didn't stop after a few bites. They would eat him alive one chunk at a time.

He rounded a corner, out of breath, lost, his hand spasming in pain and unsure where to go. There was a faint glow on a hilltop off in the distance and his eyes got wide. He realized where he was and his heart soared with renewed hope. He was at the base of the knoll where the exclusive golf course community of Smith's Landing had been built. He had made it and that was electric lights burning bright like a beacon calling for survivors. All of his uncertainty, fear and doubts fell away and he almost laughed out loud. He had made it home!

He easily outpaced the little monsters chasing him and slowed to a jog. As he got nearer, he heard music blaring and the screams of the undead at the front gate. That wasn't what he was expecting, the gate guard or the security patrols should have been on duty and keeping things under control. He dashed into the little strip mall just outside the decorative brick walls flanking the winding driveway that led to the gated community and took cover behind the Starbucks. The front gate was choked with the undead, they were ten deep trying to force their way in. Hip hop music blasted from speakers and a bonfire was burning brightly in the middle of road just inside the gates. He heard the revving of dirt bikes and the whooping of people having a party. A couple on an ATV zoomed up and down the streets driving the undead into a frenzy.

A slow smile crept across his face. His friends and neighbors were gathering all the undead, pulling in whatever ones were left in town so survivors could sneak around to the back entrance to get in. It was a great idea. He would be able to get to the rear without worrying about running into any of the undead. He swelled a little with pride. His people didn't cower and hide. They were bold as brass.

He tore off a piece of his shirt to wrap his bleeding

hand, forgot about his hunger, his cramping stomach and his utter exhaustion. He had made it and he'd been right all along. His people were living like the kings they were and he was about to be welcomed home like a returning son. His father was the richest and most influential of all the other families in the Landing and he would take his rightful place as his successor. It would have been nice to have the kids with him. He would rub their noses in it for doubting him and with his family and friends to back him up, they could have killed the animals easily, stripped them of their weapons and made them his servants. He might have to go back and get Harper. After he got inside and got established, he could lead an army back down to the Park. He'd show them. He'd teach them that you didn't treat a Lowery like they had. The thought gave him pleasure as he slipped down the side streets and worked his way through the woods to the back of the compound. He picked up a tail, some moaning undead thing that was dragging a broken leg. He tried to outrun her but he was too tired. He stayed a good way ahead of her, it wasn't hard, and all he had to do was get to the gate.

He paralleled the tall fence running along the golf course that kept stray balls in and riff raff out. He was shivering again when he reached the back entrance as it neared midnight. The long trek had sapped him of the last of his strength. All he wanted was to get inside, get back home and go to sleep in his own bed. When he approached the gate, a couple of men were standing around a burn barrel with rifles slung on their shoulders and warming their hands over the flames. Gordon sighed heavily with relief. The military were here and everything was going to be fine. He had made it.

"Hey." he yelled when they didn't see him walk up.

Both turned and nearly dropped the bottle they'd been passing back and forth between them. Gordon frowned. They shouldn't be drinking on guard duty, even he knew that. They should be alert to protect the people inside. To protect him.

"What?" asked one of them.

Gordon stood there for a moment, completely nonplussed. What did they mean *what*?

"Let me in." he said and looked over his shoulder. The old woman was still a long way off but she kept coming, slow and steady like the ticking of a clock.

"What's the password?" one of them said and took a swig from the bottle.

"I don't know, I just got here." Gordon said. "Let me in, there's zombies out here."

"No password, no entry." The first guard said.

"I live here." Gordon was starting to get pissed. "My father owns the biggest house in the Landing. I'm a Lowery, open the damn gate."

"oooooowwwwww." The second one said. "Well ain't you special. Take a hike punk, before I call up some more of the undead to chase you off. Unless you got something to trade, something we want, we ain't taking in any freeloaders."

Gordon couldn't believe it. He had come all this way only to find out some raiders had taken over. The zombie with the dragging leg was closing in, he could hear her scrapping along the cobblestones.

"Wait a minute." the first guard said. "You say your name is Lowery? You related to Richard Lowery?"

"He's my cousin." Gordon said, grasping at hope. "We're really close, best friends even. He's here? He'll want to see me."

"Yeah, he's here." the first guard said. "He kind of runs the place. I don't remember him mentioning you, though. You sure you're not just making things up? Are you sure you're not somebody's husband come back to get their wife or daughter or something?"

The man wavered on his feet and passed the bottle back to his buddy as Gordon shook the bars. The woman was getting closer.

"Do I look old enough to have a kid or even be married?" he nearly shouted. "Let me in, I'm Gordon Lowery! I live here!"

"Okay, okay, don't get all excited." the man said and weaved his way over.

He was just a kid, not more than sixteen or seventeen. He fumbled the keys and the woman started to keen, she could smell the blood dripping from Gordons hand.

"Oh shut up." the second guard said and shoved his rifle through the bars and pulled the trigger as fast as he could.

He emptied the magazine as Gordon ducked for cover and the other guard covered his ears.

"Dammit, Flame! Quit wasting ammo and let me know before you go shooting." the first guard said, mumbled under his breath and finally found the right key.

The woman was still coming. If any of the thirty bullets hit her, she wasn't bothered by them. The bone of her broken leg drug on the stones, the skin and muscle long since worn away. It made a noise like fingernails on chalkboard and Gordon wanted to scream at the man to hurry up but was afraid to distract him. The instant he turned the key and loosed the lock from the chain, Gordon shoved and sprang inside. Both men fell and the magazine he'd been trying to reload bounced away in the dark. Gordon shoved the gate closed just as the gray-haired thing slammed into it and reached for them with searching fingers and gnashing teeth. He breathed a sigh of relief and the fear flooded out of him. He was safe. This was a scenario he was used to from the Park. Reaching arms, hungry faces and a spear in his hands. He grabbed the guard's AR-15 off the ground and thrust the bayonet into her belly, slicing all the way to the breastbone. Rancid coils of guts spilled out and the men scuttled away to get out of the slop zone.

"Gross. Why'd you do that" one of them said, gagging on the smell.

The smell didn't bother Gordon, he had gotten used to it from all the hours he'd spent at the gate doing this very thing. The woman started to shriek at him so he thrust the blade into her voice box and twisted. The snapping sounds of cartilage was louder than the splashing of fresh, black blood and she was quiet. He was almost enjoying himself, paying her back for all the fear her kind had caused him over the last few days. He jabbed out her eyes and they ran down her withered, old cheeks.

"You're sick, man. Why don't you just kill it?"

"If you knew how to shoot, she'd be dead a hundred yards from here." Gordon replied and tossed him the gun. He was feeling more like his old self than he had in months. He was home, he was safe and his family was in charge.

"Where's Richard?"

"Up at headquarters." the first guard said then added, a little unsure of himself as he held out his hand. "Uh, they call me Smoke and that's Flame. Say, you won't tell him about this will you? We were just goofing, you know. We wouldn't have left you out there."

Gordon let the boy's hand hang in the air, refusing to shake it. A little trick he'd seen his dad do on occasion. It set the mood and let them know who was in charge.

"Yeah." the second man said. "We didn't know you were family. Honest. We don't want trouble with him."

Smoke let his hand drop and they both tried to sober up. Gordon wondered why they were afraid of Richard. He was a bully; he might dump your lunch tray at school but these guys seemed genuinely afraid of him. Like maybe he would do something a little more than embarrass you in front of your classmates.

"I'll keep quiet." Gordon said. "But you owe me. You understand? You owe me."

They both nodded and apologized again as he turned and walked off, wondering what the heck had just happened.

Gordon considered things as he made the long trek across the over grown golf course back to his house. Those two idiots at the back gate had nearly let a zombie inside. If he would have been on guard duty, he never would have opened the gate until it was dead. Hell, they didn't even check him for bites. He needed to have a talk with Richard. The undead were stacking up at the front gate and pretty soon, they'd be able to climb on each other and make it over the top. Mr. High and Mighty was always going on about that, said that's why they had to keep the numbers down. Gordon hadn't minded that job, though. He liked to see how many different ways he could kill them and see how bad he could butcher them before they finally collapsed. More than once he'd pictured Cody or Donny's face when he stabbed them with a pitchfork, twisted the tines and pulled ropes of guts out to spill on the ground.

He stood outside the house and watched from the darkness for a long time, his hunger and fear forgotten. It was lit up bright, the music was blasting and all he saw was teenagers drinking and smoking. No adults at all and no one wore armor. They had on their hockey jerseys or wore designer clothes. It was a party, just like any other party before the fall except this one was a little wilder, a little louder and a little meaner.

Gordon watched through the giant windows, not feeling the cold. He had been alone for weeks when he was trapped in the old military surplus store. He might as well have been alone in the Park since everyone hated him. He didn't want to repeat the same mistakes and if he wasn't careful, Richard would be making him the butt of his jokes again. Most of the kids looked older than him, they were seniors in high school and college kids but they looked soft. He hated the thought of it but the stupid brats in the park could have whooped any of their asses. They'd been living it up and partying since the outbreak and he would bet they'd never known a moment of discomfort. They had everything he had wanted all along but now he saw. Now he realized it made them weak. He couldn't be seen as weak, he wouldn't become a servant to them. He was a Lowery and his rightful place was next to Richard. They would share power like their fathers had. They must never know he'd been a scared little boy, jumping at every noise and so afraid he'd pissed his pants. They could never know how he'd been run out the park, blubbering and crying and afraid.

His uncles' place was a mirror image of theirs, the two brothers had them built at the same time to the same specs, each one dwarfing the other million-dollar homes. They were ostentatious and larger than life, much like their owners.

He didn't really care much for his cousin. They played together as kids but Richard was three years older. That was a lot when they reached high school. Gordon was still playing with action figures while Richard was sleeping with every girl that would let him. And some that wouldn't, if rumors were true.

Their fathers were brothers, heirs to a large financial portfolio that had its beginnings back in the prohibition era. Their grandfather, Gordons great grand dad, had learned quickly that paying the right men the right bribe would make sure his loads of booze coming out of Canada didn't get intercepted. He was one of Al Capones suppliers and the money pile kept growing and growing. By the time President Roosevelt ended prohibition in 1933, Ezra Lowery had already moved his money over into real estate. He snapped up properties cheap during the great depression and after the War, the Lowery Family became one of the richest in Southern Minnesota.

His and Richards step mothers were both trophy wives, more than twenty years younger than their husbands. The brothers were in constant competition and never let a chance go by to one up each other. Gordon's mom had passed away under suspicious circumstances but the grand jury could find no wrong doings on his dads' part and he was remarried six months later. Richards' dad, not to be outdone, had divorced his wife and his shrewd lawyers had made sure she didn't get a dime. His new mom was twenty-two, only a few years older than him. The new wives were gold diggers who knew their place and knew how to keep the men happy. They had won the lottery; they knew it and would do whatever it took to stay in their men's good graces. In return, they had huge allowances and spent their days shopping and looking down their noses at the working class. The brothers had been born into money and grew that money by buying and selling companies, real estate developments and stock trading. They were ridiculously wealthy, and their ventures had increased their wealth to the point that none of their children would ever have to lift a finger to make ends meet.

Richard was a jock and a bully. He was famous for his parties and popular with the girls. He was the goalie on his high school hockey team and a minor celebrity in the Minnesota town where he played as well as the star pitcher on the baseball team. Tall with a bodybuilder's physique, rumors of illegal steroid use lingered around him but were ignored by coaches and faculty. He'd taken them to State three years in a row.

He had a reputation as a trouble maker and was always in some predicament with the law. Poaching, drag racing the Dodge Hellcat he'd received on his eighteenth birthday, possession of stolen goods, drug trafficking and the list went on. The rules didn't apply to him and Daddy's money always made the problems go away, including two different underage girls who claimed Richard was the father of their children. The claims were silenced when the large checks cleared the bank and Richard carried on. He was invincible on the streets and a hero on the ice. Before the outbreak, he'd been courted by all of the prestigious colleges, playing them against one another to see who promised the largest compensations if he blessed them with his athletic prowess.

Gordon stripped out of the colorful ski jacket he'd scrounged, tossed it aside and adjusted his armor. His jeans were ripped from the possum and his bloody hand was wrapped in a rag. His hair was a lot longer than it had been the last time he'd seen Richard and he was a lot thinner. Working like a slave at the Park had toned him and put on muscle. He'd never appreciated it before; he was always the laziest and the slowest and the weakest of the kids but here it was different. From the looks of things, they'd been drunk and stoned since day one. They looked sloppy and soft. He'd bet money they'd never been outside the wall. Here he could be a bad ass. He adjusted the gun in his belt as he considered the story he would tell.

36

GORDON

Gordon found his cousin Richard sitting under an outdoor propane heater by a covered swimming pool, a bottle of Jack Daniels in one hand and his other swatted at the ass of a girl who danced drunkenly around him. A blue haired girl sat on a stool beside him. Tattoos covered nearly every inch of her skin and she had oversized gauges that formed large holes in the lower earlobes. She was tattooing a hockey mask with a joint in its mouth on Richards' heavily muscled exposed chest.

Richard took a long swig of Jack and looked up at the newcomer. He spit liquor and laughed as he recognized the disheveled boy standing in front of him. "Gordy!" Richard started making oinking sounds. The crowd gathered around the pool laughed with him as Gordon's face tightened.

Gordon hated that nickname. It came from some stupid kids' movie Richard had watched too many times about a talking pig. Gordon was heavy when he was younger and Richard would oink every time he saw him. He'd terrorized Gordon and his other cousins whenever they were together.

Gordon wasn't laughing along like he usually did and Richard took a long hard look at him. He was dirty, trail worn and wearing plastic armor that had seen some real-world abuse. A bloody rag was wrapped around his hand and he was lean and muscled. He wasn't chubby Gordy anymore. Not a little piggy. In fact, he looked a little intimidating.

"Take a break Tasha," he told the tattooed girl, pushed her away and stood.

"Sasha," she corrected him. Richard waved her off, threw his arm around Gordon and offered him the bottle. He motioned to a dreadlocked guy to turn the music down.

Gordon took it, pulled a long swig and felt the burn as the liquor made its way to his stomach.

"You look like hell, man." Richard said. "Welcome home, cuz."

The drunken teens wandered outside to see what was going on then turned their attention to Richard.

"Everybody, this is my cousin Gordon." Richard said. "We thought he was lost but now he's found."

Cheers went up and one drunk girl flashed her chest at him. Catcalls and laughter echoed in the night as he was welcomed by the group.

He was introduced to the dozen or so guys and the four girls that were at the party. They had ridiculous names like Jester, Maggot, Trish the Fish, Pole, Gargoyle that Gordon didn't try to make sense of. The ATV rider he'd seen from the front entrance and the girl with him were Skull and Squirrel. *Cause she's nuts*, Richard had whispered. They were all either high or drunk or a combination of both.

"You'll meet the others later." Richard said. "The light weights are already passed out."

Moaning drew Gordon's attention to the covered swimming pool.

"What's with that?" he asked and Richard made a flourish with his hands then hit the remote to retract the cover.

Wandering around the bottom of the dry pool were four of the undead. Only one of them could stand, the others were mangled and torn so badly they could only crawl and snarl at the teens gathered around the rim above them. Empty liquor bottles and cigarette butts littered the bottom of the pool. Raucous laughter erupted as the guy called Gargoyle stepped to the end of the diving board, unzipped his fly and whizzed a golden arc on the zombies.

"Battle trophies." Richard said and as the music cranked back up he pulled Gordon away from the crowd. He was stumbling drunk and kept his arm around his shoulder for balance and support.

"Where you been man? Honestly, I hadn't given you much thought, figured you were like the rest of them outside the gate, just moaning and wandering around looking for a handout." he laughed at his own joke.

Gordon told his story leaving out the bad parts, exaggerating the good parts and made himself out to be a double-crossed hero. A handful of the more sober teens came over to listen, Gordon was the first outsider they'd met. As it turned out, the fires and lights weren't a beacon to help others, to show them a safe haven. They were just burning stuff and as far as the lights, how were they supposed to party without lights? As they listened and passed around a bottle, he told them how he had saved a bunch of kids from a horde. He led them out of town, fighting the undead the whole way and found them a sanctuary at the animal park

"I lost a lot of them." Gordon said with feigned remorse,

his voice dropping so they had to lean in to listen. "It got real bloody and I couldn't save them all."

There were murmurs of approval and they raised toasts to him.

"I showed them how to live." he continued. "I had them start training the animals but one of them got jealous. A punk named Cody. White trash. I had a lion who was a savage, a huge beast, but he poisoned him. Killed him because he wanted my girl."

Gordon went on to describe the battle that ensued where they turned their animals loose on him and without his Lion, he had no choice but to flee. He told them about Harper and the other girls and the teens were really interested in them.

"We should go get them." somebody said. "Get Gordon's girl back and the rest of them, too. Teach that jerk Cody a lesson."

"They sound a little young." Gargoyle said.

"Old enough to bleed, old enough to breed." Maggot said and everyone snickered.

Gordon heaped praise on Richard for all he had accomplished and spread the compliments around to all the others. As he spun his tale and listened to their responses, he realized they had been drunk and stoned since the outbreak. They never sobered up, they were aimless and didn't have any plans for the future. They were partying at the end of the world and from everything he'd learned during his time at the park, he knew it couldn't last. If this bastion of hope were to survive, there would have to be some changes made. The way they looked at him, with respect and a little bit of awe, made him start thinking he could be their leader. First, he had to get Harper. She'd see he was right and she could help him turn this community into something better, not just a drunken free for all quickly running out of supplies. It could be a great place if he was in charge.

Everyone nodded along to the story, interrupting to raise drinks to Gordon or spit curses at the ones who had wronged one of their own.

"Somebody needs to teach those kids a lesson." Richard said as he wound up the tale of how he fought his way north to find them. "We could really use some new girls. If you haven't noticed, we have a serious shortage of female companionship. We could use some fresh meat around here for me and the boys if you know what I mean. Tell me more about this harem that bastard Cody is trying to keep all to himself."

Gordon described each of the girls, detailing their looks and ages, exaggerating a little on the size of their boobs. The rest of the survivors joined them and listened raptly as he spun a story of how good it would be if they captured all of them and made them do all the hard work.

"They could keep this place clean." he said. "They could fetch water and cook and whatever else we wanted them to do."

More nods, more drunken cheers.

"You mean like slaves?" Tasha or Sasha asked

"Nah, they'd be like hired help." Richard said. "Instead of money, they get paid with a roof over their head and protection from the zombies. Sounds like a fair trade."

"And like any good servant, we can do whatever we want and they can't say a damn thing about it." Skull said to the laughter of the others.

He and his father were known for forcing themselves on their cleaning staff. Mr. Abelson only hired illegal aliens who had no choice but to comply or have immigration called on them.

The party kicked into high gear when one of the girls brought out a bottle of tramadol stolen from someone's medicine cabinet. She crushed it on the coffee table and they gathered around to snort long lines of it.

Richards step mom and another one of his crew came out of a room and joined them. He had a big smirk on his face as she adjusted her mini skirt, pulling it down to cover most of her thighs. She grabbed a bottle of whiskey and gargled then swallowed. A moment later, Gordon's step mom came out of the same room, spotted the lines on the coffee table and made a bee line for them.

Richard winked at the stupefied look on Gordons face and explained it away. "They didn't want to leave."

"But that's Misty. She's your mom." Gordon said. "And my mom, too."

"No, they're not, Gordy." Richard said harshly. "They were both gold diggers and they still are. Hell, both of them are young enough to be our dads' kids, not their wives. They made their choice, they're free to leave anytime if they don't like it."

"That's not a choice." Gordon said.

"You're still young." Richard said and gave his shoulder a squeeze. "You'll figure it out. There aren't any rules anymore."

"Where *is* your dad?" Gordon asked. "He wasn't out of town on business, was he?"

Richard pointed to one of the creatures crawling along the bottom of the pool.

"He was one of men who tried to take over. Tried to tell us what to do. Tried to lay down some rules. There are no more rules, Gordy. You can do whatever you want to whoever you want. That's the new reality."

He hit the remote on the pool cover to hide them away again then walked over and to grab his step mom. He pulled her towards the bedroom and she followed along, wiping the dust from her nose.

Gordon mingled, stayed mostly sober and when Richard came out of the bedroom an hour later, he learned why there were only a bunch of jocks and a few girls left inside the gates.

Most of Richard and his teammates had been passed out at his house after a wild post-game party. The mansion sat well off the road and had its own gate at the end of a long driveway. Decorative shrubbery hid the fencing and the undead ran past it, following the sounds of screams or racing engines. The outbreak started early as it did everywhere else with breakfast and it didn't take long for most of the gated community to be affected. The first minutes of the outbreak had neighbors stepping outside to see what the noise was all about or rushing to aid bleeding neighbors. Those staring in horror out of the windows and trying to call the authorities were seen and the growing horde crashed through to bite and rend and add to their numbers. Some managed to get in their cars and flee with hundreds of undead chasing them. The sensors kept the exit gate open until most of the zombies were gone and before any of the teenagers woke late in the afternoon, the battle for Smiths Landing was over.

It took the hungover teens a long time to come to grips with what had happened but Richard rallied them, kept them in booze and drugs for days until it became their new normal.

Wake up whenever. Take a pill or two to dull the pain.

Bloody Mary's for breakfast and start the party again. When the electricity went out the generator kicked on automatically and the party continued for another week until the fuel was gone. After that, they had to be careful and turn off some of the electrical things like the hot tub and space heaters. The solar panels couldn't keep up with the demand.

When the booze and his pill supply ran out, some of the undead were still inside the fences of the Landing and outside the gates of his home. They took his fathers guns and killed them. When they started raiding the other houses for more party supplies, they found other survivors huddling inside. Men who tried to shame them for their behavior and tell them what to do. Men who tried to take the guns away and demanded they stop pillaging everyone's house. It was so long ago Richard claimed he could barely remember it; the whole incident was a hazy half memory. He didn't know who fired first, it may have even been an accident, but when the shooting was done, a dozen people were dead. They drank more, smoked more and took more pills to erase the ugly afternoon from their minds. Their blood lust was up and they took the women by force. Outnumbered and outgunned, they ran the men out of the gates. The women and girls who stayed could have followed, they weren't guarded or kept in chains, but chose not to. They grabbed a bottle and joined the party. It was better than being dead.

The houses were loaded with food and valuables. Prescription meds and stashes of weed and cocaine the upstanding citizens of Smith's Landing hid from their neighbors behind closed doors. Liquor cabinets were filled with the best booze. Freezers were full of steak and lobsters, all there for the taking. During a moment of clarity, Richard had organized a gathering of all the food and made sure the perishables were stored in freezers of the homes with solar panels. They had a lot when the job was finished. Entire rooms full of canned and boxed goods, deep freezers full of meat and case after case of booze.

Richards house remained as their main residence, there was plenty of room for them and it had more solar panels than all the others, except for maybe Gordon's place. With the big banks of batteries charged from the sun providing the power, running water and hot showers were available for all. From the unwashed smell, Gordon didn't think most of them were taking advantage of the opportunity. He would kill for a hot shower. The memory of weeks of washing in cold well water from the pump in the kitchen of the old house were still fresh in his head.

The party was winding down near dawn and as Gordon was rewrapping his hand with a fresh bandage Richard wandered over and sat beside him.

. "Who's in charge?" Gordon asked.

"Nobody, everybody, hell who cares," Richard said, shrugging his shoulders. "You wanna be in charge Gordy?"

Gordon bristled at the nickname. "Don't call me that."

"Ok, bro, don't be so uptight. You wanna be in charge? You wanna run this band of miscreants and delinquents?" Richard laughed.

"Somebody has to." Gordon said. "You can't keep this up."

"Why not?" Richard asked. "It's working out just fine. We got you here, now. A zombie killing badass. When we run out of booze, you can get us more."

"Maybe." Gordon said "But there are other things to consider. Where is the water coming from? When is it going to run out?"

"You worry too much but that's okay. Maybe we need that. Hey everybody!" Richard shouted to get their attention. "Gordon is in charge!"

Tired whistles and whoops rang out as everyone cheered and then they went back to whatever it was they were doing. For most of them, it was going back to sleep.

37

GORDON

Everyone in the Landing agreed they needed to go and teach the brats a lesson and get themselves some new servants but no one wanted to actually do it. *Maybe tomorrow, man,* was the answer whenever he brought it up. They were too busy having fun and besides, there were zombies out there. They had everything they needed and so far, no one had dared venture outside the fences. It was too risky. The quads were fast on the roads, pretty good in the fields but there were long miles of deep woods along the road. They couldn't plow their way through the underbrush and fallen trees. If they met a horde, they might be in trouble. A big pack of four wheelers couldn't get turned around fast enough. They would get overrun.

Gordon was a few years younger than the rest of them but they quickly learned that he was a stone-cold killer. He went out alone and speared nearly all of the undead at the front gate and took it upon himself to patrol the perimeter fence. A tree had toppled over and a whole section was down. They had been lucky all the undead were attracted to the bonfire and hadn't wandered along the fence line.

Using one of the side by side four wheelers and its winch, he and Skull made the repairs. Gordon gained their wary respect and Richard let him do whatever he wanted. The kid was taking care of things and as long as he didn't get too big for his britches, he would let him think he was running the show. It was easier to have him voluntarily do all the work than try to get somebody to sober up long enough.

Richard didn't trust Gordon completely. He still remembered him as the spoiled, overweight tattletale who would say anything to get what he wanted. He wasn't sure how much of the story Gordy told was true but the kid had got hard, that was obvious. He wasn't the same whiney brat. Before he committed his men to an all-out assault, especially if they really did have trained attack animals, he wanted one of his guys to check it out. He wanted a second opinion.

One of his best men was Smoke, the only guy he trusted to watch the back gate. He'd been worried about some of the angry residents that he'd kicked out coming back with guns but so far they hadn't. He didn't have much ammo left, not enough to have a gun battle with anyone. The whole development had been advertised as an environmentally friendly green community and had attracted a lot of progressive families. Richard didn't care one way or another how anyone voted but wished there had been a few more NRA members living here. At least there would have been more guns. All they found were a few pistols and the rifles from his dad and uncle. It had been weeks since he'd run them out though and they were probably dead by now. It was probably safe to stop guarding the rear entrance. Richard told Smoke to sober up and go with Gordy, he wanted a full report.

The ride down to the park only took a few hours on the

quad. It could easily go fifty miles an hour on the clear sections. Gordon had been full of bravado when they left but the closer they got, the more the old doubts and fears crept back in. He couldn't let it show, couldn't display weakness in front of the older boy. He had his nickel-plated revolver; he wasn't afraid of the undead. They were pretty slow, the cold weather seemed to be affecting them and, in a worst-case scenario, he could always shoot Smoke and let them attack him while he got away.

They parked a good distance from the back gate and snuck up through the woods. He knew Swan and Donny hunted at night so the only thing they had to worry about was the roaming fence checker. They waited and watched for a few minutes and when no one came from either direction Gordon pulled the wire snips from his pocket and cut the retaining clips down low. They slid under the wire, stayed crouched in the tall grass and ran across the field. Smoke was amazed at the gazelles and antelopes who raised their heads and watched them.

"I didn't even know this place was here." he said. "They let the all the animals run loose?"

"Yeah." Gordon replied "There's bears and panthers and wolves so keep low and keep quiet. We can see the main house from that hill up there. That's as close as I want to get."

They stood by a lone tree on the rise and shaded their eyes, trying to see the house a half mile distant. As they watched, the Twins came into view riding their polar bears. They had come from their river traps with a basket of fish.

"No fragging way." Smoke said. "They set those things on you?"

It took Gordon a moment to remember the lie he'd told then nodded his head.

"Right after they killed my lion." he said, "And look, see that crazy looking girl with the wolves? She's the worst of all of them. She's going to be my personal slave. I'm going to beat that bitch every day."

Donny followed her out of the house with Yewan padding beside him.

"I don't know, man." Smoke said. "We can't fight against that. I mean, look at them. I'm sorry they turned on you Gordon but they'd wipe us out."

One of wolves raised his head and sniffed the air then looked in their direction.

"Get down!" Gordon hissed and they both dropped below the waist high grass.

"Think they saw us?"

"I don't know." Gordon said, "But let's get out of here."

They ran hunched over and tried to stay out of sight.

"We're going to pass on this one." Smoke said as they neared the fence. "I'm telling Richard he's going to have to do without these girls."

When they stood upright both were surprised to see Harper examining the fence where they'd cut their way in. She whirled and had her blade in her hand while they both stared at her in shock. Bert stomped a hoof at them and while Smoke gaped skyward at the towering giraffe, Gordon pulled his pistol and aimed it at her.

"Drop it." he said, and a smile crept across his lips. "Or I'll shoot."

What kind of good luck was this? His Harper had appeared like a gift wrapped present.

"I'll chop your face off before you can pull the trigger." Harper spat.

Smoke glanced over at Gordon. "This was your girlfriend?" he asked.

Harper snorted in derision.

"That's what lazy ass has been telling you?" she asked, "Can't wait to hear what else he's said. I wouldn't date that back stabbing piece of crap if he were the last person on earth."

Gordons face reddened as Smoke looked back and forth between them.

"She just needs to be disciplined." he said, and moved the gun over to aim it at Bert then watched as her eyes got big.

"I said drop it." his grin came back, "Or I'll shoot."

"Don't Gordon." she said and color drained from her face because she knew he was capable of it. He would do it just out of meanness. "Please."

She lowered the blade, let it drop to the ground and raised her hands.

"You're coming with us." he announced, "Cuff her, Smoke."

"A feisty one. I think I like it." he said, and unhooked the handcuffs he wore dangling from his belt loop.

Harper tried to pull away as he neared.

"Knock it off." Gordon yelled and took a step closer. "I'll blow him away and you know I will."

Something moved in his peripheral vision and he looked back at the giraffe just in time to see its big head swinging right for him. Gordon didn't have time to react before he felt a sledgehammer blow slam into him. The gun went off as it flew out of his hand and he went sprawling backward to bounce off the fence some eight feet in the air. Smoke started to yell something but the words were abruptly cut off when Bert kicked out with a twelve-inch hoof nearly as big as his head. There was a nasty, wet crunching sound as a surprised face turned into splintered bone and bloody gristle. Smoke's neck snapped as his head was nearly knocked completely off. He was dead before he crumpled to the ground in a boneless heap.

Yewan and the wolves arrived first with Donny and Swan close behind. Gordon was trying to suck in air but all he could pull in were tiny little gasps. If he hadn't been wearing his armor, his ribcage would have been splintered like matchsticks. He grasped at the fence to pull himself up but a snarling face inches from his froze him in place. He eased back down and Lucy's growl was replaced by Swans. She looked wilder than ever and her teeth were bared. Gordon was afraid she might snap and bite his nose off.

"I didn't..." he started to say but her growl grew more insistent and Zero moved to within an inch of his face. The warm air of their snarls blew across his cheeks and he closed his eyes. He was going to die, ripped to shreds by the wolf girl and her pack. His bladder let go and Swan jumped back.

"Gross, Gordy." she spat, "You're a disgusting pig."

"Call them off, Swan." Cody said when he came up, panting from the long run.

A gentle hand on their necks was all it took and the wolves went over to sniff at the dead boy.

"Donny, can you and Vanessa help Harper catch Bert. The shot scared him, I don't want him to hurt himself."

Donny nodded and took off on a path to intercept the spooked giraffe. Vanessa swung herself onto Ziggy's back and they raced away to cut him off before he slammed full speed into a fence or broke a leg in the marshy areas near the river.

"What do you want me to do?" Swan asked.

"Stay here and look scary." Cody replied.

She smiled, pulled a tomahawk and squatted in front of Gordon.

Cody saw the handcuffs and tossed them to her. She snapped one end around Gordon's wrist, the other through the chain link. Cody scanned the horizon for the polar bears and Otis. When they'd heard the gunfire, they'd ran the other way.

"Big babies." he muttered.

He saw Bert's tall head disappear over the rise and sighed. It might be a while before they got him calmed down. The bears were probably inside the house, they'd be fine. He turned back to Gordon and crossed his arms.

"I told you I would let Swan and Donny carry out judgement if they caught you inside the fences." he said, "I think your five minutes were up a long time ago."

Gordon struggled to his feet, and grimaced at the pain. He felt like he had busted ribs, armor or not.

"They made me." he blurted out. The first words that came to mind. "Him and his buddies."

He pointed at Smoke who couldn't defend himself. Once the lie was out, Gordon knew he had to sell it before Harper came back. He had to get them to let him go before she told what really happened.

Cody held a hand up to Swan who had pulled her other tomahawk and was staring at Gordy with a smile.

"Who is they?" he asked.

"Them." Gordon said, pointing at Smoke again. "It's a big gang. When you threw me out, I found them up north. I told them about the animals and they thought it was cool."

"I bet." Cody said. "How big is this gang and what did they want? Why did you come back?"

"I told you, it was nothing bad. Honest. They couldn't

believe you were living with the animals, they just wanted to see, that's all. They wanted to meet you."

"Why did you fire the gun, then?" Cody asked examining the pistol.

"It was the savage ones." Gordon said, thinking fast. "We went under the fence to get in and one of them must have followed us. It was going after Harper so I shot at it to save her. It spooked Bert though and he attacked."

Gordon looked completely sincere and he almost believed the story himself. It was a good story. Now he had to get away before Harper could come back and ruin it.

"Uh huh." Cody said doubtfully.

"Honest, Cody. I'm not mad at you guys anymore. I found a good group. We've got electricity and everything, we just came here on a peace mission and one of our guys got killed. If you let me go, I can smooth it over. You don't want trouble with these guys, believe me."

"Yeah. I think we'll wait to see what Harper has to say." Cody said and shrugged the buffalo hide cloak a little higher on his shoulders. The December winds were biting and the first of the big snows looked like it was moving in.

Gordon kept talking but nothing he said could convince them to free him. He finally ran out of lies and stood there waiting for his judgement. When they saw the rest of the tribe returning, Harper riding high above the rest of them on Bert, Swan and Cody went out to meet them. He needed to hear her side of the story. As soon as their backs were turned, Gordon pulled the snips from his pocket and clipped the wire holding him in place. He was lucky Swan hadn't put the cuff around one of the bars. He rolled under the fence and ran for the four-wheeler. He ran like he'd never run before and he heard their shouts behind him. He threw himself inside it, hit the switch and stomped the gas pedal. The machine roared to life and shot down the road. He had the pedal floored and was going fifty before he dared to turn around to look over his shoulder. The wolves were falling away fast but the panther seemed to be gaining on him, its' sleek black fur a shadow on the road. Gordon urged the machine faster, willed it to hurry before he felt those claws rip him out of the seat. He hunched low over the steering wheel and when he looked back again, the black cat was nowhere to be seen.

He didn't slow down until he was miles away.

38

MURRAY

There wasn't much they could do about Gordon although Donny and Swan wanted to try to track him. Harper told them what really happened and they hoped losing one of their members would scare the gang off. They decided the best thing to do was stay vigilant and keep preparing for winter. When Gordon had stolen the golf cart, he destroyed all of their solar chargers so their trips into town took a lot longer and they could carry less in the saddlebags made for the bears and wagons they pulled by hand. In the spring they would figure something out. Murray thought they could rig up some big carts for the bears to pull if they worked with them through the winter to train them on the harness. On a few trips they came back empty handed. They had to abandon the run because of wandering hordes moving slowly down the main road.

No one said much about the dead boy they had buried in a shallow grave. None of them knew anything about him so the makeshift service they held had been short. They didn't have much, if any, sympathy for him. He'd come on their land, tried to kidnap one of their tribe and failed. He had paid for his mistake in a currency all too common in this harsh new world.

The days got shorter, the nights grew colder and time went by quickly as they laid in supplies for winter and everyone started getting excited about Christmas. They didn't talk about it but beneath the festive decorations and boisterous board games by candle light, there was a quiet fear of repercussions from the death of the boy. Gordon had found someone to take him in, maybe even the gated community he'd talked so much about, but he had returned for a reason. Scouting for an attack, most likely. They couldn't have planned on taking Harper; it had been a crime of opportunity. She had been in the wrong place at the wrong time. If they were the kind of people who would kidnap a thirteen-year-old girl, who knew what else they were capable of. Revenge for sure, especially with the tale Gordon would have spun for them. Cody had no doubt he'd told them some ridiculous story of slow murder and torture of their friend.

How many more were there? Could they be reasoned with if they knew the whole story? Maybe. Maybe not. All they could do was be vigilant.

Murray had expressed concern over the changes in the group to Cody but he shrugged it off, told him they had to be tough or perish.

"Maybe we should try to tone it down a little." he'd said. "Tobias and Annalise have been using that tattoo gun nonstop, they want to add some to their faces next."

"As long as they charge the batteries back up, I don't care." Cody said. "The old world isn't coming back. Every time Vanessa leads some of the zom's away from the front gate, she looks for other survivors. Donny and Swan have traveled for miles in all directions and we've been in town eight or ten times. Everybody is dead, there's no one else around here except Gordon's gang and they want to hurt us. They failed this time but they'll probably try again when it warms back up. We need be fierce and look fierce. Maybe it will scare them off."

Murray was worried that they were becoming wilder, losing their culture, but nothing could be further from the truth. They were losing the twenty-first century culture of smartphones, unlimited channel TV's and twenty-four-hour connectivity to social media but those were frivolous things. In the new world, they didn't have time for electronic distractions. Murray had rigged a bicycle up to an alternator so they could charge the car batteries and it gave them a little power when they needed it. He'd had enough foresight to download tens of thousands of books on every imaginable subject and they spent free time reading. Each of them was rediscovering how their early ancestors had lived and survived by their wits and skills. Cody had Vikings, Indian and African warriors, a ninja, and a pioneer woman in his tribe. Murray was his mechanical wizard and he considered himself a mountain man like Jeremiah Johnson. They discovered new skills and taught each other. They learned from their cultures and brought ideas to the table from all of them.

Every day was filled with work, patrols and training. Cody was learning how to hunt. Harper was teaching Donny to sew. Swan taught Murray and the triplets to become deadly accurate with throwing knives and the bond between them and their animals became closer. They honed their fighting skills, practicing for hours with spears, war hammers, battle axes, blades and arrows. They knew they were no match for a grown man in hand to hand but the weapons and the animals evened the odds. They hoped it would be enough. They hoped they would frighten anyone away who were looking for easy conquest. From the history they read and from what they'd seen so far, they didn't think anyone they met would be kind and helpful. The world had lost its thin veneer of civility, there was no fear of the law and the strong would take from the weak.

Murray tossed another log on the fire, rolled around the triplets and the foxes playing some strange game that included a lot of giggling and went to stare out of the window. It was nearly noon and still snowing, thick and wet, adding to the three or four inches already on the ground. It had moved in late last night and everyone was excited to have a white Christmas. They had given up on decorating a tree and putting presents under it. Between the monkeys and the panther, it was constantly being knocked over or the gifts torn open. It and all the presents were currently in the garage and they were going to bring it in after dinner. If they were all in the room, they could probably keep the curious animals away from it and keep it standing for a while. At least until gifts were exchanged.

Cody came in with another propane bottle, dusted the snow from his buffalo cloak and hurried it to the kitchen. The twins were beside themselves with worry and snatched it out of his hands to swap bottles. They had a cake in the oven and were afraid it would fall.

Murray pulled out his inventory notebook and made a little check mark. They had four more full bottles. Enough to keep the converted stove working until maybe mid-February if the twins didn't do a whole lot of baking. They were getting better with the dutch oven and cooking some things over the open fire.

"There's the same fifteen at the front gate." Cody said, letting Murray know that no more of the undead had wandered in overnight. "But they're barely moving. It's like they're frozen or something."

"I guess that makes sense." he said, chewing on his ink pen and staring at the ceiling. "They're probably like reptiles, they don't move around much when it's cold."

"They're still really chompy, though." Cody said. "Their mouths move well enough."

"You're going to leave them at the gate, right? Not going to kill them?"

"Yep. I think you're right about keeping them as a little deterrent for Gordy's Gang if they decide to come back." Cody said and picked up his Warhammer leaning against the wall.

"I don't expect any trouble out of them until it warms up." Murray said. "The roads are slick and ATV's aren't all that great in the snow."

"You're probably right." Cody said "but I feel better with them there."

"I wouldn't put it past him to try something on Christmas Eve." Swan said, bundling up herself to bring in more firewood. "He's a lowlife."

"Maybe." Cody said. "It's my turn to do a perimeter check, I'll be back in a few hours."

"Dinner is at early tonight!" Annalise yelled from the kitchen. "Before dark so don't be late."

"Take Otis!" Clara complained. "He's hogging all the heat!"

"Yeah, take Otis." Caleb and Landon chorused, adding their two cents. "Heat Hog. Heat Hog!"

"Didn't you just hear Ana tell me to be back before dark?" Cody asked. "I'll be gone till January if I take him. You know he's slow and grumpy in the cold."

"He's taking up all the room!" Clara said as she scrambled on top of the big, lazy furball. "Make him move!"

"You make him move." Cody said and laughed when all three tried to push him.

It was a game they played and Otis would probably amble off to a corner in a few minutes. Or not. He might ignore them as they climbed all over him.

Murray watched from the window as Cody cut towards the gate and disappeared in the falling snow. He was aware of his own physical limitations and practiced for hours on end with his throwing knives to try to make up for it. He was far from helpless; he could use them to strike from a distance since close quarter fighting left him at a disadvantage. He had machetes strapped to his chair but they were last ditch weapons. His visit with the disabled Army vet was burned in his mind and kept him focused but he knew no matter what they did, if Gordons' gang had firearms, their blades and hammers would be useless. They would be bringing knives to a gun fight. They had avoided guns so far; they got along fine without them and didn't see a real need. Besides, nobody knew anything about them, the gun store in Putnam had bars on the doors and windows and the animals got skittish around loud noises. That would have to change. They were going to have to get some and learn how to use them and teach the animals not to be afraid of them. It was doable, it only took a little time. They were going to work on it over the winter and maybe by spring time they would be ready if the other gang came after them.

He spent most mornings working in the house or, when it wasn't too cold, at his shop in the converted gift store. He was making hard copies of all the most important information in his eBooks. He filled notebook after notebook with all manner of things he considered essential knowledge. He felt that learning to grow their own food was a critical skill. The stuff on the store shelves wouldn't last forever and they needed to start now. He wasn't a green thumb and doubted if their first or even second crops would do well. It was trial and error but the books would help. It was fall when the outbreak started and the hardware store didn't have much of a seed selection. They would have to try and save seeds from the crops they planted next year. They had plenty of fertilizer from the animals and an ideal spot to plant along the fertile land on the banks of the Mississippi.

He devoted a few hours every day to working with the capuchins. They were fast learners and picked up the new tricks and skills quickly. He trained them using the Halloween dummies to attack on his command, to bite and claw and harry their opponent, using their numbers to their advantage. He also taught them simple skills like retrieving things he couldn't reach or placing items on shelves. They were eager to learn, mastery of a new trick meant a treat. Their new-found skills aided him greatly in managing his daily tasks, most importantly they made him laugh and gave him hope.

39

GORDONS GANG

It was late afternoon; the snow was still falling and everyone except Cody was back from their duties and chores. The twins were adding the final touches to Christmas dinner and had to keep shooing everyone out of their kitchen. Harper had the tree up in a corner and they kept a constant eye on it to make sure the animals didn't go after the ornaments and tinsel. Murray watched out of the window for Cody. He wasn't worried, not yet, but darkness was creeping in early and the snows were getting deep.

The animals heard the sound of engines first and heads cocked at the noise, something they hadn't heard in months.

"What's wrong with Mr. Ringtail?" Caleb asked when his fox ignored him and stared at the door, his nose high looking for a scent.

Murray shushed everyone and they heard the high revving two stoke motors roaring into the parking lot. It wasn't a friendly sound, and they heard shouts and laughter cutting through the twilight. Headlights arced across the walls and the wolves had low growls in their throats. Donny and Swan reacted first and dove into their armor. Clara tried not to cry but she knew something bad was happening. Everyone looked afraid. The twins came rushing out of the kitchen, tossed their aprons and grabbed their gear. The noise increased as the machines came to a halt and revved their engines, splitting the twilight with the angry mosquito noise. It was an aggressive sound. It was a challenge.

"Got a little something for you!" they heard Gordon shout as the engines all cut off at once. "Better hurry!"

There was laughter of young men. Drunken laughter with a mean edge. Donny and Swan flashed hand signs at each other at a furious pace then ran for the back door with weapons in hand.

"We'll flank." she said to the twins as they disappeared.

"Keep the animals inside." Tobias said, as he and his sister strode out into the cold wearing their coyote fur cloaks, beaten leather armor and sawblade axes.

"Hey, freaks." Gordon said when the tattooed twins stopped just short of the iron bars. "Where's the rest of the circus act? Too afraid to show their faces?"

The undead at the gate had turned towards the sound of the engines and were in a slow-motion frenzy to get to the fresh blood. Their mouths ground and chomped at the air but their bodies moved like they were trying to walk through thick molasses.

A dozen snowmobiles were lined up some twenty or thirty feet away and Cody was strapped cruelly across the front of Gordons. His face was battered and most of his armor was missing. Shirtless, arms tied wide to the handlebars, his head lolled to one side. Blood oozed out of a gash that ran across his forehead and down one eye. Gordon stepped away from his machine and let a chain dangle from his hand.

"Looky what we found." Gordon said and yanked Cody's head up by a handful of hair.

The eye that wasn't swollen shut popped open and he snapped at Gordons wrist, trying to sink his teeth into a vein. Gordon jumped back and swung the chain, lashing him across the chest with an ugly flesh tearing sound.

"Stop it!" Harper screamed and her hands flew to her face in horror. "What kind of monster have you become?"

The zombies made their slow way across the sidewalk, low moans in their throats and hands inched up, reaching for the fresh meat.

"Sure." Gordon told her. "I'll stop. I'll even let you have him back. I'm offering a trade. You for him."

Grins from the other riders. Rifles and shotguns were laid across their handlebars.

"I have a better trade." Tobias said "Cut him loose and I'll let you live."

There were guffaws of laughter from the teenagers.

"Shouldn't you be playing with your Lego's, kid?" one of them asked.

They were unimpressed by the skinny albino twelve-year old's, evil looking axes or not.

"Better make up your mind fast, darling." Gordon said. "At the rate these dead bastards are moving, I'd say you have maybe a minute to decide."

Cody found Harpers tear filled eyes and shook his head.

"Don't." he told her between gasps.

"Shut up." Gordon said and stepped farther away as the deaders struggled forward on their uncooperating frozen legs.

The mob pushed their way through the snow, inching closer and their hunger grew more intense. One of them toppled over and caused a chain reaction. More fell and struggled to find their feet again. Gordon shook his head, the teens on the snowmobiles laughed and drank from bottles as the other undead kept trudging forward.

"Tick tock." Gordon said, and smiled, throwing the phrase back in their faces. "Times a wasting."

Vanessa came out of the petting zoo and ran to the gate with machetes unsheathed, her dark, scarred features seething with rage. She looked fierce and wild but she was only ten and the guns that came up went back down again. She was just a kid playing dress up.

"Damn, Gordon. When you said there were some babes here, I didn't think you meant babies." Maggot said and there was more laughter.

"The wolf girl is older." Gordon said peevishly. "But you'll have a hard time taming her."

"Challenge accepted!" Skull said and raised his bottle high.

The undead grew closer to Cody, they were only feet away.

"Stop them Gordon!" Harper yelled "This has gone far enough; they're getting too close!"

"The gate isn't blocked anymore. Come on out and I will."

Cody struggled with the ropes but they cut into him and he couldn't get leverage. He was draped across the windshield and cowl, his arms spread wide and his legs stretched behind him and tied viciously tight.

There was a whisper of the air being disturbed then the zombie reaching for him toppled to the ground with an arrow sticking out of its head. There were shouts of surprise and the guns came up again and aimed in the general direction where they thought it came from. There was another whoosh of air and the head exploded on the next zombie and a long spear imbedded itself into the cowling of Jester's snowmobile. He jumped in shock and fell off the seat as chunks of blood and brains splattered across his windshield. Guns pointed the other direction and but there was nothing to see. It could have come from anywhere.

"I've got your ugly face in my sights." Swan's voice rang out and guns moved back towards the shadows to their left. The laughter stopped and the teens gripped their rifles tighter. Fingers rested on triggers but there was nothing to see, just shadows on shadows in the gloom and falling snow.

Another spear whispered through the air and another of the undead tumbled to the ground.

"Where the hell are they?" Gargoyle asked a little panic in his voice, his pistol jumping from one building to the next, looking for a target. They were supposed to kill all the animals when they showed up. It was supposed to be like shooting fish in a barrel with the gates separating them.

Tobias shoved the gate open and the four kids strode out.

"Put a spear through the first persons' head that aims a gun at us." Tobias told the shadows, as the nervous men glanced at each other. Guns wavered and didn't know where to point.

Vanessa and Harper went straight for Cody as the twins ran for the other undead and started swinging their axes. The sawblades tore into them, ripping through legs and sending arms flying with syrupy thick blood painting the snow. The teens sitting on the snowmobiles didn't know what to do, the spears and arrows coming from the shadows could be aimed at any one of them. The voice didn't say which ugly face had an arrow in its crosshairs. Gordon seethed and itched to pull his pistol but he knew where Swans bow was pointed. He knew who Donny was ready to spear next. The black rune tattoos stood in stark contrast against their pale white skin and blood splattered faces as the little kids moved like half sized demons through the undead. Tobias ripped the legs from a woman in threadbare, graying rags and Annalise spit her skull with an overhead swing. She pulled her jagged blade out with a sickening slurping sound and half the woman's hair ripped out and dangled from the saw teeth. The teens sitting on the snowmobiles didn't think the kids were so funny looking or harmless anymore. Before most of them had time to react, while they were still trying to figure out where the others were hiding, the *babies* tore through the undead in seconds leaving grizzly, mangled corpses in their wake.

Gordon backed off further when Vanessa slashed the ropes holding Cody in place and watched with impotent rage as her and Harper slung his arms over their shoulders and hurried back to the gate.

His superior numbers and firepower had been rendered useless by a bunch of tweenagers. His crew sat helplessly on their machines and looked on as his prize was taken away.

"This isn't over." he told them, as they latched the gate behind them. "You killed Smoke. We owe you."

"You killed him." Cody said and separated himself from the girls, used the bars to support himself. "You killed him when you came back."

"I could gun you down right now." Gordon said, his voice cold anger. "I could shoot you all."

"Then do it." Cody said and pulled himself taller, the feeling in his legs starting to return. "Go ahead, Gordon. Grab for your gun."

The snow fell thick between them as they stared at each other, bitter hatred and cold anger. Cody had been so easy to capture it was almost laughable. They had been at the back gate with plans of sneaking in when Mr. High and Mighty came strolling along. He didn't even see them until he had a dozen guns in his face. It was easy to strap him to the front of his snowmobile like a big trophy then put the fists to him. Easy and fun. It galled him how fast he lost control of the situation.

"I can finish him now." Swans voice came faint but clear from somewhere off in the shadows, maybe from a rooftop.

Gordon's eyes darted toward the sound and he hunched his shoulders.

"Let's go." he finally said and straddled the machine.

He had no doubt an arrow was centered on his back until he was out of range.

40

GORDON

Gordon was livid and embarrassed and knew they were laughing at him. At his grand plan that was supposed to be foolproof. It had been so perfect. They should be taking home their Christmas prizes of animal trophies, new servants and Harper. He knew she would come around and grow to like Smiths Landing after a little while. She'd get over her stupid giraffe in a week or so and everything would be fine. Instead of a victory celebration, there would be derision and ridicule from Richard. He ground his teeth as they flew down the road, past the abandoned golf cart and the first house where he'd spent the night after they ran him out. As he flew past the little church, he suddenly braked hard and cut his engine. At first, he didn't think the others were going to stop but when they did, he had a smile of his face.

"Yeah, it might work." Skull said, slipping away from the stained-glass window. "But who's going to bell the cat, Gordon. Who's going to lead them in?"

Gordon looked around at their hostile faces and knew

none of them would volunteer. They didn't trust his plans anymore.

"I will, of course. You just make sure the hole is open and you're far enough away they don't smell you."

They looked at each other, shoulders shrugged and nodded. It might work and since none of them were going to be in danger, why not? It might knock some sass out of those brats.

He and Skull looped the chain through the front doors and hooked it to the back of Gordon's snowmobile while half the gang went to cut the fence and the others filled empty beer and whiskey bottles with gas. They stuffed rags in the necks then circled the church to wait for the signal.

"Throw 'em hard so they break!" Skull yelled at the others. "Then ride like the devils on your ass. You want to be out of hearing distance by the time he rips the doors off."

"Don't worry about that." Jester said. "We'll be long gone. We'll meet back up at the cutoff to the Rolling Hills Estates a few miles north of here."

It only took a few minutes to toss the firebombs through the windows and start the blaze. They ran to their snowmobiles, rushed to get away and Gordon was alone again, sitting on his machine and getting ready to do something really brave or really stupid. He wasn't sure which. He was having second thoughts. Something could go wrong. Anything could go wrong. Hell, *everything* could go wrong. He tightened the helmets chin strap, looked at the lighter he'd stolen from Cody months ago and his resolve hardened. His hatred was stronger than his fear. He took off a glove, flicked the zippo and the flame burned strong. He stared at it for a moment then lit the rag on his bottle. The wick had been in too long, was soaked with gas and his whole hand went up in flame. He yelped, nearly dropped it in panic then threw it as hard as he could against the doors. There was a crash and a whoomph as the bottle smashed and covered the ancient wood in hungry fire. The dead inside had been milling around but like the others, they moved slow and listless. The fire would thaw them out and he would lead them to the kids' front door. Fast, aggressive and hungry, they would ruin any celebrating the brats were doing.

The fire got real hot real fast and it felt good at first. It didn't take long and he had to move away, his snow dampened clothes were starting to smoke. Gordon fired up the Snowmobile and goosed it. The treads dug in and he shot forward. He nearly flipped over the handlebars when the chain snapped taut but the old doors tore loose and he regained control. He quickly unhooked it and fought the urge to leave now. Get out while the getting was good but he kept his hand off the throttle and watched the door. He waited for the undead to see him and give chase as the fire reached the roof and burnt bright in the night sky. He could hear the crackle of the flames and the hissing of melting snow but not the hungry sounds they made when they were chasing prey.

"Hey! Dumbasses, I'm out here!" he yelled with more bravado than he felt and revved the engine, worried they might stay inside and burn up.

One of them stumbled out to the stoop and zeroed in on him. His hair was starting to smoke and his jacket was singed but he recognized fresh blood. He shrieked and sprang down the stairs, landing only yards away from the idling snowmobile. Gordon screamed and hit the throttle and was nearly thrown off the machine as it careened out to the road. He'd never seen anything move so fast. He'd never come across a zombie that had been inside since the beginning. One that wasn't chewed up from animals, broken down from ceaselessly chasing the living or worn out from the elements. They poured out of the church and came for him, some on fire, some just smoking but all of them fast and hungry. The snow on the road was packed down by snow-mobiles and the dead were sprinting for him, clothes and hair aflame Gordon had to slow down not to leave them far behind. It only took a few minutes to cover the distance back to the Park and he saw the gaping hole they had cut in the fence line. He left the hardpack and shot through it with those things screaming and reaching for him only a hundred yards behind. He raced across the field towards the house. They would probably all be inside, they shouldn't be expecting another attack. They were probably fussing over the beating he'd given Mr. High and Mighty. He had to get close but now too close. Donny and that psycho Swan were deadly with their primitive weapons and he was a big target.

Drawn by the noise and flames, two huge hunchbacked shapes loped along through the darkness. They smelled the seared flesh, remembered the taste of cooked meat and followed the shrieking horde through the hole in the fence.

41

THE TRIBE

Almost as one, the animals stiffened and turned their heads. Otis sniffed the air, abandoned his spot by the fire and joined Yewan and the wolves by the big picture window. Daisy and Popsicle were enjoying the snow, rolling around in the yard and both stood and stared to the north. The little capuchins abandoned their game of chase with the triplets and scampered over to Murray, each trying to hide under the blanket covering his legs.

"They're back." Swan said.

Cody stood, brushed Harpers hydrogen peroxide and cotton swabs aside.

"They've come to kill." he said. "If not us, then the animals."

"Then we kill them first." Swan said and shrugged back into her gear. "I knew I should have put an arrow through his head."

Cody thought furiously but there was nothing they could do. They didn't have any place to hide and running blindly away in a snowstorm would only get them lost and frozen. They'd be easy to track anyway. They could try to talk but he knew how that would end. More beatings, butchered animals and the girls being carted away. Maybe all of them. Had Gordon's gang degenerated to slavery?

The others were throwing on their equipment and they knew the stakes, too. The animals were growling and chuffing and Yewan was pawing at the front door. In the distance they heard the rev of a snowmobile coming in from the back of the Park.

"Hit them hard and fast." Cody said as he jumped into his spare armor. "They won't be able to shoot anything while they're riding. With the animals charging them, maybe they'll be too scared to get off and take aim."

Donny threw open the door and Yewan bounded along beside him as they leaped from the porch and melted into the darkness. Swan barked a command at her wolves and they flew past the twins as they swung bareback onto the Polar Bears, battle axes in hand and a war cry on their lips.

Vanessa and Harper ran for the barnyard to get their companions as they strapped on their protective armor. Halfway there the saw the headlight of a lone snowmobile in the far distance dancing across an open field. They heard the screams of the undead, too. They were faint and far away but they were coming. They were being led in and from what they could hear, there were a lot of them.

Cody almost didn't catch up to Otis as he jumped off the porch and ran toward the intruders. He caught a handful of fur, swung up on his back, bent low and urged him to go faster.

When he topped a rise, Gordon saw the panther first and knew Donny and his damn spear had to be close behind. Yewan was running straight for him, standing out in stark contrast against the snow. A second later he was gone, the headlight beam picking up nothing but falling snow.

Gordon didn't know what to do. If he turned now, the horde would follow him. If he got any closer, he might have an arrow sunk in his chest or a wolf tear him off the machine. He crouched down low, hiding his whole body behind the front cowling and windshield.

A little closer. He told himself. *I want the horde to be on top of them.*

He rode down into the next small valley and gunned the machine towards the top. He would turn once he was over the rise. The horde wouldn't see him and that would be close enough. He craned his neck around to see how close they were and was satisfied as he saw them streaming down the last hill. When he looked to the front again, he screamed and involuntarily jagged the handlebars. A nightmare visage with a soot blackened face was jumping for him, a tomahawk in each hand. The machine turned and she missed plunging them through his face shield. She twisted and sunk the spike ends of her hatchets into his back, tearing deep into his heavy coat and imbedding in his plastic armor. Gordon was ripped off backwards and landed with a grunt when he hit the snow. Swan rolled to her feet, had a snarl on her lips and dove for him. Lucy got to him first. Gordon got an arm up as the wolf tried to tear into is neck and she bit down on plastic instead. While Lucy tried to crush his arm, Swan aimed her spikes at his face. Gordon screamed again, was jerked sideways by the wolf savaging him left and right. Her tomahawks bounced off his helmet and before she could choke up on them and start using them to slash him to ribbons, a spear whizzed by them and into one of the undead only yards away. Zero leaped past them to plow growling into a keening blood hungry child. Donny retrieved his spear without breaking stride and aimed for the next one running through the snow.

"Take care of him, Lucy." Swan said then joined Donny to fight the more immediate threat.

The polar bears crested the hill with the twins screaming their battle cries and urging the beasts to go faster. Their war axes would drink deeply from the blood of their enemies this night. Vanessa was right behind them and Ziggy knew what to do. All of the animals did. Their keepers and their wards were in danger and they knew no fear. The unnatural things that smelled of death but didn't die still had to be destroyed and they didn't hesitate. Bert ran right through them, stomping and breaking as many as he could. Harper swung her morning star and sent gouts of slow rotting brains and blood splashing across the snow. The undead screeched and reached for her but Bert drove them down.

Cody rode into the fray swinging his hammer as Otis plowed into the middle of the horde, snapping his massive jaws and ripping them apart. He reared on his hind legs and slashed with long, sharp claws. He bellowed his rage and Cody rolled off, got his back against the bears and started swinging with both hands.

Yewan fought silent like her master. She didn't waste energy on snarls and growls, she ripped and tore and bit as Donny spun his metal spear to impale faces or crush heads.

A group of three lunged at Cody and he met them head on with skull popping blows from his hammer. The heavy steel crunched through bone, destroyed the brain and the zombies dropped. He spun, swung his hammer like a baseball bat and shattered the head of another. The third one was almost on him when Otis turned with a roar and raked a paw across its face to send its head flying away with a streamer of black goop painting the snow.

Donny withdrew his spear from the face of a well-dressed old lady, sent hundreds of pearls flying from her broken necklace and drove the butt of his spear backwards through another a chomping mouth and out the back of its head. Yellowing, splintered teeth joined the pearls and the zombie joined the growing pile of unmoving corpses.

The battle raged as animal and warrior worked through their ranks. There was no order to the fight, only chaos, the undead cared about nothing but biting and spreading the virus. They shoved and clawed at each other to get closer to the untainted blood and were met with tooth, claw or steel.

Vanessa guided Ziggy with her knees and used her spear to thrust through heads until it was ripped from her grasp. A machete filled each hand and she continued the fight, slashing without mercy with a war cry on her lips. The ostrich danced and slashed, her wings up, her talons tearing open the undead and her powerful beak caving in their heads.

Swan worked beside Zero and the pair were merciless. Her arms moved like machines as the wolf tore into them and she caved in heads. They were on the outskirts of the mayhem; she didn't dive into the center of the mob like those riding their animals did. That didn't slow down the fight, though, they kept coming to her, mindlessly chomping and reaching for her pure blood.

Gordon still screamed, his terrified voice lost in the battle cries of the animals and children and the shrieking of the undead. The wolf was jerking him around like a rag doll, the only thing preventing her from ripping his arm off was his armor. They rolled over to the idling snowmobile and slammed against it. Stark raving terror and uncontrollable panic was blinding him to everything except the snarling wolf shredding his arm. Blood poured freely from the punctures and every time she snapped and bit, more armor was torn away. He tried to push himself up and his hand fell on his machete strapped to the inside of the cowling. Lucy shook her head and ripped loose the last bit of plastic protecting his arm. She spat it out and sprang again for him and he swung with the strength of a man knowing he is about to die. The blade bit deep into her shoulder and she yelped in pain as the blow knocked her aside. She found her feet and turned to attack again

The hulking, hunchbacked shadows had been pacing on the outskirts of the fight, waiting to join until they saw weakness. Saliva dripped from their toothy maws as they smelled the living, breathing, warm blooded animals and humans. They hadn't had a warm meal in months. They couldn't catch the rabbits and the deer smelled them from long distances and bounded away before they could get close. They'd been feasting on the undead and the smell of freshly blooded meat had the hyenas drooling. They weren't picky: human, bear or giraffe, which ever fell first, they would be there to finish it off and eat their fill of meat where the blood still ran hot. The cry of pain from one of the wolves sent them running for the sound. It meant weakness. It meant little resistance. It meant fresh meat.

Swan spun towards the sound of one of her pack in pain. Gordon had a machete and swung wildly at Lucy but missed. Her wolf darted aside and readied herself to spring again but blood was spurting from a slash in her shoulder. She yelled for Zero over the screams and shouts and roars and snarls of children and bears and wolves and he came. They ran for Lucy but when she saw the laughing shapes leap out of the darkness, everyone heard her shrill cry of warning over the pandemonium of battle.

Diablo and Demonio sprang, the scent of Lucy's' blood hot and thick driving them wild.

Gordon fell over the snowmobile then threw himself onto the seat. He snapped the throttle all the way open and launched away in a high-pitched flurry of noise and kicked up snow as both hyenas blindsided the injured wolf. She turned her teeth against them and slashed and tore at the one snapping at her spurting shoulder as the other clamped bone crushing jaws around her haunch. Swan shrieked in fury and fear as she landed atop the spotted beast splintering Lucy's hip. She drove twin spikes into its massive humpbacked shoulders and felt them bottom out against bone. It yipped a bark of pain and swung it's gaping, blood drenched jaws around to rip her off but it couldn't reach her leg. She clamped her knees and held on as he bucked and twisted in a frenzied effort to throw her off. Zero launched himself at its throat and with Swans spiked tomahawks pulling him off balance the wolf tore into the exposed flesh, found the jugular and ragged viciously back and forth. Demonio shrieked a high-pitched hyena shriek and ran. He bound after the snowmobile, chasing the light away from the pain and the hurt. Zero was pulled off his feet and dragged along but locked his jaws and ground them deep into the muscle as hot blood splashed across his muzzle. Swan pulled a spike, held on with the other and drove it back down into the undulating shoulders. She repeated with the other hand, pulling them out and driving them in, stabbing over and over, trying to sink one into its head. Blood covered her legs and thighs, the thick heavy snow blinded her and the hyena ran after the fleeing headlight and through the hole in the fence. He followed the road where he could run the fastest for a while but he couldn't out run the girl on his back or the wolf with its jaws locked on his throat. He dove into the woods, running in blind panic and pain through the brambles and thick undergrowth. A plunging paw caught one of Zero's bouncing legs and ripped him loose. A mouthful of muscle, fur and veins tore free and came with him. Demonio stumbled, lost his footing then plowed muzzle first into the snow. Swan tumbled free, slammed up against a tree and lay stunned for a moment. She heard Zeros challenge to something, shook her head and choked up on her blood slicked hatchets, the lanyards the only thing that kept them from flying free.

Diablo stopped in his tracks when Demonio didn't rise and fight. He had the she wolf in his oversized muzzle, intent on dragging her deeper into the woods to feed in peace. He was confused when his brothers' prey stood and snarled but his brother lay still, his life pouring out into the snow. Zero laid his ears back and bared his teeth, the rumble coming from his throat vicious and promising death. Diablo dropped the dying Lucy and crouched, ready to answer the challenge. He was twice the size of the bloody wolf and would gorge himself on both of them. Swan pushed herself to her feet and crouched beside Zero, a snarl on her lips and hate in her eyes. Diablo took a step back. He was a killer of opportunity and didn't like to fight very hard for his food. Lucy whimpered as he snatched her up and ran.

42

TRIBE

The clouds scuttling across the moon threw the valley of death into deeper shadows but enough light reflected off the snow so they could see their enemy. A few were still moving, those mauled by the bears, but Donny and Vanessa were darting from corpse to corpse thrusting spears through heads. Cody was leaning on his Warhammer, still breathing hard as Harper tried to fuss over his wounds that had torn open again. The twins were arguing over who killed the most and were debating about taking trophies. Ears or something.

"No ears." Cody yelled over at them. "Come on, you know how bad that would stink?"

They reluctantly agreed then went after Donny and Vanessa to make double sure the undead stayed dead. The bears and Yewan sniffed around but they ambled away from the killing field, the smell was too much for them.

"Where's Swan?" Cody suddenly asked.

Everyone looked around then at each other.

"The wolves are gone, too." Vanessa said.

"Who saw her last?" Harper asked "I lost track of every-one; it was hard to keep Bert under control."

Donny pointed away from the piles of dead, near the snowmobile tracks where she and Gordon had been fighting.

"You think Gordon snatched her and the wolves went after?"

"Swan getting whooped by that moron? I doubt it." Annalise said. "It would take more than him, even if she was unarmed."

Donny shook his head vehemently and pointed at the churned-up snow and the blood starting to freeze. He looked closer at it and held up an almost frozen piece for all to see. It was red, not black. Human or animal, not zombie. They looked around and there was a lot of it. Way too much to come from one person. Or animal. The snowmobile track was still visible and as they followed it past the where the fight took place they could see the prints of two animals. A blood trail ran along with both sets of tracks but there were no human prints at all.

"What the hell made those?" Tobias asked as he placed his own booted foot in the snow beside one of them. "They're not from Lucy or Zero. It's huge."

"Hyenas." Cody said. "And one of them had something in its jaws."

The imprints were filling in quickly but they could see the smeary blood and wide drag marks in the scattered snow.

Donny signed with his hands and they watched. He was the best tracker and hunter and he could read the tracks better than anyone.

"He says the thinks Gordon has Swan and the hyenas had a wolf each in their jaws." Harper said.

"I don't believe it." Annalise said. "No way, no how could Gordon take Swan."

"No way." Tobias agreed. "She'd beat him stupid with her bare hands."

"Unless he shot her." Vanessa said. "There is a lot of blood."

43

SWAN

S wan chased after the hunchbacked beast, her fury raging too much for the tears to seep through. Zero ran beside her as they followed the trail though the underbrush. The blackness was thick in the woods where the snow fell heavy and the evergreen trees blotted out the meager moon light. They ran until her lungs burned. They ran until her soot blackened face was whipped and scratched from slapping branches. They ran after the monster, following the tracks when they could and Zeros nose when they couldn't. The snow fell heavier and muffled their sounds, it blanketed the forest in silence. It was thick and wet and soon she was soaked to her knees. They ran deeper and farther than her and Donny had ever hunted and the woods stretched on. They ran until they found Lucy cooling in the snow. What was left of her. Swan fell to her knees with great anguished sobs she could barely get out from her tortured lungs. She pulled the wolf mother close and buried her face in the fur. She had never known such ache and tears weren't enough. Crying wasn't enough. When Zero loosed his pain and howled his sorrow at the moon, she joined him.

44

CODY

Cody leaned heavily on his Warhammer and tried to ignore the pain of his bruised ribs, throbbing eye, rope burned wrists and tender nose. Reminders of the beating Gordon had given him. Now that the fight was over, the adrenaline rush gone, he felt weak and tired and hurt all over. It felt hopeless. They could never catch him, he was miles away by now. The snow would cover any tracks he made before they could chase him down but he had to try. He couldn't give up if there was a chance, no matter how slim. Maybe she'd managed to get away from him. Maybe she was lying on the side of the road injured and freezing to death.

"We have to go after her." Cody said.

"You're not fit to go anywhere." Harper told him. "You can barely stand."

"We'll go." Tobias said.

Donny shook his head and pointed to himself and Yewan. The three started arguing in the Pidgeon sign language he used and the twins were getting louder in their defense of why they should go too. Cody closed his eyes for

303

a moment. It only made sense, Donny and Yewan could cover more ground faster than anyone else and the Panther was a lot better at following commands than the bears were. They might decide they wanted a swim in the river and there was nothing the twins could do to stop them.

"Enough." he said. "Donny, you go."

He nodded and set off at a fast jog, pacing himself. He knew it might be a long night with miles to travel.

Cody stared at the bodies of the undead littering the ground. They'd fought well, despite the odds but it was hard to feel elated at the victory with three of their own missing and most likely dead. They'd have to burn them or drag them down to the river but they would keep for now. They'd be frozen solid and easier to move by tomorrow.

"We need to find out where they came in. Can you guys backtrack the trail and see how bad it is? If you can, just pull the fence back in place, we can repair it properly tomorrow. I'll check the back gate." Cody said.

Vanessa and the twins hurried to their animals to mount up and ride.

"I can cover more ground than you on Bert." Harper said. "You should go to the house and let Murray patch you up. You're bleeding again."

"Bert hates the cold." Cody said. "You need to get him back in the barn before he gets sick."

He didn't know if the giraffe would get sick or not but he didn't want to argue with her. He whistled for Otis and they started the long trek across the fields. He needed some time to himself. He needed to rethink his so-called leadership. He'd learned a lot during his hour of captivity and it changed his whole world view. He couldn't turn the other cheek anymore.

The boys were apparently the only survivors in a place

called the Landing. It was one big nonstop party and most of them hadn't been sober in months. They had realized they could do whatever they wanted and there was nobody to stop them, there was no reason to follow the rules anymore. They wanted more girls because the few they had weren't enough and from the armor they wore, he assumed they were hockey players. Unlike the tribes which was a mishmash of all kinds of different things, the teens all had the same gear, almost like a uniform.

He knew the Riders wouldn't quit. They'd been embarrassed by a group of kids they thought were their inferiors and had loosed a horde on them in retaliation. They'd be back. Gordon was consumed with revenge and he'd dragged all those other boys into his web. He knew they'd keep coming, they were just as bad as him, probably worse. All of them had pointed their rifles at him. All of them had laughed and cheered once he was bound hand and foot and they started throwing the fists to him. All of them had taken pleasure in watching the beating and one boy had put a cigarette out on his chest. They were drunk and stupid and mean and he had no sympathy for them. He knew boys like them before the fall. Bullies who thought giving freshmen swirlies in the toilet or random wedgies walking down the hall was the height of hilarity. They were mostly harmless and sometimes their pranks were even funny as long as they didn't happen to you. They towed the line, though. They knew not to really hurt anyone, not to take it too far or there would be repercussions. They could get suspended or banned from the team. They could get a record and not be able to get into their college of choice.

It was different now. It had been months and the only law of the land was whatever they said it was. They would have killed him and that thought kept running through his mind. He had been strapped shirtless across a snowmobile in freezing weather. The ropes were so tight on his hands and feet that they had turned purple. It took a long time for the blood to return and they stopped stinging. Another twenty minutes and he probably would have lost them to frostbite, that is, if he even lived that long. They would have killed his people. They turned a horde of the undead loose on them. If Swan was still alive, if she recovered from whatever Gordon had done to her, they would kill her too. She would force them to do it because she would never submit. She would fight them until her last breath and curse them with it.

Cody Wilkes was unable to stop them. He was weak, still bound by the teachings of his old life. He still tried to follow the rules. Still tried to be someone his mom would be proud of. That way of thinking, that life was over. It had to be or they would die. He had been reluctant to accept that things would never be the same again. Everyone he'd ever loved before the tribe was gone, it was all any of them had and his weakness had nearly cost them everything. He was wrong when he thought they could lock those gates and ignore the rest of the world. Wrong when he naively believed in live and let live.

He had no idea where the Riders came from, no way of taking the fight to them. They had gas cans strapped to the machines so it had to be miles away. Twenty? Fifty? He didn't know.

They had powerful snowmobiles and he understood the genius of using them. They may have been limited to only riding when it snowed but they could go anywhere when it did. The Christmas snow wouldn't last, it was still getting warm during the days. It would start melting away in the morning. January was when the snows blew in and stayed for the rest of winter. In another few weeks they would come before the hard-cold set in and they would linger until spring thaw. When that happened, the Riders would be unstoppable for the next two or three months. They either had to run away or be ready when they came back and he knew they'd be back. They wanted the girls. Gordon knew the few dozen zombies he let in wouldn't be able to defeat them, he'd been there for at least part of the battle. He'd seen the Tribe cutting them down.

He would return to the scene of his crime and he wouldn't like what he found Cody vowed to himself.

He and Otis came to the back gate and he found his buffalo robe nearly buried in the snow. He brushed it off and swung it over his shoulders. The weight felt good and he wrapped it tight, holding in the warmth. He continued along the fence line towards the river, his mind still puzzling things out and coming to grips with the way things were. They had been alone and isolated and had tried to be good, to do what was right. Murray had voiced his concerns that they were acting too much like their animal companions, getting too uncivilized, too wild. Murray was wrong, though. He needed to become more like Swan and the twins. He needed to embrace the animal in him and not be concerned with things like mercy or forgiveness. In the animal world, you fought, you killed you moved on. You didn't dwell on what was right or wrong. You did whatever you had to do to live even if something else had to die.

When Swan wanted to kill Gordon up before they voted to banish him, he was pretty sure it was just an act. She was putting on a front to scare him. She was still a thirteen-year-old girl on the inside. She could have killed him with an arrow tonight but she hadn't. She wasn't a cold-blooded killer no matter how hard she tried to convince them she was. Somebody had to be, though. Somebody had to be the executioner.

Things were different now. No one outside the Tribe could be trusted. If he were faced with the same situation again he had to be fearless enough to destroy the threat, not let it loose to come back and attack. He had to become more like Otis, unburdened with complicated thoughts.

He was failing them with his old way of thinking, he understood that now. If he didn't change, they would be walked on, taken advantage of, imprisoned and enslaved. He had to be just as cold and devious as the enemy and he had to learn to show no mercy. Offer no quarter. Cody Wilkes couldn't do it though. He had to let go of his old life, embrace the one thrust upon him. This life was hard, dirty and bloody. It could kill you for being decent, for trying to help the wrong people. He would have to be more discerning in the future. Learn to trust his instincts. He'd had qualms about Gordon from the first moment he met him but had pushed them aside to do the right thing. Never again. His mistake had cost them dearly.

He went back to the spot of his first kiss with Harper. Back to the place where Derek talked to him about what it meant to be a man. Where he gave him his first beer and the old Zippo that he'd lost. Back to the spot where his mom said her goodbyes to Derek and floated his body down the river. He knew she was still out there somewhere wandering around, still leading the horde away, but that wasn't his mom. Not anymore. He believed the undead were soulless. When they died the first death, the spirit departed and left a shell that didn't know it was dead.

He wished he was strong like Otis, the mighty oversized Kodiak. The word lingered in his mind. *Kodiak.* Feared. Respected. Nothing in the wild took anything from the big bears. Nothing crossed them. Other animals ran. Ran in fear for their lives. Cody squatted on the riverbank and put his hands in the water. It was cold. It was pure. It rolled on and on, an unstoppable force taking anything that stood in its way with it. If his tribe were going to survive in this ruthless new world, he needed to lead them in a ruthless new way. He needed to do what they couldn't.

He rose and stripped off his weapons, armor and clothes until he stood naked in the falling snow. The old Cody had to put away childish things, to die and be baptized into something new.

He dove into the cold, slow moving waters of the Mississippi and swam for the bottom as the frigid river worked to force the air from his lungs. Numbness settled into his muscles as he found mud then dug his hands and feet into it. He forced himself downward, let out a little air so he could lay on the bottom and faced the surface. The cloud of muddy water was swept away and he lay there still and silent and felt the mighty river gently tug at him. The clouds slid away from the moon and the world at the bottom of the river brightened. He could see the snow falling and disappearing as it hit the surface. He willed his weakness away, demanded the river to take it and carry it to the ocean. When he came out of the water, he would be a new man he told himself. He wouldn't surface until he was sure he had the guts to be as hard as he needed to be.

At church, he'd seen the miracle of baptism. He'd seen drunken Willie Hodges finally join his wife after she'd come alone ever since Cody had known her. Willie was a mean drunk and a lay about that liked to smack her around. They lived in a run-down trailer and everyone said he was white trash, and that she deserved better. When he finally got saved and came up out of the water, he was a changed man. He put down the bottle, got a steady job and went to service every Sunday. He had become a good man. Everyone said it was a miracle and Cody needed one now. He would stay on the bottom, in the mud, until he was sure he had it. Until the old Cody was gone and a new one emerged.

They attended a Baptist church and the preacher liked his fire and brimstone sermons. In Sunday school, when he was little, they'd learned about Jesus and love and charity and helping the less fortunate. When he started staying upstairs with his mom for the grown-up sermons, the preacher spoke of an angry God who gave men power to destroy their enemies. Bad men were used to do good things. The icy waters slowed his heart and he knew he needed air, the edges of his vision started turning black, but he waited. He prayed his weakness away and willed himself to become who he needed to be. To have what it took to save his Tribe. To be a bad man so he could do good things. He would wait until he died if he had to before he rose up too soon. He wasn't cold anymore and the river seemed crystal clear. He saw a face in the moon and the mud wrapped around him felt warm, like an electric blanket. A fish swam lazily by a few feet above his face and there was a sudden explosion on the surface. Otis dipped his head in the water so fast the fish didn't have time to react. Sharp teeth clamped down and before it could thrash its tail, it was jerked out. Swift, violent death in an instant. Cody was so startled he almost gasped in a lungful of water but held still. In less than a second, even the ripples disappeared and the face in the moon was still smiling down. The fish was gone, as if it never existed. He had his answer. Some things died so others may live. On the verge of passing out, he pushed out of the mud toward the surface and kicked his legs upward.

Cody Wilkes never emerged from those icy cold waters, what remained of the innocent boy was swept away in the current of the mighty Mississippi. Disappeared like the fish. A ruthless warrior that came to be known as Kodiak waded ashore.

45

TRIBE

"Cody's coming." Murray said from his spot by the window. It had been hours and the twins were already discussing going to look for him. Relief flooded their faces and Harper ran to the door to open it. She threw her arms around him then exclaimed and dragged him over to the fire to warm up. It was roaring in the hearth and Otis nudged the triplets out of his favorite spot.

Cody looked around the room, at the unopened presents under the tree and the table still set for Christmas dinner then asked the obvious. "No word from Donny?"

Murray shook his head and looked at his watch again for the ten thousandth time. It was nearly two in the morning. The snows had finally stopped and the thermometer showed twenty-nine degrees.

"If he found her, he wouldn't try to bring her back. It's not ten below zero, it's not a killing cold but he would get her inside someplace." Harper said again, same as she told the others before. "A nice, warm bed with plenty of blankets."

"There's no use going to look for them, either, Cody." she added. "We'd never spot them in the dark and the tracks are long covered."

He nodded, didn't offer an argument and turned his back to the fire to face them.

"It's my fault this happened." he said. "I didn't want to change. I wanted our old world back and I thought any other survivors would too. I was wrong and I see that now. People like Gordon don't change. They don't suddenly turn into nice people; they just get meaner and we have to be as ruthless as them if we're going to make it. My kindness, us giving him chance after chance to fit in has ended in disaster. I should have let Swan and Donny kill him. I should have killed him myself. If you think I'm still fit to lead, I won't make the same mistake twice. The Tribe is all we have. It's what keeps us alive and we can't let outsiders take us down."

"Of course, you're fit to lead." Harper said and the others joined in. "It wasn't just you, we all gave him second and third chances."

"Not us." Tobias said. "I wanted to throw him out months ago."

"Then call me Kodiak from now on." Cody said. "It'll be a reminder every time I hear my name of who I have to be."

"Can I have a warrior name too?" Landon asked "I can fight."

Murray watched the banter as all of them thought of new names they liked but it was all in fun, something to joke about. He noticed something subtlety different about Cody. Or Kodiak as he wanted to be called. He couldn't put a finger on it and point out exactly what it was but he wasn't the same boy who had left to make a perimeter check earlier that afternoon. Maybe it was the way he carried himself as he ignored the cuts and bruises and rope burns. He was a little harder. A little more predatory and his eyes never stopped moving.

46

RICHARD

They drank heavier than usual and the mood was black once they finally made it back to Smiths Landing. Richard had a celebration planned but it was more like a funeral party. They had returned half frozen, miserable and empty handed after the long, cold ride. They had risked their lives for nothing and had run away from a bunch of little kids like whipped dogs. They had no plundered booty, no animal heads as trophies, and no girls as new play toys. Gordon tried to turn their defeat into a victory, tried to brag about leading the zombies in to teach them a lesson but Richard was scathing with his reply.

"I thought I sent you down there to get girls, Gordy. I wanted you to bring them back, not turn them into more zombies!"

Nobody stood up for him. Nobody admitted they thought it was a good idea at the time, that they all wanted a little payback.

The more they drank the angrier they became and for some reason Gordon got most of the blame. He was supposed to know the lay of the land, he had lived with

315

them for months. He should have known they would have tricks. The only thing he'd warned everyone about was the animals. They were dangerous. They were vicious. They were unpredictable. They needed to shoot them the instant they saw them. Once the animals were down, the brats would be easy to control. They hadn't seen a single one of the so-called fearsome beasts and had been outsmarted by a bunch of ten-year old's. It didn't sit well with any of them.

"Maybe they're hibernating." Squirrel said, commiserating with them. "Maybe they're not dangerous in the winter."

"Well those damn kids were. Pinpoint accuracy with those spears and arrows." Jester complained, "and we had no idea where they were coming from. We were sitting ducks."

"We do things different next time." Richard said. "Next time we do it my way."

"I say we leave them alone." his step mom said. "They don't have anything we need."

Richard eyed her coldly and she dropped her gaze. She had spoken out of turn and bit her lower lip. Richard wasn't kind when he was angry.

"They have something that *I* need." he said, his eyes boring into her. "I want this Harper girl everyone is saying looks so wonderful. This beauty queen who hasn't been used up."

The words cut her but she knew better than to argue. Her husband was still stumbling around in the empty pool and that was all the reminder she needed that he could be cruel. If she knew what was good for her, she would keep her mouth shut.

Gordon started to protest, Harper was his girl, but

stopped mid-sentence when Richard turned to stare him down, dared him to say something.

"You had your chance." he continued, then turned to address the room. "They killed Smoke in case you've forgotten. He was my best friend. They can't be allowed to get away with that. They started this war and we're going to finish it. Next time, I'm leading us down there. Next time, the Landing doesn't get its ass kicked by a bunch of little kids with oversized pets. Next time, we teach them who's in charge."

Richard raised the bottle then took a long pull of the tequila. He had sent his guys down expecting an easy victory and a few new girls but it had become more than that with the second defeat. He wasn't used to losing, not in Hockey or baseball or life in general. Lowery's were winners. Period. He absolutely positively would not let a bunch of middle schoolers embarrass him.

He had misjudged Gordon's ability to lead. How hard could it be? They had superior numbers, superior firepower and the snowmobiles made it too easy. They could go anywhere; they weren't confined to the roads or trails. If they ran into a horde, no problem. Take a left and go around them. Even the animals, the much-ballyhooed killer animals hadn't made an appearance. Squirrel was probably right; they were all hibernating. It was too bad Smoke had gotten killed and not Gordon. Smoke had a head on his shoulders, he could be trusted.

Richard decided he would ease up on Gordy a little, let him think he was in charge of something. He'd let him strut around like he was important because the idiot got things done around the Landing. He liked to brag about how he'd survived in the wild and how he had killed more of the undead than all the rest of them combined. He talked big talk but so far, Richard was unimpressed. Gordy seemed to be fine as long as he was inside the walls. He fretted about the fences and supplies and that was good, somebody had to. He didn't drink much or argue over whose turn it was with the girls so he had his uses. He'd proven that he couldn't be trusted with any big plans though, any war plans, and there certainly would be war. Gordy couldn't think on his feet, he couldn't adapt and overcome.

Now that they'd been outside the gates, now that they'd seen it wasn't so scary out there after all, there were whole new opportunities to explore. The undead were slow in the cold and the snowmobiles could take them anywhere so he started working on a plan of his own.

47

DONNY

Donny ran, following the snowmobile tracks out of the hole in the fence and down the road. He paced himself and the big cat loped along beside him. The trail got confusing with all the undead footprints and other riders tracks but one set was a little fresher, a little less obscured by the falling snow. They had left him behind, his path much clearer and newer than the others. It was obvious Gordon wasn't trying anything evasive, he was on a straight line right back to where ever he came from and Donny picked up the pace. Maybe he would have to stop to refill or maybe Swan would figure out some way to slow him down. Maybe he could catch him then.

Yewan stopped by the side of the road and waited. Donny looked back then slowed his pace. He tapped metal on metal.

Come.

Yewans yellow eyes watched him, a black shadow on white snow and flicked her tail. Donny stopped and retraced his footsteps to see what was intriguing the panther. He spotted the paw prints halfway down the slope and there was a splash of blood still visible. They hyenas had taken off through the woods but he wasn't interested in them. He wanted to chase Gordon and Swan. He placed a hand on Yewan and tapped the metal again.

Come.

The cat ignored him and sprang lightly down the incline and disappeared into the woods. Donny glared after her but guessed she couldn't smell Swan and Gordon, probably only the metal and gas of the machine. She could smell the wolves though and Swans smell was all over them. She was following that scent. He couldn't leave her, she was no match for the two hyenas and he didn't want to follow her, he wanted to chase Gordon. He finally slammed his spear in frustration and plunged in after her.

She was sniffing the body of one of the huge hunch-backed creatures when he burst through the brambles that grew thick at the side of the road and into the woods. The snow wasn't as deep, the evergreen and spruce trees acted as natures canopies. The darkness was deeper, though. The same trees blotted out the moonlight. He spotted boot prints, small ones, and his eyes grew wide. One of them must have been carrying Swan. There were wolf prints, signs of a scuffle then all three sets went deeper into the forest. Donny was confused by what he saw but Swan had to be chasing after the Hyena, if it was chasing her, it would have caught her in a few quick bounds. He placed his forehead against Yewans, thanked her, then they were both running again, this time he let her lead.

They followed the prints and the smells across fields and back into woods. They wound down by the river and through the yards of long abandoned houses. They found the half eaten, half frozen body of Lucy but the trail continued, the wolf and the moccasins followed the giant paw prints of the Hyena.

The moon was waning and the heavy snows had tapered off when he found them. Yewan was sniffing a mound of snow at the base of a massive downed tree. Zero chuffed from inside the snowbank when he stooped to see what held her interest. He dug through and found them curled up in the hole the oak had left in the ground when it tumbled over. The roots, covered in years of vine growth, and the snow had made a cave and the two were huddled together. He crawled in with Yewan right behind him. She didn't care much for the cold, she'd been fighting and running most of the night and it was warm and cozy inside.

"They killed Lucy." Swan whispered and snuggled in closer to Zero, giving them room to lay down.

She was drained, completely exhausted from the fight, the long run and the heartache.

"Close the door." she mumbled and drifted back to sleep.

He obliged, piling the snow back up to block out the cold and spread his cloak over them. He was worn out too and within minutes they were all sound asleep.

48

DIABLO

Less than a mile from the tree where Swan sheltered, Diablo lay beneath an overturned boat near an empty cabin on the riverbank. His long tongue licked gingerly at the wound in his shoulder where the wolf had torn the skin and underlying muscle. It throbbed incessantly, eliciting a whine from the savage creature. His body was covered in bites and claw marks from the she-wolf's vicious attack. He'd never encountered another creature that was so fast and powerful and fearless. Even wounded with both of them tearing into her, she had punished him with fangs and claws. The cold and the snow perplexed the beast. It was arid, dry and hot in the warmer climes of the southwest where'd they'd been raised.

His clan mate was gone. He felt the loss and emptiness; they were social animals and rarely wandered by themselves.

He kept his senses alert. He was alone now and aware how other predators perceived a wounded animal. They would smell the blood and smell weakness. They would think he was easy prey. They would find out different.

Diablo was a predator never seen in this part of the world and even wounded he was a match for anything that roamed the wilds.

Thirstily, he lapped mouthfuls of snow, seeking to parch his dried throat and rumbling belly. He'd have to hunt soon, the few bites he'd had of the wolf weren't enough. He'd tired of carrying her mile after mile but the ones following him wouldn't let him stop and eat. They kept coming. Even after the dropped her, they chased him for more miles before they finally stopped. After he could no longer sense them, he traveled farther. They were a danger; they had killed his clan mate and they were hunting him.

He crawled from under the shelter of the boat and instinctively sought higher ground to increase the chance of scenting some prey. The rotted ones on two legs were easy pickings, yet he didn't smell any of them on the wind.

He limped slowly, the battle then the long run from the fight had greatly exhausted his energy reserves. His body burned calories much faster in an effort to keep him warm.

Unfamiliar smells caused his nose to twitch as something drew near. He exaggerated the limping motion of his walk, hoping to lure whatever predator that stalked him in closer. He whined, made a pitiful, helpless, wounded sound and sniffed the wind to know where the attack would come from. Soon he would feed.

The limbs above his head were filled with the flapping of wings as crows and ravens lighted on the icy, snow-covered boughs. They were too high and too quick and fell into the *not food* category. He ignored them.

The sounds of many feet crunching in the snow caused him to turn and face his downwind side. They stood there watching him. A multitude of eyes from a dozen different kinds of animals.

Diablo didn't know what these creatures were. Most had unfamiliar scent patterns, more new things in this strange new land.

The scavenger animals stared at the wounded hyena. They were many in number and had learned to work together to bring down their prey. They were an unnatural selection of coyotes, raccoons, opossums, stray house cats, foxes and pigs gone wild. There were a few dogs still wearing their collars mixed into the bunch as they slowly formed a circle around the injured Diablo. They acted like a pack even though they were all different and this confused him more. How could such strange and diverse creatures hunt together?

He growled to warn them, low and rumbling from his thick chest. The pack alpha, a large mixed breed bullmastiff answered the growl and stepped forward. This Diablo understood. His former master had pitted him against such an animal many times in the past.

Diablo struck quick and the two slammed together, each pawing and ripping, snapping and biting, trying to sink teeth and tear flesh in a bloody mix of fur and fangs. The bullmastiff had been a family pet up until the fall of man. He was powerful and strong, twice the size of the coyotes in his band and had never lost a fight. He was the biggest, the most ferocious and led the mixed band of animals because they all shared the same hunger. The same craving, the same addictive need for the infected meat of the shuffling dead. He was fifty pounds lighter than the Hyena and he didn't lack courage but he had never encountered a beast like Diablo.

The mastiff never had a chance.

The hyena had jaws that could snap water buffalo bones and when he clamped down on the dogs neck, he didn't bite and tear. He didn't rag him back and forth. He crushed down with the force of a hydraulic press and the Mastiff went limp. Diablo ground his jaws until the head popped off and the body fell to the snow. He growled at the band of animals again then held the dog in place with an oversized paw as he bit open the belly, snapped ribs and gobbled down the still beating heart. He stuffed himself on the entrails and never took his eyes off the surrounding pack. A coyote darted in to grab a bite and Diablo slashed at him. The coyote yipped and melted back into the hungry animals to lick his wound.

The hunchbacked creature stood in defiance, wolfing down the flesh of the dog as the pack stared motionless at him. His shoulder was bleeding freely but he ignored it. He was asserting his supremacy, daring any of them to attack.

His appetite momentarily sated, he turned and limped through the forest, seeking a new place to rest and heal his injured body.

The remaining animals quickly stripped the flesh from the corpse of the dog, leaving only bones for the birds to fight over. They picked up the trail of the hyena and followed the scent of their Alpha.

49

KODIAK

The tribe fretted and worried all the next day. They fixed the fence, took care of the animals, milked the cow and fed the chickens, but mostly they stayed in the living room and waited. The sun made an appearance in the cloudless blue sky and the snows were melting fast. They had tried to follow Donny's tracks but it was already too late by the time they could no longer sit still and wait. They couldn't follow what was no longer there. Annalise puttered around in the kitchen and made comfort food, the triplets played with their foxes and the wolf cubs and everyone else tinkered with their armor and weapons to make minor improvements. Yesterday's battle haunted some of them: it was the first time they had experienced the violence and brutality of kill or be killed in such a chaotic fight. They all had close calls whether it was a zombie clamping filthy teeth down on protected arms or losing their grip on a blood-slicked weapon. They remembered how it happened, too.

Gordon.

They didn't understand how anyone could be so cruel,

so evil. He wasn't alone, either. Every one of the snowmobile boys had been willing to kill them and it was all for nothing. They weren't starving, they didn't need a protected place to stay, and they didn't need anything. In fact, they had much more in their gated community than the tribe had. They had electricity and hot running water and guns.

They were slowly coming to grips with something Kodiak already understood. Some people didn't need a reason to hurt someone, they did it because they could and they couldn't be reasoned with. They only understood and respected superior strength. Fear was the only thing that would keep them away and they didn't fear the children or the animals. They had been over confident and had been outsmarted but they weren't afraid. They were angry. They would be back for revenge; they had no doubt about that.

"Donny and Swan are back." Murray said from his watch on the window and the room emptied to run outside and greet them.

Zero was favoring one paw and had drying blood in his fur but most of it wasn't his. Swan was wearing the hide from one of the hyenas draped over her shoulders. It was huge on her. With the head acting as a hood, the tail dragged the ground. They hugged and didn't have to ask about Lucy, she told them and most had tears in their eyes when they heard.

"You two get inside, get some dry clothes." Harper told them. "Vanessa and I will stretch the hide."

Swan shrugged it off, still bloody with bits of hanging flesh, and handed it to them. It would make a fine cloak once it was cleaned and cured and the hatchet slashes were sewn.

Donny handed him his old cigarette lighter, the one Derek had given him.

"It was at the church." Swan said. "We saw the smoke when we came out of the woods, it was still smoldering. It had been full of zombies, that's where he got them."

So, Gordy had stolen it, too. He should have guessed. One more reason for payback.

They celebrated Christmas a day later but a cloud of apprehension and sadness hung over them and continued for weeks after. As the weather stayed a little above freezing, the zombies started returning, stumbling into the parking lot and congregating at the front gate. They were too slow to lead off, it would take forever so they wound up spearing many of them. The warm spell would be over soon, though. A white Christmas in Iowa was never a sure thing but zero-degree temperatures in January were.

They talked of leaving but they would have to travel far to be out of the reach of Gordon and his gang and who's to say there wasn't someone just as bad or even worse a hundred miles down the road. They did what they could to fortify the house and had drills to see how quickly they could gather and put the wood shutters over the windows. There was no way to monitor or protect the fence line, it stretched for miles so the house became their fortress. Their last stand. Swan had extra arrows placed in strategic locations and they added perches on the roof where she could have a clear shot at those below. Vanessa and Donny used up all the supplies they had to make spears and then started carving more from tree limbs.

Kodiak oversaw it all but knew it was futile. He put himself in Gordons place and asked *what would Gordon do?*

Gordon would come with the next snow because it was the way they traveled and the threat of the undead was low.

Gordon wouldn't be overconfident next time.

Gordon would be careful.

Gordon would have a sniper shoot anyone that popped up, especially the animals.

Gordon would set fire to the house.

Gordon would win.

The snow melt turned to ice and it stayed frigid halfway into January. Kodiak was healing quickly and spent long hours away from the rest of them. Sometimes he roused Otis from his favorite spot in front of the fireplace and sometimes he went alone. The sun was bright in the sky but it didn't give off much warmth. The breeze from the north brought the temperatures down and they kept the fire roaring to ward of the cold.

His buffalo robe kept him warm as he made preparations, sometimes using Otis, sometimes working by himself. He didn't answer them truthfully when they asked him where he'd been all day. *Just double checking the fence line* he would say. *It's our weakest point.*

They were all busy. The cold made every task harder and they took much longer but they were doing all right. Sometimes Kodiak had to remind himself of that. They had managed to survive when almost everyone else hadn't.

Them.

A bunch of kids who should have been dead the first week.

They had toughened up, all of them had grown hard. Six months ago, he couldn't imagine seven-year old's getting up at the crack of dawn, dressing themselves and going out to milk the cow and feed the chickens. Somebody would have called child protective services. He couldn't imagine the twins walking into school with braided hair and covered in Celtic tattoos. Somebody would have been going to jail for allowing it to happen. He grinned when he thought of Donny and Swan walking down the hallways with their wolves and panther padding quietly by their side, faces blackened with soot and blooded weapons in their hands. Somebody would have called a SWAT team. Or Vanessa with her tribal scars and spears wearing little more than a loincloth and feathers riding an ostrich like it was a chocobo from a video game. He could imagine the gasps and wide eyes of the other kids as he and Otis lumbered into a classroom. It would be a heck of a show and tell.

They had done more and grown up faster in the past few months than most people did their entire lives. They had spilled the blood of their enemies, fought and killed and had faced death more times than they cared to remember. He was proud of his tribe.

It felt like it was warming up a little, there wasn't much wind but it was coming from the south and it didn't have the same frosty bite. Kodiak grabbed his robe off of an abandoned car and surveyed his handiwork. Otis saw that he was finally ready to go and hauled himself to his feet to nuzzle him. It had been a while since he'd had his ears scratched and nobody could do it as good as the boy. He knew just the right spots. Kodiak smiled, scratched his friend and listened to him grunt in pleasure then stretch his neck so he could get to the good spots under it. The sky was darkening and the clouds were heavy and hung low in the sky. Some of them were almost a deep purple color. The air was still and it looked like snow. A lot of it. They started the long trek back home as Otis hurried along with his pigeon-toed walk. He had a spot in front of the fire waiting for him.

50

TRIBE

It was full dark by the time they made it back to the house, even though it was barely four o'clock. The snows were coming in from the north, thick fat flakes that covered the ground quickly. It fell heavily on Piedmont house and showed no signs of slowing as the twins brought out the bowls of venison chili and their first attempt at home made cheese. It was lumpy and had the consistency of runny playdoh, not at all like orange shredded cheddar they used to pile high on Coney dogs. Tobias looked defiantly around the table, daring them to say something, anything at all, about his cheese. It had taken him nearly a month to make it and he was determined to eat it no matter what. Under his glaring eye, they all complimented him on the chili and made their excuses to pass on the gooey bowl of yellowish slop.

"Good. More for us." he said, and tried to spoon some into Annalise's bowl. She covered it and jerked it away quickly.

"Uh, I'm on a diet." she said.

"Since when?" he asked. "If anything you need to gain weight."

She ignored him, shooed one of the monkeys off the table and started in on her chili.

"Fine." he said. "The animals can have your share. You don't know what you're missing."

He set it on the floor for the foxes and cubs who were there begging and they backed off after one sniff. Neither would touch it.

Swan started giggling, tried to disguise it as a cough. Her face was turning red from trying to hold the laughter in but it was contagious. As they watched Tobias try to get any of the critters to try it the snickers and coughs got worse. Cody was fit to burst, his eyes bulged from holding his breath and holding in the booming laugh that was going to break free any second. One of Murrays' monkeys finally took a proffered piece of it and stuffed it into her mouth. She screamed her high-pitched monkey scream, spit it out and ran and they couldn't control themselves any more. The dining room erupted in raucous laughter, purifying laughter that had tears running down their faces. Every time they would taper off to catch their breath, someone would scream like the Capuchin and it would start again.

"You guys suck." Tobias said, but even he finally admitted the cheese was pretty rancid.

Candlelight, children's laughter, the warmth of the fire and love filled the rooms as a soft, yellow light glowed through the windows pushing away the darkness and the falling snow.

Kodiak listened to their even, steady breathing over the sounds of the wind whipping through the eaves and couldn't sleep. They had gotten into the habit of winding down and going to bed early, usually shortly after nightfall, because they got up early. It was the real first snow in weeks, the first chance Gordon would have to come after them, and it was turning into a regular blizzard. Would he wait until the weather was calm? Would he come in the daytime? Was he wrong and maybe they weren't coming at all? He had an uneasiness settling over him and he knew he wouldn't be able to sleep. He couldn't leave his tribe unguarded and vulnerable.

What would Gordon do?

Gordon and his band of goons would probably use darkness and the storm as cover. They would come like a thief in the night because they didn't want to kill everyone, probably just him. They wanted the girls. They could be sneaking up on the porch right now with cans of gas. They might be planning on burning them out and taking them prisoner as they fled. They might have gunners at every door waiting for the animals to panic and...

He sat up and Otis chuffed at him. He felt the tension in his companion and didn't hesitate when Kodiak threw aside the blankets and clicked his tongue for him to come.

When they stepped out onto the porch, he almost changed his mind. The gusts pulled at him and whipped snow across his face. The moon and stars were hidden as the storm gained strength and started to dump its full fury on northeastern Iowa. The wind howled out of the northern sky, eliciting mournful moans and creaks from the old house and it promised more. He thought about the long walk ahead that would probably be for nothing, the weather was turning worse and only an idiot would be out in it. He thought longingly of his bed that would still be toasty warm near the fire. Then he thought of all they would lose if he was right, if Gordon would want to use the storm to his advantage. If he decided to do the easy thing and go back to sleep, they would have no advance warning. Gordon had already tried to kill Otis once; he had no doubt the bear would be their first target. He rubbed his ears where he liked them to be rubbed and made his decision. He pulled the hood up on the buffalo cloak and started down the steps.

"C'mon, Otis. I guess we'll be fools tonight even if no one else is."

Kodiak set across the park in a steady jog, one he could keep up for hours and set a quick enough pace where the bear wouldn't get distracted. They made it to the old stone church with its caved in roof, shattered stain glass and fire scorched walls and sought shelter from the wind. He'd been working on and off, making his crude defenses for weeks. He knew when they came, it would be in the snow and it would be cold. They had heated snowmobile suits and hand warmers and all he had was Otis but it was enough. The road curved in a long, looping horseshoe around a bend in the river and from the church, he could see them coming from a long way off. It wasn't far as a crow flies but if they followed the road, it was a mile or two. He had a windbreak with good visibility and between the bear and the buffalo robe, he wasn't worried about freezing to death.

Otis was snoring softly within minutes as Kodiak settled in beside him and watched for headlights. Would his traps work? Would they stand a chance when it finally went down? Was he wasting his time waiting for something that might not happen?

His thoughts wandered. Their survival was a miracle in itself. Of all the places he could have been, he was in one of the safest spots in the world. They hadn't seen another living adult in the months since the outbreak. If it had been a Monday, he'd have been sitting at school stealing glances at the pretty girls he'd never had the nerve to talk to. He would have been watching the clock, wishing for lunch so he could feed his growling stomach and looking forward to after school. He and his friends would race to their homes and fire up the game consoles and wage war with and against each other. Now, he was getting ready to wage another kind of war. One that didn't have a reset button if you got yourself killed.

He was angry. He was defiant. He was tired of it all. He had worried about the threat the Riders posed for weeks. His stomach had been in knots at the thought of what he would have to do to keep his tribe safe. Even after he came up from the water, baptized and changed and convinced he was right, the old Cody nagged at him.

He was going to hurt them.

Hurt them bad.

Probably kill a few of them if his ambush worked out.

He would be a murderer.

He didn't want this. He wanted to live in peace. He'd tried to help Gordon. Tried to do what was right. He didn't have a beef with the others but they had made their choice and they would have to live with it. Maybe die for it.

He'd made peace with his decision. He told himself he would feel no more remorse for them than a bear felt for a fish when he killed it. He didn't do it for meanness or spite, he did it to survive. Kodiak was doing the same thing. He wouldn't have to hurt them if they weren't coming for him. He wouldn't have to kill them if they would have stayed home and left him alone.

He was warm and comfortable wrapped in his robe, soaking up the heat coming off Otis and he must have dozed off. It took him a moment to recognize that the lights cutting through the snow far up the road weren't reflections. He heard them then, the wind carried the high-pitched whine of screaming engines and Otis raised his head.

They were coming.

They were coming!

He sprang to his feet and raced to the old maple tree. He grabbed the cable TV wire and yanked it tight. It popped up from the road, sending the covering snow flying away as he tied it in place about three feet above the surface. He ran to the next tree, pulled thicker electric line into place and locked it in position less than a foot from the asphalt.

Otis stood, shook the snow from his fur and sniffed the wind.

The mosquito buzz of the two-stroke engines was getting louder and he could make out the individual headlights. They were running single file and spread out for a long way. He'd hoped they'd be bunched up, running in a tight pack down the road so he could take most of them out but his ambush wouldn't get them all. Maybe only two or three if he was lucky.

It won't be long, he thought. He felt the churning in his stomach, his nerves raw and on edge. He would do what he had to tonight.

He'd hurt them.

He'd kill them.

He'd do it so maybe the others wouldn't have to. He felt a twinge of regret, not being able to say goodbye because he was pretty sure he knew how this was going to end. He couldn't get all of the riders and it was too late to abandon the plan and run. They'd see his tracks and follow. They'd kill Otis for sure, him more than likely, then continue to the house where they were all nestled under their blankets by the fireplace. Warm and safe.

He had to take the battle to them, maybe if he did enough damage, they'd get scared and turn back. Maybe he could tell them the others were waiting with similar ambushes and they'd all be dead before they made it to the house.

He pulled the last cable tight, tied it off, gripped his Warhammer and waited. Otis felt his tension, growled and started chuffing. He sensed a fight was coming, he could smell the machines and hear their angry buzz over the wind and whipping snow. He stood on his hind legs and roared a warning.

A panther answered and Kodiak whirled to see them running out of the woods by the church. They materialized in the snowy mist like phantoms. Yewan, ebony black against the pure white snow and Donny: armored and armed with his spear with only his eyes visible through the protective gear. They hurried toward him and he felt a new chill run down his spine. His brother was here. The hunter and his cat.

Behind him came Tobias and Annalise, battle axes in hand, cloaked in coyote hides, astride their polar bears. The big bears puffed out white smoke as they galloped along, the twins had their faces painted for war like Vikings of old and Kodiaks heart swelled.

Swan appeared other worldly in her hyena cloak, its ears sticking up, its head covered hers and Zero loped alongside her. Both were painted for war and wore collars of hyena fangs and claws; hers for decoration, his for protection. She wore red slashes of paint on her soot blackened face and Zero had red handprints on his hindquarters. The beads and feathers and acorns twisted into her dark hair clacked together like a wind chime.

She had her bow slung over a shoulder, a quiver of

arrows protruding over the other and her tomahawks hung in their holsters. She wore a grim expression and Kodiak wasn't sure if she looked like an avenging angel or a demon from the pits of Hell. Maybe a little of both.

Vanessa and Ziggy followed behind, ready for whatever was going to happen. She had her spear in one hand and with the other she tried to reassure Ziggy who was agitated and unaccustomed to the severe temperatures.

Bert faded into view out of the snow with Harper riding high on his back, a morning star in her hand.

Kodiak wasn't surprised to see them but he had been prepared to fight the Riders alone. Prepared to die alone if it came down to that.

But he wasn't and he realized that he'd never been alone. The tribe had been there every step of the way since this all began months ago. From the time they'd comforted him over the loss of his mother and through all his decisions, good and bad, they'd been there. Solid and dependable. More than friends. More than family. A tribe.

"We knew what you were doing." Swan said "And we know why. It's not your fight to fight alone. It's all of ours."

The headlights dancing through the trees were getting closer, they were on the long curve just before the straight stretch and his traps.

"We have to hurry." Kodiak said and snatched up the wooden spears with the road flares attached a few inches down from the points.

He handed them up to Vanessa on the side-stepping ostrich and pointed up the road. "Light them when they stop. Aim for the gas cans strapped to the machines."

She nodded, gigged Ziggy and they raced off to find a place to get out of sight.

"The rest of you spread out, both sides of the road."

Kodiak said. "Remember, they have guns. We have to hit them hard and fast. If one guy starts shooting, he can kill us all."

They melted back into the shadows of the woods, disappeared in the snow storm, and each shivered in anticipation.

51

GORDON

Gordon and the other Riders flew down the highway, the snowmobiles eating up the miles on the covered roads. They were built for whatever winter threw at them: top of the line, high dollar machines that were popular in the north. They drove fast, warm in their heavy suits and motocross gear they wore beneath them. He could taste the victory already and he smiled under his full-face helmet at the thoughts of revenge. The plan to attack tonight had been Richards but he'd helped by answering hundreds of questions. It was a good plan, he approved. With most of the animals either hibernating or penned up in the barn, they would only have a few to deal with. They all crashed out in the same room, gathered around the fireplace, and at two in the morning they would catch them sleeping. They never locked the doors and they would wake up to the sounds of gunshots putting down their animals. They'd never expect it with the storm raging, it would be a quick and easy victory. They could tie up the boys, maybe beat on them a little if they got sassy then break in the new girls. He knew he'd never get first dibs on Harper or any of the others for that matter. He'd come to terms with it, though. They'd get tired of her after a few months and then he could move in and claim her as his own. He'd get Richard to tell them to leave her alone. They were family so he probably would. He was looking forward to seeing Skull or Gargoyle have their fun with Swan. Those two were pretty rough on the girls back at the Landing and Richard had to tell them to tone it down more than once. If they kept it up, they were going to break them. That would teach the wolf girl to get on his bad side.

The snowmobile handled like a dream, the heated seat and handlebars dispelled the cold, the fairings kept the wind off him.

He carried a .32 caliber revolver tucked inside the pocket of the snowsuit. Richard had called it a popgun with its little bullets, but Gordon liked how small it was and easy to hide. He'd turned down the big guns offered to him by the other guys. It would do just fine for the job he had in mind.

He couldn't wait to hear Cody beg and plead. He planned on sitting on top of Otis's bullet riddled body with Cody trussed up at his feet listening to Harper scream and cry as they took turns with her. He wanted to laugh at his pain and when the time was right, he'd shoot him in the knee caps with his little pop gun. It wouldn't kill him but he'd never run again and he'd never be able to win a fight. One little tap to the leg would send him tumbling to the ground.

They were getting close; the old church was just ahead. He was near the rear of the pack, right in front of Richard. His cousin wanted him close in case he had any questions. He took another sip of whiskey from his camelback and didn't even grimace. He was getting used to the taste. Like the others, he was half lit from the alcohol in his hydration bag. He was sixteen now. He drank and smoked, took turns with the girls and popped pills the same as the rest of them. He was a man.

Pole was in the lead and knew the fun was about to begin when his headlight caught the church they'd burnt down. They were just around the corner and the back gate was only another mile beyond it. He came out of the bend, took another sip of tequila and goosed it. The machine shot up to fifty miles an hour then slammed into something solid. He didn't see the cable stretched across the road. It caught the snowmobile right above the skis and sent it tumbling end over end before it snapped. Pole flew through the air, arms waving frantically and bounced off a telephone pole. His leg bent in places it wasn't supposed to bend and he screamed when he felt the bone break and spear through his flesh and snowsuit. His machine continued to spin and roll, fiberglass pieces and bits of metal flying in every direction, headlight flashing like a strobe. He howled in agony at the pain and nearly passed out when he saw the sharp, bloody end of his bone sticking out of the snowsuit.

Jester was right behind him, dodged to the right to miss the wreck and caught the second cable strung across the road. It caught the tip of his fairing and rode it up, smashed through his windshield and caught him across the chest. He was going thirty when it snapped his ribs, sent him flying in one direction and the snowmobile in another.

Two more riders, reaction time dulled by booze and blowing snow, the vibration of the machines and the warm electric suits, jerked the handlebars to avoid Jester who was flying right towards them.

They slammed together and Cappy's gloved hand slid over the thumb throttle, revving the big Polaris to redline. It answered instantly. The studded track dug in, lifted the front skis skyward and powered the machine up and across Maggots back. The steel barbs shredded the seat, his snow-suit then sent chunks of muscle and flesh spraying across the snow.

Cappy tried to scream but choked on a mouth full of alcohol as he held on for dear life. The machine launched into the air, hit the same cable and snapped it. The flying end caught the wildly spinning track, tangled in the sprocket and jerked the sled towards the tree where it was tied. Cappy went flying the other direction, landed hard and the camel back flattened. It shot a half liter of booze down his throat. The impact knocked the air out of him and his coughing fit turned into drowning as he sucked the tequila into his lungs.

The rest of the machines slid to a halt, helmet visors were flipped up and they started yelling questions at each other.

"What did they hit?"

"What the hell just happened?"

A war cry erupted from the wood line, a flaming spear shot through the darkness, an arrow from a compound bow drove deep into a rider's heart and screaming children on polar bears charged out of the night swinging saw bladed battle axes.

"Shoot them! Shoot them!" Gordon shrieked in panic and fought to rip his gloves off so he could grab his own gun.

The Yamaha behind him erupted into a geyser of flames and someone ran past him beating at a burning suit, trying to tear it off.

Two shadows leapt from the ditch line, one with a spear and one with claws, and a rider trying to pull his rifle from its scabbard was knocked sideways off his machine. Snarling white fangs sank into his shoulder as claws tore his snow suit to ribbons. The man tried to scream but vomited blood inside his helmet when something hard and sharp tore through his belly. Donny withdrew his steel shafted spear from the man's stomach, twisted it to cut lose the trailing bits of guts and let Yewan finish the kill.

Skull tore his AR-15 out of its bag and aimed at the big, brown bear that felt like it was making the ground shake as it thundered towards him. He squeezed the trigger, heard the bear roar in pain and fury before an arrow knocked his aim off. It hit the hard plastic of his hockey pad and shattered but it caused his bullets to go wide. The boy they had tied to the front of Gordon's machine leaped for him, a wicked looking Warhammer swinging for his face. Skull jerked the gun up just in time to block the hammer from knocking his head off, iron smashed against metal and plastic, sent the rifle flying away. He grabbed the boy by a handful of hair as he fell over the seat and pulled him down into the snow while flaming pieces of plastic rained down all around them.

Swan sent arrow after carefully aimed arrow into the bunched-up machines, silent death coming at them from the shadows.

Richard couldn't get his gloves off to pull his pistols; they were velcroed to his suit to keep out the cold. In his panic, he pawed at the slick, waterproof material and kept slipping. This wasn't supposed to happen. Half his guys were already down and screaming, being mauled by crazy looking kids in war paint and monster animals that were supposed to be hibernating.

Another flaming spear came out of the dark and another snowmobile splashed bright orange, lighting up the night in a ball of flame. Roiling black smoke from burning plastic joined the wind whipped snow to shroud them with a haze that was hard to see through.

The fight was over before it even began, he had to go. He had to get away. He'd just seen half-naked kids riding polar bears and swinging homemade axes cut down one of his men. How did you fight something like that? Gordon had lied, this was no easy way to get a few more girls, and this was a slaughter. He stopped trying to pull his gun and hit the throttle of the idling machine.

Kodiak twisted his hammer, tried to hit the hand curled in his hair but it was knocked aside. Skull was three years older, fifty pounds heavier and still heavily muscled. He head-butted the boy with his helmet then rammed his face into the Kevlar track. Blood exploded from Kodiaks nose and Skull jerked him back to slam it again and again but was suddenly lifted off his knees and flung through the air. Six inch long claw as big as cigars shredded his armor, slashed through flesh and tossed him some ten feet away next to one of the burning snowmobiles. Otis towered above him silhouetted by flames with blood matting his shoulder where the bullet had hit. He roared, the polar bears answered and the savage growls of the wolf and panther drowned out the screams of terror and war cries of fury.

Snowmobile engines revved to life adding to the cacophony of horror as riders tried to escape from the nightmare. Otis clawed at a passing rider, sent him tumbling towards the ditch then dropped to all fours to chase a fleeing machine.

Kodiak wiped the blood out of his face and saw Skull reaching for the rifle. He rolled to his feet, double fisted his hammer and raised it over his head as he catapulted high in the air. He drove it straight down against the rider's helmet, putting all his strength and all his weight behind the blow. It was a solid hit, cracked the plastic and slammed him back down to the ground. He swung again like he was wielding a baseball bat and trying to knock one into the stands. Chunks of the helmet broke away and the rider stopped reaching for the gun. He pushed himself unsteadily to his knees and tried to crawl away. He had no more fight left in him. The helmet pieces fell to the snow as he hung his head and in the dancing firelight, Kodiak saw blood oozing out of his ears. The boy was helpless, was trying to crawl away but was headed back into the madness. Gordon's gang member had tried to shoot him, had hit Otis at least once. The boy had tried to break his skull and blood still cascaded from a gash across his eye. Kodiak gripped the long, iron handle, raised it high over his head and aimed for the back of boys' neck. It would be like slaughtering a pig, all he had to do was bash his head. It was unprotected. The boy would never even feel it. Kodiak held the Warhammer high for a moment then let it fall. He kicked him instead, knocked him flat again.

"You're going the wrong way, idiot." he said then ran into the smoke, looking for targets that could fight back.

Richard spun his snowmobile out of the cluster, ducked low behind his windshield and raced around the roaring bear for the open road. Otis slashed out, splintered the front of the machine and swept his paw across the boy's chest. His massive claws sent him flying, sheared through the snowsuit and raked four deep gouges across his ribs. His machine careened through the ditch and came to a halt with its nose against a tree. Richard hit the ground, staggered to his feet and ran, clutching his wounded chest. He fled towards the forest, hit the ditch and stumbled. A wolf came out of the darkness, ripped into his leg, pulled him down. His screams were lost in the night, mixed with the others as the wolf shredded his clothes, anxious to get at the flesh beneath. The snarling beast was jerking him around like a rag doll but he managed to get his knife out of its sheath and slashed at the thing trying to rip his leg off.

Swan dropped her bow when she heard Zero yelp. She had a tomahawk in each hand as she left the woods and ran to the ditch to join the fight. Zero had backed off, a long gash across his muzzle but his teeth were bared and he had a rumbling, snarling growl deep in his throat. Swan hurled one her tomahawks as she leaped down the embankment and slid to a halt by Zero, her own growl on her peeled back lips. The spike slammed into the boy's shoulder, buried itself to the head and he looked up at her in shock and surprise. Richard turned his hunting knife towards her, stared at the soot blackened face, the spotted hyena hide she wore over her shoulders, and knew he was going to die. These kids weren't human, they were something else. Something vicious and wild. Another snowmobile exploded into flames and the screaming albino twins were slashing at anyone they saw. Their bears ran them down after they had smashed through the clustered snowmobiles, scattering everyone in panic. Nobody was firing their guns, nobody was fighting back, it was complete chaos and the feral children were butchering them one by one.

He dropped the knife and held up his hands.

"Please." he said "Please..."

Swan stopped short of driving the blade into his skull, put a hand on her wolf to stay his spring. To stop his killing lunge.

His terror filled eyes were wide, his hands held up in a feeble effort to protect himself from the wolf girls' terrible anger. From the gleaming tomahawk in her hand.

"Please..."

Swan hesitated, ground her teeth. He flinched and gasped when she snagged her other tomahawk out of his shoulder then stepped back.

"Run." she said.

It was a limping, ungainly run that left a trail of blood melting the snow behind him but he fled as fast as he could.

Vanessa lit the flare and tried to spot another gas can, another target, through the swirling snow. She heard the twins yelling their battle cries, the roaring and snarling of the animals, the screams of men in pain. The winds lashed the flames and illuminated the ambush area in dancing orange light. Dark smoke whipped through the pandemonium of battle. One of the riders had managed to strip off his burning suit and armor, dig out his pistol and fired as he ran straight at her. Bullets whizzed by her head, splintered bark from the tree, but she didn't cower and hide. She let her spear fly, its duct taped magnesium flare sending a shower of red fire out of the end. It flew true, hit him square in the chest and sunk deep. He dropped the gun, sank to his knees, gripped the spear and stared in shocked disbelief. His insides were on fire, he was glowing pinkish red and smoking. She came out of the woods, small, dark and silent, running at him with a machete.

He was being killed by ten-year-old.

A dark-skinned girl with scars and paint on her face.

She had a tight mohawk, feathers and beads around her neck and he was so stunned he didn't feel the blade as it sliced open his neck when she ran past.

Gordon screamed his frustration and jumped on a sled that didn't look damaged. The crazy twins and their bears had scattered everyone and smashed most of the machines. It wasn't supposed to be like this. They had the numbers and they had the guns. It wasn't fair. They were losing and everyone was running as fast as they could. He didn't know where his cousin was, he thought he saw him take off a few minutes ago, and he really didn't care. Pole pulled himself along in the snow, trying to get back to the sleds, a mangled, broken leg left a blood trail behind him. Gordon goosed the machine to knock a twisted snowmobile out of the way and almost didn't see the crawling boy in the confusion. He heard the snarl of Swan behind him and didn't have time to go around. Pole would understand, nothing personal, he would have done the same thing. He bumped over him, dodged around Donny and Yewan as they appeared out of the smoke and pressed the throttle. The machine shot forward, out of the reach of Swans tomahawks and Yewans fangs. He saw Cody when he passed by the burning sled and cut the skis.

He grinned maniacally as he bore down on him. It was small revenge but it was all he was going to get this time. At least he would accomplish something on this messed up mission.

Kodiak heard the quick revving buzz of the engine, threw himself out of the way as Gordon sped by. The handlebar caught his buffalo robe, jerked him off his feet as the snowmobile jagged sharply and caught the rear end of a burning sled. One of the skis on Gordon's machine hooked something solid and snapped off. The fiberglass and plastic fairing exploded as he fought for control. It nearly jerked his arm out of its socket but the machine righted itself and he leaned his weight to the opposite side to keep it moving forward. He breathed a deep sigh, threw a hateful look over his shoulder and gave gas again. The machine would ride with one ski. It might be hard to handle but that was okay. It was better than being dead. He turned around just in time to see a giraffe appear out of the darkness and a flail of spiked steel coming straight for his head. He threw up his hands barely in time to stop it from impaling his face and screamed in terror as he went sprawling off the sled. The tough, padded armor saved him from two shattered arms but the plastic tore free on the spikes. They gouged through his flesh, leaving bloody rifts in both arms. The machine came to a halt a dozen yards up the road and he scrambled to get back to it. To get away from these lunatic children. To escape.

A huge yellow and black head swung for him and once again the giraffe sent him tumbling away. Harper spun in her saddle, hopped on to Bert's long, sloping back and slid to the ground, using his tail to slow her fall. Gordon tried to clear his head, tried to stand but she knocked him flat before he could get to his feet. Harper stood over him, her blonde hair whipping in the wind, her face painted like the rest of them, her morning star ready to bash his head in if he tried to move. He heard other snowmobile engines revving and fading as they took off through the woods or down the road, running for home. Swan and Donny came out of the smoke and snow, bloody wolf and bloodier panther padding slowly beside them. Kodiak appeared, him and Otis both bleeding but they walked steadily forward. He heard more cries of pain, more engines starting up. Headlights split the night and shot down the road, injured riders crouched low and fleeing for their lives. Leaving him behind. The fires behind the kids turned them into shadowy wraiths as Gordon crabbed slowly backward, away from the girl with the toma-hawk. Away from the boy with the spear. Away from the animals who would shred him alive and feast on him as he died. The twins materialized out of the snow, white on white and splashed with red.

Harper kept pace, not trying to stop him, just watching

him with an inscrutable look on her painted face. Gordon's eyes flashed to each of them looking for mercy but saw none. He remembered his gun and fumbled with the zipper of his suit. As Kodiak approached, he pulled the pistol from his pocket, pointed it before anyone could react and squeezed the trigger. Fire erupted from the barrel and the bullet hit Kodiak at nearly point-blank range. He stumbled as it struck, felt the burn as it plunged through the thick buffalo robe, his plastic breastplate then buried itself into his chest.

Barely.

The children's response was instant and Gordon would have been speared, flailed, hatcheted, macheted and slashed to ribbons with sharp toothed axes if Kodiak hadn't yelled for them to stop. Donny was the quickest and barely altered his thrust to snap Gordon's wrist instead of plunging the steel through his faceplate.

They heard the bone break, saw the pistol spin away to be lost in the snow. Kodiak reached under his chest plate and plucked the flattened little bullet out. It was still hot so he let it drop the ground and sizzle in the snow. The fire in the background was slowly dying out, but there was enough light to illuminate the panic and terror on Gordons face as he cradled his broken wrist.

"I'll do it." Kodiak said. "I'll carry out the judgement."

They backed off, formed a half circle as he approached and adjusted his grip on the hammer. Their bloodlust was still high, these men had come to kill, rape and enslave. They didn't have pity and they wouldn't show mercy. Gordon started to keen, a drawn out high pitched *nooooooo* coming from somewhere deep inside him.

They heard someone crying, a girl, and turned to watch as a naked woman staggered out of the smoke, most of her hair burnt off and smoldering bits of Gore-Tex snowsuit fused to her skin. They smelled her then, the sickly-sweet smell of burnt flesh as she stumbled and sobbed, her body raw, blistered and red. They slowly lowered their weapons and their faces softened.

"She came to kill us, too." Swan said. "She deserved what she got."

Her heart wasn't in it though and when the girl fell, Swan was the first to run help her.

52

DIABLO

Diablo slunk through the tree line, his senses alert. The smell of burnt fuel irritated his nostrils and he sneezed. There was another scent though, blood. His acute nose homed in on it and he approached stealthily towards its source.

Behind him, the Savage Ones followed. The crows, ravens and vultures soared overhead in oblong circles. The raccoons, opossums, feral hogs, stray cats, dogs and foxes followed in his wake. Some of them had felt his ire when they got too close. Powerful jaws crushed fragile bones and his laughing bark warned them to keep their distance. The fallen became food for the many as they fought over the scraps of whatever unfortunate had met Diablo's wrath. Yet they followed still, drawn by his power and commanding presence. They had been eating the undead for months and it changed them. Subtly altered the way their brains worked. The virus that turned the humans into frenzied flesh eaters almost instantly was caused by microscopic man-made nanobots. It didn't affect the animals in the same way, it didn't turn them into undead monsters. The more of the infected flesh they ate, the more they wanted. It was addictive, easy to hunt and plentiful. It slowly changed them over time. It didn't make them undead, it made them crave the same thing the undead craved. It made them hunger for human blood. The more dead flesh they ate, the more living flesh they wanted.

Diablo crept forward, his infected shoulder was stiff, weeping pus, but it would hold. He was the most fearsome creature roaming these woods and even wounded, he would shred any animal that crossed him.

He eyed the roadway warily, keen night vision taking in the machines that man rode and the rapidly filling depressions in the snow where the blood scent emanated. He growled a warning at his followers, letting them know this was his find. He would feast first; he would have the choicest bits. The hearts and kidneys and liver. His wounded body craved the blood enriched protein and drool ran from his massive jaws as he crept slowly forward. He feared no creature but man. Man meant pain. Man meant beatings with leather straps and shocks with cattle prods. He inhaled the scent of his enemy, the wolf, but it was an old scent, faint and fading. He had no desire to tangle with the wolf again, but he didn't fear him either. The scents of the bears and the other animals still lingered but his nose told him the danger was long past and the spoils were his.

He dug into the first cavity, ignoring the pain from his wound. He found the body beneath and with his powerful jaws ripped through the clothing until he reached the flesh. It was hard, nearly frozen but he forced his muzzle through, sharp canines snipping through flesh and tendon to the warmer treats inside. He sensed the approach of the others and growled another low warning. They watched him feast, keeping plenty of distance between them. He gorged on the internal organs; his muzzle coated in blood until he had eaten the choicest bites. He moved on to the next, the Savage Ones quickly fell onto the remains he left behind, snarling and biting amongst themselves as they fought for position around the corpse. The rotten ones they'd been feasting on were scarce lately and their empty stomachs drove them to near madness. Some of them were devoured in the frenzy by their own pack as their first taste of untainted blood pushed them over the brink.

Diablo, sated at last, moved towards the shelter of an abandoned car and put his back to the vehicle. None of the ravenous beasts would flank him. He watched as they devoured his scraps. There was more meat not far from here. The ones who'd caged him. The ones who'd hurt him. His instincts told him he wasn't prepared to attack there yet. He would heal then seek out the weaker ones inside the fences to fill his belly.

He rose to his feet, turned back into the wood line and disappeared. They would follow, his scent was unique to these woods. These things didn't concern him. Sleep and the warmth of a den beckoned. He set out in search of a suitable place, the snapping and snarling, the crunching of bone and ripping of flesh echoing in his ears as he disappeared into the forest, leaving the carnage behind him.

53

SMITH'S LANDING

Richard slammed the door behind him to the startled looks of the girls who had stayed behind.

"Where's everyone else?" Misty asked then shrank back from the baleful glare, his torn suit and the blood running down his leg.

A few of his guys had made it back before him and they didn't look injured. They were the ones who ran away first. Cowards. He'd deal with them later. He hobbled to the bar, grabbed a bottle of tequila and turned it up. He chugged deeply, the fire making its way down his throat to burn in his stomach. His leg throbbed and blood flowed freely from the spike hole in his shoulder. The alcohol gave him the illusion of warmth and dulled the pain. The whole miserable ride back it had taken every ounce of his willpower. Every jostle and bump in the road made him hurt more.

"Gordon" he muttered under his breath, turning the name into a vile curse word. "He did this."

He flung the half empty bottle against the wall. It shattered and the gold liquid soaked into the expensive rug covering the floor. He should have known better than to let that lying little weasel talk him into the raid. His libido always overrode his good sense. Girls were his weakness and Gordy had promised him girls. An easy victory and beautiful girls. He hadn't said they were wild and untamed like that painted up wolf girl who stabbed him. He had escaped, he was alive when others were dead and he was trying to forget how he begged for his life from a twelve-year-old. Those kids weren't normal, they were as savage as anything he'd ever seen and she was like a honey badger, vicious and unforgiving. He'd watched the rest of the battle from his hiding spot in the tree line and they scared him. He'd rather fight a horde of zombies than face them again. Their animals were even worse, he'd seen the polar bears grab someone and rip his arm completely off. His whole damn arm. And those pale white savages riding them, they scared him more than the wolf girl the way they swung their axes, splitting helmets and cutting down his men. He was glad they were separated by so many miles and he was thankful for the storm. It would cover his tracks, they wouldn't be able to follow.

"Get over here, Tasha." he spat at the pale faced girl.

Or maybe it was Sasha. He couldn't remember.

"Get some bandages and get me sewn up."

He looked at the hamburger that was his calf, which the wolf had ravaged. This was gonna hurt.

The rest of the Riders trickled in one by one or in pairs and Richard realized he had been lucky. He only had a hole in his shoulder, bear claw slashes across his chest and a chewed-up ankle. The others were scattered around the living room, the few that were left anyway. They were all wounded. Broken arms, broken ribs, broken legs and cracked skulls. Frostbite, slash marks, bite marks, arrows that punched through armor, missing fingers, gut wounds that probably wouldn't heal, third degree burns, jagged gashes and then there was Squirrel. The pretty little party girl that thought everything was a joke, who lived in a constant state of inebriation, was a blackened mess. She'd been splashed in gas, caught fire, panicked and ran. It wasn't that bad at first, only her jacket was burning. She had Everclear in her camelback and when it caught fire, she'd been engulfed. If she would have dropped into the snow and unzipped her suit, she would have been fine but she didn't. She ran and it melted into her. She probably wouldn't survive either but if she did, her good looks were gone forever.

His crew would be incapacitated for months. He'd lost friends. Their loss meant more than Gordon was worth. He hoped he was dead. He hoped the bear had killed him or that he'd had his head bashed in by the Warhammer the boy in the buffalo robe carried. The last he'd seen of him, he was on the ground with the kids and their animals gathered around him.

They'd had guns but barely got a shot off. They'd had superior numbers and powerful machines but a few cables across the road had stopped them in their tracks. It had been a perfect ambush and he should have known better. He'd done something similar a thousand times in a hundred different video games. It never occurred to him that the kids would do it in real life.

The girls that stayed behind couldn't wrap their heads around what happened. Little kids and big animals had killed or maimed everyone. How did Richard let that happen? Were the men of Smith's Landing really that weak or were the tweenagers almost God-like warriors?

Richard sat in a recliner, his leg elevated, and surveyed the oversized living room that had been turned into a hospital ward. He'd heard their stories as they told what happened to them, how they had gotten injured. He called BS on every one of them. None of them had stood to fight like they claimed. None of them had been brave, him included. They all ran. Moans and groans and curses filled the house. Nearly every one of them were wounded and he still wasn't sure who was dead. More survivors may be coming.

He looked at Skull. Blood trails ran out of both ears, his head was puffy and misshapen, his nose flattened across his face. The boy with the Warhammer had done a number on him. He chewed Oxy like it was candy.

Maggot was busted up bad from Cappy running over him. He looked terrible, his back looked like someone had taken a cheese grater to it before they bandaged him up. He was black and yellow with bruises and stared blankly at the wall, drool pooling on the couch from the corner of his mouth. He kept moaning that his guts hurt. Richard tuned him out. There was nothing he could do for him except pump him full of drugs and alcohol.

Gargoyle was gone. The panther had killed the shit out of him. He'd miss Gargoyle.

Boonie was dead, that crazy wolf girl had punched his ticket. He was pretty sure Rooster was dead because he was pretty sure it had been him getting his arm ripped off.

They'll just have to rot out there, he thought. No way was he going anywhere near those crazy bastards and their animals. If they ever left the compound again, no one would ever be allowed to go south. Ever.

Cowboy and Shaggy were chewed up from the psycho albinos on the polar bears. Jagged sawblade axes had sliced through their snowsuits and found soft flesh. Cowboys back had been laid wide open. Shaggy's was no better but at least he wasn't crying about it like Cowboy was.

Bong lay passed out next to his namesake. He couldn't even tell them what happened. One minute he was riding, the next he woke up freezing cold, all alone with an arrow in him and his helmet cracked open. *At least a concussion there*, he thought. Bong was brain damaged enough already without taking a hit like that.

He took another swallow from the bottle as he watched the girls tend to the broken boys of Smiths Landing.

He listened to Pole moaning from his place on the floor. The compound fracture of his leg had him drifting in and out of consciousness. The girls were afraid to try to set it, they didn't have any experience in such things. Pole would be lucky if he didn't die of infection and if he survived, he would walk with a limp for the rest of his life. His hockey days were definitely over.

Juicy was missing two fingers from his right hand. The boy stared at the bloody bandage with an unbelieving look on his face. Part of him was missing. A ninja with a razor-sharp staff had sliced him as he was trying to aim his gun then disappeared back into the smoke. He didn't even know if he was remembering it right but he knew he never wanted to mess with the kids again.

Richard guzzled more booze and told Trish to get the Oxy from Flame. He needed one. Or maybe two.

The front door burst open and Gordon staggered in.

He looked scared. He looked around at the wounded and his eyes met Richard's. His cousin glared at him.

Gordon shed his snowsuit and moved over to stand over one of the heater vents. His pulse raced and his heart pounded. His broken wrist throbbed and the holes in his arms from Harpers ball and chain had soaked his thermal shirt."

"I figured you for dead." Richard said. "And truth be told, I wouldn't have been one bit sorry. You were supposed to know these kids, Gordy. You promised us it would be an easy raid but we got our asses handed to us."

There were mumbles of agreement from around the room.

"Yeah, well you guys left me behind. I had to fight them off by myself. At least I put a bullet in Cody, he's probably dead by now and so is the bear."

He snorted and turned his back on his cousin, falling back on the old standby when someone was winning an argument. Righteous indignation. Twist the truth and put the blame on them. He needed a drink to calm his nerves

Richard eyed him suspiciously. "So, you shot him and the rest just let you go? Sounds like a Gordy story to me."

"No, they didn't just let me go. I kicked ass and got away in the confusion. We could have won if you hadn't chickened out." The lies slipped easily from his mouth but no one was listening and wouldn't have believed him if they were.

"Look around you idiot! No one was in any shape to fight. Half the guys were dead before we even knew we were under attack! I've got friends laying out there in the snow, food for the animals and it's all on you!"

Richard tried to rise but his wounded leg screamed in protest. He slumped back into the chair with a groan.

"Sasha, take a look at my wrist." Gordon ordered.

"Do it yourself," she answered.

She was pouring hydrogen peroxide over the bone sticking out of Pole's leg. He screamed as the liquid hit his exposed nerves. Misty and Trish held him down as she gave a sharp tug on his ankle, pulled the bone back into place. She felt it slip into position then cleaned and stitched the torn flesh as best as she was able before wrapping it in a splint. She moved onto the next boy. It was gonna be a long night.

54

PIEDMONT HOUSE

The mood at breakfast was somber, they were lost in reflection over the fight. Murray had cooked when the twins didn't show any interest as they sat around the fire cleaning gore out of their weapons. Each of the tribe had gone to sleep as soon as they made it home last night, the adrenaline rush gone and the long walk back sapping the last of their reserves. They had won, a decisive and absolute victory, but it felt hollow. It had almost been too easy. Most of them didn't even have a scratch and they had put a lot of people in the grave.

The crying girl, her body burnt and scarred, her hands melted lumps, had sapped their fury. Their determination to kill them all and be done with it. She had changed everything, shamed them when they realized they were getting ready to butcher the injured and unarmed. They couldn't kill Gordon or the rest of them in cold blood, couldn't sink spears into helpless people.

Kodiak wondered if all survivors felt guilty for being victorious. If maybe that was why so many soldiers committed suicide, they couldn't get the images of what they had done out of their heads. He didn't know how things could have been different, it was kill or be killed, but it was a lot bloodier and uglier than any movie or video game. It wasn't clean and easy.

Instead of killing them, they helped the injured, the ones who hadn't already ran away, and sent them back to where ever it was they came from.

Even Gordon.

Outside, the snow continued to fall in big fluffy flakes. The storm had passed, almost as if it had spent its fury during the battle, dying out as the adrenaline faded and the spilled blood froze.

Murray and the triplets had a million questions about the fight.

The tribe ignored them.

Harper promised details later. Much later. It just didn't feel right to talk about it.

"They won't be coming back," was all Kodiak said. "We hurt them pretty bad."

He had been hurt the worst, his face felt like mangled hamburger.

"I'll have to teach you how to fight." Swan had said and made faces as Harper cleaned and closed up the wounds.

It almost didn't seem fair. They had killed a half dozen of the gang, broken the rest of them, some permanently damaged, and he was the only one who'd been seriously injured. He couldn't see very well out of his swollen eye that got slammed into the snowmobile track but at least it hadn't blinded him. Harper said the scar gave him character so that was okay. The others had bumps and bruises, sore muscles, a sprain and Otis had a gouge in his shoulder but the bullet had passed right through. He'd acted like a big baby when Murray cleaned the wound and stitched it up but it gave him an excuse to be fussed over and hog the floor in front of the fireplace, as if he really needed one.

The traps and their vicious ambush had worked. There was so much confusion among Gordon's people they had broken and ran almost as soon as the fight started. Harper hadn't even been in it. The first gunshot startled Bert and it took her a while to get him to stop running and get turned around.

After breakfast they lounged around the fireplace playing games, reading or brushing their animals. Kodiak stared out of the window, questioning his decision to let Gordon go once more. When it came down to it, he couldn't, he wouldn't kill him in cold blood, even after everything he'd done. He might be a killer but he wasn't a murderer. There was a big difference.

He was proud of his tribe. Proud of the way they'd stood in the face of superior numbers and firepower. Proud of all the long hours spent with their animals, not even training them for battle, just being with them. Being their friend and teacher.

Swan sat in one of the wide windowsills, sharing the ledge with Zero. She cradled River, the cutest of the wolf pups, while his brother and sister tussled on the floor nipping and biting each other, fearsome growls emanating from their tiny bodies. She thought about the life she'd taken. His blood still stained her tomahawk. It was dried now, dark and rusty looking, nothing like the bright red spray that splashed her face when she buried her blades. She'd thought revenge would be easier to swallow, but she felt empty inside. A few months ago, she'd have laughed if someone told her she'd be a fearsome killer and run with a pack of wolves. If she was like this a few months ago, she'd be all over the headlines and sitting in a jail cell. But so would Gordon. He'd shot Kodiak and they'd simply let him leave.

They had it coming, she thought, *they could have just stayed away.*

This world didn't favor the weak. In the bright light of the day, she wanted to disagree with their decision to let Gordon go. He needed killing. He was too dangerous to let live but the crying girl had stopped them. She had made them see the stain it would leave on their souls. Maybe the snow would take care of the problem for them. Maybe the snowmobile had left him stranded and the crows and ravens would feast on him in the spring. Maybe one of the zombies would get him. She'd love to see him at the gate, clawing and snarling, his eyes dead and flesh rotting on his bones. She savored the thought, nursed her hatred. She liked the idea of catching his zombified corpse and putting him in one of the animal enclosures. He'd make great target practice for her bow and tomahawks, as long as she didn't hit him in the head. When the pups grew older, she'd use him to train them to attack. She smiled at the thought. River yelped and she snapped out of her nightmare daydream. She'd been squeezing the poor thing.

Geez, Swan, what's wrong with you? She nuzzled the cub and whispered her apology softly in his ear. River relaxed and nestled against her chest. She took a deep breath and tried to clear her head of thoughts of Gordon and his gang. She had to let go of her anger. She wanted love in her life, not hate. Peace, not war.

Tobias and Annalise faced each other over a game of checkers, each trying to outmaneuver the other as they stared intensely at the board. Popsicle and Daisy lay in a pile under one the windows, seeking to take advantage of the drafty nature of the old house. They would have preferred to be outside in the snow, but the urge to be near their children over rode their own desire. The twins showed no outward indication that just a couple of hours before they'd been screaming ancient war cries and cutting down running men with battle axes. Tobias smirked as he watched his sister make a rookie mistake; he double jumped her, said *king me* and she crowned his checker. She held her poker face for a moment but grinned broadly as his jaw dropped when he saw he'd been drawn into a trap. She effectively hemmed in his King and he couldn't use it until she moved her blocking pieces. And if he knew her, those pieces would be there until the end of the game.

Vanessa sat with Donny, Yewan lay at his feet. The panther licked her paws and forelegs, purring contentedly. Vanessa sang softly as she braided his hair. He ignored the dull throb from his bruised shoulder, thankful it wasn't his head. The fight had been chaotic and he didn't know how many men they had battled. They had moved from one to the next as fast as they spotted them, stabbing or clawing, knocking them aside and moving on. He'd lost track of the others, the snow, the dancing fires and the smoke made it hard to see. It was easy to know where the twins were, they never shut up. He'd seen Swan ghosting in and out of view a few times swinging her tomahawks, Zero always by her side. He was pretty sure the snowmobilers' armor protected them from the worst of their blows and most ran away out of sheer panic. Some fought back, the boy with a pistol in each hand had him in his sights. No doubt he would be dead, not getting his hair braided, if Yewan hadn't struck when he did. He shivered as he thought about the sickening crunch of the boy's neck when she had closed down on it with those powerful jaws. He wanted to feel remorse, he wanted to be repulsed at the thought, but it eluded him. They had done what needed to be done to protect the tribe. There was no dishonor in that. He finally had a place. He finally had a family that loved him. He had Yewan, a companion and protector. He felt no remorse, he felt peace. It radiated out from somewhere deep inside him. He glanced at his sister, his friend, as she sang softly and braided a trophy into his hair. A small metal piece from a snowmobile, a reminder of the Gordon war. He took in his tribe scattered around the parlor, each dealing with the aftermath of the battle in their own ways. It took the end of the world to find his place in it and he vowed to never let it go. He'd killed for his tribe and he'd die for them if it was required.

Harper stared at Kodiak from the comfort of the recliner she lay in, nestled under a thick blanket, a book in her hands. She worried about him, he tried to take on too much. He and Otis would have fought the Riders alone if they hadn't seen through his ruse. They would have died out there and become food for the Savage Ones. She loved him for it but cursed his stubbornness at the same time. She felt sleepy and sad. She didn't know how many they'd killed; how many survived the long ride back to wherever they'd come from. Cody, *Kodiak*, she corrected herself, told them to help anyone they could and send them on their way. She hadn't wanted to count the bodies lying in the snow when they finally left that cursed place. She'd be fine if she never saw the burnt-out church again. She sent up a little prayer that the fallen found peace and the injured made it back safely. She sighed contentedly as her sleepy eyes passed over each of her brothers and sisters, her tribe.

The triplets were giggling madly. They had taught the monkeys to ride on the foxes and it was a constant source of amusement or annoyance to watch them play.

Vanessa hummed softly to Donny while she tied off the

little braid that hung behind his ear. Her spears had flown straight and true, she had probably even saved lives by adding to the confusion and chaos. Her Daddy would have been proud. She tried to forget the burning woman, tried to justify it. She never would have been hurt if she hadn't come to hurt them.

She felt a little guilty about riding Ziggy in the snow but she had proven herself when they rescued the children and leaving her behind had felt wrong. She was brave in a fight and she felt safer knowing she was close by. Now she was nestled in her stall with thick hay to keep her warm. She'd clucked and gave Vanessa that funny sideways look of hers while she had sung to her and told her how brave she was and how much she loved her. Vanessa felt like she understood the intent, if not the words, and was sad to leave her in the barn for the night. She needed to go check on her and the rest of the barn animals. She finished the braid, hugged her adopted brother and dressed for the snow. She had some salve for the big ostrich's feet and wanted to spend some time with her. Maybe they could move south in the spring time, someplace a lot warmer. She hated the cold.

EPILOGUE

SMITH'S LANDING

The house stunk of decay. Used bandages, empty whiskey bottles and dirty clothing littered the floor. Unwashed bodies and the lingering gangrene smell from Poles leg hung in the air. He had never regained consciousness, just a drowsy fever dream state. They didn't know how long it would take for him to pass, but the infected, pus filled wound smelled worse by the hour. He wasn't going to recover and all they could do was make him comfortable.

Richard hobbled with the assistance of his grandfather's old blackthorn cane. He was healing slowly but he was healing. The rest weren't so lucky. Tasha and the other girls had saved most of their lives but the crude splints and the lack of knowledge meant bones would heal crooked and the injured boys would be in pain for the rest of their lives. It was a disaster of the highest order and Richard placed the blame squarely on Gordon. If he hadn't shown up, hadn't gotten himself thrown out of the animal park, none of this would have happened. He should have been more suspicious. He should have interrogated him as to why, exactly, did a bunch of little kids want him gone. He tucked the pistol behind his belt, put on his heavy coat and limped his way to where Gordon sat watching a movie.

"We need to talk cousin." Richard told him, then under his breath "Outside, where the others can't hear."

"About what?" Gordon asked, his eyes never leaving the screen. "It's dark, can't it wait till morning?"

Richards face twitched in barely controlled rage and it took him a moment before he trusted his voice.

"About moving to a different house." he said, as nonchalantly as he could, "and other things. We need to make some changes."

Gordon sighed, hit pause. "Sure."

"After you." Richard insisted.

Gordon stood and put on his own coat, careful not to jostle his wrist. He led the way to the double patio doors, stepped outside into the cold night air and turned to look at his cousin. Richard leaned heavily on the cane as he limped past him and over to the patio table. The propane heater was on and the covered area actually wasn't too chilly. There was a dusty bottle of wine and a single glass on the table top and Gordon started to relax. He knew what this was about. Richard needed him to step up. Take charge again since his men were either crippled or stayed too drunk all the time. It had been nearly a week, the guys needed to get over being mad at him, it wasn't his fault the raid had gone wrong.

There was only one chair and Richard sat heavily with a grunt then rubbed the bandages covering the gashes on his chest.

"These things itch like crazy." he complained and picked up the bottle to fill the glass.

"This was one of dear old dad's favorites." he said. "A French Red from nineteen seventy-two."

Gordon looked around for another chair but they were all gone.

"You won't need one." Richard said. "You're not staying long."

He hit the remote on the pool cover and it slid smoothly back. The dead inside were slow but they weren't frozen. Mouths full of rotted teeth started gnashing and hands slowly went up, reaching for them.

Gordon's eyes darted around, looking for an exit. He didn't like the way this was going. The single chair and single glass took on a whole new meaning.

"So, what did you want to talk about? It's cold out here."

Richard pulled a pistol out of his jacket pocket and laid it on the table. His hand remained on it, ready to snatch it up.

"You damned near got us all killed. For what? Hurt feelings?"

"Hey, don't put this all on me, you wanted to get those girls and so did all of the other guys, and don't forget about Smoke. You wanted revenge for that too."

"We wouldn't even know about them if you hadn't come in here spouting off about it. You said they were weak and easy targets. You said they were just little kids who would be a pushover. You lived there for months and you didn't know how vicious they were? You had no idea they were so savage? My God, they ride polar bears! You didn't think to mention that? You led us right into a trap, Gordy. They kicked our asses! My boys are crippled or dead, our machines are trashed. No, this is all you *cousin*." He hissed the last word.

Gordon swallowed hard, eyeballed the hand on the gun. He had to spin this.

"Calm down, man. Everything is gonna be fine. We'll

get another chance at them, catch them off guard. We'll have those girls and our revenge. I'm really sorry about the boys that died but think about it. Less people to feed and drink up the booze. Less people to share the girls with. It's not so bad if you think about it like that."

"They were my friends!" Richard shouted.

"My friends, Gordy." he said quietly, "And you're stupid if you didn't learn a lesson from that ass kicking we got. Ninety percent casualty rate if you didn't notice. Ninety percent of our entire community is dead or maimed. Countries have unconditionally surrendered for less, Gordy. I'm just glad they don't know where we live. They could walk in here and finish us off. Hell, one of them alone could. We're broken, Gordy. And you did this."

Richard raised the pistol and on cue, the rest of the gang hobbled and limped out. They wanted to watch the show. Gordon heard the half-frozen moans of the undead behind him and realized what was happening.

This wasn't an argument.

He wasn't being told to leave.

They were going to execute him.

He hadn't thought to ask who the others were crawling around in the empty pool but from the eager and evil smiles on their faces, he knew they had done this before. He was going to be their Friday night entertainment.

"You gonna jump or do I need to shoot you first?" Richard asked. "Either way, you'll become one of them. You won't bleed out before you turn. Just ask dear old dad."

There was no way out. The rest of them were in a semi-circle behind Richard, out of his line of fire no matter which way he tried to run. He'd get shot and then tossed in, there was no way around it. No amount of begging, no swearing to change, no leaving and never coming back promises would work. Nothing would change their minds.

"Can I go off the diving board?" Gordon asked, trying his best to act cool. To buy a little time so he could think of a way out. "You know, walk the plank? I always had a thing for pirate movies."

There were murmurs of approval. That would be different. They usually had to shoot whoever was sentenced to the pool and push them in before they died.

"Yeah, Gordy." Richard said. "You can walk the plank. After all, we're family."

Gordon nodded and reached for the wine glass. Richard tensed, almost pulled the trigger, but relaxed when his cousin raised it in toast.

"I'm sorry." he said, "I didn't mean for any of this to happen."

Nobody softened.

Nobody looked down at their feet and started having second thoughts.

Nobody cared.

He put the glass to his lips, drained it and moved to set it back on the table. When he was close, almost out of the line of fire, he struck out at the gun. In the same instant, he spewed the wine he'd been holding in his mouth into Richards face. He kicked him in his wolf chewed leg as he pulled the trigger but the bullet went wild. Richard was blinded by the alcohol and excruciating pain of all his stitches being ripped open. He screamed and fought for the pistol as the others ran to help.

Gordon ripped the gun out of his grip, twisting and snapping his trigger finger backward and clubbed him across the face with his splint. They both roared in pain but Gordon managed to grab the chair and jerk it forward, throwing Richard to the concrete inches from the edge of the pool. He scrambled backward, away from the reaching arms, but when he grunted to his feet Gordon had the gun pointed at his belly.

"Goodbye, cousin." he said, and pulled the trigger.

Richard only screamed for a few minutes as they all stood around, stunned by the turn of events and wary of the only person holding a pistol.

"There's a new sheriff in town." Gordon said, watching them. "Any objections?"

No one said anything.

"Go get Pole." he said.

There was a moment's hesitation and he waited. This was the deciding moment. If they did what he said now, they probably always would. If they didn't, he'd gun them down until he ran out of bullets. The two healthiest of them finally broke off to drag him out as gently as they could. He was burning up with fever and delirious.

"Toss him in." Gordon said and motioned to the pool.

They wouldn't. Gordon waited.

"He's dead anyway." Misty said. "You'd be doing him a favor."

"She's right." Jester said. "Just do it before you get us all killed."

They did.

His eyes sprang open a few minutes later and he jumped to his feet, clawing at them. He kept falling and it didn't take long before the bone was sticking through his pant leg again. He didn't seem to notice.

As they filed back into the house, Misty came over to him.

"Let me check your bandages." she said. "You've started bleeding again."

He sat back down in his favorite chair as she fussed over him and Jester set a cold beer down beside him.

"Here ya go, boss." he said, giving him a slight nod.

"Things are going to get better." Gordon said. "Winter will be over soon. Let's drink up, heal up and get ready for spring."

They raised a toast to that.

AUTHORS NOTE

We hope you've enjoyed this tale of the children and their companions. This story grew from their interaction with Jessie and Scarlet way back in Zombie Road 5. Wesley has written a few stories set in the Zombie Road world and wanted to expand on the kids who had managed to survive in the wild animal safari park. As of this writing, May of 2019, we are hard at work on the second book in the series.

I wanted to take a moment and really, really thank a few people that made this book happen.

First off, Wesley. All he had to work with was a few chapters from the Zombie Road book and a couple ideas I threw at him. From that, he created the whole safari world and most of the characters in it. He gave them personalities and names and made us care about them. He can be reached at Bisley356gnr@yahoo.com

Next, the cover artist. Erick doesn't usually do book covers, he is a tattoo artist with incredible talent. I'd already commissioned two different covers from two different artists and they were rather dreadful. With a release date looming, my daughter showed him what I was going to have to use, there was no time to hire another artist. He said "hold my beer" and two days later, he had created the cover that graces the book. Beautiful. He's agreed to do the next two covers for the trilogy and I can't wait to see what he does with Swan and her wolves. Or Donny and his panther. Or should it be the little kids and their foxes? Murray and his monkeys? Vanessa in full African battle rattle riding Ziggy as she cuts down the undead? Harper and her giraffe? The twins with their sawblade axes charging through a Walmart on their polar bears? We may have to write more books just to get to see the covers!

Erick Holguin owns the Tattoo Dojo in Atlanta and has been inking for over nine years. If you need skin art, check out him or any of his talented crew. His portraits and detail work are world class. Follow this link and book in advance. A guy with his skill set stays pretty busy. https://www.thetattoodojo.com

Tamra Crow is my third set of eyes and editrix extraordinaire and Valerie Lioudis helped sort the cover layout.

If you would like to sign up for the Simpson newsletter, and get a free book with a few short stories, follow this link: https://subscribepage.com/r2r8no

Although to be honest, it's not much of a newsletter. I don't fill your inbox with spam, just a note a few times a year letting you know when there is a new release or if there is major news about the game or movie that we're working on.

To keep abreast on the latest goings on, join us in the David Simpson Fan Club group on Facebook https://www.facebook.com/groups/265507950527733/ It's a pretty active group and I'll answer any questions you may have.

The obligatory author website (that doesn't get much love) is www.davidasimpson.com

As always, if you could leave a review, that would be awesome. Amazon really does place a lot of emphasis on the number of reviews a book gets, it's how they decide whether to promote it or make it more visible for shoppers.

Have fun, live life and don't get hit by a bus

David A. Simpson

5/19/2019

59748291R00213

Made in the USA
Columbia, SC
07 June 2019